I0761129

ALSO BY

Christina Hammonds Reed

The Black Kids

THE JOHNSON FOUR

THE JOHNSON FOUR

A Novel

CHRISTINA HAMMONDS REED

BALLANTINE BOOKS · NEW YORK

Ballantine Books
An imprint of Random House
A division of Penguin Random House LLC
1745 Broadway, New York, NY 10019
randomhousebooks.com
penguinrandomhouse.com

Copyright © 2026 by Christina Hammonds Reed

Penguin Random House values and supports copyright. Copyright fuels creativity, encourages diverse voices, promotes free speech, and creates a vibrant culture. Thank you for buying an authorized edition of this book and for complying with copyright laws by not reproducing, scanning, or distributing any part of it in any form without permission. You are supporting writers and allowing Penguin Random House to continue to publish books for every reader. Please note that no part of this book may be used or reproduced in any manner for the purpose of training artificial intelligence technologies or systems.

BALLANTINE BOOKS & colophon are registered trademarks of Penguin Random House LLC.

Hardcover ISBN 978-0-593-72448-4
Ebook ISBN 978-0-593-72449-1

Printed in the United States of America

1st Printing

First Edition

BOOK TEAM: Production editor: Robert Siek • Managing editor: Pam Alders • Production manager: Sandra Sjursen • Copy editor: Rachelle Mandik • Proofreaders: Evan Stone, Tricia Wygal, and Cameron Schoettle

Book design by Kim Henze Walker

The authorized representative in the EU for product safety and compliance is Penguin Random House Ireland, Morrison Chambers, 32 Nassau Street, Dublin D02 YH68, Ireland. https://eu-contact.penguin.ie

For my baby and his favorite person—
how wondrous the world with you in it!

PART ONE

1968–1970

CHAPTER ONE

1968

I AM THE PICKANINNY PRODIGY CHRISTMAS JONES THE THIRD. I WAS alive for approximately eight years, although it's been so long, I'm not quite sure that's right anymore. There is a good chance that I am ten, and forgetful. In North Carolina, in the year 1923, I was born to a fourteen-year-old in a field. She squatted deep in cotton, her thin dress in brambles, and out I came covered in the stuff of life. I think maybe there is a chance I remember this moment, my head landing in the dirt by my mother's small brown feet as a haughty earthworm scooched by. I say haughty because the earthworm had no respect for personal boundary, or space. He crawled right up to my baby eyeball, completely unaware of his place in the food chain and entirely unafraid. I could feel his gaze upon me, and so for the first time, I opened my eyes to stare right back. We had a brief moment, and then, having been born, I began to cry.

Christmas is not the name my mother gave me, but I have forgotten both her name and my own. If I close my eyes and think really hard, I believe it was Edward, or perhaps Tobias. Tobias is a very nice name and I should like to have been called it, however briefly. Mr. Farraday gave me the name Christmas Jones, that day he took me from the orphanage and I was born again. Later, we decided together that I should affix "the Third." It has a great weight behind it, as though my name has been passed down through the generations, from my father's father to him, and then on to me. Mr. Farraday thought it was a name befitting his extraordinary baby nigger. This is how I was billed, "Christmas Jones the Third, the Pickaninny Prodigy." Mr. Farraday was never very good at naming his acts.

Anyway, I was born, I was a brief sensation, and then I died. But this story is not about my short life, fame, or brutal death, or even the many years I spent wandering the woods near where I was hanged; it's about how I came to live with the Johnsons, and thus how I came to find myself loved for two (almost three!) glorious years, before I destroyed it all.

You must believe me when I say that I didn't mean to do what I did to the Johnsons. To pull them apart like a cruel little boy plucking the legs from an unassuming spider. Sometimes, I still hear Rocco screaming in horror as bone slammed against metal. Other times, I see the sheer joy in River and his friend's faces unaware of what lay ahead. When I allow myself to think of it, I feel myself slipping somewhere very, very dark indeed, where my heart is torn asunder in my chest, and the very hairs stand at sinister attention on the back of my neck. Except of course that, being dead, I can't feel anything at all.

BUT BEFORE THAT, there was this. This is how I was found:

Before Detroit was broken, when people still offered it their dreams, Odysseus Johnson packed up his three sons and drove them several hundred miles to audition for the Man under the group name the Johnson Three. It wasn't a very original name.

For months they practiced. Odysseus choreographed a routine like the ones the kids did on TV, a little shimmy here and a doo-bop there, finger pops and snaps to accent it all. I should interject here that I was not yet familiar with television, but I have since come to love it. The Johnsons have a box big enough to sit on, wooden and warm, and at the flip of a switch the world turns on. On comes *The Flintstones*! On comes Walter Cronkite! If you sit very close and press your nose to the screen, they are all little itty-bitty dots, like life but fuzzy, and everybody looks to be in a dream. It is not a good thing to be neither here nor there in the world, neither in heaven with the baby angels, nor a real boy of flesh and blood, but goddammit if I ain't glad that I got to stick around to watch television.

The boys were not much more than a year apart with the biggest gap being the eighteen months between Roman and Rocco. Roman was the oldest. River, the youngest and the cutest and . . . well, unless you've been living under a rock, you know who River was. Rocco was my best friend.

Anyway, Roman, Rocco, and River killed it at that audition. Everyone in the room clapped for almost a full minute when they were done. There was just one problem. Rocco wasn't quite right in the head. He could sing like a dream, and he hit every last one of Odysseus's dance moves, but when he stood still, when the man, Black and shiny like his wingtips, was just talking to them, sizing them up, he and everybody else could tell that Rocco was special.

"Is your boy Rocco a retard?" the gentleman said to Odysseus.

"I am not re—" Rocco began to interject angrily before Odysseus interrupted him.

"No sir," Odysseus said.

"He ain't all here though, right?"

"Rocco just a dreamer, is all," Odysseus said. "Sing for the man won't you, Rocco?"

Rocco sang. His voice was tonally perfect, sweet and innocent and pretty as a bluebird's. He stared at the wall behind the man as he sang.

"You can stop now, son," the gentleman said. "Beautiful voice you've got."

He smiled kindly at Rocco, who kept singing. Roman elbowed his brother in the side, hard.

"You're a fine family. A mighty fine family," the gentleman continued. He was right too. All the Johnson boys were handsome and well behaved, all of them good boys. Odysseus looked at his work and was satisfied.

"I'd like you to audition for the boss man himself," he said. The boys began to jump around.

"Except I think maybe the group would work better with just Roman and River. We could bring in another boy, I think. . . . Yeah. That would work," he said, as if to himself.

River, Roman, and Odysseus looked at one another. Rocco stared out the window at a butterfly as it passed by. The butterfly was orange with white and black polka dots, a Painted Lady, which is Rocco's favorite type of butterfly. Rocco can tell you all about different kinds of butterflies if you let him. Everybody calls him a retard, but ain't no retards I know of that have thousands of butterflies floating around their heads so that at any old time they can pick one from another and say, "That right there's a Sad Duskywing. Isn't it a beaut?!"

"The boys . . . it's the Johnson Three," Odysseus said. "They're a package deal, you dig?"

"Of course. Of course," the gentleman said. "Is that how you boys feel?"

Sixteen-year-old Roman and thirteen-year-old River looked at each other, then over at Rocco, then up at their father.

Roman stepped up to the gentleman with the wingtips. "We the Three Musketeers, man. One for all and all for one." He had just read the book in school and it had appealed to his youthful sense of honor and adventure. Plus, Dumas was Black, and he could dig that.

River walked up next to his brother. "We ain't doing nothing without Rocco, sir." River was always the most straightforward of the bunch.

"It was a pleasure to meet you boys," the gentleman said. "If you ever change your minds, you know where to find me."

Odysseus and the boys piled into the car, with Odysseus up front and all the brothers in the back. They sat quietly as Odysseus drove them around the city, under the lights, past the shiny ice-cream shop, beyond the movie theater with its fancy marquee. Rocco lifted a hand to the window and touched Canada in the distance.

Roman threw the first punch. River followed. The two boys both punched Rocco while he wailed, tears dripping down all of their faces. Odysseus looked at them in the rearview mirror and didn't say a word until they reached the Wonder Bread sign. There, he rolled down the window and the entire car smelled of fresh bread.

"That's enough, now," Odysseus said, and because they were good boys, they stopped.

FOR THEIR JOURNEY, Emmeline Johnson had packed a cooler full of sandwiches and sardines, whoopie pies from the corner store, and exactly four bottles of Coke, one for each of the Johnson men. Now, Odysseus was generally a man of discipline. He walked around the neighborhood twice a day, after which he did a series of push-ups and sit-ups in the basement, with the sun before the boys awoke, or bathed in moonlight after they'd gone to sleep, though it was not uncommon, after they'd all been tucked into bed, for one of the younger boys to sneak down to the basement and be used as a weight, a tiny brown body raised up and down like an offering in the pale moonlight. Odysseus drank sparingly, and smoked not at all. He was abstemious when it came to food, preferring to eat the same meal every day—grits for breakfast, chicken for lunch, fish for dinner with some greens on the side at each. And because Emmeline generally prepared for the boys what she prepared for Odysseus, they usually ate the same.

"Gotta keep your mind clear," Odysseus told the boys whenever they complained. "Too much of anything make your brains soft."

All this enforced abstention is why River drank his Coke before they'd even gotten properly on the road, why Roman snacked himself sick on sardines on the way back, and why Rocco quietly ate his brothers' whoopie pies (saving his own, of course) before Emmeline even realized that they hadn't made their way with him from the kitchen counter to the cooler. Combined with the Motown-sized hole in all three of their hearts, this brief gluttony led them to the brink of carsickness in the family's 1961 Cadillac DeVille. Odysseus vacuumed and washed the car once a week, allowing neither neighborhood stray nor wayward ball anywhere near it, upholstery still like butter, nearly as beautiful as the day he and Emmeline walked into the showroom and bought it from the one salesman smart enough not to ignore them.

All of this to say, Odysseus pulled by the side of the dark country road so his three musketeers wouldn't vomit all over his baby, even though something about the place didn't feel right, not at all.

Roman exited the car first, with River at his heels. They stumbled into the weeds with the high beams as their spotlight. Roman heaved, pitching himself forward as he tried to avoid fish guts on his brand-new Chucks. River bent over and swayed, moaning quietly to his maker, a pendulum willing the sick to come. Rocco had to pee. Odysseus let him wander just a bit farther to relieve himself with some dignity, just slightly out of view.

"Stay close, boy!" he yelled.

It should be noted that I have imagined most of what happened over the next few minutes, until I finally made Rocco's acquaintance. Just because I am dead does not mean I am all-knowing. Not exactly, anyway.

Odysseus reached his arms above his head, breathed in, and puffed his chest—a grizzly, watching, ready. On these roads, at this hour, there were plenty of things to fear, but none more than the right truck full of the wrong drunks and a few feet of rope. As though the woods could hear his thoughts, they howled and swayed, and with a gust, spit out River and Roman, but not Rocco.

"Where's your brother?" Odysseus asked.

"Pissing, I guess," River said.

"What'd I tell you about that?" Odysseus gently slapped the boy upside his head.

"Urinating," River corrected. Odysseus was of the mind that if his boys were to be anything one day, they needed to use the proper words for things.

Roman had sullied the edges of his new shoes, and he'd just about had it with this trip anyway; he sulked off to the side.

"Rocco!" Odysseus shouted, and the name bounced around in the darkness until an owl chorus replied in five-part harmony, "Who?"

Odysseus looked once more up and down the country road. "Shit. Come on, boys, we have to go get him."

"Rocco's always messing everything up," Roman complained before Odysseus grabbed both of his boys' hands in his and all three ventured into my woods.

If you are scared, my woods are dark with tree branches like claws and the howls of monsters. I cried on my very first night there because I had never been anywhere alone for so long. First, I had been in the orphanage, with all the other unfortunate children all around me, but we didn't much know that we were unfortunate because we had two sets of clothes, three meals of grits, one another, and the kind Negro nuns with brims like birds—down the dark hallways they gave the appearance of floating swans.

Then, when Mr. Farraday took me from that place, I had all of the other acts around me and they were nearly as good as the orphans. But I'll tell you about those some other time.

Anyway, like I said, I had never been alone for very long at a time, and that first night in the woods, as I lay between life and death, I cried for many hours, until I began to be quite certain that the woods were in fact trying to talk to me. The squirrels scurried around my feet and said, "Don't cry." The caterpillar lazed around my stump and said, "There, there." And even the wolves, cliquish as they tend to be, with a great few howls said, "You'll be OK." Eventually, I understood myself not to be alone at all.

There is no way to skirt around describing myself, and I suppose it's best you get an accurate picture, lest you judge Odysseus or the boys unfairly. My right arm ends in a charred stump, and I have to keep my snapped neck propped up with the hanging rope as a brace, wrapped 'round like an indigenous neck ring; but my smile is big and bright, I'm told my eyes dance, and my chest is strong. The nuns used to say I was a very pretty child, and the audiences too. I think perhaps I still am, even if now there are parts of me missing. While Rocco sang, I kept time on my thigh, which is diaphanous as a woman's stocking on a clothesline.

Rocco shimmied and shook for me, singing almost as good as the Boy himself, "*Stop! The love you save may be your own!*"

Rocco was the huskiest of the Johnson boys, and on the short side. Even though he was older than River, he was the shortest of the bunch. And while the other two were a deep brown like watered soil, Rocco was closer to desert sand (at least as I imagined it, having not yet been to the desert), with hazel eyes that seemed to grow darker or lighter depending on the world around him. Rocco looked the most like Mr. Odysseus, who stood silently off to the side, a few yards behind the boys, watching.

Upon seeing me, River began to tremble, and with a yelp, let out a steady stream of urine, not piss, he thought, and hoped Odysseus wouldn't notice.

Roman heaved once more, this time quite directly on his new Chucks. Already, he was near as tall as Mr. Odysseus himself, so there was quite a way down for his sick to go.

At the end of his performance, Rocco bowed for me, and I slapped my remaining good hand on my thigh with such enthusiasm that in a moment of both pride and jealousy (for it had truly been an exceptional performance), River and Roman momentarily forgot their fear.

"Ain't you something!" I declared.

"Well shit, Rocco!" River said.

At the sound of River's voice, I stood up to face them. I would like to think that Odysseus and the boys could tell I was a proud boy in the way I carried myself, chest forward, body erect, one hand on my hip like Peter Pan in a stage play, my charred stump hidden in my pocket. I used my good hand to push my head up on my neck, adjusting both just a bit straighter.

"Hello, Mr. Johnson, sir. My name is Christmas Jones the Third," I said.

"What the hell kind of name is Christmas?" River asked.

"Don't be rude, River," Odysseus said.

"Your boy Rocco's just informed me that you are part of a traveling group of entertainers. I'm an entertainer myself," I said, and with that I began to dance.

"Normally, this is where I'd use my hat as a prop, but they took it," I said offhandedly, continuing the movements with the hat in pantomime. Then I started to sing. The ditty had the sound of the field holler deep in its bowels.

I could tell that Mr. Johnson didn't like me much, or even at all. Rocco, Roman, and River clapped out a beat while I cake-walked, and when I bowed, the Johnson Three gave me a standing ovation.

"That was great!" Roman said, and Rocco nodded enthusiastically. "You're even better than us!"

"We have to get going, boys," Odysseus said, in what I now know to be his stern-but-protective voice. "It's too late. C'mon, now."

Odysseus turned his body back toward the car, expecting the boys to follow his lead.

"Mr. Johnson, sir," I asked, "I was wondering if I might come with y'all? As you can see, I'm an experienced performer and, pardon me for being forward, but I think I might could be an asset to your troupe."

Odysseus stared long and hard at me before him. He had come out to the city to audition his boys, and now here he was in the woods being auditioned for. I could tell this was not how he'd expected his day to go, not at all. And what was he to tell Emmeline if he brought home this here little ghost?

"I'm sorry, but I can't. I really can't." He did look awfully sorry, but not sorry enough.

"Daddy, please!!!" Rocco begged.

Roman looked a little skeptical, as though he wasn't sure it was a good idea either.

I began another song in hopes that Mr. Johnson might be further persuaded.

"*There was a boy, a very strange, enchanted boy . . .*" I started.

"Nature Boy" was one of my absolute most favorite new songs. Well, I suppose maybe it's not so new anymore, but it came out after I died. Honestly, it's very hard to keep track of time when time means nothing anymore. I'd first heard the song from somebody who'd died hiking through the woods not too long ago. To be honest, most of us who died in my woods hadn't wandered very far at all. Something unnatural tethered us to the place where we took our last breaths. Like you could somehow, if you tried hard enough, still remember what it was like to be, if only you stayed closest to where you last were. They were my woods and they were our woods. Trees grew larger, roads went from dirt to paved. Now we watched as teenagers carelessly tossed the cigarettes once carefully hidden inside rolled-up sleeves. There had even been a fire or two just since I'd lived there. Then, all of us dead marveled at the life as it slowly reemerged.

Anyway, the dead hiker sang "Nature Boy" quite a bit, even if he only wandered from one end of the forest to the other. He sang it whenever he was sad, or bored, or happy. And eventually he got into an argument with another spirit about whether Nat King Cole was the very best, or Frank Sinatra, and then the two men fought as though they were flesh. We all had a good laugh because Sinatra and Cole were probably sound asleep in their fancy beds as the two dead men tried and failed to land punches in their honor.

All this to say, I did a very good job singing a very good song, and I so very hoped this man and his boys would like me. I had always wanted to be part of a family! With brothers! None of the other families that had come through the forest fit the bill. Too many children. Or they were too old, with nobody for me to play with. Or they were mean to one another, something rotting deep within. I couldn't feel much at all, but I felt the Johnsons. They made me feel as though I had skin again, and the sun was shining down upon it. I would've done anything to keep them.

"You're very good, but we really must be going," Odysseus said.

"Pleeeeeease!!!" Rocco said.

"He's so little," River said. "We can't just leave him!"

"Boys, what am I going to tell your mama? What about our neighbors? What if somebody's looking for him?"

"Nobody's looking for me! I promise!" I said.

The boys begged and pleaded with Mr. Odysseus to take me home with them. How desperately I wanted to go to wherever it was they were headed. Home! I wanted to go home.

"C'mon, boys," Odysseus said, and headed back up to the car.

I'm not entirely proud of what I did next, nor do I regret it; I stowed away in the trunk. Odysseus is, and was, not the kind of man to put a little boy in a dark trunk next to luggage for hours, even if the boy could easily poke his head through the leather bucket seats and join them inside, even if he could no longer feel any pain at all. It had been years since I'd last been away from my little bit of forest, and when I eventually poked my head through, unable to contain my excitement, River and Roman were leaning against their respective windows, asleep. Rocco's eyes widened, but I put my index finger up to my mouth and whispered, "Shhhhh!"

He grinned and didn't so much as say a peep! Already we had shared secrets, like brothers!

Finally, after many hours, the car came to a halt, and Mr. Odysseus popped open the trunk. I looked up at him sleepily from where I'd been resting my head on a little blue suitcase and smiled.

"What the—" Mr. Odysseus said a very adult word just then that I have been told not to repeat. River and Roman scrambled over to the trunk to see what it was that had caused their father to curse like that right in front of them.

"Oh shit!" Roman said. River started laughing.

"Mama, look!" Rocco said, as soon as Ms. Emmeline Johnson came to the door to greet her boys. Ms. Emmeline was the most beautiful woman I have ever seen in my entire life, Negro or otherwise. And it's not just her kindness and warmth that makes her so, though she is very kind. I have seen many men of all races turn their heads to watch her walk down the street, so striking a woman is she, even with her slight limp. I don't understand grown-ups much, even after all these years of watching them, but if I were a grown-up, I would very much like to be married to her, I think.

"My name is Christmas Jones the Third," I said.

"This is our mama," River said. River was the spitting image of Ms. Emmeline, with their shared big, beautiful eyes and long lashes like a fawn just woke up, blinking at the world around it still new. He was wiry most everywhere except for the soft puppy belly that threatened to push over his soiled corduroys. Oh to look like you belonged undeniably to someone! To a mama!

I didn't know just how much I'd wanted a mama until right that moment. I rushed over and, with a yelp of pure joy, wrapped my arms around her neck. Then, Ms. Emmeline's skin felt like a faucet in the dead of winter, frozen until a rush of heat poured through her core and cracked her right open and she plum dropped to the ground!

When she finally came to, Rocco was cradling her head and screaming while River and Roman yelled at him to shut up.

"Emmie, dear!" Odysseus repeatedly snapped his fingers in her face.

In the corner, I wrapped and unwrapped my noose, a nervous habit, letting my neck hang down low, then raising it back up again.

"Oh no, I killed her!" I wailed. "I killed her. I killed her. I killed her."

CHAPTER TWO

"We have to establish boundaries," Odysseus said to Emmeline. "I can't just have the little ghost popping up behind me while I'm washing my nethers."

It was true that on that very morning, as Odysseus washed down the length of his body, taking special care near his darkest parts, just as he had begun to hit the highest notes of his register with, "*Unimportant are all these things I can do,*" the little ghost boy had popped his head right through the shower tiles to finish the lyric with a harmony: "*'Cause I can't get next to you.*"

Odysseus startled and slipped, everything swung this way and that, and he landed with a loud thud on the tile floor. Emmeline heard and came rushing in her curlers, silk robe wrapped tight around her, as she herself hadn't had time to dress. Luckily, Odie hadn't broken anything other than his pride.

"The boy has a name," Emmeline said with a sigh.

She hadn't wanted Christmas in her house. After she'd fainted, those first few minutes when he wrapped his tiny arms around her, after eventually getting her boys tucked in and settled away, and Christmas with them, she and Odie had argued well into the night about what exactly they were going to do with a little ghost in their house. Odysseus thought they should ask him to leave.

"Where's he gonna go?" she asked. "We can't just dump him out into the world all by his lonesome like that!"

"He's dead!" Odie said. "It's not like he needs us for anything. Not really. He can just go back to where he was."

But Emmeline couldn't bring herself to do that to the child. Not after what she herself had been through.

Emmeline Johnson had spent most of her own childhood loveless and lonely. Not the ordinary loneliness that comes with being a mere misfit or misunderstood, but the deep and abiding loneliness that came with abandonment. When she was not much older than the little ghost boy, Christmas, her own grandmother had dropped a newly crippled Emmeline off at the St. Joseph's Negro Sanitarium never to return.

"I told him not to marry that woman." Emmeline's grandmother had shaken her head, still in disbelief, tears streaming down her pale face. The both of them were still in their funeral attire. Emmeline looked down at the patent leather shoes pinching her feet. She couldn't feel much else, but somehow she could feel that. This was how they'd said goodbye.

Emmeline had spent months in the sanitarium's halls learning to be bipedal once more, convalescing in her small corner cot while the others came and went. The place was a catchall for all manner of Negro malady, and a wheelchair roll through its corridors revealed any number of terrible things that could befall a person, from the madwoman who ran around naked with her rather pendulous breasts to the shy young man with cauliflower blooms where his face should be.

Here, Emmie learned not to be afraid of difference, of death. Mostly it was tuberculosis. Their Negro lungs thickened with the white plague, with stick and blood, and Emmie began to be able to tell, by a cough in the distance, when the reaper would come.

"Mr. Thomas is dead by Thursday," she'd whisper to the night nurse.

"Be a child," the nurse would snap back, as though there were anything else Emmie could be.

During the war, the night nurse, Clarabel, had tended to the German POWs and injured Negro soldiers, and even though she hadn't been allowed abroad, her cold fingertips were battlefields.

Nurse Clarabel was Emmie's favorite, and every so often she would sneak Emmie caramel treasures that later lodged themselves in Emmie's loosening baby incisors.

The hospital itself was several acres of land, red brick surrounded by green field. Occasionally, the night nurse would trade shifts and become briefly the day nurse, and it was as magical as any eclipse. If Emmie begged hard enough, Nurse Clarabel would take her outside on her lunch and the two would sit and eat quietly together.

Nurse Clarabel was in love with the groundskeeper. He would come over and quietly clip the hedges around them, just to be near her. He had the strongest arms Emmeline had ever seen, with skin that stretched over coursing veins, thick as the roots of a knotted tree. Emmie thought to be lifted up by him would be a wonderful thing. If she were Clarabel, she would ask him to lift her into the tallest trees where they could both sit and watch the world. This seemed to young Emmie the most romantic thing one could do for another person, to lift and be lifted, love as flight.

Occasionally, something dark would come over Emmeline, and she would find herself uncontrollably angry. When the madwoman screamed down the hallway, breasts flopping, marvelous afro between her legs, Emmie would yell, "Nobody wants to see them old saggy titties!"

When the boy with the cauliflower face would speak too quietly, she would yell, "Speak louder, ugly!"

When the day nurse brought her porridge that was not still warm, she would launch it across the room such that poor unsuspecting, syphilitic Maurice, with his missing nose, had to wipe the gruel out his very eyeballs themselves.

"Haven't I suffered enough?!" he'd shout to nobody in particular.

Even her beloved Clarabel was not spared. When she would take too long to bring her an extra blanket, Emmie would scream, "You can't do nothing right, you ole Black bitch!"

At the end of the dark days, Clarabel would tell Emmie how she'd find her soaked in sweat, mumbling in her sleep, "Mama! Mama! Mama!"

There were also what Nurse Clarabel called "those poor polio babies," with their legs bent like wishbones. Emmeline would venture around the corner and see four of them in their iron lungs. Negro children were not supposed to be susceptible to the disease, and yet here they were, brown baby heads attached to stark white mini-pods, these ventilators that hinted at space or the very depths of the ocean itself. They were the lucky ones. The iron lungs had been purchased by a wealthy benefactor and were the only ones available to Negro children for miles and miles.

Bettina Woodson was Emmie's age. Her father was a young doctor in the hospital and when his rounds were done, he would sit with his only child and annoy the ever-living shit out of the nurses.

"That man tries my patience, Emmeline. He really does. I swear, he annoys the ever-living shit out of me," Clarabel huffed as she changed Emmie's dressing. Late at night, Emmeline would wheel her chair over to Bettina's small head and they would make up stories above the push and crush of the machine.

"Why you here?" Betty asked. Lungs weak, she spoke in little waif sentences.

"One day, my mother and father and I were about to leave our castle—"

"You ain't . . . live in . . . no castle, Emmie."

"Shut up. You wanna hear the story or not?"

"Fine." Betty sighed. Though it was generally hard for her to say no, being stuck in the machine and all.

"We were in search of a new kingdom. The queen, my mother, told the little princess, that's me, that the new kingdom would be even more beautiful than the old kingdom. But an evil old witch cast a spell on our chariot, and while we were on our way to the new kingdom the chariot turned into a dragon. The dragon breathed fire and swallowed the queen and king right up. And only the little princess remained, having scratched her way out of the beast's intestines and into the stars."

"The dragon's what crushed your legs?"

"Exactly," young Emmeline said.

"What kind of car was it?" Bettina asked.

"Ain't nobody said nothing about a car!" Emmeline said, blinking back tears.

ONCE EMMELINE WAS finally able to walk more than a few steps, she waited until she was strong enough to show Bettina. She debated whether it was cruel to show a girl confined to a cylinder that she could move. Emmie herself would've been quite nasty about it, and called her friend a show-off, or worse, but Bettina was a better person than she. She wheeled herself to the polio room, the entire time readying herself for her tentative steps, excited to demonstrate her new mobility.

"Look! It's only a matter of time before I get the hell out. Maybe my grandmother will come back. Or maybe somebody will adopt me now that I'm not a cripple no more!" Emmeline walked all the way around

Bettina's cylinder as she spoke, holding out a hand to grab it if she should fall, never mind that might could've taken the both of them out for good.

"I'm never getting out of here." Bettina sighed. She closed her eyes and refused to look at Emmeline any longer.

Emmeline sulked back to her bed, annoyed that her friend hadn't been happier for her.

She hadn't been to see Bettina in two days when she heard the whispers. The doctor's daughter was gravely ill. There was a chance she wouldn't make it through the week. Nobody was to enter her room without permission. Emmeline waited until the exact briefly chaotic moment when the nurses changed shifts before she snuck in.

"Bettina?" she said to her friend. "It's me, Emmie!"

She walked closer to the iron lung. "I'm sorry, Bettina. I'm so sorry."

She wasn't sure what for, exactly, but it seemed there were always a great many reasons to be sorry. Emmie tried hard to be good. Maybe Bettina had given up hope after watching Emmie walk again. Maybe Emmeline had been cruel and broken her friend's heart.

"I won't leave you, Bettina, I promise. We can get old together here. It's not so bad, is it?" Emmeline said.

"Get away! You're going to kill her!" The doctor came up behind Emmeline and smacked her upside the head, then grabbed her by the collar and lifted her up off her feet and out of the room. Once outside, the doctor thwapped her on the bum repeatedly.

"You are not to go back in there, you hear? I see you around here, I'll kill you myself."

The nurses all paused in the hallway. Dr. Woodson was known for being kind and gentle, and nobody had seen him lose his temper with anyone like that before. Much less a child.

"Yessir," Emmeline said through her tears, and promised to stay away.

═══

WHEN THE GIRL died, the doctor refused to let them move Bettina's body for several days. They begged him and even got the groundskeeper to go in there for a chat, man-to-man. The groundskeeper had lost his parents in the 1918 flu and knew loss as much as any of them. The groundskeeper was kind but firm, and much, much stronger than the implacable doctor.

It was as the two were talking that Emmeline first saw dead Bettina at the door watching her father wail.

"I've got to comfort Papa," Bettina said sadly.

Her friend was the first apparition Emmeline had ever seen. She had thought them to be myths and the stuff of scary stories. But she wasn't afraid. She pinched her arm the hardest anyone ever had (and because she often got into her dark moods, she'd had plenty of arm pinches).

"Emmie, stop that! You're gonna hurt yourself!" Bettina said.

It was the first time Emmeline had seen Bettina outside of the iron lung. If ghosts were real, if there really was another spirit world overlapping their own, why hadn't Emmeline's mother come to her after the accident? When she had lain by the side of the road for hours alone, across from the still-smoldering car with her parents' bodies. Why hadn't her mother or father comforted her then? Or when her grandmother had cruelly abandoned her to this place?

"Where's my mother?" she asked Bettina.

"What? I don't know," Bettina said. "My poor papa looks so, so sad."

═══

ALL THIS AND more was why Emmeline wasn't the slightest bit afraid of the little ghost boy, Christmas, even if she had been a bit startled. She hadn't told Odysseus or the boys this fact of her childhood. The year she kept company with her dead friend, wandering around the grounds, the two of them were finally able to run and play together outside. Ultimately, Emmie couldn't keep her promise, and she did leave Bettina after all. Bettina refused to leave the hospital, wanting to be near her papa, who, after only a week off, returned to the place to do his rounds. Everyone said the good doctor was but a shell of his former self; the nastier gossips said he was going mad, with tales of him animatedly talking to himself at lunch and on breaks. Others knew he was talking to Bettina. Emmeline wasn't the only one who could see her. Some people just seemed to be more attuned to these things.

Eventually, Nurse Clarabel adopted Emmie, after it was clear that nobody else was coming. Together, she and the night nurse migrated up north for a fresh start after the groundskeeper broke Nurse Clarabel's heart after all.

At her new school, the other kids laughed at her limp, and the scar ran down the length of both legs, marking her skin like seamed stockings. So Emmeline learned to fight with the best of them. She imagined the poor little dead boy, currently sleeping upstairs next to her Rocco, had done more than his fair share of fighting, both in life and death.

"No. He's staying here," she said to her husband as Odie ran through a list of nice but firm ways to tell the ghost to git. "We'll figure it all out somehow."

"You'll be safe here," Emmeline said to Christmas earlier that day, and meant it.

Nobody had ever said it to her.

CHAPTER THREE

SO FAR, ROMAN FOUND THE GHOST AS ANNOYING AS BOTH HIS LITTLE brothers. He had a habit of trailing Roman around the house asking too many questions, or popping his head through a door just as Roman was thinking some deeply private thoughts while looking at the *Jet* "Beauty of the Week." At least Rocco and River had the good sense to make a bit of noise when they barged in uninvited.

That very morning as Roman sang "You're All I Need to Get By," his voice cracked at what should've been the most climactic "*Neeeeed.*" He tried the note again closer to Marvin range (he had been doing Tammi just for shits and giggles), and again it was just out of reach. He tried once more and the stupid note split right open like Humpty Dumpty.

The little pick had appeared in the bathroom and sat down next to him on the counter, like a nosy little brother he couldn't shove out of the way. Christmas repeated the lyric in perfect tune, with perfect pitch, as though Roman had only to copy him and all would be all right.

"Like that," the little ghost said.

"No shit." Roman sighed. "I can't do it."

If Christmas was hurt, he didn't say anything.

"Do you have hair on your underparts?" Christmas said.

"What the hell kind of question is that?" Roman asked.

"That's what happens when your voice gets low!" the boy said, and giggled.

"How do you even know that?" Roman said.

Christmas looked pensive. "I've seen lots of people grow up."

The little boy had a habit of playing with his intestines the way some kids twiddled their hair, or sucked on a thumb. In the three days he'd lived with them, Roman had noticed that Christmas often tried to sound happy, but every so often he would trail off, and it was as though he were elsewhere, lifetimes away.

"Jesse Elijah was the pickaninny before me, and when his voice got deep, apparently, Mr. Farraday had to get rid of him on account he couldn't sing well no more with his man voice."

"Don't say pickaninny!" Roman sighed.

"What else would I call him?" Christmas asked.

"I don't know . . . but it's offensive. Nobody with any sense uses that word anymore," Roman lectured the little boy, who let his head drop all the way to its most unnatural angle as he took Roman in.

"Where did Jesse Elijah go?" Roman asked. "After your guy got rid of him?"

"Not sure. I never met him," Christmas said. "But luckily Mr. Odysseus probably won't get rid of you. Since you're his son and Jesse Elijah wasn't kin to nobody . . . Like me, I suppose."

Emmeline and Odysseus had argued for days over the boy's presence. Roman's bedroom was the closest to theirs, and since he had his very own, only he had been privy to their private words by pressing his ear up against the walls. Admittedly he hadn't been able to hear much clearly, but the muffles had definitely sounded angry. From what he could gather, his mother didn't want to send Christmas back into the world all by his lonesome. Roman's mama was a good one. Of course she wouldn't leave a little boy alone in the world. Even if he were dead as a doornail.

═══

ROMAN WAS HANDLING the presence much better than River, who had up until now downright reveled in his standing as the baby of the family and was loath to give it up. Christmas upended the natural order of things in the Johnson home.

It didn't help that after the initial shock wore off, Emmeline looked at the little ghost boy as tenderly as Odysseus eyed him with suspicion. All three of the Johnson boys were mama's boys. And now here was another one vying for her attention?! Roman tried his best to be charitable. The kid was dead, after all. And a brutal death it appeared to have been.

"How did you die?" Rocco had asked at dinner after the boy had been with them for almost a full week.

"You can't just go asking people how they died, Rocco," River said.

Roman thought that River was too harsh with their brother, especially since everybody knew Rocco wasn't always the best with social graces and the like.

"It was very, very sad," Christmas said, trailing off. "I don't want to think about it right now."

"You don't have to, baby," Emmeline said protectively.

"Do you scare people?" Rocco asked.

"I don't mean to . . . usually," Christmas said.

"Have you ever killed anyone?" Rocco asked.

And Christmas's eyes went wide.

"He's just a little boy, how could he kill somebody?" River said, clearly annoyed.

"Aren't some ghosts bad?" Rocco asked.

"I don't wanna be a ghost." Christmas sighed.

"Do you need to seek revenge? Do you need us to help you?" Rocco asked.

It was the most Roman had heard his brother speak to a stranger in some time. Rocco usually got all kinds of quiet around people who weren't part of their family.

"Enough," their father had said uneasily. Roman figured Odysseus probably would've stepped in sooner, but he too must have noticed it was the most Rocco had spoken to a stranger in a long time, maybe even ever. Still, Roman really did want to know the answer himself—why was the boy still part of this world? And why had the Johnsons been the ones to find him?

Now his mama sat on a slatted lounge chair, and Christmas next to her, watching.

Usually, kids from around the whole neighborhood hung over, or peeked through, the slats in the fence of their neighbors, the Taylors, as they watched the Johnson Three practice. Sometimes they were even bold enough to actually climb up and straddle the top of the Johnsons' side of the fence. They'd hoot and holler, shouting suggestions and occasionally, when there were lulls, when Roman's daddy went inside to do something or another, throw rocks at the Johnson boys. It was a love/hate thing, Roman reckoned.

His mama said folks were just jealous. But dammit if it wasn't as though the neighbor boys spent an hour scouting for the sharpest, pointiest rocks they could find. Tracey Taylor had the best arm of the bunch and thus became the leader. That, and his house was their launching pad. Roman wanted nothing more than to go next door and fuck them all up. He was bigger than Tracey Taylor, no question. When the onslaught inevitably arrived, poor Rocco shielded his whole body, curled up into a ball, and started moaning. River, that little freak, kept on practicing, dodging rocks as though it were some kind of game. Once, Odysseus came out and actually witnessed a rock fly dangerously close to River's head and River still did nothing.

"Keep going!" Odysseus snapped at Roman, who'd stared, fists balled, toward the fence. "You keep your focus through whatever gets thrown at you? You boys will be unstoppable."

"Or brain-dead," Roman mumbled.

"Get up, son," Odysseus said gently to Rocco, who was temporarily distracted by a ladybug crawling across his hand.

Rocco tentatively brushed his pants off and stood up from his protective stance. But he still placed his arms around his head as he sang and moved his legs along with River's playing.

"This is bullshit," Roman mumbled, but he knew better than to say it louder.

Today they practiced uninterrupted, a brief ceasefire with the terrorists next door, if not quite a détente. Mostly, it was that Tracey Taylor knew better than to throw any rocks at them when Emmeline Johnson was watching. He wasn't that stupid. Roman's mama did not play when it came to her boys.

They were about to start their version of "You're All I Need to Get By," the one song Roman had stumbled on in the bathroom that very morning.

"Roman's part should go down half an octave," Christmas interjected right as they were about to start. "It'll make the sound more rich. And then he can sustain the note for longer."

Roman glanced over at Christmas, who gave him a wink.

"Oh, that does sound smart!" Emmeline said, though she hadn't a lick of musical ability as far as Roman could tell. His mama sang as though she were blindfolded and trying to pin the tail on the donkey, except the donkey was the scale.

Roman, River, and Rocco looked at their father expectantly. On the other side of the fence, something rustled. Probably the Taylor kid and the others listening in, getting ready to resume fire as soon as Emmeline stepped away. Could they hear Christmas? Or see him? Or did they just assume it was one of the Johnson brothers?

"Try what the kid said." Odysseus threw up his hands and shook his head. "I'll be right back."

Roman definitely never thought he'd see the day his father would listen to musical-arrangement advice from a dead eight-year-old, but he guessed the little pick had been labeled a prodigy for a good reason after all.

"Yeah, try it!" taunted a voice on the other side of the fence.

"Shut the hell up!" Roman yelled over.

"Language, RoRo," Emmeline said as she stood up from the lounge chair. "I'm going to go make you boys some lemonade."

Roman suspected maybe his parents were just going inside together to make out, or worse, which he had caught them doing exactly once, and he'd have drunk Clorox afterward if he could.

"Yeah, *RoRo,*" the Taylor boy mocked as soon as Emmeline was out of earshot.

Christmas might've just saved Roman from further embarrassment, from being kicked out of the band, which might as well have been like being kicked out of the family itself! But Roman wasn't entirely sure he wanted to be saved. He was starting to stretch beyond the confines of his body, and his voice was only the half of it. He'd even begun to notice little spidery veins along his upper thighs and butt, as though his very skin were grabbing at this newer version of him, begging him to stay in childhood a little longer. Fuck that, he thought. He was ready to be grown, for whatever the world was to throw at him.

They were only a few verses in when a rock smashed into the side of Rocco's head. Poor, sweet Rocco, who didn't never hurt nobody.

"Oh hellll no," Roman said. One did not fuck with Rocco in Roman's presence.

Rocco began to cry in pain. Roman geared up into action. River quickly followed Roman's lead. No longer would the Johnson Three turn the other cheek. No longer would they choose nonviolence. Both parents out of sight, Roman snatched up the massive rock that had hit

Rocco. River scrambled to find a few more rocks that had been launched by their tormentors over the weeks.

"By any means necessary, motherfuckers," Roman said, and launched the big rock across the fence to where he approximated the Taylor kid's position.

River too threw the pile of rocks at his feet one by one over the fence. Though, bless him, Roman's little brother couldn't aim to save his life. But the kid did have heart. Rocco rocked and wailed as the battle was valiantly fought and his brothers avenged his injury.

Christmas looked from Rocco to River then back to Roman. He too picked up a rather substantial rock, almost a boulder, and threw it effortlessly with his one remaining arm. Roman and River looked at the pick in awe.

"You can throw?" River asked. "How can you even hold anything?"

"Ooooowwww," somebody cried out on the other side. "Mama! Mamaaaaa!"

And then, before Christmas could answer, the Johnson Three hauled ass back inside the house, where their parents were most definitely making out.

═

"YOUR SONS DONE hit my boy," Lorraine Taylor snapped as soon as Emmeline opened the door. Roman held a cold compress against the slight bruise on Rocco's face.

"Hello, Lorraine," Emmeline said to their neighbor, her words soaked in disdain.

There was already bad blood between the Taylors and the Johnsons.

First was on account of the fact that the Taylors' dog, Spike, had torn out of their house and bitten poor Rocco several years back when he was out minding his business watching butterflies on the Johnsons' lawn. Spike was a floppy Bassett hound, and his bite hadn't much hurt, but poor Rocco had still suffered, and was insanely terrified of dogs now, especially the ones with stubby legs and long ears.

Second, Mr. Taylor didn't never cut his lawn, and Odysseus fumed that it made the whole neighborhood look bad. Made it look like Black folks couldn't be trusted to take care of their property, he said. When he'd finally had enough and went over there to cut it himself, Lorraine came out hollering and Odysseus snapped that since neither her boy nor her husband could be bothered to take pride in their house, Odysseus would. Lastly, for whatever reason, Lorraine Taylor, and a few of the others in the neighborhood, seemed to take it kinda personal that the Johnsons didn't much go to church. But as far as Roman could tell, after whatever happened in their childhoods, neither his mama nor his daddy had much use for the whole shebang. There were other things too, some things the adults gossiped about that Roman heard in bits and pieces. Mostly, from what Roman could make out, both Mr. and Mrs. Taylor were trifling.

"Did you hear what I just said? Your boys hurt my boy." Lorraine pointed to Tracey, who put on his most pitiful face. He was bleeding, but still, Roman was ready to punch it right then and there.

"They did it first, Mama!" River interjected.

"They always attack us when we're out there just trying to practice and mind our business," Roman added. "Look at what they did to poor Rocco. Never mind that we gotta be onstage with him looking like this."

Rocco just stood there silently with a rag full of melting ice dripping down his face.

"Shhh," Emmeline said, "grown folks are talking."

"But it's true, Miss Emmeline! I saw it!" Christmas joined in. Lorraine Taylor glanced inside the Johnson house to see who'd spoken. Her face blanched at the sight of the little boy with his intestines splayed open and the tragic crook of his neck, the sickening stump. After a week with Christmas, the Johnsons had gotten used to it, but Roman remembered that first day in the forest when River had soiled his pants, and even he'd upchucked.

Lorraine Taylor took a step back, nearly tripping over herself in the process. "You got evil up in that house, Emmeline Johnson!"

"Only evil thing around here is your bad-butt little boy, always throwing rocks over at mine," Emmeline responded.

Tracey Taylor had the goddamn nerve to poke his head inside the Johnsons' door to see what his mama was talking about. The gash on his face wasn't nearly as bad as the one on Rocco's, Roman thought.

"What you talking 'bout, Mama?" Tracey said.

"Don't tell me not a one of you can see that haint?" Lorraine said, all shrill-like.

Christmas moved closer to the front door, damn near close enough to touch her, and said, "Hello!"

Lorraine Taylor startled back, falling straight onto her caboose, her legs splayed so that she looked like a Thanksgiving turkey. A single sensible brown pump remained on their front step, and Tracey quickly gathered it up for his mama and awkwardly tried to put it back on her foot. It seemed as though the ghost boy did it on purpose, as far as Roman could tell. Christmas was helping a brother (or brothers, as it were) out.

"Don't be ridiculous, Lorraine," Emmeline said, pretending to have no knowledge of the little ghost with whom, just hours earlier, she'd been sitting, the both of them laughing and watching *Days of Our Lives*.

"But I saw it. I know what I saw," Lorraine Taylor whimpered as Tracey helped her to her feet.

"You all right?" Roman said to Mrs. Taylor, surprised his mother hadn't asked. Emmeline must've been real mad to not even offer to help the woman to her feet.

"Grown folks are talking," Lorraine Taylor snapped, and steadied herself on Tracey's arm.

"Ain't no such thing as haints," Emmeline said. "Now, get on out of here with that country stuff."

Oblivious to all that had just transpired at their front door, Odysseus walked past with the last suitcase to be placed in the station wagon and nodded a hello over at Lorraine before saying, "All right, boys, we better get a move on, we got a competition to win."

"You mark my words, Emmeline Johnson, something wicked's coming your way with that little haint hanging 'round like that," Lorraine Taylor said over her shoulder as she hobbled back toward her house.

"Break a leg!" Their mama blew kisses, which River pretended to catch through the back window.

"Break your legs!" Christmas yelled.

CHAPTER FOUR

1969

THE BAR GIGS MADE ROCCO FEEL AS THOUGH HE WERE SUFFOCATING. There were too many people. Too many noises, alcohol-soaked anger, laughter that came up from the very bottom of people's bellies. Too many sour smells, sweat and spilled drink and smoke. Sticky floors and small stages. It felt like a full-on assault to every single one of his senses. Their costumes were already plenty itchy enough. After each gig, Rocco wanted to scrape his skin clean off. Everything was too-too. Too-too to count.

"One, two. One, two," Rocco muttered as he practiced Odysseus's choreography backstage. He had to get it perfect. To his left, Roman was a half-step offbeat. Roman was always a half-step offbeat.

Daddy said bar gigs meant money and exposure, both of which were what they needed to get to the next level and pay for a demo. Bar gigs were the best way to make good money fast. Rocco heard his parents arguing over it at night.

"I don't want you bringing my boys around bars. Lord knows who, or what, they're gonna be exposed to."

"I'll be right there with them, Emmie. I won't let them out of my sight. We'll perform and come straight home."

"How are they gonna get up for school the next day?"

"They're young. They can get by with a little less sleep."

"I don't like this, not one bit," Emmeline said.

Rocco's mother and father had been arguing more than he had ever heard them argue before in his life. Over their new bar gigs, but also over money. Their father kept closing up his millinery early to get them to gigs. Several of their regular customers had stopped Emmeline on the street to complain and had threatened to take their business elsewhere.

"I don't know why I can't take the boys and you stay and run the shop," his mama said.

"Most of these bars really aren't no kind of place for a lady," his father said.

"But it's an OK place for my children?" his mother snapped.

"You know I wouldn't let no harm come to them, Em," his dad said. "You know that."

"Fine, Odie. I'll keep shop. And you can take the boys here, there, and everywhere."

"You don't know what you're doing."

"Teach me, then," Emmeline snapped.

"What would it look like, me having my wife work all of a sudden?" Odysseus said.

"It'll look even worse you lose our business 'cause you ain't never there," Emmeline said.

"*Our?*" his father scoffed.

Then his mama would let loose some of her not-mama words and Rocco, River, and Roman would crowd at the top of the stairs to listen in wonder at how their beautiful mama had one of the filthiest mouths they'd ever heard in bars or elsewhere.

The first bar they'd been to was small and not very crowded, and though the floors were sticky, Rocco surprisingly liked being under the lights; he imagined himself a sunbeam, or a rotisserie chicken, and chuckled at the idea right in the very middle of their first song.

The next bar was larger, in a city a little ways away, where Roman said the patrons were already sauced even though the sun had only just gone down. Groups of well-dressed men clustered around smoky tables in the basement beneath the stage. On their way through the men, to the small closet that served as a dressing room, Rocco took note of the knives in black sheaths on the side of their pleated pants. Where there were knives, there were probably guns.

"What are they doing?" Rocco asked loudly.

"They're number runners," Roman whispered.

"What is that?" Rocco asked. How could numbers run? Or did the men run with numbers? And why? Why did it seem that so much of the world of grown-ups made sense to everybody else but not to him? Or just the world in general, for that matter?

At the bar after that, the Johnsons got up on the stage and as soon as Rocco could begin the countdown, for Rocco relished the countdown, a man slid his chair out from under him, raised it above his head, and slammed it down on the head of the man next to him. The boys struggled to dance and sing as the men were both dragged from the bar by a huge bouncer.

"Keep going," their father whispered, and Rocco stood frozen.

But Rocco was thrown off and couldn't remember where they were in the song. Or any of his steps. He felt like what the kids at school sometimes called him, a retard. Never mind that he was one of the top of his class in almost everything. Well, except for recently, when he'd started falling asleep in class after so many late nights performing. But even when he was fully awake, Rocco always got tongue-tied whenever teachers called on him. Except for when he was singing, or with his family, his words always felt just out of reach.

Until Christmas's arrival, Rocco had been so very lonely. Christmas knew what it was like to move through the world as though you were nothing at all, just a bit of cellophane. To have nobody see you or hear you. To speak and not always have your voice. Christmas was his first real friend. His best friend, other than his brothers, anyway. Somehow, Christmas always understood what he meant to say, even if it did come out all garbled up, or not at all. And besides, Christmas had a whole lot to say. If Rocco couldn't find his words, Christmas had plenty enough to give him.

Together, they could lie on the grass just under the great white sheets pinned to the clothesline and watch the butterflies as they flitted this way and that. Sometimes his brothers joined them, but River could hardly sit still, and Roman was increasingly grumpy these days. Hormones, according to their mama.

"Rocco! The butterflies are full of all kinds of drama today! Lemme tell you, Miss Francine has been up to shenanigans!" Christmas would call over and, ever one for a good recounting of shenanigans, Rocco would lie in the grass under the sun next to him.

"Rocco, what I tell you? No matter what's happening offstage, you keep on singing, you hear?" their father said on the way back. "Can't get distracted come the talent show. Got too much riding on it."

If it were either of the other boys, Rocco knew his father woulda been yelling at them right now. Knew sometimes River and Roman resented how gentle his parents were with him and not them.

"He sure did whup that man real good, though, didn't he?" River said after a brief silence, and they all nearly fell out the car with laughter.

═

THE WINNERS OF the talent show would get $60. All the best local acts would be there, vying for the top prize, not to mention the winner got their picture in the *Gazette*. With that $60 they'd finally have enough for a demo. Trouble was, Rocco didn't want to go. It was too much pressure, too many people judging, and all that money meant just about everybody in town would be there.

"I can't. I can't . . ." Rocco started smacking his head as the hour to leave for the talent show drew near.

"Rocco, stop!" his father said. "What's wrong with you, boy?"

"I can't." Rocco began to wail and smack his head harder. The very thought of yet another bar and all those people, all that chaos when he would much rather spend the evening out under the stars with Christmas made his head hurt, wrecked his insides, and yet he didn't want to let his brothers down. But he couldn't give voice to any of that. Not right now. Right now there was only, "No-no-no."

"Mama!" River called up the stairs. "Rocco's doing it again!"

Just then, Rocco's mama dramatically came down the stairs and gave a little twirl.

"What you all dressed up for?" his daddy said skeptically.

"We're coming too," his mama said.

"I helped her pick out the earrings," Christmas said proudly.

Roman gave a whistle, and their mama beamed. She sat down on the stairs to buckle up a pair of sparkly heels that Rocco had never seen before.

"I already told you these bars ain't no kinda place for a lady."

"Ain't no kind of place for children either, but we're not letting that stop us, are we, boys?"

"Christmas and I will be in the front row, baby," Emmeline leaned over and said to Rocco, briefly touching her forehead to his. "Don't need to look at nobody but us."

"Yes ma'am!" Christmas said.

"Johnson family outing!" Roman said, and laughed.

"Oh boy, oh boy, oh boy!" Christmas exclaimed as they drove from their house to the venue.

It was his first time accompanying them on a performance at night, as Rocco's mama had tried to make sure the little boy had an appropriate bedtime for his age, and adult supervision, which didn't much make sense to Rocco, since Christmas was dead anyway. What did it matter? But nobody argued with Emmeline. Not even Christmas. He seemed perfectly content to be mothered.

In the parking lot, the Johnsons looked around in awe of all the men and women exiting their cars and heading toward the bar.

"Packed house tonight," Odysseus murmured.

This bar was the loudest yet. But this time, Rocco had Christmas and his mama at least.

The boys recognized a few of their frequent competitors among the folks grabbing up instruments and costumes and readying for battle. There was a larger-than-life lady comedian who told jokes that had the grown-ups, and Roman, nearly falling off their seats, but Rocco didn't really understand why.

"Do your best to blend in, Christmas, OK?" Odysseus said, having agreed to his presence very, very reluctantly at Emmeline's insistence. "We don't need you scaring folks before we even get started."

"Yessir!" Christmas yelled, and then caught himself and whispered in lowercase this time: "yessir."

"Ooh, would you get whiff of all that reefer?!" his mama said, and laughed.

"What you know about that stuff, Mama?" Roman said.

"I lived many lives before I was your mama," Emmeline said to Roman, who opened his eyes real wide and burst out laughing.

"What's reefer?" Rocco asked, but nobody answered.

"River, what's reefer?" Rocco whispered, but River was too busy getting himself in the zone to perform and shushed anybody who dared speak to him. Roman said River was a little diva. Occasionally, Roman was right.

The boys readied themselves backstage next to the Sertrelles. Minerva, Joan, and Kiki were rail thin with what other folks called "that good hair" that they wore half up, half down, with a huge nest at the top. Rocco really wanted to stick his finger in to see what exactly made their hair reach the heights it did, but when he started toward them, Roman swatted him away. Rocco thought they looked like angels. So did Christmas.

"Hey, Minerva," Roman said.

Rocco noticed his brother's voice go lower by an entire octave.

Minerva just gave a half wave and kept on toward the stage.

"We're gonna get you this time!" River said to Kiki before they went on. Kiki just popped her gum in his face.

"What are you doing?" Roman elbowed River.

"Trying to psych them out," River replied.

"Leave them girls alone," Emmeline said. "You perform well enough, you don't need to resort to those kinds of shenanigans to win."

"They're really something." Christmas looked at the girls as they glided in formation across the stage.

Rocco nodded. It was hard to concentrate on anything at all at the moment. His nerves buzzed from all of the conversations going on all at once, the battling colognes, cigars, and cigarettes. He tried not to tense up.

"You know what Mr. Farraday told me to do first time I performed with the revue?" Christmas said to Rocco. "Imagine them all in their underwear! Or pretend you're singing to a crowd full of babies!"

"Babies are very loud." Rocco sighed.

"I'm going to go up front. If you get nervous, just look at me and I'll be right there to cheer you on, OK?" Emmeline said, and gave each of her boys a kiss on the top of the head.

Roman seemed as though he couldn't care less about any of it. His tongue hung half out his mouth, drooling at the Sertrelles, even though they'd seen their act a bunch of times already.

"Wish they hadn't booked you boys after them." Odysseus paced back and forth.

"Why not?" River asked.

"It's hard for a bunch of boys to go after pretty girls in a room full of drunk grown men."

"So? We're better than them!" River said confidently. "Mama just said—"

"Your mama is trying to make sure you boys turn out to be good people."

"Aren't you?" Roman said.

"Yeah. But I want you win too," his father said, and then they all burst into laughter.

They had beaten the Sertrelles in the last three competitions in which they'd faced off. But Rocco thought River shouldn't be too cocky. In the two contests they'd lost, the Sertrelles won first and second, and the Johnson Three hadn't even placed. So really, the Sertrelles were more consistent.

The girls finished their set to thunderous applause, and whistles that echoed off the walls.

"Marry me!" a man shouted out, and reached up to pat poor Minerva's behind even though she wasn't much older than Roman. She dodged and swatted the man away as he continued to grab at her. Then Minerva blew him and the rest of the crowd a kiss before jogging offstage.

"Asshole," Minerva mumbled as she moved past the Johnsons, the fringe on her minidress swinging back and forth.

"That wasn't right," Roman said to her sympathetically, but once again, Minerva just walked on by.

"You're up!" the stage manager said, ushering them forward.

"Bring back the girls!" the man up front yelled before they could even introduce themselves.

"Hi. We're the Johnson Three," River declared, and Rocco began to count them in.

They were doing well. Really well. Except that the men didn't care at all. They weren't fighting as they had in the other bar, but the patrons were talking over them and loudly. It was very rude. Rocco heard his mother trying to shush the people around her, saying, "Can y'all please stop talking? Those are my babies up there!"

Rocco felt a frustration burning deep inside him. Deep enough that it overtook everything else, even all of Odysseus's training.

"Be quiet!" he yelled at the crowd, and stomped his foot, interrupting their song.

A bread roll smacked him upside the head with the force of a baseball, thrown by somebody who definitely had been in the Negro Leagues, or least should've been. Rocco thought he actually saw stars around his head, like he was in one of those Looney Tunes cartoons they watched on the weekend. Why was he always the one to get hit by things? A beer bottle was thrown at River, who ducked, but only just barely. It smashed to the ground and spilled its bubbles and wheat on the ground near Roman's feet.

"Who did that?" Emmeline stood up and yelled. "What? You think you're all big and bad, throwing things at little boys?"

Before their father could do or say a thing, Christmas appeared next to Rocco. He floated up in front of Rocco, took the bread from the ground, and pelted the offender back. Then he went over to the man who had tossed the beer bottle and flipped his chair upside down.

Most of the patrons who could see Christmas screamed and ran toward the exits. Others sat wide-eyed. Still others didn't see him at all and just sat there looking very confused as to what exactly all the fuss was about. The stupid men who had heckled the Johnsons assumed that the people next to them were responsible for their comeuppance and thus threw punches at unsuspecting innocents.

"Oh fuck," Roman said, too close to the microphone.

Soon grown men were pushing and shoving. One man even stubbed out his cigarette on another's silk tie. Emmeline stomped on a very drunk man's foot with her sparkly heel after he barreled into her.

"Stoppit!" Christmas yelled into the crowd and the windows and floor shook. A wineglass exploded. What was left of their audience stood, jaws on the floor, wondering what, or who, it was before them, Christmas being dead and kinda gory and scary looking, if you didn't know him.

"Go on." Christmas nodded to the Johnson Three.

Rocco counted them down and then they began, again.

At the end of the night, when the crowd voted, the Johnson Three won first place. Rocco wasn't sure if it was because they deserved it, or because of Christmas scaring folks, or because those folks felt badly about everything, or because the crowd had so thoroughly thinned out by that time that nobody was there who even remembered that the Sertrelles, or anybody else for that matter, had even performed before the baby ghost had appeared.

Still, now they had $60.

"You did it, boys." Odysseus beamed as he held the cheap trophy given to the winners. Emmeline rushed over and gathered Roman and River in an embrace.

"Mama, you were about to throw down!" Roman said to her, and laughed.

"They were not about to disrespect my babies on my watch," Emmeline said, grabbing her husband affectionately by the arm. "I haven't had that much fun in ages!"

Emmeline hugged Rocco to her and kissed both his cheeks. "You OK, baby?"

She was sweaty and smelled like cigar smoke. Rocco gently pushed her away.

From a distance, across the parking lot, the Sertrelles waved. Enthusiastically, Roman waved back at them.

"Oooh, Minerva, ooh." River made kissy faces mocking Roman, who promptly shoved him. Rocco barely dodged out of the way.

Rocco's mother leaned her head on his daddy's shoulder. His daddy drove one-handed as he wrapped his other arm around her. His parents looked so very happy together in that moment. Rocco hoped one day to be loved by somebody as wonderful as his mama.

"We're recording a demo!" River yelled out the window.

"Whooopeee!" Christmas shouted, and Rocco joined him, because joy was infectious.

CHAPTER FIVE

A WEEK AFTER THEIR TRIUMPH AT THE BAR, MS. MINNIE FLUELLEN AT the house across the street from them up and died, and her peoples were over for days.

"Do you see Ms. Minnie yet?" Rocco asked Christmas.

"Not all dead people become . . . like me," he said.

Their mama thought the boys should hold off on practicing for as long as the folks across the street were grieving, not to mention that after their encounter with Lorraine Taylor things were still a little tense. She'd spread news of the haint and the Johnson Three like their neighborhood's very own Paul Revere, warning all the upstanding Black folks within several blocks that the Johnsons were harboring something unnatural, possibly even sinister. They'd decided it was best to keep Christmas inside as much as possible, at least until everyone who'd heard the rumors decided Ms. Lorraine was crazy as a coconut. Everybody already knew she was a busybody. But with Ms. Minnie's passing, there was so much hooting and hollering and wailing outside that after two days even Odysseus figured wouldn't nobody pay the little pick any mind. Maybe they'd think the dead boy was just their grief making a sandbox of the mind.

"So they're gonna hear the boys singing and laughing, and everybody over here watching them, while they're over there thinking about poor dead Minnie?" Rocco's mama said.

"You and I both know Minnie wasn't no saint. And it's been two days already. Not practicing ain't gonna stop the woman from being dead," Rocco's daddy said.

His mother swatted his daddy's butt and said, "You so bad, Odie!"

"Me bad? Your temper's the one got us into this mess with Lorraine." He laughed.

A few moments later, Rocco, Roman, River, and Christmas were outside practicing. Then, Christmas did a dance move that stopped River dead in his tracks.

"Again!" Rocco said.

Christmas shimmied a bit to the left, then again to the right, then leaned his body all the way back way up on his tippy toes, and picked himself up again with a twirl to finish it off.

River tried to do it. Roman, too, but instead he just fell flat on his face.

"You gotta lean all the way back," Christmas said. River tried again.

"We should start using it in our choreography!" River said.

Odysseus didn't much care for Christmas's moves, River could tell. Maybe it had something to do with the fact that Christmas had once been a baby minstrel and these had been a pickaninny's moves.

"I'll think about it . . ." he said. "All right, let's start at the top!"

"But . . . Daddy!" River started. There was something special about Christmas's footwork. Something River could feel himself the very moment he imitated him and lifted his body skyward. Maybe the pick's moves wouldn't be bad if they just modernized them a bit? Wasn't exactly like the Johnson Three was about to bust out a rendition of "Mammy" while doing it.

"From the top!" Odysseus said, ignoring him.

The boys continued practicing and eventually they noticed they had an audience. Not just the usual neighborhood crowd, but must've been Ms. Minnie's folks from out of town, all dressed in black, smoking cigars and drinking, while they watched the Johnsons. They didn't seem very mournful at all to River, but what did he know?

"Them boys is good," a large, greasy man in an impeccable suit said. The man had a mustache that went across the whole length of his face, not just the mouth part. He wiped sweat from his brow.

"Thank you," Odysseus said.

"The other one part of the act too?"

"The other one?" Odysseus said.

The man gestured over to Christmas.

"You can see him? Not everybody can," Odysseus asked, eyes wide.

"It's my job to see talent everywhere." The man shrugged as though it were perfectly natural to see a dead child dancing and singing in his world. "They ever been to the Apollo?"

"Not yet. We're working on it."

The man took out a card. Turns out Mr. Vic Hadley was Ms. Minnie's brother-in-law come to pay his respects all the way from New York. He had a friend who was responsible for booking acts at the Apollo.

"That's in Harlem!" Christmas murmured approvingly. "Hot dog!"

All the major scouts checked for new acts at the Apollo's amateur nights, Mr. Vic Hadley told them. "I'd be more than happy to introduce y'all."

"You'd do that for us?" Odysseus asked.

"Ain't but ten minutes of my time. Way I see it, we Negroes gotta do whatever we can to help each other out, lift each other up. That's what them rich white folks do. You got a demo?"

"Not yet. Working on that too," Odysseus said.

"May I use your phone?" Mr. Hadley asked.

"My man Theo will hook you up," he said after hanging up the phone.

"Theo Celestine?" River's eyes widened. "You two know each other?"

"Went to school together. He still heaping mad at me 'cause I dumped his sister before moving to New York," the man said with a laugh. "Theo's expecting you next Friday. Ten A.M. sharp."

AT TEN A.M. the next Friday, the entire Johnson clan crowded into the unassuming building, standing atop well-trod Persian rugs that smelled of weed and sweat. River excitedly imagined all the musicians who had come before them giving it their all in that very same room, singing, playing, tambourine shaking, to the point of exhaustion. The fanciest thing about the place was the velvet red chair upon which Theo Celestine sat, like a starship captain, cigar in hand.

"That's not good for our voices," Rocco chastised him.

River elbowed Rocco, but he was right. River could already feel the smoke in a tickle in the back of his throat, pushing his notes downward.

Theo Celestine laughed and placed it down. He was an avuncular presence, with graying hair that went in a stripe right down the center of his head (still in a conk, even though wasn't hardly anybody but James Brown doing that still).

"Vic says you got something special here," Celestine said. The man's voice was silky as a scarf and slippery as butter. "The thing is, these things cost money. It's not cheap to record. We gotta pay the session musicians and engineers."

River pictured the man's silky-smooth voice as a tall playground slide he was convincing the Johnsons to go down.

"What's the cheapest we could go and still make a decent-sounding demo?" Odysseus asked.

"If we could get y'all live that might take a few bucks off it. Or if we did something very stripped down. Usually, for demos, we ask for half upon signing a contract and half after you're done recording. So, you got a bit of time to get everything together, depending on how soon you want to get in the studio."

"Soon as we can," Odysseus said.

That very morning, with the money from the contest, and a bit of money their parents had set aside for this very moment, the Johnson Three gave Mr. Theo Celestine the deposit on a recording session at Brodie Records.

"All right, Mary Jean, now that you've decided to show up to work, let's book these kids," Celestine said to the girl at the front desk.

Two weeks later, the Johnson Three, and Christmas, sang with all their might in the small recording studio, accompanied by the session players Celestine had secured for them. Nothing too fancy, just a guitar player, drummer, and a piano player to do a few simple arrangements.

Silently, Celestine worked. Every so often, he shouted out a suggestion for Roman here, or had River come in a half beat sooner than he had been. If his father minded the man messing with their arrangements, he didn't say a word.

As they took a quick break, Rocco sat down next to the pianist, who was a man about their father's age with a big wooden peg where his left leg should've been.

"Did you lose that in the war?" Rocco asked, pointing downward.

"Rocco . . ." Roman said.

"Nah. Leg survived the war. Didn't survive no diabetes. Had to get it amputated," the pianist said.

"You ate too much sugar?" Rocco asked. He was unusually chatty that afternoon, hopped up on the excitement of performing.

"Rocco . . ." River interjected.

"Born with it," the pianist said.

"Then how come—"

"Let's take it from the top," Theo Celestine said through the speaker on the other side of the recording studio glass.

"I can feel it sometimes. I forget it's not there," the pianist said.

"Like a ghost leg?" Rocco asked.

"Exactly."

"Well, you're very good," River said.

"So are you." The pianist chuckled and leaned in to whisper, "And your little friend over there too."

He gestured at Christmas, who was trying and apparently failing to remain as inconspicuous as possible.

"Y'all are great," the pianist went on, picking out his fro, and then placing the pick back in his hair. "I mean it. Just know that y'all are the real deal. Whether other people say so or not."

It had never occurred to River that they wouldn't.

═══

HOURS LATER, THE boys' mother glowered at their father across the dinner table. "Are you kidding me?"

Odysseus looked up from cutting his roast. "I just wonder if the boys can do better."

"This is something!" Celestine had stood up suddenly and said during playback. "This is really something!"

Right then and there, Celestine had excitedly offered them a record contract with Brodie Records.

"We aren't as big and bad as some of these places, but we take care of our peoples, you know what I mean? At Brodie we're a family. Some of these folks would screw over their own grandmamas for money. All skinfolk ain't kinfolk. And half of these white producers don't quite know what to do with Negro voices. It's not their fault . . . it's just . . . different with them," Celestine said.

Still, their daddy wasn't sure.

"What do you mean? Mr. Celestine was lovely, and he's excited about the boys! Brodie's close enough and they got a great track record. The boys wouldn't have to disrupt their lives even more than they already do!"

"I don't know, Emmie."

"What could you possibly not know?"

"I think the boys can do better. Brodie's small. You were there! You saw how small it is. We don't want them getting relegated to race records. It's a fine place for a demo recording but for an album . . . I'm just . . . I'm not sure. Plus, I don't even think they have distribution."

Their parents argued into the night, but River found himself not thinking about Celestine, or Brodie, or even the Apollo itself, where, true to his word, Mr. Vic Hadley had gotten them a place on amateur night in three weeks.

He interrupted Rocco and Christmas, who were talking about something the butterflies told them earlier.

"Say, Christmas, can you show me how to do that thing you do again?"

River knew Odysseus would never let them use the move, not now. But maybe one day, eventually. Just as Theo Celestine had known the Johnson Three were something, River knew this here footwork was something.

"OK. You gotta make sure you lean back just enough, like this." Christmas demonstrated.

And soon, up on their toes they went.

CHAPTER SIX

THE TRIP TO THE APOLLO WAS THE LONGEST THE JOHNSON THREE HAD taken yet. Rocco almost peed his pants, and the humidity had River sweating like a hog. Their mama sat up front, whistling along to "(Sittin' on) The Dock of the Bay" and only hitting every third note.

"Oh boy!" Christmas said, crawling over Rocco's lap to look out the window.

"Sit still, Christmas," Emmeline said gently. "You can't distract Odie while he's driving."

"Jesus. Did you put on deodorant?" Roman said to River. "You're gonna scare away our fans, smelling like a barn animal up in the Apollo."

"I can't smell you," Christmas said kindly.

"You can't smell anything!" Roman said. Which was apparently true, but River thought it was shitty to rub it in the dead boy's face.

"Knock it off, Roman," his mama said, and reached back to pat River on the hand.

Christmas looked rather hurt, but said nothing.

"We're here!" Rocco shouted loudly. "We're in New York!" and River felt every single hair on his funky body tingle with excitement.

═══

THE APOLLO WAS not nearly as imposing from the outside as River would've guessed, sandwiched as it was between a shoe-repair shop and an adjoining steakhouse that advertised their steaks nearly as loudly as the Apollo marquee itself, which read, 25 MEN AND 1 GIRL: JEWEL BOX REVUE.

After they'd unpacked and finally settled in the hotel, River fell backward onto the bed, arms outstretched. They'd been cramped up in the car a godawful number of hours, River's arms and legs feeling like he'd been boxed up and shipped through the post.

"Don't you want to check out the venue beforehand?" his mama said with a gleam in her eye, even as the clock neared midnight. And of course they did; it was the Apollo, after all.

At the box office, the big wooden beads at the end of the cashier's cornrows clack-clacked percussively as she looked down at River, Rocco, and Roman and said, "Little young, aren't they?"

River thought she looked impossibly chic. A real city girl!

"It's a special kinda night," Emmeline said protectively.

In response, the lady popped her gum loudly and handed them their tickets.

Inside, they sat way in the very back of the theater, so that they could hear what the audience would be hearing tomorrow, according to their daddy.

Onstage, women with legs for days shimmered in outsized sequin-and-feather headdresses prettier than a peacock's plumage. Holding court in the middle, a man with a thin voice and an even thinner mustache led them all.

"Someone must've paid handsomely for those headpieces," Odysseus said appreciatively.

"I thought it was twenty-five men and one girl?" Christmas asked.

"Those are men!" Roman sniggered. "And that man's a lady!"

River leaned in closer to see what the hell Roman was on about. And sure enough, his brother was right! Those were men's legs gliding gracefully across the stage, Black and white, all together.

River hadn't even known that men could, or would, do such a thing. And yet, how wonderful they were. How imposing the only lady was as she strode across the stage, big as any man. He sat thoroughly transfixed. Around him, the audience whooped and hollered excitedly, men and women. Though mostly men, River noted.

"Don't go getting any ideas, Riv." Roman laughed.

"Shut up, Roman," Odysseus snapped at him. Rocco's eyes went as wide as dinner plates. Their father rarely spoke to them like that, and Roman quickly went silent.

The rest of the performance was sour and sweet. Sour 'cause Roman had ruined it for River, but only just a bit. Why was he always such a dick? And still, how glorious all twenty-six performers were!

That night, in bed, River dreamed himself up there onstage with them, leg elegantly outstretched. At least until Rocco kicked him awake, and then he lay still, listening to all the occasional shouts and sirens, that wondrous cacophony of the city below them, like so much jazz.

═══

AMATEUR NIGHT AT the Apollo was no joke. Everybody knew that. And the boys were to be up first, the acts to follow being a bit more established. Some even had record deals already! River had actually heard the final act on the radio, even all the way out by them! How was that an amateur? How were three little boys supposed to compete with that? Mr. Vic Hadley, ole dead Ms. Minnie's kin, said there were 1,500 seats there! Apparently, the booker trusted Vic enough to book them without hearing them himself, unless the booker didn't much care if they were good or not, as long as they were entertaining. The Johnson Three had only ever performed in front of as many as a hundred people max. Maybe two hundred. River had no aptitude for estimating crowd size.

Snapping her brand-new Nikon like crazy, Emmeline made the boys pose for photo after photo to commemorate the occasion, merrily yelling across the din, "Act natural!"

Now there would be photographic evidence if they failed.

River began to hyperventilate backstage. Around them, the other acts primped, did vocal exercises, and argued as they rehearsed their dance moves. The world was full of many talented people; who was River Johnson in the middle of all that magic?

"Breathe, Riv," Roman said. But River could hear the nervous quiver in even his brother's voice.

Up front, a squat comedian in a badly tailored suit warmed up the crowd with all manner of ribaldry. The jokes were decent enough, in River's opinion, but not enough to get the energy level up. Or perhaps he wasn't old enough to understand them really. Or even worse, the crowd was in a mood tonight.

People were dying all over the world. Assassinations and hijackings and random weird men killing famous people in their own homes, the horrific images playing over and over on the nightly news. Sometimes, it made even River feel tired and hopeless, and impossibly old, even though he was still just a kid. It was hard to laugh sometimes, with everything going on in this world of theirs. Still, wasn't that their job? To make people smile in the middle of it all? It was so much to ask of him.

"Maybe we shouldn't do this? Maybe we're not ready?" he whispered to his father, lest the other acts hear him. He thought of Rocco's freak-outs at their last two bar appearances. How could his brother handle a crowd this big if he couldn't even handle a few drunks?

"You wanna quit before you've even tried?" Odysseus said. "Did I raise you to be a quitter?"

"No sir."

"No sir," Rocco repeated.

"And do you want to disappoint your dear mama, who came all this way with us to see you perform at this positively venerable space?"

"No. But . . ." River started up again.

"No buts. You're gonna get up there and perform for those people like we just drove a thousand miles to do."

"Yessir," River said. Then he ran to the nearest trash can and dry-heaved.

"Jesus, Riv," Roman said, looking a little green around the gills himself.

Before they could huddle, or have a pep talk, or whatever it was that people did before playing one of the most important shows of their lives, a man yelled, "Go, go, go, go! You're on!"

The boys nervously trotted onto the stage.

"Rub the tree, boys!" the audience yelled.

River reached over to rub the famed Tree of Hope.

Feeling like butter on a fresh biscuit, River thought he might melt right then and there, it was too damn hot onstage. Didn't help that their costumes weren't exactly made of the most breathable fabric. River stared out at all thousand-plus people. Roman took it upon himself to walk up to the front of the stage and say, "Hey. Um. We're the Johnson Three."

Somebody booed loudly.

Rocco looked at both of his brothers.

"One. Two. Three!" he said. Rocco loved the counting part; even the Apollo couldn't stop him from that.

How much larger everything sounded in a place like this! The house band's instruments felt both all up in River's ears and very far away. His voice felt like his own, but also like he was a giant looming over the seats. His brothers stumbled over their steps at first. Roman's voice cracked at their first chorus. But eventually, the Johnsons found their groove. River felt himself relax into the song and he smiled at the audience. He winked at a teenage girl in the front row, who seemed to be especially feeling it. He felt the sweat drip down his leg and collect in a small puddle of nerves somewhere down his calf.

And then they were done.

The boys looked at one another, then out at the crowd. There was what felt like the longest silence ever, in which River thought he might die of embarrassment. Roman looked over at River and mouthed, *What do we do?*

Then Rocco began to applaud quite enthusiastically for himself. For themselves.

And the audience responded in kind. It wasn't the jump-out-of-your-seat, rush-the-stage level of applause that they'd hoped for. Not the whooping and hollering that came from having given the audience a damn near religious experience. But a polite applause from an audience not known for handing those out, unless you'd earned at least some modicum of respect! And the Johnsons had. At one of the most important venues in the whole wide world!

River walked over to Rocco and Roman, and the three of them took the deepest of bows before they were beckoned offstage.

The other acts were mostly good. Some of them were admittedly better. More polished. With the confidence that came with being older, or maybe just the coordination. Two poor souls got booed right off almost immediately.

The Johnsons didn't win, but at least they didn't get booed off. That was success enough, wasn't it?

After the show, a man approached them as they were packing up to go.

"You kids were great!" The man was barely larger than River, but something about him felt big. His big salt-and-pepper curls ebbed just above his temples, and his dark eyes took up half his face. He was slightly unkempt in that way very rich white people allowed themselves to be.

"Thank you, sir," they murmured, unsure of what this man wanted.

"Do you have management?" he asked.

"I'm their manager," their father said.

"And I'm their mama," their mama said.

Christmas stood between Odysseus and Emmeline. Some folks looked at him for a minute, while others kept it moving, many colored folks of a certain age having ghosts of their own.

The man didn't seem to be able to see Christmas though.

"Nice to meet you. My name is Mr. X."

"Like Malcolm?" River asked.

The man laughed, a little too heartily in River's opinion.

"Power to the people!" he said, raising his fist with a chuckle. "No, it's short for Wexler. The boys at school called me Wex, then X. It just kinda stuck around."

River nodded as though he understood, though he didn't entirely. The man couldn't have been inside a classroom in many years. And why'd he have to go and put "Mr." in front of a nickname?

"I'm normally based out in California, but I like coming out here to check out the acts every once in a while. I think these boys have got something really special, if we just tease it out a little bit."

We? River thought.

"I own several nightclubs throughout Los Angeles. We can get the boys to perform there. People will see them. Big people. The right people. Plus, I'm an entertainment lawyer. Well, you could say I'm a little of everything, I guess."

River looked off to the side at old dearly departed Miss Minnie's friend Mr. Vic Hadley. A Negro gentleman stood next to him smoking a cigar. The man looked sleek, important. Or maybe, River thought, all New Yorkers just looked that way.

Mr. X listed off a few of the names he'd worked with. Names they recognized. Names that nearly anybody with half a brain cell would recognize. He told their origin stories as though stardom were an everyday occurrence and not the stuff of legend itself.

"I'm not just blowing smoke up your ass here," Mr. X finished.

"No sir," Odysseus said.

The boys looked up at their parents excitedly. River thought his father's voice sounded a little too measured. Wasn't this everything they'd been waiting for?

"Appreciate it," Odysseus said. "California's a mighty big move."

"Sure. Sure," Mr. X said. "Y'all can discuss it as a family. But I wouldn't take too long . . . this industry's awful fickle sometimes. You boys got a demo I can take with me?"

Odysseus was ready for that exact moment with the demo they'd pressed over at Brodie just weeks before. He gestured to Emmeline, who quickly whipped it out of her purse. Mr. X examined it in his chubby hand.

"Good. Here's my card. If you guys make it out my way, please do give me a call."

"Whooopee!" River said after Mr. X had disappeared around the corner.

"What about Mr. Celestine?" Rocco said.

"Celestine's small potatoes compared to California!" Roman exclaimed. Even Mr. "I'm Too Cool for This" himself seemed to be swept up in the excitement.

Mr. Hadley and the sleek gentleman, who, up close, looked a bit like a meerkat River had seen on a nature show that morning, sauntered up next to them in the spot Mr. X had just vacated.

"He'll get you there," Vic Hadley said.

"Mmm-hmm," the meerkat said.

"Can't trust 'em all, but X is as good as his word."

"Mostly," the meerkat concurred.

"Say, you want me to take a photo of you all? Not every day you get to play the Apollo," Vic Hadley said.

"Would you?" Emmeline passed over her camera.

Oldest to youngest, the Johnsons linked arms and smiled, Christmas along with them.

"So . . . is the haint coming with you?" River heard the meerkat whisper with a chuckle to Odysseus.

═

THE NEXT DAY, Odysseus opened the worn damask curtains wide, letting the bright sun flood the small room. One by one the boys shadowboxed the morning light, bleary-eyed and bad of breath.

"It's too early!" Roman grumbled. He was right. The sun wasn't even fully up and the night before they'd not gotten back to the hotel until well after midnight.

"Gotta get on the road early," Odysseus said, and even their mama groaned.

As Odysseus navigated the Caddy through the New York City streets, River marveled at all the life before him. On their way in, he'd been focused on the show, but now he could really look at the city inhaling and exhaling all around them. In Harlem, children readied games of hopscotch on the sidewalks with big pastel chalks. Grown men argued over dice games on the stairs. A woman pushed a pram down the street looking positively glamorous.

"I stayed right there back when it was a boardinghouse," Emmeline said as they passed by a row house. "That's the very first place I lived in New York!"

"And that's where me and your mama first made eyes at each other," Odysseus said, pointing at another. "At a rent party for—Emmie, what was his name again?"

"George, I think it was, or was it Alain?"

River had never seen his father drink before, and it was deeply weird to think of his parents before they were parents.

"Your mama was the prettiest girl in the whole room and didn't want nothing to do with me at first on account she thought I was broke."

"Weren't you though?" She giggled. River couldn't remember the last time he'd heard her sound this carefree.

"Told you I wouldn't always be."

"That you did . . . I'm still waiting, Mr. Rockefeller. Besides, it wasn't that I'd thought you were broke, it's that I'd seen you cutting up."

His mama started a deep belly laugh that seemed to come up from the very past itself.

"Hush, woman."

"Oh, I do miss this place sometimes, Odie, don't you?" Emmeline gazed wistfully out the window.

"Ain't nowhere like Harlem," Odysseus agreed.

"Mr. Moses left Mr. Powell and me to come to Harlem," Christmas said.

"Who's that?" River said.

"They used to be my family many years ago," he said wistfully. "For a little while."

Then the little boy stared out the window as though he were very, very far away in another place entirely, and they all knew not to bother him.

===

SOMEWHERE IN BROOKLYN, River watched middle-aged white men in newsboy hats yelling at each other in a language that sounded like opera, even though he was pretty sure somebody was about to kick somebody else's ass. Sure enough, soon as they were about to round the corner, the first punch was thrown.

As they traveled along the water for what felt like an eternity, River spotted a few fishermen struggling against the ocean for something worthwhile. He wasn't sure he'd want to eat anything they caught. He wondered if perhaps their father had gotten lost, he was pretty sure the ocean was the exact opposite direction from home.

Finally, they saw it, the wooden rocket tilted on its side across the horizon that read ASTROLAND!

"Surprise!" Odysseus said. "Wasn't gonna let you boys leave New York without a little fun first."

Rocco jumped up and down in his seat as they approached the boardwalk.

"Hot dog!" he said.

"But we didn't bring any swimsuits!" River said.

"Don't be a killjoy," Roman said, and practically ran out of the car as soon as it was parked, propelled seemingly by the sight of two brown-skinned girls in bikinis.

Coney Island was everything River hoped it would be. They gorged themselves on Nathan's Hot Dogs and ate pink, fluffy sugar, like clouds melting in your mouth. Roman shot down several galloping cowboys. River and Rocco aimed a steady water stream to get a boat to the other side. At a huge tank, about the size of an aquarium, a ride called the Neptune Diving Bells took them thirty feet underwater, where they looked through the portholes at two real-life porpoises swimming back and forth! It would've been thrilling, except that a boy next to them screamed, right in River's ear, thinking they were sharks.

"They're not sharks, they're porpoises!" Christmas said to the boy, and the boy's eyes grew wide and he promptly shut up.

River wondered what it might be like to swim back and forth like that when the whole ocean was supposed to be yours. What did the porpoises say to each other all day? Were they in love, or were they sick of each other? Or maybe it was both?

At the Astro Tower, as they waited in line, River decided to broach the topic of California with their father.

"I've been thinking . . . I wouldn't mind moving to California," he said.

"California!" Christmas exclaimed. "I love California!"

"You been?" River asked.

"Once, a very long time ago. To be in the pictures!"

"You were in the movies?" River asked. River wasn't sure if the little boy was a pathological liar or if he just had a fantastic imagination.

"Just one," Christmas said wistfully. "It was lost in a studio fire, I'm told."

"Huh," River said. There were enough people buzzing around them that the Johnsons and Christmas went unnoticed. Otherwise, some might think it odd, a whole family carrying on a conversation with an invisible member. Though River could've sworn one old man turned all the way around to look and stumbled headfirst into a trash can, like something out of Laurel and Hardy!

"So, you want to move to California?" Emmeline chuckled.

"If we needed to," River said, trying not to sound overeager.

The truth was that school had gotten a little rough recently, especially after they'd appeared in the *Gazette*.

"River Johnson walk around thinking he all special and shit," one of the older boys had said, and just like that, the others pounced.

The newest insult was that River had a bit of swish to him, according to Loren Jessup, who had raised his voice octaves higher and swayed side to side, imitating River. He wouldn't have dared to do that the year before, but something had shifted. The rules were changing quickly, even faster than their bodies, and something about junior high felt more ominous.

Never mind that half his class thought the Johnsons crazy because of the rumor about the little ghost boy haunting their house. It was crazy sounding, he could admit as much. River would've thought it was weird if it had been anyone else. And the other half of his class wanted to know every single thing possible about the afterlife and what the little ghost boy could do. Could he walk through walls? Did he kill people?

"Of course he doesn't," River snapped. "He's just a little boy."

On the Cyclone, Christmas squeezed into the empty space next to Rocco. "I've never been on a roller coaster before!"

The roller coaster had been Roman's idea, and River didn't think it was a particularly good one, given their recent gluttony, but he didn't wanna deal with Roman calling him a wimp.

"Hold tight, boys," Odysseus yelled from the platform as the Johnson brothers were strapped in, their mama and daddy having decided to sit this one out.

Emmeline ran up closer to the coaster to snap another photo as the ride started.

"Say cheese!" she shouted, and off they went.

As the roller coaster's gears started to grind, sending them upward, Christmas turned around to look at River and gave him a thumbs-up. A white girl seated two cars down saw Christmas and promptly fainted. Though really, River thought she was being a bit dramatic. Was seeing a dead boy on a roller coaster any scarier than being whipped up and down and around on a rickety, man-made wooden machine operated by a teenager?

"Jesus, the good part hasn't even started yet, Julie!" the boy next to her said.

Rocco squealed with delight as they shot up in the air.

"I think I'm gonna be sick!" River said, just as the cotton candy, hot dogs, and flavored ice in his stomach all began their ascent.

"Don't you dare!" Roman yelled over at him.

"Oh boy!" Christmas said.

Odysseus and Emmeline stood down below and off to the side watching. A lever was released and River and his brothers went up, but his stomach went down. Then, the Johnson boys were propelled through the salty ocean air, twisting, turning, and plummeting, held by mere straps that didn't feel nearly as secure as River would've hoped.

CHAPTER SEVEN

THE SMALL MAN HELD HIMSELF LIKE A GIANT AS HE GREETED ODYSSEUS in the stuffy office just off Sunset. It had taken Odysseus forever to find the rather absurd streamline modern building made to look like a ship, a great big globe sitting upon its spire and signage announcing itself, CROSSROADS OF THE WORLD. Around that structure, with its portholes and upper deck, sat buildings in a variety of international architectural styles, the very world itself as a studio backlot meets shopping center. It was in an office on the top floor of one such building, in the middle of Hollywood, that they found the craggy, if dapper, Scot.

Building a Negro family in America seemed to Odysseus a bit like blowing glass. He considered it his job to take all that pressure, that heat, and make something beautiful. This is why he'd decided the Johnsons should move to California a month after their Apollo performance.

Crossroads of the World indeed.

"What brings you here?" Martin McAvoy said, flicking a piece of lint off his well-tailored suit.

Odysseus was loath to ask a white man for anything. Back home, the banks he'd frequented had been Negro-owned and -operated; everything in their community had been. They'd built their own independence, their own little slice of heaven.

The white soldiers had found themselves bolstered by the GI Bill. Doors opened even to the poorest and dumbest and most ignoble of them. Micks and guidos became white and middle-class, with Uncle Sam's gratitude, but not the Negro. All the war had done for the Negro was make him uppity, according to white folks. Still, Odysseus scraped and he climbed and he created. He sewed just as his mother had taught him, but also he discovered the beauty of millinery, learning from the hatmaker who had the shop next door to his tailor shop, and when the man grew too old to want to continue, Odysseus took over the milliner's shop too. His creations attracted women of all races to drive for miles for a specialized fitting. "His hats are like wearable art!" the white women gushed to each other. This is how he became a credit to his race.

Excepting that the loan officers in California didn't see him as such.

"How's it going?" Emmeline asked him after a week.

"Great! Got some great leads," he lied, and he could tell she knew he was lying, but his wife wasn't cruel and thus didn't pour salt into the wound.

"You wanna speak to the boys?" she said after a long silence.

River was first on the line.

"You been practicing?" Odysseus asked. It seemed as good a way to start as any.

"Can we get a house with a pool?"

Odysseus laughed. "Let's not get ahead of ourselves."

"Have you seen any famous people yet?" River demanded.

"How's Rocco? Put him on for me."

"Hold on."

"Hi," Rocco said.

"How are you, son?"

"Good."

"You miss your old man?"

"No," Rocco said, and Odysseus laughed. He could hear River and Roman bickering in the background. How much he missed the warmth of home. Of family.

"I wanna talk to him too!" Odysseus heard Christmas say in the background.

"Hi, Mr. Odysseus! This is my first time talking into a telephone! Do you like California? Is it very sunny? Don't you worry, sir, I'll take good care of Ms. Emmeline while you're gone . . ."

Odysseus felt himself start to choke up. He hadn't expected it to be the little pick that made him cry, but something about the boy's little voice pricked something in him.

Odysseus had enough money to pay for the mortgage back home and the bare minimum in California. He needed much more to put together a decent down payment for the kind of house to which Emmeline and the boys were accustomed. At the first boardinghouse in which he'd landed, the plain-faced white landlady eyed him suspiciously but didn't refuse his money. When he returned to his room the next day, having ventured out to get the lay of the land, his suitcase was unzipped, and a pair of socks had rolled under a chair. The woman had not even bothered to conceal that she had flipped through his weathered Green Book, had touched the photos he'd brought with him of Emmeline and the boys, as well of his dear mama who had been dead many years.

He'd quickly moved on to a second boardinghouse, where another Negro passing through told him about a construction crew in need of more hands. A month later, with few options left, he joined them. The plan had been to go to California and get a new millinery shop up and running, buy a house, and the boys and Emmeline would follow. But Odysseus couldn't hardly set up shop if he couldn't find a lender, and he didn't want to leverage the shop or house back home until he knew he'd be able to make a go of it in California. In the meantime, he decided he would work on this crew during the day, make enough money to get by, and ask around for leads.

Odysseus dug, swung, and hammered, building somebody else's dreams. Several of his fellow newly-arrived Negro crewmen occasionally invited him to lunch at Fox's or to drinks and a show after work at the Hotel Carver. He didn't have much in common with most of these men, other than a homesickness that sometimes seemed baked into the very nature of living as a Negro in this country, but they were a comfort nonetheless. It was here that he learned of a man named Martin McAvoy who would loan to Negroes and had connections. Best not to know too much more about him, the others said.

"What's your business?" McAvoy said.

"My boys are part of a singing group . . . sir," Odysseus said. He hated how obsequious saying "sir" to white men made him feel. He'd made it a point to do so as minimally as possible after the war.

"They good?"

"Very. Trying to move 'em out here. Get my business up and running in California."

Out of the briefcase he'd brought with him, he pulled newspaper clippings. Of his millinery's grand opening. Of the boys' recent win at the talent show, and of the hometown paper's coverage of their trip to the

Apollo. Back home, he had been a very successful business owner, all built from the ground up, he said, reciting the spiel he'd given dozens of times by now. He had a proven record of success, and he intended to replicate said success right here, in this land of citrus groves and movie stars. All he needed was a storefront. Prime real estate from which to grow a future.

"Why not go to a normal bank?" McAvoy said finally, after lingering for some time on the newspaper clipping of the boys at the Apollo.

"You know," Odysseus said. He did not want to tell this man much more about himself or his family.

The man nodded.

"Do you sing too?" McAvoy asked. It was not the question Odysseus had been expecting.

"No . . ." Odysseus said. "Well . . . in the car, the shower, that's about it. Why?"

"A man should sing. At least when he's alone." McAvoy chuckled. "Can't trust a man who doesn't sing at all. Can you?"

Odysseus laughed.

"I'll give you the money," McAvoy said finally, after some consideration. "I should warn you, the interest will be quite high."

"I'll pay it all back and then some," Odysseus said.

"I haven't even told you the terms just yet." McAvoy laughed.

"Why do you help Negroes?" Odysseus asked the man abruptly.

"Your money's green as anyone else's." McAvoy shrugged. "You'll need a good real estate agent. I got a gal."

Odysseus felt uneasy, as though he'd just struck a deal with the devil himself. But at least this devil was an integrationist.

And so, the holding pattern ended, he thought, soon their new lives would begin! He went down to Colorado Boulevard and browsed through a record shop with a few of the Caltech kids playing at being hippies. He decided on the new Sly and the Family Stone record and bought a new record player.

"Emmie! I've done it!" Odysseus yelled into the phone as around him the others in the boardinghouse helped ready dinner.

"It's really happening?" his wife replied.

"Goddamn right it is!" Odysseus shouted, even though he generally preferred to keep his language clean around his wife, as Emmeline was a lady. No matter that she could curse like a sailor herself.

"*Higher! Higher! Higher!*" he sang along with Sly later that night, blasting the record at full volume until the white woman downstairs banged the ceiling with a broom. Then he got out his sewing machine. The boys would soon be needing new costumes.

With McAvoy's help, he closed on a house on Mar Vista Avenue in Pasadena not too much longer afterward. The street was lined in beautiful oaks and stood right at the foothills. The real estate agent told him that in the fall and winter, the mountains nearby were covered in snow and a little bit magical. Her words.

"I'll take magic," Odysseus said.

"More and more Negroes moving into the area," she said, her expression unreadable. Odysseus couldn't tell if the real estate lady meant it disapprovingly or not. She had just sold him the house though, hadn't she?

"That so? Well, as my wife said, 'If it's good enough for Jackie Robinson . . .'"

"More of you on the other side of Lake, though," she continued, smoothing several escaped strands of her blond chignon. Whatever else there was to say about that, the both of them let hang in the air.

He stood, hands on his hips, surveyed around, and decided that it might just be one of the prettiest streets he'd ever been on. The house stretched the budget well past the breaking point, but Odysseus was certain he could make it back eventually. His family deserved beauty, same as anyone else.

Alone, in the near-empty house, Odysseus listened to his new Sly record as loud as he wanted. He hammered a nail into the hallway to hang the picture of the Johnson Three at Coney Island, preparing to fly. If you looked close enough, Christmas was visible in the glimmer of light where there ought not be next to Rocco. Where would the little pick fit into their lives here in California, and how?

There would be time to worry about that later, for now there was Sly.

"Welcome home," he said.

CHAPTER EIGHT

IT SHOULD BE NOTED THAT THE JOHNSONS WERE NOT MY FIRST FAMILY.

Right after my mother died, I spent time on the streets as a little beggar child. I was barely old enough to hold a broom, which I sometimes did as I swept the floors in front of the occasional business for a few coins, or a biscuit or two. Oftentimes, I sang a little ditty that my mother had taught me, or something coming from the crystal sets playing from within one of the stores. Customers would stop to listen to me sing, and while sweeping I'd dance a little with, or around, the broom. It was a way to break the day up. And sometimes, if I got lucky, I'd get a piece of taffy; once I even got a cream soda!

The kindest of all the store owners was Mr. Harold Powell. I think he was my very first real father, though I hope Mr. Odysseus won't be offended. Mr. Powell and his very good friend Moses stayed in the apartment above their store, and let me stay inside by the fire when it got cold, then eventually I moved in altogether. Moses was a gentle man, with one of the brightest smiles you ever did see, lithe and elegant as a ballerina. He was also a learned man, having graduated high school, and thus he helped Mr. Powell keep the store's books. Mr. Powell was good with people and knew when to haggle and when to let somebody put it on credit, and he knew how to avoid any trouble with the white folks who would occasionally stumble in from the other side of town.

Together we would listen to "Ain't Misbehavin'" or some Gladys Bentley, or Blind Blake, or Blind Sammie, or Blind Willie—all the blind men, really. Unless Mr. Moses was feeling especially sentimental and then we might listen to Cole Porter's "What Is This Thing Called Love?" Or "Let's Misbehave." The apartment was always full of music! Mr. Powell would play the fiddle, and Moses and I would sing and dance into the wee hours, when we finally would will ourselves to bed, because Mr. Powell had to open the store bright and early to get money from the workers before they left for the fields.

Moses wanted to go to New York and would often sigh and say things like "Wouldn't Harlem be grand? Or the Village? I mean, the parties alone . . ."

Then Moses would go off and daydream and Mr. Powell would grumble that this was his daddy's store and his granddaddy's store and his great-granddaddy's, who had been the very first free man in their family. He wasn't leaving it for nothing or nobody. Not even New York.

"But it would be safer there," Moses would say. "For all of us."

Mr. Powell and Moses were the very first I'd known of family outside of my mother, and between the two of them there was more joy than I'd ever thought possible for a colored person in the South. We would go to church together. Moses would sit with me and teach me as much as he knew from school, or he would tell me stories he had heard about the rest of the world and how he supposed it to be. Moses was prone to flights of fancy, and sometimes the two of us would dress up like pirates, or put on plays in which he'd act out any number of parts. Mr. Powell was not as fanciful. Mr. Powell would tell me to "get off that!" and "don't ask so many questions, boy!" and he would generally grumble about any number of things, but at the end of the day, after all the money in the register had been counted and it was a particularly good day, he'd leap up and say, "How 'bout we make root beer floats!" Then all three of us would have entirely too much sugar until our bellies ached.

Now, I guess Mr. Powell was older than Moses, because Mr. Powell would bellyache about how his back and knees hurt from standing all day at the store, and Moses would massage his body and laugh whenever Mr. Powell yelped out at the slightest pressure.

"Oh, you old man!" he'd say.

And Moses would sometimes privately complain to me how Mr. Powell was stuck in his ways, and how he insisted on staying in this godawful place when there was a whole world out there waiting for them. He mentioned how all the most exciting new Negro writers and singers and actors were convening in New York right this minute, and how you could stay at salons and drag balls until all hours without a care in the world. He badly longed to be a part of it all.

At first it started off as low grumbles from Moses, but then it got louder and louder still, until the two of them would shout at each other over me, and I had to cover my ears because I couldn't bear it.

One night, when Moses thought I was asleep, he whispered to Mr. Powell, "I can't live like this anymore."

And Mr. Powell whispered, "Don't I make you happy? Isn't that enough?"

And I could hear Moses say, "I really want it to be. I do."

Moses tiptoed out very early one morning, when it was still pitch-black and even the birds were still asleep. I opened one eye and caught his. He walked over to me and leaned down and gave me a kiss on the forehead.

"You are the best, and likely, only son I'll ever have. Please take care of him for me."

"Don't go! Don't go!" I sobbed loudly. I had just lost my mother not a year before and I couldn't bear the thought of losing another adult I loved.

My sobs woke up Mr. Powell, who jolted from his slumber and nearly stumbled over his nightgown trying to see what, or who, was bringing the ruckus. He lit a candle as Moses stood frozen in the middle of the apartment, and I continued to wail.

Mr. Powell slowly looked Moses up and down as both of them adjusted to the light. Moses looked at Mr. Powell mournfully. I think this is perhaps the first time I saw what a broken heart could do to a person. In a matter of seconds, Mr. Powell looked years older, suddenly frail.

They didn't say anything to each other for a good long while.

"Go on then!" Mr. Powell snapped. "You goddamned fairy. Go!"

I went to grab ahold of Moses's leg, and he let me cling to him for a moment before shaking me off. Nothing was going to stop him then, I knew.

I followed tearfully behind him as he walked down the stairs and outside. There, Moses looked up once more at Mr. Powell standing in the top window.

They held each other's gaze for just a moment.

"Be good, OK!" Moses said. "Come find me if you can one day."

Then Moses turned around, kicking up the dust all around him, and headed in the direction of what I assume was the nearest train station.

Mr. Powell was not the same after that. He drank a little too much, and we never had the fun that we did before when Moses and Mr. Powell and I would all make merry and sing and dance to Moses's records. Mr. Powell did not care as much about my schooling as Moses had, given that he himself had left school early to begin work in the store. He wasn't unkind, but he would cry sometimes at night, and then I would sit at the foot of his bed and pat his leg, telling him, "Everything will be all right, Mr. Powell. He'll come back. I promise."

But before Moses could come back home, a horrible thing happened.

Mr. Powell was arrested. The police came barging into the store, claiming that he was indecent, morally depraved, a sodomite! "Is it true that you've been living here with this little boy in your quarters?" they asked.

"He's my adopted son. He helps me around the store," Mr. Powell snapped. My heart leapt at the word "son."

"You're contributing to the depravity of this delinquent."

"What the hell are you talking about? Get off me!" Mr. Powell yelled. "This is my property, you can't just barge in here like that!"

But they could and they did. Mr. Powell sat in jail for many days. And I tried my best to keep the store going, but I was just a little boy and I didn't quite have a head for numbers, or people, just yet. Customers bought things on credit and I let them. And bad folks, or desperate folks, stole stuff too.

It turned out that a very rich white man wanted Mr. Powell's store. The store was in a prime location, being the only store around for miles, and even though it catered to coloreds, I guess that white man saw that there was money to be made, even from colored people. Mr. Powell was given a choice between selling his store to this man for peanuts or going on trial for indecency.

While Mr. Powell was in jail, as I swept in front of the store, I sang to keep myself company. One of the many songs that Moses used to love. The good people of the town would give me a bit of money in passing, because they all knew about the plight of Mr. Powell. But between all of them, nobody had nearly enough to bail Mr. Powell out, and they were afraid to even try, given the inevitable wrath of the rich white man.

The white man let me stay in a closet at the back of the store, only to let me out at the hour when people headed home and would stop to gather around me at the front of the store. This brought more customers in who might've otherwise walked right on by. When the store belonged to Mr. Powell, I'd performed any manner of song I wanted, whenever I wanted, but the white man had other songs in mind. He beat me when he felt like it, which was often. But he kept me fed and clothed and, being an orphan, I didn't much have anywhere else to run, and everyone was poor then, it being the Great Depression and all.

Often, as I drifted off to sleep in my closet at the back of the store, I missed Mr. Powell and Moses deeply and thought of what Moses might be doing in New York, if he knew about what'd happened to Mr. Powell. I hoped he might return in a very fancy New York car, wearing New York clothes, and save Mr. Powell and me both, but he never did.

As the months went on, and it became clear that nobody was coming, I dreamt of what it might be like to one day have a family just like the Johnsons. I never saw Mr. Powell again. He was a very good dad. Moses too. But, as I discovered with the Johnsons, having fathers was not nearly as wonderful as having brothers! Brothers to sing and play with, to talk to and laugh and argue with until the wee hours of the morning. Brothers who farted in each other's faces, and borrowed clothes without asking, and gave one another purple nurples until somebody screamed out, "Mom!!!!!!!"

Brothers of my very own!

I would do absolutely anything for them. All of them.

And I did.

CHAPTER NINE

"ODIE, I DON'T FEEL COMFORTABLE DRIVING ALL THAT WAY ALL BY MY lonesome with three children," Emmeline said in a lowered tone.

"I hate to ask y'all to make the drive. I really do." Odysseus's words slowly trudged through the lines. It sounded like he hadn't much slept since he'd arrived in Los Angeles. River stood right up against his mother, straining to listen in, at least until she shooed him away.

"Tell him you're not going all the way out to California unless it's on an airplane!" River whispered to Rocco, who stood beside him.

"I'm not going to California unless it's on an airplane!" Rocco repeated on River's behalf.

"What did I say about staying out of grown folks' business?" Emmeline scooted them all out of the kitchen and shut the pocket doors.

River spent miles pouting across state lines, mad as hell that they were not going to ride an airplane as Odysseus had promised. As they drove, occasionally Roman shoved him and he shoved back, and their mama yelled at them to stop. They did, because they all knew their mother was more stressed than she was letting on.

Christmas floated across their laps, looking from window to window, hanging his body out like a puppy, taking everything in.

"Woo-hoo!" he yelled. "Would ya look at that?"

"Knock it off!" Roman said. Every time Christmas crawled across them, there was a faint chill in the very marrow of their bones.

"Boys, please be quiet. I'm trying to think," Emmeline said.

"We could be on a plane right now." River sighed. He thought of the pilots with gleaming white hats, gold wings on their breasts, how regal they looked, and the glamorous stewardesses who could, at this very moment, be serving him a Shirley Temple across the clouds.

On the radio, Dionne Warwick sang, "*L.A. is a great big freeway, put a hundred down and buy a car . . .*"

"This song is dumb," Roman said, and reached over to fiddle with the radio.

"Stop it, you jackass! That's dangerous while she's driving!" River said.

Their mother didn't say anything.

Roman settled on the Four Tops' "Bernadette," and all of them, including Christmas, joined in finding the harmonies and yelling, "*Sweet Bernadette!*"

River was the first one to notice his mama was not just a little stressed but actually scared. The dramatic desert dusk in its moody blues and purples and pinks had distracted the rest of them. Emmeline bit her lip so hard that a drop of blood manifested, almost indistinguishable from her lipstick.

"What's wrong, Mama?" River asked.

She reached back and patted his hand. "We just need gas is all." It was meant to be reassuring, but he knew his mama.

The first gas station they pulled up to smelled like fresh paint. A sign that swiveled high above their heads gleamed, as though not even bugs had managed to squash themselves in its light, no dust had settled on its chrome. FULL SERVICE! it read.

As they pulled up, "Baby, I'm Yours" emanated from the speakers. The gasoline attendant on duty was clean-shaven, almost handsome. He looked bored and his uniform looked crisp, still bright, as though the day had been an easy one. Not many cars went through here, River guessed.

The attendant perked up as they pulled the car into the station. Emmeline quickly checked her hair in the side mirror, smoothing down her dress before rolling down the window as he walked over to the car.

"Don't say anything, boys. OK? No matter what he says. Don't speak."

"*And I'll be yours, until two and two is threeeeeee,*" River sang.

"What part of 'be quiet' don't you get?" Roman snapped.

The young man dipped down to Emmeline's open window.

"What do you need?" the kid said.

"Just gas, please. Thank you, sir," Emmeline said.

It did not go unnoticed by River that the gas-station attendant had not called his mama miss, or ma'am, or lady, or even said so much as "Hello, hiya, how do you do?"

"That'll be five dollars and forty cents," the attendant said.

"That's not what's on the sign!" Rocco said.

"Shut up," Roman whispered.

"Shh." Emmeline took out her pocketbook and silently handed the attendant a good two dollars over what was listed above them.

He made a show of counting it before pocketing it.

"Where are you headed?" he asked, peeking in the car.

"California!" Emmeline responded too brightly, in a voice River knew she reserved for white people.

"I always wanted to go to California, myself." The attendant dawdled, looking over the car, the boys, Emmeline. "How is it?"

"This is our first time visiting."

The attendant hummed along with "Baby, I'm Yours" in the background; still, he didn't budge from his spot or make as if to move toward the gas tank.

"I'm sorry, but we're in a bit of a hurry. If you don't mind?" Emmeline's voice was gentle, as though the attendant were a newborn kitten and she was cradling him with her words.

"Oh, I don't serve niggers," the kid said nonchalantly. River bristled in his seat. Roman balled up a fist.

Christmas woke up from where he had been resting across their feet as though the word had sounded an alarm. What did ghosts dream of? River wondered. He would have to remember to ask Christmas soon.

Emmeline opened up her car door without saying a word. River had never seen his mama pump gas before. He wasn't sure she knew how. Roman opened the door on his side.

"Lemme do it, Mama."

As far as River knew, Roman had never pumped gas before either.

"Get back in the car, Roman."

"But Mama?!"

Emmeline glared at him, and he did as he was told. Emmeline took off her scarf and laid it upon her seat. Then she walked over to inspect the pump.

"You can't touch that," thc kid said.

"How am I supposed to get gas then?" Emmeline said, her frustration finally creeping through.

The kid shrugged and kicked a rock. A smirk tugged at the corner of his mouth.

Emmeline continued on to the pump and began to lift it.

"Hey! I said you can't touch that!" The kid snatched it from Emmeline's grip.

On the passenger side, Rocco began to wail. Roman rushed out the car toward his mother.

"Get in the car, Roman!" Mama's voice trembled.

"I suggest you do as your mama tells you, boy," the kid said. He reached across Emmeline for the nozzle.

"Please, sir. Just give me back my money and we'll be on our way."

The kid looked at her. "I've changed my mind. I think I'll help you after all."

Before Emmeline could say another word, the attendant took the gas nozzle and began to spray it all over her pretty travel dress, the one River knew his mama had chosen especially for their journey to a new life.

The boys rushed to open the car door, when, just then, the kid dropped the gasoline hose and began to raise up off the ground. The attendant grew red, his features distorted, his eyes began to bulge. The gasoline slowed to a trickle across the concrete. Christmas had the kid by the neck. He floated as his intestines wrapped tighter still around the attendant's windpipe. This was the closest River had ever been to violence. A human life as a period. Or, perhaps, an exclamation. The attendant's shoes were shiny on his feet. River wondered who had shined them.

River froze in place. Roman too. Rocco stopped wailing.

"Help . . . me . . ." the attendant gasped down at them.

"Christmas, stop!" Emmeline yelled. But Christmas squeezed and raised the boy higher still.

"You'll kill him!" Roman said.

Rocco walked toward Christmas and the attendant. He got to where he was right up under them. River's brother seemed to stare hard and long at the attendant and then at Christmas. None of the rest of them could understand what he said next, though there was a musicality to the gibberish. One might even have called it a lilt, if one were being generous. River knew Rocco and Christmas had their own strange means of communicating. Regular words often eluded his brother. Except for when they were singing. That and when he was with Christmas.

Christmas dropped the attendant to the concrete and the kid curled up into a ball and shivered. River watched as Rocco walked over to the white man and stood above him and said, clear as day, "Help my mama, sir."

The attendant slowly rose, still sputtering. A blood vessel in his left eye had burst, filling those baby blues with red. He walked over to the fuel tank and opened it. River stared up at him while he worked. His hair was mussed from the struggle. His uniform rumpled from the thrashing. Every once in a while, he would catch River's eye, and then quickly glance away.

Their mother went to the trunk, where she slipped her travel dress over her head and used the parts that weren't soaked to wipe the gasoline off her body. Standing in her lace pink slip, she then stuffed the dress into the space between suitcases. River knew how much she'd loved that dress. His daddy had made it for her as a present two years ago and she'd lit up like the Rockefeller Christmas tree when she'd opened it. Now Emmeline quietly grabbed a plain blue dress from the suitcase and buttoned it up as quickly as her fingers would allow. The boys stayed in the car, watching the white man service their car, his head bowed.

"What are you?" the attendant eked out, as though they were magic.

They were the Johnsons, on their way to California, River thought. And Christmas. Four little Black boys in a station wagon, hurtling toward their futures.

When Emmeline returned to her place in the driver's seat, her hair readjusted, her arms and legs dried off, the attendant backed away like a frightened animal.

River knew he wouldn't apologize, that the attendant would never speak of this to anyone, and even if he did, who would believe him? The only consolation was that the attendant had now been forced to attend.

"Do you boys have to use the bathroom?"

"No, Mama," they said.

"Are you sure?" she said.

"Yes, Mama," they said.

The attendant had been pretty, almost like a girl, River thought. He was briefly ashamed of himself for lingering over the attendant's nice hands, his perfectly straight teeth, the shape of his shoulders and biceps, well formed like a budding movie star.

As they pulled away, all River could smell was the gasoline that still soaked his mother's travel dress, permeating the whole car even from inside the trunk.

"May I roll the window down, Mama?"

It was too heavy for River's eyes and nose. When she said yes, they all rolled down their windows, and the air flowed in around them. One by one they finally remembered how to breathe.

CHAPTER TEN

THE CALIFORNIA I ENTERED WITH THE JOHNSONS WAS VERY DIFFERENT from the last time I'd been, when I danced in the pictures with a little blond girl who eventually became very famous. Talkies were still relatively new then, and that Los Angeles still had lots of land with more orange groves than people. Now there were many new freeways! Freeways are big roads that twist through and above and under all parts of the city like none I'd ever seen before, and on them drivers honk and almost crash and then yell out the window, "Fuck off!" which is what happened to Ms. Emmeline as we nearly missed our exit at somewhere called Fair Oaks.

The Johnsons went to a part of Los Angeles called Pasadena, which had lots of trees and was nestled right up against foothills of a tiny snow-capped mountain. Palm trees are very funny indeed because they got lots of trunk with nothing even on most of them. They kinda look like they're flashing you. Or like the actress Marilyn Monroe with her dress blown up around her bottom. A dead man I met briefly in the forest claimed to have met her after her passing and said she was very nice, but much sadder than he'd expect from such a beautiful woman. I asked him, "Why shouldn't beautiful women be sad?" and he laughed at me like I'd said something funny, but I didn't get it.

Pasadena was very pretty, but not quite as glamorous as Hollywoodland, as far as I could tell. Mr. Johnson had bought a house with tiles the color of clay, which he told Emmeline was called Spanish. I'd never been to Spain, but if this is what the houses looked like there, I figured Spain must be quite lovely indeed.

River, Rocco, and I ran through the house until Roman yelled at us to knock it off and to help Mama take in all our stuff.

In the new backyard, the trees had oranges and lemons and limes, and these funny little fruits called loquats. Ms. Emmeline had us pick them while she and Mr. Odysseus talked about grown-up things upstairs. Then afterward they both came down in a very good mood, and they taught us to squeeze the lemons and add sugar until they made lemonade, which looked divine. If only I could still taste!

Two days later, I thought I'd be content to sneak with the Johnsons only so far as to see what River and Rocco's new school looked like. Mr. Odysseus was to drop Roman off at the fancy all-boys Catholic school that Mr. X had practically commanded Roman attend. Meanwhile, Ms. Emmeline would take Rocco and Roman to public school nearby. If Rocco and River's school was the one any ole kid could go to, I could hardly imagine Roman's! It was much larger than the crickety wooden schoolhouse I'd attended only sporadically before my mama died. There, all of us crammed into the one room, reading aloud off books with broken spines and sitting for hours on hard benches that the local fathers helped carve in the off-season. Those benches were quite uncomfortable indeed and often left splinters in your hands or, if you were particularly unlucky, your caboose! But I loved being around the words and numbers and other kids and, most especially, our teacher, Ms. Littlefoot, who would come calling even to the most wretched of houses if you hadn't gone to school that day.

That morning, I'd hidden in the back of the car behind Rocco, and when River looked over at him, I held my finger to my mouth and said, "Shush." River was still a little afraid of me because of what happened at the gas station, I think.

At the Johnson boys' new school there were lockers and a swimming pool, even a big field of freshly mowed grass meant for exercise, or play, or both!

The boys and girls were white and yellow and medium brown with rosy cheeks and freckles and blond curls and long hair dark as night. What they weren't, of course, was Black.

River and Rocco were the only Black boys in their grades, and I wouldn't have liked that much myself, even though I no longer had reason to fear white children, or anyone at all.

My very best friend in the forest had been Becky, who was quite white indeed, with her long blond pigtails and the limp she acquired while dying. At first me and Becky weren't friends because I didn't stop those men from doing what they did to her. But I was only newly dead myself then, only a few years in, and I hadn't yet known that there was anything I could do. Plus, I was still afraid then.

When Becky had finally gotten up from where she'd been left on the forest floor, she looked at me with wild eyes, feral. Her body was a scream, and all around us the trees shook and lost their leaves, and even the chatty squirrels went silent because critters and lost souls alike knew that what happened to Becky was truly awful.

All this to say that I suppose that the first day of being dead might be a bit like the first day of school. There were plenty of new people and animals to meet and things to learn and instead of getting a new pair of shoes you took on a whole new form. Instead of being afraid of getting lost down a corridor, you had to learn the good parts of the forest, where there was soft mulch and friendly deer and the other souls who let one another be, versus the part of the forest where the trees were gnarled and rotted and the souls there took sinister forms that made your skin crawl, even though you didn't have any skin at all.

On my first day, when I finally stood up, my innards had fallen out and the world was at a forty-five-degree angle. (Rocco was learning about angles in class right now.)

The shock of it had caused me to faint, and when I awoke the second time, I hoped I would be alive, but no luck. I sulked for a week, until finally the butterflies approached. They fluttered.

"Poor dear," Myrna said. She was the oldest of the bunch, a Pipevine Swallowtail and one of the prettiest old ladies you ever did see.

"Most unfortunate," Alfie concurred. He was a Silvery Blue, and a bit of a dandy I'd come to find out.

"They'll get what's coming to them," the yellow one, Joanne, said. I never did find out what kind of butterfly she was before the lizard Torbert ate her later that week.

"Don't lie to the boy," Myrna said. "It doesn't do anybody any good. Being human is nasty business sometimes."

The butterflies were my first friends, and so I thought I might do the same for Becky. Be Becky's butterfly. But when I got closer to her, she kicked up a mound of dirt in my face. "Don't you dare come near me. Not one step closer."

I had been waiting quite a while for somebody my own age to talk to. Even if she was white and meaner than a box of snakes. Days later, I decided I'd win her over the only way I knew how. With a song and a dance.

"Best leave the girl alone," grumpy old Eric said. He was the oldest man I had ever seen. He liked to walk around the forest naked as a jaybird, his old balls hanging like bells.

I could feel Becky's eyes on my innards, on the crook of my neck, on my stump. I was suddenly quite self-conscious. I didn't like when people looked at me like that. It was even worse when they themselves weren't even alive.

And so, I began to dance. Then sing.

"Coon!" Rutherford called out. Ole Black Rutherford had met his end over a pittance of a gambling debt, but he fancied himself better than me.

When I was done, Becky broke out into a faint smile.

"Disgraceful," Rutherford spat. "*No* shame."

"That was wonderful." Becky clapped. "I'm Becky."

That was the beginning of our friendship. Before Becky, I hadn't known how desperately I needed a friend my age. I often felt myself coming undone with loneliness. Wasn't friendship a few stitches and some stuffing to sew you up and make you feel whole? This is what I intended to do for Rocco.

═══

"YOU SHOULD GET on the table and sing," I said to Rocco as he licked the peanut butter from the corner of his mouth. Across the cafeteria, River was already surrounded by a gaggle of girls. Nobody else saw me in the corner sitting with Rocco. River shot over a very disapproving glance.

Rocco reminded me an awful lot of myself on that first day. I thought of Becky and how delighted she'd been when I performed. This was what Rocco needed to do to win everyone over, I was sure of it!

"Everybody loves when you sing," I said. "You'll have your pick of friends afterward."

"I don't know," Rocco said, uncertain.

The girl next to him looked to see if he was talking to her.

"Trust me," I said. Backstage all the ladies had pinched my cheeks afterward and rubbed my head and the men clapped me on the back and

I felt it was a kind of home. And wasn't that just what Rocco needed right now?

After a bit of back-and-forth, finally, Rocco climbed up on the bright-red table and began to sing. He shimmied and shook and leaned. He made the exaggerated faces and clasped his heart, like I taught him. "Sonny Boy" had been quite the hit in its day and I was surprised none of the other children joined in.

At first, everyone went about their business, until eventually they didn't. Rocco's voice rang out loud and clear and echoed across the normally cacophonous cafeteria walls. Soon, everybody stopped what they were doing to watch.

"Don't forget the finale," I whispered to Rocco.

He still needed a bit of practice with the routine, I thought. The details were off. His smile wasn't broad enough, he wasn't selling joy. But he'd done good. Before Rocco could do the big finale involving the backflip, a voice rang out, "Stop!"

In the corner, River was getting redder by the minute. He'd started up toward Rocco when Ms. Horner stood up in front of Rocco and said again, gently, "Stop."

She held out her hand and said, "It's time to get down now. We don't dance on tables, Rocco."

Rocco looked at her, then over at River and back at me. I shrugged. I wouldn't argue with a teacher. Rocco took her hand, stepped down, and a few kids clapped. Most of them laughed. Some did nothing at all. River stormed out of the cafeteria and into the hallway. Rocco followed after him.

"How could you do that to him?" River yelled at me amid the bright-yellow lockers. It was as though we were in the middle of a bunch of bees or dandelions or both. "There's no way Rocco decided to do that on his own!"

"He was great!" I said.

"That was . . . offensive," River said.

I huffed. "That was my crowd pleaser! You had me teach you those very moves!"

"Not like that!" River said, imitating my jazz hands and "cooning face," as mean Ole Man Rutherford had called it in the forest. "This isn't like 1890 or whatever."

"Hey! Just how old do you think I am?" I swear, River was so rude sometimes!

"That shit is racist," River said.

I straightened myself up and began to fiddle with my small intestine. "Excuse me, but I think I know better than anyone what racist is."

River opened his mouth, but not a word came out. He shook his head, turned around, and went back into the cafeteria.

"I'm right here," Rocco whispered finally.

Just then, two white boys approached Rocco and shoved him against the lockers, hard. The boys were ruddy-cheeked, with cherub faces and eyes green as leaves in spring.

"Retard," I heard one of them snigger as they walked away.

I froze and looked at Rocco, who dusted himself off and stood up, walking in the opposite direction. I followed him, my eyes never leaving those boys.

I thought back to that first day with Becky in the forest.

"Why didn't you do something? Why didn't you stop them?" she'd cried. I remembered how she'd felt. My anguish when I finally awoke in the forest, remembering the smell of whiskey on their breath and how I screamed for Mama, who had been dead for many years by then. One day these mean ole boys would turn into men, and if I had any say in the matter, so too would Rocco.

"Why didn't you save me?"

I hadn't saved Becky. But I would do whatever it took to keep Rocco safe, because he was my friend, my family, my brother!

CHAPTER ELEVEN

THE RUMPLED BLOND TEENAGER ANSWERED MR. X'S DOOR IN NO BRA and the biggest bell-bottoms River had ever seen. He'd already feared they were overdressed in their best matching multicolored suits, and the girl's appearance just confirmed it. Never mind that the suits barely fit anymore; Odysseus had had to let out every single hem. The girl blew a pink bubble, then laughed when it popped on her face.

"What do you want?" she said laconically.

"We're here for the party. We're the Johnson Three. The talent," Odysseus said. If his father was insulted by the manner in which the girl had spoken to him, an adult, he didn't let on. Emmeline looked over at Odysseus, eyebrows raised, and River could tell his mama was having second thoughts about this whole thing.

"Dad!" the blonde yelled, and it echoed in the marble entryway.

"Jesus, Talia. How many fucking times do I have to tell you not to do that?"

Mr. X appeared at the door beside her. He smelled of alcohol.

"Lovely to see you again, Mrs. Johnson. Apologies for my language." Mr. X smiled at Emmeline and clasped her hand. "Do forgive us. My children are positively feral. How is California treating you so far? How long has it been?"

"A little over a month," Odysseus said.

"Nowhere like it, right?" Mr. X said, not waiting for a response. "Couldn't pay me to live anywhere else."

Odysseus politely laughed.

"Come in, boys." Mr. X clapped River on the back as though they were old pals. River hated when old white people did this to him. He could never tell if it was because he was a child or because they were trying to prove they weren't racist, or both. River felt that to still be a child was to often not be afforded any dignity, and being a Black boy . . . well . . .

Inside smelled heavily of cigarette smoke. It watered River's eyes as they passed through the rooms of revelers. A heavily made-up lady spilled her drink on Roman's shoe and then reached down to wipe it off.

"So sorry!" she slurred, and wiped the black leather with her cocktail napkin.

"Get up, Linda!" some man who must've been her husband snapped and yanked her up. River didn't think men should yank their wives like that, especially not in front of other people. He had never seen Odysseus do anything of the sort to Emmeline. River would never treat his wife like that, even if she annoyed him.

"I'm sorry," River said to the white lady, even though he hadn't done anything at all.

White men were going to the moon, again, and the Johnson Three were going to be the pre-moon entertainment for a party of rich white people watching. A very famous producer would be attending this party. He had seen them at the showcase, heard their demo, and been very impressed, Mr. X said. This was their chance to really wow him as astronauts bounced once more among the moon holes. The man had famously eccentric hair and an ear for launching stars. The plan was that they would perform after the takeoff. Then, Mr. X said, you could ask a man anything, 'cause anything felt possible. The producer hadn't arrived yet, but he would.

"In the meantime, mingle," Mr. X said. As though it were as easy as that.

"We'll be right back, boys," Emmeline said as she and Odysseus went over to the bartender, to talk grown-folks things with grown-folks drinks.

Roman found Mr. X's son, Tad, and several boys from school. River looked at how quickly they circled him like the rays on a sunflower, with Roman's fro at the center. Roman had never been popular before, but maybe it was different now. Somehow, in California of all places, Roman increasingly was. River couldn't tell if his brother was about to have fun, or be devoured, or both. His father knew a few people here and there who had come by the shop, and Odysseus went over to say hi and grab a drink. Rocco and River sat on the stage by the pool. It was where River felt they belonged.

═

THE BOY WHO sat down beside River had red glasses like an alarm announcing his delicate face. His lips were bright pink like he'd just finished a lollipop, or a popsicle, and his eyes looked watery, an almost unnatural deep blue like the ocean just after a storm. River had the feeling of having met him before, in another world, or maybe another life.

"I'm Milton. I'm in your math class," the boy declared.

Oh yes! That's where River knew him from! Still, he'd never taken him in before, not like this.

"I'm River."

"Everybody knows who you are." Milton laughed.

This was not just because River was Black, and thus stuck out, but because he was popular. He smiled easily. He laughed at jokes and told a few of his own. He kept secrets and shared none of his own. And here, at this new school, he pretended not to notice when conversations would occasionally go uncomfortably silent upon him entering, like vertical blinds being shut. He'd sing and eventually their tongues and bodies would loosen up to his imitations of Stevie Wonder, or Nat King Cole, or Frank Sinatra. Song was a method of disarmament. The pale boy stared at River as though he could hear him speak.

Did I say any of that out loud? River thought.

"I never noticed you had freckles before," Milton said to River, and pointed in his face. River backed away from Milton's finger and Rocco reached over to grab it. Rocco was still a big brother, even if it was in his own weird way. For a moment, River had forgotten Rocco right beside him.

"It's OK, Rocco," River said, and gently patted Rocco on the arm.

"Nice to meet you, Rocco, my name's Milton." The boy pushed up his glasses with the hand that was not in Rocco's death grip.

"Like Milton Bradley," Rocco said.

"Exactly . . . I come in peace."

Milton mimicked an alien. He snatched his fingers from Rocco's grip and threw up the peace sign. Then he switched to the Mr. Spock sign. "Live long and prosper."

That was all it took for River and Milton to get sucked into a conversation in warp speed. Everything they liked about *Star Trek* and everything they thought was stupid. They both loved Uhura's legs, and every so often, Milton's leg would lean against his and River would feel a sharp current through his body, as though he himself were preparing for liftoff. Milton had nice teeth, straight as piano keys, and River felt quite immediately as though he might like to play them.

But why? River had plenty of other friends, and even a few to talk *Star Trek* with. Why should this one feel so easy? And a white boy at that? He didn't even mind when Milton whispered—

"What's wrong with your brother? Is he retarded?"

"No! He's really smart, actually. He just has a harder time with some things. Like people . . . and talking sometimes."

Milton looked over at Rocco, who had wandered into the corner and bent over to inspect something in the bushes.

"He's just . . . different. He's smart though. He knows all kinds of things about bugs. Mostly butterflies. Bugs are his bag," River said with a chuckle.

"Are butterflies bugs?"

"Fucked if I know." River laughed. He felt he wanted to know everything about Milton right now, and also as though he had always known him somehow.

"Why haven't I seen you at lunch or outside of class?" River asked.

"Most of the time I don't want to be seen." Milton let his knee fall and bump against River's. "Sometimes it's not bad though."

River felt his face grow hot.

"I . . . I have to pee," he said.

He quickly rushed away from Milton and through the adults who were getting ever rowdier.

River felt as though if Milton touched him once more he might scream. But why? The adults yelled at one another over melting ice in crystal glasses. Across the room, his father and mother looked somewhat trapped in conversation with Mr. X and a woman who was presumably Mrs. X, or at least, the most recent one. Emmeline briefly caught River's eye and winked.

"Excuse me, missus, which way is the bathroom?" River asked the adult nearest to him.

"Aren't you too cute?" Drunk Linda patted his head. "Upstairs on the right."

He climbed up the stairs and pushed against the first door he saw, relieved.

Except, it was not the bathroom. Mr. X's daughter, Talia, and three glassy-eyed friends sprawled across the bed and floor, definitely drunk, maybe more.

"Oh, I'm sorry," River said.

"Don't be." Talia motioned at River to enter. "Close the door."

"I'm looking for the bathroom." River did not want to be in this white girl's bedroom. Even if it was 1969 and the world was changing and the secrets of the universe were about to crack wide open on channel eight in a matter of minutes.

"You're cute," a brunette with droopy eyelids said. She looked a bit like an Afghan hound. The girls all gave the impression of escaped show dogs. As though they'd made their way off plush beds and through brambles, on the lam from their rightful owners.

"You can use my bathroom." Talia nodded toward a doorway. River didn't especially want to pee where girls could hear him. But as he was about to explode, he didn't much have a choice. He entered the powder room with all its markings of a girlhood being outrun. He peed into the pink toilet while staring at a tasteful floral print, then washed his hands next to a lavender brush with long blond strands tangled in its tines. The room smelled of perfume and, underneath, a hint of metal, blood. He'd peed quietly and quickly.

When he emerged from the bathroom, the girls looked even less like a slumber party and more like a coven. The girl who looked like an Afghan hound looked at him mischievously.

"Is it true what they say about Black guys?" She peered from behind her long bangs.

"What?" River didn't know what she was talking about.

"About your . . . you know," the girl who looked like a poodle said.

"Um . . . I should get downstairs. They should be on the moon any minute."

It wasn't exactly the moon River wanted to return to, but Milton. Was it possible to miss a brand-new friend this quickly? Was he that lonely? He, who had so many friends? Who was only a few months into a new school and already the most popular boy in his class, even if there had been that stumble after Rocco's antics? He should've protected his brother. Roman would've. Roman cared for Rocco more than he did River. Where was he? Roman could get him out of here. But Roman was downstairs with those boys from school he insisted he hated.

Talia scooted to the edge of her bed.

The Afghan rushed to the door and blocked it.

"We want to see it," Talia said.

"I don't want to miss the landing, please," River said.

"Then show it to us," the Afghan said. She slumped against the door, her head heavy with whatever had been in her glass.

River started toward the door.

"If you don't, I'll scream and tell my father you tried to touch my boobs. You guys are trying to get signed right? That's why you're here."

River didn't know what to say to any of it. He wanted desperately to run from this place and never return.

"Hurry up if you don't want to miss the moon," the poodle said.

River thought of yelling for help. Clearly the girls were out of their minds, and he wasn't. Why shouldn't he be believed? And yet . . . even at his age he knew exactly how the world worked, how it would be, what would happen if a white girl opened up her mouth and screamed.

He did as they said. He pushed down the tears welling in him. Everything in him surging up.

"Oh shit, he actually did it!"

"Now, that's a rocket," the Afghan said with a laugh.

The girls giggled and he felt the urge to throw something, to push them out of the way, to pull Talia's hair and break the fancy perfume bottle on her dresser. But he was his mother and his father's son, and Roman and Rocco's brother, and they had a dream. What would Christmas do if he were here? Something like at the gas station? He would give anything to see Christmas use his large intestine to string Talia up by her neck.

I am a man, he thought to himself. I am a man.

He repeated this as he quietly buckled up his pants and went back downstairs where everyone had gathered, pushing up against one another and the big wooden television. He saw Milton sitting on the edge of a couch. Milton waved. River's father and brothers stood toward the back of the room, which buzzed.

And then, just like that, as soon as it started, the launch was over, cut short by a camera's failings. The newsmen tried to make sense of it, then apologized as though it were their fault on Earth millions of miles away.

Mr. X frantically rushed over to Odysseus, Emmeline, and the boys. "Go! Sing something! Now!"

River didn't much feel like performing. He wanted to stand onstage and scream. He wanted to run. His first few notes were wobbly, too tentative. He could not shake the feeling of violation. Nobody had touched him though. What did it mean if nobody hurt you? If you never actually said no?

He saw his father grimace and then he felt it—the rage. He sang as though it were the last time. As though it were the end of the world. He danced as though he were possessed. He looked at Milton smiling in front of the stage. His mama looked proud as can be right in the very front of the crowd. Then he looked over at Talia, the Afghan, and the poodle, clapping. He felt something urgent rush through his highest notes. Roman looked over at him and grinned. Even his big brother's ole sourpuss had lost itself in the music, the feeling. His brother could be such an asshole, but at times like this Roman, Rocco, and River moved in perfect harmony, as though each were merely an extension of the other, together their bodies a song.

Everybody danced. A few jumped into the pool. The crowd seized and shook and floated as though the Johnson Three, and not the moon, had always been the main attraction. As though they, the Johnson Three, were the men on the moon. They played an encore, and then there were no more songs. River left the stage reluctantly.

When the set finished, a sweaty Mr. X rushed over to them.

"That was magical!" He beckoned over the famous producer with his electric hair, his ear for stars.

"Didn't I tell you?" Mr. X said.

"Yeah. They're real." The producer was subdued, but it was clear even he had felt something undeniable.

While the adults talked logistics, Odysseus's arm proudly draped over River's shoulder, and River caught Milton's eye across the room. A woman hunched around small Milton's shoulders was leaning into him as she increasingly came undone. Milton's mother was Drunk Linda! She had clearly had too much, and they were leaving. River wanted to rush over and say goodbye, or just to talk to him, to be near his new friend one last time. But there would be plenty of time for that at school, wouldn't there? Emmeline whispered something into Rocco's ear as he squirmed next to them.

Mr. X beckoned Talia over.

"What'd you and your friends think, darling?"

She smirked at River, who felt himself take a step back. He felt hot all over. He felt shame. He stared at the ground.

"They were great, Daddy. They're gonna be huge." She giggled. Her words were drawn out, sedated.

"Is she stoned?" Roman whispered to River. He shrugged.

"There you have it!" Mr. X kissed Talia's forehead. "If Talia says so, so it will be."

River thought he might be sick.

CHAPTER TWELVE

THERE WERE MORE CONTRACTS THAN ODYSSEUS HAD ANTICIPATED. Really, he thought it would just be one big contract that he'd sign on the boys' behalf after having looked it over for a bit, the way he'd done at Celestine's before they'd geared up to record the demo. Instead, the record executive in front of them presented him with three contracts per child and one for the group overall. One for any songwriting rights, one was an artist agreement, and one was a producer contract, Mr. X explained. "Just making sure to cover all the bases."

"It's a lot to go over." Odysseus hesitated. "I think maybe I'd like to take it home with me and give it a good look first?"

"Sure. Sure. It's just that the sooner we get it signed, the sooner these boys can get to work," the record executive said.

"It's all aboveboard. I can assure you," Mr. X said. Everything was happening at a blistering pace. The party had only been not even a full two weeks earlier.

Odysseus thought briefly that he was perhaps in over his head. He was a small business owner, and a successful one at that, or at least he once had been. But this was different. This required the ability to see both the aboveboard and below-board machinations that went into the making of a superstar. Odie was not the man for that, not really. He was an honorable man, and he was fairly certain none of these people would consider themselves particularly honorable. Weren't half of them rumored to be connected to the mob in some form or fashion? How could Odie possibly go up against that? But who else but himself could he trust to protect the boys, make sure they were getting what was owed to them?

Next to him, River bounced his leg rather violently.

"I'm sure it's all good!" he said excitedly.

"No doubt." Odysseus smiled the executive's way to give the impression of trusting him much more than he did. "Still . . ."

Roman pulled the contract closer to him. "I don't get why we gotta go through all this . . ."

Rocco rocked back and forth in his chair, then stood up abruptly and paced around the room.

"He OK?" the man asked.

"Just needs a bit of thinking space is all," Odysseus said.

"Look, I don't mean to rush you boys, but I have a tee time in forty minutes all the way in Burbank," the executive said.

There was still time to back out. To move back home. To say to hell with it and let the boys just be boys for a little while longer. Longer than Odie or Emmie or even Christmas ever had to be children, that's for sure. Maybe Emmie was right to have her reservations about what this industry might do to their children, but who knew how much longer Roman, Rocco, and River had with these perfect little voices and what these voices could do? Roman's was already starting its descent. The boy thought he was hiding it well enough with the pick's help, but Odie could tell. He knew exactly where each son's notes rose and fell in his ear. Could feel in his tympanic membrane itself how Roman's strained against time.

Roman slumped in the chair next to his father.

"Sit up straight," Odysseus whispered.

"I'm starving," Roman whined.

"OK," Odysseus said to himself as much as anyone. "OK."

He scribbled across the pages, signing Roman, Rocco, and River up for something larger than he'd ever dared to dream for himself. He felt the charge running through River. The ambivalence in Roman. Felt Rocco's thought land on the butterfly at the window. He knew his boys much more than they thought he did. They were his.

"And here . . ." The executive flipped the page and Odysseus dutifully signed.

And with that, his boys also belonged to the record company.

Across from them, the executive popped open a bottle of ridiculously expensive champagne and poured it into four etched crystal glasses as the boys' eyes grew wide.

"I'm too young to drink," Rocco said. "It's illegal."

The man laughed heartily as though Rocco were joking, which the Johnsons knew he definitely was not.

"Nonsense," Mr. X said. "You can go back to being a teetotaler tomorrow. Isn't every day you boys sign a record deal!"

Without so much as a glance over at his father, Roman reached for the glass in front of him. River and Rocco looked over to Odie for permission. He nodded and they grabbed theirs up as well.

"Cheers!" the man said. "Welcome to the rest of your lives! We're gonna make a lot of money together, aren't we?"

"Yessir!" River said as he tried not to burp. The boy never could handle carbonation.

Rocco made a face as the alcohol hit his throat. He immediately spit the champagne back into the cup. "That's gross."

"All right, gotta go," the man said, and lifted up a bag full of shiny clubs.

He headed out the door as Odysseus and the boys stared after him. Should they chug the champagne? Sip it on the way out? Leave it there for the secretary to clean up and pour out? Was that rude?

Mr. X stood up and Odysseus and the boys followed the white men out of the office.

"Helluva Christmas present, right boys?" Mr. X said as he walked them down the hallway to the elevator. "Rest up for these next few weeks. Then we get to work!"

"Yessir," River shouted, a little too loudly.

"We really did it," River whispered in the elevator on the way down.

"You really did it," Emmeline said. She had stayed downstairs outside at the meter, the Johnsons having come up short on coins for parking off Vine. Not to mention that the little pick was with them and Odie wanted not one thing to go wrong before they signed that contract. Emmeline wrapped her arms around Odie and leaned him right against the parking meter wrapped in festive tinsel.

"Don't pretend like you didn't doubt me, woman." Odie forced a laugh and hoped she couldn't tell. He tried not to think about which pieces of his progeny he might've just signed away in that office. It would all be OK, he reasoned.

"Me? Doubt you? Never!" Emmeline smooched him right there on the street as their children happily sang about being sex machines under the dangling candy canes, the California sun making halos of their afros.

CHAPTER THIRTEEN

1970

THIS?! THIS IS WHERE THEY THINK MY ROCCO NEEDS TO GO? EMMELINE scoffed.

A strip mall didn't seem a fitting place for a psychologist's office. Emmeline didn't like that any old person just going to do their laundry or buy doughnuts could see them enter. It seemed a private undertaking, not one you smushed between errands, not something you did somewhere where half the signs read 20 MINUTE PARKING FOR CUSTOMERS ONLY. Wouldn't it be nice to fix a brain in twenty minutes? Not that her Rocco needed fixing. This was simply at Mr. X's recommendation. Now that they were a signed act, they needed to prepare Rocco more after he'd had a few tiny incidents at performances around town. The lights were bright, the crowds were loud, the smoke wouldn't let go of your lungs, or clothes, no matter how much you tried to shake it. That would be a lot night after night for anyone, much less a young boy.

To the appointment, she had worn not her nicest dress but one of them; her fingernails were freshly painted and hair shellacked just-so. Rocco's pants were freshly pressed. She would not have this headshrinker thinking she was neglectful. Not of herself, or Rocco. She was not a bad Black mother. And none of the fights at school had been Rocco's fault, of this much she was certain.

The waiting room was full of magazines, on parenting, psychology, beauty—the faces on them shining, smiling, and pale. All-American happiness and all-American misery. She settled for an article in *Good Housekeeping,* though quite honestly, she didn't give much of a damn how her house was kept. The lady across from them fidgeted too much, like a child. *Sit still,* Emmeline wanted to tell the woman. Then she saw the weeks-old *Time* magazine the woman was reading from December 5,

1969, with Lt. William Calley Jr. on the cover: "The Massacre: Where Does the Guilt Lie?"

The woman caught her eye. "It's terrible isn't it? Ignoble."

"That's war," Emmeline blurted, then caught herself. She was not in the habit of sharing her opinions with white folks.

The woman murmured and Emmeline couldn't tell if in assent or dissent.

"I'm Beth," the woman said, extending her hand rather aggressively.

"Emmeline Johnson," Emmeline said.

"Pleased to meet you," Beth said.

Right then, a little pug-nosed brunette, her hair in messy pigtails, swung open the door, and behind her, the good doctor, who was not at all what Emmeline had expected. Only a tad taller than Emmeline herself, broad-shouldered and erect in posture, his face a little weathered, the doctor looked like a man who had labored outside at some point in his life. Scruff, though not quite a real beard. Like he'd be more at home on a boat than in this office. And when he glanced at her, she felt everything pause for just a minute. But only just. What would it be like to languish on his couch?

He said something to the fidgety woman and her girl that Emmeline couldn't hear because Rocco was telling her about a kind of butterfly.

"In Palos Verdes," he said. "We need to go there. It's not far. I don't think."

"Mmm," Emmeline said distractedly.

"You must be the Johnsons," the doctor said warmly.

The doctor was a handsome man who knew he was, and it was Emmeline's experience that they were usually the very worst kind of man, as though attractiveness absolved you of any number of sins. But he was a psychiatrist and, as Emmeline understood it, was supposed to help you figure out the origins of your malcontent—mother, father, the world itself. How could a man possessing that kind of beauty possibly understand what it was like for everyone else, much less her baby boy, whose best friend was quite dead, who sometimes spoke to butterflies. Emmeline hoped Rocco knew better than to tell Dr. Takahashi about Christmas.

He approached Rocco gently, as though he were used to skittish children. Emmeline noted how he somehow knew not to touch the boy, not yet.

"Nice to meet you, Rocco. Mrs. Johnson." Dr. Takahashi shook her hand, and his hands were mostly smooth with calluses dotting several of his fingertips. "Shall we go inside, Rocco?"

"I will be right here," Emmeline said to Rocco. He nodded his head OK. She peered into the room and saw a velvet orange sofa, very antique-looking and a strange thing upon which to place a troubled child. Not that Rocco was troubled. The door closed between them.

"Let me give you my number," Beth said.

Emmeline had forgotten the white woman was still there. Beth searched around for a piece of paper and, finding none, pulled the subscription card from the magazine. Emmeline handed her a pen from her purse.

"Maybe we can get the kids together sometime," Beth said.

Emmeline thought the two of them were a little too old for playdates, but she didn't dare say so aloud. And if Rocco, in one of his fits, should hit or scratch a little white girl, what then?

"It's just that . . . Edie doesn't have any friends. They said they couldn't accommodate her at school. It's absurd, right? Shouldn't all kids be able to go to school?"

Emmeline nodded. Rocco had always been lucky enough to go to school and to have his brothers there with him. She didn't want to imagine what school might have been like for him otherwise.

The little girl began to twirl herself around in circles.

"All right, darling, we'll go," Beth said. Then to Emmeline: "I mean it. I'll call you. Or you call me . . . Either way. Lovely to meet you, Emmeline."

The woman grabbed up her daughter's hand and said, "Doughnuts, my dear?"

The girl shrieked in response. A joyful shriek, Emmeline guessed. And with that they left the office.

Emmeline picked up the *Time* magazine Beth had left behind.

My Lai was sickening, but it was not shocking. Emmeline didn't live in the same world as the white lady across from her who had been so shaken. She had grown up with tales of Black bodies mutilated and strung up like Christmas lights for white folks to delight in. Every morning she awoke to a little boy who floated through their house with a twisted neck, gnarled arm, spilling guts. Even in their comfortable suburb, in her America, violence was always at the door.

As much as Odysseus wanted fame for the boys, Emmeline wasn't sure. To be famous was to be adored. But it was also to be the target of racist abuse. It was to be rich, but look at all the girls and boys it broke. Agents took, and managers took, and fans too, until those young Black kids had nothing more to give. She didn't know if she was the kind of parent who wanted to set her boys up for a lifetime of that. Of giving pieces and hiding pieces until you weren't sure what was you. And Rocco was such a sensitive boy. All of them were, even if they tried hard not to show it, even if Odysseus didn't realize it. Her little Black boys moved through the world as pieces of china, delicate as Christmas's exposed innards dangling from his little brown body.

"Mrs. Johnson?"

She looked up to see Rocco standing before her, and with him Dr. Takahashi. Had it been an hour already?

"Are you OK, baby?" She patted Rocco gently and he nodded.

"We had a good time getting to know each other, didn't we, Rocco?" Dr. Takahashi smiled at Rocco, and to Emmeline's great surprise Rocco smiled back, and how!

She raised her eyebrows at the doctor, who, it seemed to Emmeline, smirked at her disbelief. She rose from the seat and the magazine fell to the floor between them, its pages flapped open to massacre. They both reached quickly to pick it up. Their fingertips brushed against each other. There was nothing sexy about what was before them, and yet, Emmeline's face was on fire. She quickly folded the magazine shut as the doctor pulled his hand away. Emmeline didn't want Rocco to see any more brutality than he had to. Let him be a child for a bit longer, she thought.

"Same time next week?"

She nodded. "What do you think . . ." she asked the doctor.

"Let me spend a bit more time with him, first?" he said. It calmed her. His not wanting to rush a diagnosis. "I'd actually like it if you could come in next time too."

"Oh, I see," Emmeline said. "Yes. I guess we can make that work."

She felt the tips of her ears hot as coals. What did the doctor want with her?

Emmeline was embarrassed by the amount of space Dr. Takahashi took up in her head that week. She had plenty of other, more important, things to think about. Even her dear, sweet River had grown rather sullen over the last few weeks since their performance during the failed moon landing, although that was adolescence, she supposed. Whenever she tried to pry him open, he clamped back down on her fingertips. "Leave me alone!"

That night, Emmeline decided to make her famous salmon croquettes, Odysseus's favorite. They hadn't had nearly enough family time recently.

"Come home in time for dinner," she told Odysseus over the phone.

"Emmie, I can't make any promises," Odysseus said. He had been staying later and later still, just in case any customers should wander in in need of a hat, or a tailor, desperate for customers. Millinery emergencies were generally few and far between, Emmeline thought but didn't dare say.

"Everything won't fall apart if you close up on time," she said with a sigh.

Christmas helped her make dinner. He had to concentrate very hard to hold anything, otherwise his hand would pass right through. Still, he was able to help her mix the breadcrumbs and seasoning well enough.

"May I go to school please? I promise I'll be quiet. Nobody'll know I'm there," Christmas said as they placed the balled salmon onto the pan.

Maybe if she let him go one day a week when she went to do errands? Christmas didn't have to listen to her at all, really. But he did. He was a good boy.

"Let me discuss it with Mr. Odysseus, OK?" she said.

It wasn't the first or even the third time the boy had asked. As a consolation, she and Christmas had started lessons. She taught him about any and everything and he devoured it all. He was a smart boy. Likely he would've been something grand had he been allowed to grow up. Sometimes, when he did especially well on his lessons, she would be overcome by the sadness of it all and start to cry. He would wrap his little ghost arms around her and say, "What's wrong, Mama?"

Where were her other kids? They should be home already. Roman was spending too much time with Tad Wexler and all those rich private-school boys that she hadn't wanted to expose her kids to in the first place. He kept picking up River and Rocco later than he should.

"Let's make the table up special!" she said to Christmas. The two of them put out the nice candles and even the embroidered lace runner that was one of the few things Nurse Clarabel had left to Emmeline when she died, orphaning Emmeline a second time. Emmeline considered putting out the wedding china but decided against it, given that whatever feats of coordination the Johnson Three exhibited onstage somehow did not translate to real life. The *thud, thud, crash* of their clumsier boyhood movements was the reason for a not-insubstantial number of broken glasses.

"You look happy," Emmeline said to her youngest as River bounded into the room with Rocco trailing behind.

"What? I'm whatever," River said, as though she'd just insulted him.

"Go wash up, I made your favorite for dinner."

"Cornish hen?" River said.

"What? No. You've always loved the salmon croquettes," his mother said.

"Have I?" River said impishly.

"Hello, my second-born." Emmeline kissed Rocco on the top of his head, and begrudgingly he let her.

Eyes watery and unfocused, Roman smelled the way he did after their bar gigs when he finally arrived a good hour later than he was supposed to. She sniffed the air around him.

"RoRo, have you been smoking reefer?"

"No, Tad does," Roman said.

She saw River raise his eyebrows but say nothing. When did her boys become unknown to her? They were spending entirely too much time with grown people in grown spaces. Getting home at all hours before having to turn around and get up for school mere hours later. It was no wonder they were ornery; they hardly slept, hardly spent time with kids their own age. Roman's new friendship with Tad Wexler seemed to largely be a friendship of convenience. Emmeline trusted neither the boy nor his father, not one bit.

They finally sat down to the dinner table two hours later than usual. Odysseus still had not come home.

"He's not coming," Roman said.

"He will," River said.

"Tell me about school," Emmeline said.

"You already asked that," Roman said.

"But you didn't tell me anything," she said.

"Wasn't anything to tell," Roman said.

"I have a friend now," Rocco said. "Laurie. But her brother doesn't like me."

"Everybody knows Laurie's brother is a racist piece of shit," River said.

"Language," Emmeline said. "Don't hold her brother against her if she's a nice girl, Rocco."

She was slightly worried about Laurie's brother, but she was happy for Rocco's first friend in this new place so she chose to overlook it. How much damage could the boy do in school anyway? And River wasn't too far away. He would look after his brother, as Roman had before him.

"Laurie is very nice. She's one year older than me and has a pet turtle. She talks a whole lot and wants to be like Barbra Streisand when she grows up, but she's a bad singer. I told her so," Rocco said.

"Rocco, you can't just say things like that aloud," Roman said.

"She thought I was very funny." Rocco shrugged before glancing forlornly down at his plate. "Our food's getting cold."

"I'm starving," Roman said.

"This is ridiculous," River said.

"Fine. Eat," Emmeline said. She felt a migraine pushing at the edges of her temples, slowly rolling in like the fog. It would only be a matter of time before she could barely keep her eyes open.

Odysseus finally strolled in as they were finishing up. Emmeline thought her husband wore his age heavier here in the Golden State, even as he'd shed all those Midwestern layers.

"I thought you said we were having dinner together as a family?" he shouted from the foyer as he threw his coat on the coat hanger.

"I told you to get home at a reasonable hour," she scoffed. How dare he!

"I came home early for this," Odysseus complained. "I still had stuff to do. Woulda just stayed at work if I had known y'all were going to go right ahead and eat without me."

Emmeline sighed. She had tried. She really had.

"Go on back to work then," she said, and left to go lie down in the dark.

Minutes later, the door creaked open and Odysseus stepped inside and lay down on the bed next to her. He kissed the back of her neck, then her right shoulder. Emmeline found herself caught between recoil and want.

"Please don't have your nasty outdoor pants all on my bed," she said.

"I'm sorry about dinner. I didn't know how important it was to you."

"You knew. You just didn't care."

"You're looking for a fight now, Em. I'm here."

She stiffened as he kissed along her back.

"Heat it up for about fifteen minutes at two hundred. Any longer and you'll dry it out."

"That's all you have you say?" Odysseus got up and left the room in a huff.

Did Dr. Takahashi have a family? she wondered. Did anybody notice when he came home late? Did he like salmon croquettes? Was he a man who broke promises? She hadn't noticed a ring. The doctor had such elegant, slender fingers.

CHAPTER FOURTEEN

"IN FIVE, FOUR, THREE, TWO, ONE." THE WILD-HAIRED PRODUCER began the countdown.

The studio was smaller than the boys thought it would be, not much larger than the one in which they'd recorded at Brodie's. Padded, carpeted, and locked, with microphones everywhere, it was not nearly as glamorous as Roman had imagined. He felt as though they were classroom goldfish, or the trained chimpanzees at the Detroit Zoo, whom they'd visited at Rocco's insistence the year before. White men with long hair propped their bare feet up at the soundboards, or were they sound mixers? Roman didn't know why there were so many people crowded around. Like ground control but with more pot, more cigars, more whiskey, more laughter, the cacophony of levity and gravity.

The song they were recording was about missing your baby. "Baby" was the hot word right now—all the hit singles had it. The songwriter paced the floor as the boys performed. He was in desperate need of a shape-up, Roman thought, but maybe on account of he was so in demand he barely had time to do anything but work. The man had five hits on the national charts right now and he wasn't all that much older than Roman himself.

As Roman sang, "baby, baby, baby" again and again, he thought of Darla, the girl he'd been sweet on back home who was just about the nicest person he'd ever met and head of the debate team, to boot. What was she up to right now? What were his friends back home doing? Probably sleeping; it was late as all get-out.

"Hit the word harder, like you mean it, for fuckssake!" the increasingly frustrated songwriter bellowed.

All Roman wanted to hit at the moment was his pillow.

Odysseus threw the Johnson Three a thumbs-up through the window. All session long he'd been gesturing to them. Roman could feel his father's love and drive and frustration through the glass. Windows where they could see and hear all of you and you could hear only what they wanted you to of them. The hippies conferred among themselves. Rocco sat down on the floor. River did too. Roman paced to keep himself awake. He did not want these men to watch him rest.

"Get up, kid," one of the session musicians said. A drummer, who looked to be not much more than a kid himself. Most of the others inside the fishbowl were brown and paid by the hour.

"We're tired," River whined.

"Not yet. You ain't tired until they say so," the drummer ba-dum buh-ed and laughed. A warm, brotherly laugh.

Roman watched through the glass as a man quickly walked over to Odysseus and whispered something in his ear. His father got up abruptly and walked over to the mics.

"Boys, I gotta take care of something at the shop. Mr. X has kindly offered to take you home. Make sure you behave yourselves, you hear?"

Roman knew that whatever it was, it had to be something serious for their father to leave them here with a bunch of relative strangers.

"Yessir," River said.

Rocco moaned. He wouldn't be able to keep going much longer, and River and Roman both knew it. They were in serious danger of one of Rocco's tantrums.

Luckily, it never got to that point. They ran through the song two more times with what clearly felt to Rocco like diminishing returns, until, finally, the white men in charge debated and discussed it among themselves. Then they decided it was OK for the Johnson Three to go home. They clapped one another on the back and spoke into the microphone about what a great job the boys had done. Roman wished he had gone to football tryouts.

Outside, as Mr. X wrapped up something businessy inside with the owner of the studio, the musicians and mixers stood around smoking cigarettes and passing a flask between them. Rocco sat in the back of the drummer's station wagon. River leaned against the wall, pressing the bottom of his shoe to the stucco like he fancied himself on some album cover, and Roman stood among the men, imagining himself one of them.

Whatever was in the flask burned as it went down Roman's throat. River took the smallest of sips and made a face: "Ugh."

He wasn't wrong. It tasted gross, but Roman liked how he felt as it went down. Just a bit of heat, and then it was as though he were himself slightly blurred. He took another sip and another. He felt his whole body relax and begin to sway with the rhythms of the world around them.

His mother might smell it on him when they got in. But by now the smell of the older men had settled in their hair and on their corduroys, the hours of cigar smoke, the pot, even the sweat of the men as they played note after note for hours. It all lingered in Roman's nostrils. The funk had dissipated in the night air, but only slightly—the smell of men at work, all of them creating. If Mr. X even noticed the liquor on his breath when they got in his car, Roman doubted he would care.

"Li'l man's getting drunk," somebody said, and laughed.

Roman laughed along with them. It felt good to just be. To be out of his head. To release hours' worth of vocal strain, physical strain. The tension of having to be one of Odysseus Johnson's perfect sons.

One of the studio musicians (the tambourine player maybe?) passed Roman some grass. It made perfect sense to Roman that the tambourine player would be higher than the rest. Roman had never smoked grass in front of his little brothers before. River looked at Roman, eyes wide, but luckily the little snitch didn't say anything. It was only when the drummer reached down to give some to Rocco that even Roman sheepishly said, "Nah, man. He's too young for that stuff."

"And you ain't?" the bassist said, and all the grown men laughed.

When the flask came round again, Roman tilted back his head and chugged.

IN THE CAR on the way home, Roman sat up front next to Mr. X when the younger boys crammed into his Ferrari Dino, their brown arms and legs all folded into and over one another like the branches of a gnarled tree.

"Too tight," Rocco said, and leaned forward, his breath hot on Roman's shoulder.

"We'll be home soon," Roman said.

"Here." Mr. X handed a small bottle to him.

"What's this?" Roman asked.

"Mouthwash," Mr. X said. "I can't bring you home to your mother smelling like that, kid."

Mr. X pulled over to the side of the road mere blocks from their house so Roman could rinse and spit.

Bleary-eyed and in rollers, their mother answered the door. It was two in the morning. She looked the boys all up and down, then she looked over at Mr. X.

"Where's your father?" Emmeline suddenly jolted awake. "Is everything OK?"

"He had to go to the shop," River said. "Some sort of emergency there."

"Thank you so much for bringing the boys home safe," she said to Mr. X.

Roman knew that she meant it to be a polite way of telling the man good night, but Mr. X didn't take the hint. Mr. X kept talking and Roman could see his mother fighting to stay awake as he went on about what they'd recorded that night, how talented her boys were. Roman took it as his cue to sneak past her and run into the shower, where he could wash the night away.

"You left my boys with strangers?!" Emmeline shouted at Odysseus an hour later.

"They were OK," Odysseus said. "It was an emergency. Somebody tried to break into the store."

"Did you know Roman was drinking?" she said, ignoring the bit about the store. "They all came home stinking of Lord-knows-what, but I could smell the liquor on his breath."

Roman snuck into River and Rocco's room across the way. They all listened at the door as their parents went at it until the dawn began to break.

"You shouldn't have drunk," River said.

"Shut up," Roman said.

"Do you think they're gonna get a divorce?" River said.

"You're so dramatic, Riv," Roman said. "Sometimes grown-ups just fight."

"Just fight," Rocco repeated softly.

But even Roman could feel that something was increasingly different about his parents' fights in California. Here, their pettiest fights had taken on arms and legs, and menaced like the monsters in *Night of the Living Dead.*

When Roman asked about it the next day, his father told him not to get in grown folks' business. Never mind that he'd just let them spend all evening with grown men doing and saying grown-men things, largely unsupervised.

"And if I catch you drinking again, boy . . ." Odysseus said, an unfinished threat.

Roman nodded. He had zero intention of letting his father catch him.

The baby song was rushed through production and pressed in a matter of days! When they weren't in the studio recording, Mr. X had them making the rounds at all the local radio stations. The record company was getting the single to all the local disc jockeys and Mr. X, certain of a hit, wanted them to come with him to record bits for the station intros. At one such station, Roman could have sworn he saw Mr. X hand the DJ a fat wad of cash when he thought the boys weren't looking.

"Hi, I'm Roman."

"I'm River."

"And I'm Rocco!"

"We're the Johnson Three. And you're listening to 93 KHJ," the three of them said in unison.

The radio-station manager gave them a thumbs-up.

"Now we gotta drive to KDAY," Mr. X said as they stumbled into the sunlight on Melrose.

Soon enough, the song was on the local radio, climbing the charts! Mr. X said it was only a matter of time before the regional and national radio stations picked up the single, before they were famous beyond L.A.

Already they'd begun to recognize a gaggle of diehard fans at their shows, a group of teen girls who shouted lyrics, reached out their arms, and swiveled their hips, growing in number after each of their gigs. Not just girls, but women too. In Roman's opinion, they were the best part of the whole thing. He didn't get whatever it was River seemed to get from performing when they would tumble off a stage and River looked somehow both rabid and beatific. Hell, even Rocco seemed to get lost in the song when he let himself. Closest Roman had come to that was after a concert when a grown woman had licked his ear.

Outside another radio station, Roman squinted up at a man in coveralls momentarily surveying the city, sandwich in hand, sitting next to his roller. Behind them was just a third of an image, but he recognized it all the same.

"That's us!" River said, jumping up and down.

Rocco began to jump alongside him, waving his hands so excitedly Roman thought he just might take flight and join the pigeons atop their very billboard.

"Hey mister!" the three of them shouted up at the man, trying to grab his attention as they waited for Mr. X to pull around to take them to yet another interview.

═══

A MONTH LATER, Roman, Rocco, and River nervously peeked out from behind the curtain at the teenagers buzzing in their best dresses from JCPenney and May Company and Bullocks, readying themselves to dance. A girl in bright-red platforms shook her limbs and cracked her neck, as though she were preparing to pirouette or sprint. Another girl squealed at the sight of them.

"Let's give 'em a good show tonight," the director said, as if that wasn't always the goal.

He went over the particulars of the introduction, where they were to be, which camera to look into and when. The track was going to be playing over the loudspeakers. There would be a bit of lip-syncing. But they had to make it look as though they were singing live.

"Get ready, boys." A white man with shaggy hair, tinted glasses, and a nose that formed a near perfect right angle clapped them on the shoulder.

"That's the Real Don Steele," River whispered to Roman as the man in charge walked toward the studio audience.

"Holy shit," Roman whispered.

"Holy shit," Rocco echoed.

Upon finding out they were going to be on *Boss City,* their mama and daddy had called up half the old neighborhood to tell 'em, never mind that it was on a local channel.

Now their parents waved to them from just offstage, beaming. It would've been embarrassing if the boys'd had their wits more about them. As it was, even River, who usually got all weirdly calm and super-focused before these things, looked just about ready to piss his pants.

"If you get uncomfortable, just look over at me," Roman whispered to Rocco. "The lights will be really bright. We just have to get through the songs, OK?"

A walking pouf of a makeup woman smattered a heavy dusting of too-light powder over River's nose, Roman's too. Rocco put up his hands to prevent her from touching him.

"Too-too," he said. She pouffed in his general direction.

"On air in five, four, three, two, one . . ."

CHAPTER FIFTEEN

"YOU THINK YOU'RE HOT SHIT BECAUSE YOU WERE ON TELEVISION?" Laurie's brother, Wayne, shoved Rocco. "You think that means you can go sniffing 'round my sister?"

It was Monday, just a little over a week since they'd appeared on *Boss City* with the Real Don Steele and, until this very moment, Rocco was still riding high on the fact that he, Rocco Johnson, had been on live television! And better yet, that people had not only watched but liked him! Maybe now he could make some real friends of his very own instead of eating lunch with his baby brother like a loser.

Wayne grabbed Rocco's arm and pressed his fingers into Rocco so hard that he yelped.

"I'm a peaceful person," Rocco said. He didn't know what else to say.

"Knock it off, Wayne," Laurie said. Her dark hair was in two messy pigtails punctuated by pink ribbons. Her smile was slightly crooked, and her bell-bottoms were frayed at the bottom and covered in a slight layer of dirt, as though they'd been a slightly taller sibling's hand-me-downs.

"Don't mind him," Laurie told Rocco. "My parents dropped him on his head a few too many times, I think."

The two of them had taken to eating lunch with each other on the days when Laurie actually made it to school. Otherwise, Rocco ate lunch with River, who begrudgingly let him. Not wanting to provoke Wayne further, Rocco headed toward the cafeteria, where River would be holding court at the best lunch table, the one reserved for only the most popular kids. And Rocco.

When Rocco sat down to lunch with River, it was like looking at another version of himself, who he could've been. He and River looked more alike than not. Their voices were so similar that sometimes, if the sentences were brief enough, they confused even their parents over the phone.

At their old school, he used to sit with River and his friends all the time. After a while, River's friends would sling their arms over him and rub his head affectionately, and included him not only in their stickball games but any mayhem they got into. So long as he didn't tell the grown-ups. And sometimes even when he did.

Now he could see his brother's body tense up.

"Hi, Rocco," his brother's friend Milton said.

Milton was always nice to him, but most of the other boys at the table seemed as though they didn't want him there, his own brother included. Though overall, they had been nicer since the television appearance.

"Hi," Rocco said.

There was an awkward pause for a moment.

"So . . ." Milton started, "anybody else excited as I am for *On Her Majesty's Secret Service*?"

Around him, the boys began to fiercely debate whether the new Bond could possibly be anywhere near as good as Connery. Rocco tried to keep up, but he kept getting distracted by the sound of Bruce's chewing. Bruce was pale with super dark hair and a runny nose and teeth so big and bright they looked fake. He chewed and he smacked and opened his mouth wide enough that you could see every pretty, pearly tooth before he licked his lips, loudly. Rocco felt every bite like pinpricks across his body.

"Tell him to stop," he said to River.

River looked over at him but said nothing.

"Please stop," Rocco finally snapped once it was absolutely unbearable.

"Rocco, don't," River whispered.

"Don't!" Rocco said, looking over at Bruce. He began to tap his knee to get his feelings under control.

Bruce had no couth, as their mother would say, no home training.

"You're supposed to chew with your mouth closed!" Rocco said.

Bruce laughed. He took another bite of his meatloaf and then proceeded to lean his mouth to Rocco's ear and chew louder than anyone had ever chewed before, his spittle flying onto Rocco's cheek.

Only one boy laughed, and River looked panicked.

Say something, Rocco pleaded to his little brother with his eyes.

Bruce proceeded to take a very large gulp of his milk, slurping it through his straw, and Rocco felt every muscle in his face twitch and tense.

Finally, when he could stand it no more, Rocco stood up and shoved Bruce out of his seat. Bruce hit the floor with a hard thud, and the other boys at the table laughed. Then Rocco ran away.

Alone, Rocco was shoved into walls. Sometimes in the bathroom, he was cornered and called a freak. Sometimes he would excuse himself to the bathroom just because it was the only place where he could hear himself think, at least when there weren't other boys smoking inside. The acoustics were good in the bathroom, so he sang in the stalls. He sang to remind himself who he was. Once to his utter surprise a voice in the stall next to him joined in perfect harmony, as only someone who had been in the same womb could, the alchemy of brotherhood. They sang together while washing their hands, wiping them too. They finished the song in the bathroom, then opened the door and walked their separate ways down the long halls back to their respective classrooms.

═

"I WANT TO go to school." I cried and stomped, and a vase broke and dirt spilled out all over Ms. Emmie's floor. I knew I was throwing a tantrum, but also, I couldn't not, because I'm only eight. Or maybe ten? And sometimes ten-year-olds throw tantrums. The door to the kitchen slammed, the rage in me somewhere building, blinding.

"Stop." Ms. Emmie was always calmer with me than the other boys. Any one of them would've had their behinds smacked, their television privileges taken by now. She treated me more delicately, I knew. As though I were an actual piece of glass and not merely a boy you could stick your hand through. Although, come to think of it, she couldn't spank me even if she wanted to. And I'm quite sure, on some occasions she did.

Emmeline sat down beside me. She had her thinking face on, which meant that she turned up her upper lip as if to kiss her nose.

"Every third Friday is a half day," she said. "You can go in three days with Rocco. I think he'd like that . . ."

"Yipppeee!!!!" I ran all through the house and back and went to hug her tightly and felt my heart against hers, our actual chambers together, hers beating, pushing against mine so that I remembered what it was to have a heartbeat. Lub-dub. Lub-dub.

"Promise me you'll be good," she said.

"I promise! I promise! I promise!"

I didn't know then how hard it would be—to be good, to keep a promise, the fragility of human beating.

═══

ON WEDNESDAY, AS a surprise, Odysseus had the boys' finished record framed. Emmeline squealed as Odysseus proudly unveiled the custom beveled gold frame.

"But now we can't play it!" Rocco said.

"We have a whole box of them." Roman patted him on the shoulder and laughed. "I think we can spare one."

It was one of the rare moments outside of practicing and performing that Roman was actually home, instead of off with Tad Wexler, or whomever.

Together, they crowded around as Odysseus hung it next to the photo of them at Coney Island.

"Soon, won't just be the frame that's gold!" River said cockily.

Rocco ran his finger over the vinyl where their voices were. The three of them harmonizing right there on this little round disc. He liked the feeling of the grooves against his fingertips. He did it again with his thumb to see if the music felt different with another finger. Somewhere in the dark lines against his finger was his voice, belonging momentarily to whoever paid for it. That something that came from him could be so captured made Rocco feel both more and less real.

"Where are you and where am I?" he said aloud to River, who stood next to him.

"All over it," River said, then laughed heartily. "Don't you know? We're everywhere now, bro."

═══

NONE OF THE other kids could understand why Milton, of all the boys, should be River's favorite. River and Milton would talk in the library together, in the boys' bathroom, in the halls. River who smiled broadly, who did everything right. Who was destined to be a big star. Everyone could see how he shone. Why would he shine his light on a boy who looked pale and sickly with glasses as big and bright as a stop sign? River heard the whispers, but he paid them no mind.

Milton said he should be nicer to Rocco, and so River tried to be. When Rocco repeated what he said, or started on an outburst, or laughed a little too loudly, or talked longer than he should about whatever he was hyperfocused on that day, when River had enough and was about to open his mouth and say shut up, Milton pressed his knee against him. Then River felt high and whatever Rocco said was not a series of verbal farts but a song.

"Milton Bradley!" Rocco would shout whenever he sat down to join them, and it irritated the hell out of River, but Milton would smile wide and say, "Hello, Rocco Johnson!"

Sometimes he and Milton talked until late at night; sometimes they pressed their thighs together under the lunch table.

On Thursday, Milton picked a piece of lint off his sleeve and River wanted to place it right back so he could pick it off again.

═══

ON FRIDAY, ROMAN removed the ribbon on the Oldsmobile before driving it to school that morning. Odysseus and Emmeline had surprised him the night before, after the birthday cake, after he had grown faintly afraid that all he was getting was a new telescope. He'd tried his hardest to appear grateful for whatever they would give him. Seemingly sensing his disappointment, his father said, "You know things have been hard, getting the shop up and running. And buying this house."

"Yeah," Roman said.

"Let's go outside and try the telescope out. It'll be fun," his father said. His mother and his brothers had followed behind them in a row like baby ducks. The stars outside were brighter than they'd been in some time. Still not as bright as back home.

"Point out the Big Dipper for me," Odysseus said.

Roman was taking his time searching for the ladle in the sky when he heard his dad opening up the garage door behind them.

"It's not a spaceship, but this'll get you somewhere," Odysseus said.

"What?" Roman turned to see the glint of the new car in the garage. He leapt straight up. "That's mine?!"

His brothers began to jump around too. River reached out to touch the leather seats.

"Hands off my new car!" Roman said.

"Happy seventeenth birthday, son," his father said. "Plus, now you can pick up your brothers and it'll make things easier on your mother and I."

Roman wanted the car so badly that he didn't even mind that it came with babysitting duties. A car meant freedom. It might even mean girls. He couldn't wait to show Tad. To show off to the other boys. He had gotten all kinds of shit for being Black, but now he was a Black boy with a song on national radio and a brand-new car. All those asshole Catholics could go suck on an egg.

═

WHEN MILTON PICKED a piece of lint off River's sweater, sometime between second and third period, River shoved him against the lockers.

Milton looked at River like a kicked puppy.

"I don't know what got into me," River mumbled.

But he did. He thought of Mr. X's daughter and how humiliated he'd been. The shame of somebody touching him when he hadn't given them permission. The shame of doing something he hadn't wanted to do. In front of others. Desire. Talia had forced him to do something he didn't want to do. But why hadn't he wanted to do it? Wasn't that what all normal boys wanted? Why was it that a pretty girl made him feel heavy, when Milton made him feel light? He was angry at himself. At Talia. At poor Milton, who had done nothing more than be his friend. His best friend. The best he'd ever had.

He could not stop thinking about what he'd done all through the rest of his classes. He tried to make eye contact with Milton repeatedly over lessons about SOHCAHTOA and Sherman's March. In gym, as captain of the dodgeball team, he picked Milton for his side even though it was common knowledge that Milton had two left feet, bad depth perception, and zero killer instinct. River bounced balls off the other boys' heads with glee, taking out his classmates one by one, going only slightly gentler with the girls. In the back of the gym, Milton and Laura Walton held their weapons and chatted until the gym teacher yelled at them, "This is not a goddamn slumber party!"

Gym was his last class of the day, thank God. Some kids had to sweat and run and go to their other classes smelling of pubescence.

"You all are funky as hell," Jordan Covington, the prettiest girl in school and damn near the meanest, said as the boys and girls traveled the short hallway into their respective locker rooms. "And not in the good way!"

She wasn't wrong.

In the locker rooms the other boys splashed their faces and snatched up their backpacks. River lingered. Milton did too.

═══

WITH ALL THE boys at school and Roman ready to pick them up in his new car, Emmeline finally said yes to an invitation to Beth's. Beth lived in a rather giant Queen Anne on Markham Place off Orange Grove Boulevard. She stood out on the porch casually tending to a rosebush in a way that seemed as though she'd just been looking for something to do before Emmeline was scheduled to arrive. Suddenly quite self-conscious, Emmeline struggled to parallel park in front of the woman's house. Would the neighbors think she was the help? What did it matter? she asked herself. She knew who she was.

If Emmeline had anticipated struggling to find things to speak about with Beth, she needn't have worried. Beth flitted from topic to topic, sharp of wit and loose of tongue, which was a winning combo as it meant Emmeline herself didn't need to search for things to say. They laughed easily together. Emmeline found herself growing ever more relaxed.

"I know it's only two, but you want wine?" Beth said after they'd eaten all the pastries and drunk all the tea. "I swear I'm not a lush!"

"Please!" Emmeline said.

═══

ROMAN FELT LIKE a god. If high school was the animal kingdom, between having a brand-new car, and being on the radio, he found himself no longer prey but a lion.

He found himself talking more in class. Making jokes when he otherwise would've remained silent. In English, they were reading *Lord of the Flies,* a book about a bunch of fucked-up deserted white boys and a conch shell.

"Conch shells look like vaginas," Roman said after reading the room, taking a gamble, and laughed. The others laughed with him.

"Don't act like such a retard," Sam Mullen said. The lone dissenter. Sam Mullen was a loner who thought himself smarter and more sophisticated than all the other boys. He was a nobody. A nothing person. Not rich enough to be intimidating to the other boys, no street cred for being one of the scholarship kids. He wasn't even actually the smartest; Roman's marks beat his by far. Still, Roman grew mad that Sam hadn't recognized his new place in the social hierarchy. A boy not to be fucked with. Roman was no Piggy.

Tad jumped up to defend Roman's honor: "Shut up, faggot!"

"Boys!" Miss Henry intervened half-heartedly. Everybody knew she'd just gotten dumped by their chemistry teacher.

ROCCO AND LAURIE walked down the hallway together. With Laurie he didn't have to talk much; she did enough talking for them both. He listened and nodded and mostly felt the absolute glee of the first stages of friendship, a real live friend. And a girl at that!

"Don't forget. You said you would sign my magazine for me." Laurie thrust two copies of *Teen Beat* into his face. "And one for my cousin Mallory, who is the most annoying person in the world."

"OK," Rocco said.

"I've never been friends with a famous person before," Laurie said.

"I'm not famous," Rocco said.

"You were on television!"

She then began to go into great depth about just how annoying her cousin Mallory was.

Christmas, given permission by Emmeline to attend school that day, trailed them, whispering in Rocco's ear.

"She hardly even takes a breath!" Christmas exclaimed.

Rocco laughed.

"Hey, retard! What are you laughing at?" he heard from behind him, and turned to face Laurie's brother, Wayne.

"I WORRY. WILL anybody ever love Edie?" Beth said offhandedly, a half bottle in. "I mean, obviously we do. But you know what I mean . . ."

As far as Emmeline could tell, the little girl mostly communicated in grunts and shrieks.

"You know the first psychologist we went to said she's the way she is because of something I said or did. He said for me to think really hard about anything I might have so much as thought about Edie that could've caused this. And the only thing I could think of was that sometimes I wanted to be the one going off to work. That I wanted to be talking with brilliant people all day and not just changing diapers and getting spit up on, you know? Glenn and I met in law school. I was higher ranked in our class! The shrink said that's what did it. That the baby could feel my resentment and that's the reason Edie's . . . like this . . ."

Beth fought back tears, and Emmeline gently scooted the sugar dish out of the way so she could reach across the table for her hand.

"I was a teacher before I got married. I liked it. Loved it even," Emmeline said. "I felt . . . useful."

She paused, choosing her words carefully so as not to press on any of the white woman's open wounds. "It's hard reorienting yourself around the kids. Men don't have to. Not like we do. The man sounds like a quack!"

"Right?" Beth said, wiping away tears.

Just then Edie started screaming at the top of her lungs and Beth rushed over to calm her down as the girl flailed about.

"It's awful not being able to tell what's wrong," Beth said as she wrapped her arms around Edie to keep the girl from hitting her. "At least your boy has his words."

Emmeline knew she didn't mean anything by it. But something about the woman's words scraped under the skin near her very heart itself. Her Rocco was not anything at all like Beth's Edie. Not at all. Her boy was in school right now. He was atop a billboard on Sunset Boulevard right this moment.

"Oh shit! Ow! No!" Beth cried out, and released the girl, who ran into the house.

"Oh Beth! You're bleeding!" Emmeline said, looking at a fresh wound across Beth's forearm where Edie had just bitten down. "Where's your iodine? Let me help."

═══

IN THE LOCKER room, River took a tentative step toward Milton.

"I'm sorry for what I did earlier," he said. "I don't know what came over me."

"Yeah, you said that already," Milton said, staring down at his feet. Two bits of paper towels plugged both his nostrils. He sounded a bit like the Chipmunks Christmas album. Milton had been absolutely pounded in the face with a ball by Jerry Sawyer, so much so that his nose bled.

"Does it still hurt?" River asked.

Milton looked up.

"I mean . . ."

═══

ROMAN TURNED ON the car radio as the other boys crowded around the Oldsmobile. By chance of fate, or kismet, or perhaps even divine fucking intervention, there they were.

"Hi, I'm Roman. I'm River. And I'm Rocco! We're the Johnson Three. And you're listening to 93 KHJ."

Logan gave him the nod as he walked past. Roman nodded back but felt annoyed that Logan hadn't acknowledged him more.

Sam Mullen walked past and Roman turned the volume up as high as it could go. Tad and the others had spent the rest of the day mercilessly teasing Sam after their exchange in English. Roman now had minions. Or groupies. Or maybe just friends. Either way, his brothers could handle waiting a few more minutes.

He relished their harmonies echoing out over the school parking lot, took glee in the gloss of his new rims.

═══

EMMELINE DIDN'T PICK up when Odysseus called the house. He decided to hang up and try again one more time. There was a restaurant in Hollywood just by the billboard the record company had paid for advertising the boys' single. Wouldn't it be a gas to sit and eat under it, their boys looming larger than life, in the very heart of Hollywood itself? He'd already called and made reservations for nine that evening. It was much later than they'd normally eat, but it was the only reservation the place had available. He couldn't wait to surprise her, to see the look on the boys' faces when they pulled up. Hell, even the little pick could come with. Even if the little dead boy couldn't eat nothing, Odie could practically hear him now looking up at the sign and shouting, "Oh boy!"

═══

"C'MON, WAYNE. STOP trying to start shit," Laurie said, annoyed.

"I thought I told you not to hang 'round my sister." Wayne stepped to Rocco.

"Leave me alone," Rocco said. Normally he would've kept his mouth shut. But he was very tired. They'd stayed out performing until two in the morning the night before. And the venue had been so uncomfortable. Shrieking girls. Floor sticky with spilled drinks. Stage lights that made him feel like his skin was aflame. Never mind that the room itself was asymmetrical, with weird corners that truly drove him nuts. To top it off, River had gotten the crowd to sing "Happy Birthday" to Roman. Rocco hated all those off-key notes drunkenly yelled at full volume. His big brother, however, ate it right up.

After all that, Rocco hadn't wanted to go to school, he'd needed a day to recover, but Emmeline insisted.

"It's a Friday," she said. "Just make it through one day and you have the weekend. Plus, Christmas can go with you."

"Oh boy!" Christmas had said.

In front of Laurie's locker, Wayne lunged at Rocco.

═══

RIVER AND MILTON stood across from each other. Rocco would be waiting for him by his locker by now, or perhaps he'd already made his way out front to where Roman would be waiting in the new car, but a few minutes more wouldn't hurt anyone. He could handle one of Rocco's tantrums, or Roman's bitching. And besides, he was not his brother's keeper.

"Rocco's gonna get pissed if you're late," Milton said.

River shrugged and gently touched Milton's face by the chin, tilting it upward.

"Do you think it's broken?" he asked.

He heard Milton stop breathing for a moment. Felt the held breath in his own lungs.

It was River who leaned in first.

═══

"RIVER!" ROCCO CALLED out to his brother for help as Wayne began to pummel him.

═══

BUT ROCCO NEEDN'T have worried, for there I was.

CHAPTER SIXTEEN

"I WISH I'D NEVER BROUGHT YOU INTO MY HOUSE!" ODYSSEUS SLURRED his words as he knocked back something brown and bittersweet. "I should've known nothing good would come of adopting a goddamn pick. A spook! A haint! A minstrel!"

"Stop it! Just stop!" Emmeline yelled.

Suddenly, the streetlamp flickered and the sidewalks buckled as Christmas began to bawl. River felt Christmas's sadness and grief as a rolling earthquake. They all did.

Across the street, their nosy white-lady neighbor came out to look up at the sky.

"I was only trying to help!" Christmas sobbed.

Upstairs, Rocco lay catatonic in their bedroom, where he had been ever since they'd gotten home.

Odysseus picked the drink back up from the side table. "What do you think they're gonna do to Rocco now?"

As he and Roman sat next to each other on the stairs, River's leg shook violently. Nerves? Or fear? Or something else entirely? Roman placed his hand gently on it.

"I wish I'd never been born!" Christmas shouted, and the windows in the house cracked.

"You're dead, kid. Go be dead!" Odie said, and everyone, including Christmas, went silent.

Then, just like that, Christmas disappeared.

"Christmas?" Roman leapt up from where he had been sitting on the stairs.

"Where'd he go?" River said.

They all stood there openmouthed.

"It's that pick . . . this is all his fault . . ." Odysseus started.

"Fuck you, Odie," said Emmeline. "He has a name. Christmas is a little boy. And now he's all alone."

River had never heard his mother curse at his father in front of them before.

"Where'd he go?" River panicked.

"Christmas!" Roman yelled throughout the house.

But he was gone.

Just then, the phone rang and Emmeline rushed to pick it up. Principal Wallace needed Odysseus and Emmeline to come to the school immediately.

═══

THE BULLY, WAYNE, was in the hospital. It was bad. Really bad. But it had been an accident, a horrible, tragic accident. Everyone thought Rocco was to blame. How were they supposed to explain to Wayne's parents, the principal, and everyone else that a boy without a body, and a small one at that, had done this and not Rocco?

"Rocco's not dangerous," Emmeline pleaded with Wayne's parents as they sat across from one another in the principal's office. "Please!"

River sat outside, listening. He'd been called in, with the other kids, to recount his side of the events. But he hadn't seen much, just Wayne crumpled up on the ground screaming and Rocco sobbing and covering his ears. Milton said the same. He didn't know what Laurie and the other boy had said, what they had seen, if they even had words for it.

It didn't matter anyway. The principal listed off the other instances in which Rocco had outbursts at school.

"We can't have Rocco on school grounds right now," the principal said. "River can empty his brother's locker for him."

Rocco's locker didn't have much in it. A few books. The issue of *Turok: Son of Stone* where they disturb the dinosaur's burial ground. So that's where that was! A half-empty pack of Doublemint. The few stragglers still at school stared at River as he collected his brother's scant belongings. When he caught their eye, they looked down and said nothing.

═══

RIVER'S PARENTS ARGUED with each other deep into the night. River tiptoed up and out of his room, glancing over at poor Rocco, who didn't even so much as budge, even when River accidentally walked into their dresser and dramatically stubbed his toe. Roman slept on the twin bed next to Rocco, holding his brother instead of sleeping comfortably in his own bedroom.

"Where you going?" Roman whispered.

"To piss," River said.

In the hallway, River pressed his ear to the slightest crack in his parents' bedroom door.

"How could you not tell me about the gas station before this, Emmie?" his father said.

"Don't act like you didn't know what he could do. You saw what happened at the bar that night! Besides, he was only trying to protect us!" his mama yelled. "Because you made your whole family drive halfway across this damn country without you! And for what? Look at us now."

"Everything I did was for these damn boys and you know it! For the band."

"Ohhh the band! The band! The goddamn band!" his mother said in a mocking tone that River had never known her to use before. "None of this would've happened if you hadn't moved us here. If you hadn't insisted on splitting the boys into different schools because you were listening to Mr. X, or whoever-all talking in your ear."

River made the utter mistake of sneezing then. A sneeze he thought was quiet enough but apparently not, because his parents stopped arguing and walked over toward him. He froze in place.

"Go to bed, River," his father said before shutting the door right in his face.

═══

ODYSSEUS OPENED THE door to them and said, "What's this about, Officers?"

As though it weren't obvious.

Rocco fought against them and shrieked and clung to Emmeline, who clung to him as though he were the intestines spilling out her very own body.

"This is all a mistake," Odie kept saying as Rocco flailed about.

Roman tried to stand between the police and his mother and brother, until one of the police officers knocked him down, out of the way. Emmeline heard her eldest hit the floor with a sickening thud. The police officer placed the weight of himself on Roman to keep him down.

"Are you trying to join him, boy?" the officer said menacingly to Roman.

With Rocco still in her arms, Emmeline tried to turn her back to the officers. They'd have to go through her before they dared touch her other child.

"Ma'am! Ma'am!" A button from her blouse popped as the cop wrestled Rocco from her arms, and her slip spilled into view.

Odysseus yelled, "Don't touch my wife!"

But he didn't physically intervene. He was a Black man of a certain age who had seen what could happen when one dared to touch a white person, much less law enforcement. He was afraid of what the officer would do to them all, Odie said when Emmeline confronted him later. Emmeline would try to remember this when the fury overcame her in the days, months, and years to follow.

River, God bless him, tried to reason with the officers: "My brother wouldn't hurt anybody. I swear! It was all an accident. He's really scared. If you calm down, he'll calm down."

"We're the Johnson Three," Roman gasped, and tried to reason with the officer kneeling into him on the ground. "We're on the radio. We're not criminals."

"I don't give a fuck who you are," the officer replied.

And as they finally placed handcuffs on her child, Emmeline yelled at her husband, "Do something, Odie!"

"Mama!" Rocco yelled, fingers dug into the doorframe as the officers pushed him into the dusk.

Outside, her poor baby called for each of his family members by name as the police paraded him to the patrol car in front of a bevy of neighborhood gossips.

"Don't let them see you break down," Odysseus whispered to her.

Emmeline was ready to break something over her husband's head right then and there. How could he possibly care about optics at this point? How little it mattered if those white women whispered among themselves, "There goes the neighborhood!"

"Where are you taking him?" Emmeline yelled. She couldn't hear the officer's response over her child's cries.

"This is your fault!" Emmeline said to her husband as the police car pulled away and the two of them rushed to Odie's beloved Caddy to follow.

═══

WOULD THEY HAVE arrested Rocco in the manner that they had were he not a Black child? Even the boy's own sister said Rocco himself hadn't hurt her brother. That, in fact, it was her brother who had repeatedly bullied and assaulted Rocco. That if anything had happened, it was self-defense. Still, by all appearances, Rocco had hurt a white boy. It should've come as no surprise to anyone that he would have to pay.

═══

THEY WERE TOLD they'd get more information on Monday, and a court date.

"Rocco's just supposed to stay here until then?" Emmeline replied incredulously.

Odysseus sighed. "I guess he has to go in front of a judge for his first appearance and then the judge will determine the bail. But the judge isn't around on weekends. Lawyers neither."

"That can't be right. They can't have everyone just sitting around all weekend like that. Plus, he's a child. Don't they do things differently for children?"

Odysseus shrugged. "I'm just telling you what the man said."

"Call Mr. X," she said. "He'll be able to help, right? Doesn't he know people?"

"I don't know, Em," Odysseus said. "Maybe we should keep him out of this? I don't want this to get out and then folks stop working with the boys."

"Are you serious right now?" Emmeline raised her voice, then lowered it again when she saw several women look over at the two of them. "He's the whole goddamn reason we're in this place," she whispered.

The aggressively antiseptic space was starting to give Emmeline a headache. She retrieved a scarf from her purse to block the smell as best she could. Then Emmeline pulled her purse in closer, feeling woefully out of place carrying the Pierre Cardin that Odysseus had gifted her the year before. When she finally raised her head and got a good glance at the other people around her, she realized she looked a whole lot like the rest of the people in the precinct, waiting. Anxious mothers and wives. Communal misery in mostly Black and brown. The white folks stood off to the side not daring to sit down next to them on the benches.

Across from her, a Mexican woman repeated frantically to the woman at the desk, "No hablo inglés!"

How much worse it must be to not even understand what was going on around them. Not that any of them did really.

"Well, Mr. X and 'em certainly can't make their money off the Johnson Three performing if Rocco's in jail." Emmeline's voice slathered and slipped around in her disdain.

Odysseus didn't respond.

"What is his number?" she asked, after some time had passed. "I'll call him myself."

"Just calm down," he said. "Getting yourself all riled up isn't going to help."

"No," she snapped. "I'm not just going to let my child sit in there!"

"Emmeline. Drop it. Now."

"I swear to God, Odie, I'm never going to forgive you for this," she spat.

"Will you stop it, woman? I'm trying to think."

Emmeline was sick of waiting for her husband to get it together. She would handle this herself.

"We need a lawyer," she responded. "I'm going to call Beth. Her Glenn's gotta know somebody."

Emmeline walked over to the payphone and took a coin out of her bag. She didn't know the woman that well, but who else could she turn to?

"Beth. I'm sorry to bother you like this. May I ask a huge favor?"

═══

COME MONDAY, THE judge set Rocco's bail at something they couldn't afford. Not yet. Or rather, they would have been able to afford it had they not spent so much money to get to California, on this new house in this snotty neighborhood, on sending Roman to that stupid private school just because Mr. X had recommended it.

Beth's husband sent a pretty, pantsuit-wearing associate to their aid. The woman argued valiantly that Rocco wasn't a flight risk and didn't have any priors, that he was a *child.* What happened was not an intentional act, not an attempt on the bully's life, but rather a playground brawl gone horribly tragically awry, and should be treated as such in determining bail, the associate tried to reason with the judge. Then the young lawyer said that this was a sensitive case, and they had reason to believe that Rocco was mentally retarded.

"No, I'm not!" Rocco shouted in response as the judge slammed the gavel down over and over again to no avail.

"I'm so sorry, Mrs. Johnson," the woman said afterward as she went to hug a distraught Emmeline.

The young lawyer smelled of freshly cut gardenias. She had done everything she could. It wasn't her fault, Emmeline reminded herself. While baring fangs at the judge, the lawyer had been gentle with Emmeline. And how intoxicating it had been to watch her work. If the young lawyer had been a man, perhaps, or, more likely, had the Johnsons not been Black, how easily Emmeline could have pictured a different outcome.

"Will you take Rocco's case moving forward?" Emmeline said.

"It's not really my area of expertise. I do more transactional work normally," the woman said honestly. "And you'll need somebody who has experience arguing for civil rights for the . . ."

The lawyer leaned in to whisper, as though saying a bad word, "For the um . . . mentally retarded—"

"Rocco's not that," Emmeline interrupted.

"I'll give you the information for some great reputable bail bondsmen," the lawyer said.

"No need. I'll get us the money," Odysseus said as he got up from where they sat waiting.

"You're going to leave me here?" Emmeline grabbed Odysseus's wrist as he headed toward the doorway.

"I promise I'll be back as soon as I've got it."

"Like your promises mean anything," she said, and let go. Her hunger rolled around inside of her, growing legs. There was a vending machine down the hallway.

═══

SOMEHOW, ODYSSEUS HAD, in fact, gotten the money before the end of the following day. Emmeline didn't want to know how, or where, he'd gotten access to such a sum so quickly. It didn't matter. All that mattered was that Rocco could come home.

His eyes blinking, as if to readjust themselves, Rocco stumbled out of the jail. He said nothing and looked spectral.

"Rocco, baby?" Emmeline had Odysseus pull over minutes into the car ride home. She climbed into the backseat next to her child and held him to her.

"I'm so sorry, baby," she whispered, tears rolling down her face. "I'm so sorry."

She expected him to say something to absolve her. It hadn't been her idea to move to California. Or to split the boys into different schools. She hadn't been the one to uproot them from everything and everyone they'd ever known. Except that she had made the one decision that had changed everything, hadn't she?

"You'll be safe here," she'd said to the baby ghost, standing her ground even as Odysseus argued against it. She couldn't possibly have known what would happen. Or maybe that was the real problem. She should never have promised safety. She of all people should have known better. None of them were safe, not ever, not really.

Instead of responding, Rocco just closed his eyes.

Once Rocco was safely situated back home, having made bail, and "safely" being a relative term, given how easily rattled and nonverbal he had become in the aftermath of his arrest, Emmeline realized she might have another ally in this fight, and had taken it upon herself to go to Dr. Takahashi's office.

"Something horrible has happened," she said. "Please. Please. I'm begging you. If there's anything you can do . . ."

Aaron Takahashi had been shrinking the heads of many of Pasadena's elite for the past ten years of his career. Among the children whose heads he shrank was the child of Judge Gordon Markman. Judge Gordon Markman could be counted upon to be fair, to actually be honorable, as it were.

"Don't worry, Mrs. Johnson," Dr. Takahashi said. "I promise I'll do everything I can."

She hugged him right then and there, in spite of herself. And he, perhaps sensing that she needed to be soothed, held her until Emmeline pulled away, abruptly.

"I'm sorry," she said.

"Why?" the doctor said. "You have nothing to be sorry for."

"I should get going," Emmeline said, not knowing what else to say or do. She wasn't used to being vulnerable in front of other people. Dr. Takahashi simply nodded and awkwardly put his hands in his pockets.

"I mean it," he said. "I'll do everything I can. I promise, Mrs. Johnson."

And true to his word, he had. He had connected them with another great and deeply sympathetic lawyer (also the parent of a client), who had somehow finagled to get the case in front of Judge Markman.

This is how justice works for the wealthy and the well-connected, Emmeline thought. What a difference the right access made. Speaking of the wealthy, she noted that Mr. X had been increasingly hard to get hold of for a time.

An uneasy quiet descended on the Johnsons as they awaited Rocco's sentencing, seeming to sink into the very bones of the house itself. For a while, they'd done everything they could to put on a brave face for Rocco's sake. Even tried to cheer him up. One weekend, they'd even piled up in the car and driven all the way to Palos Verdes to see the blue Morpho butterfly that Rocco had wanted to see ever since they moved to California. But when even that didn't elicit so much as a "wow," they'd given themselves over to the quiet, save for River's practicing.

═══

ONE MONTH LATER, instead of sentencing Rocco to juvenile hall, a fate that Emmeline knew her boy couldn't withstand, Judge Gordon Markman sentenced him to a psychiatric facility for two years, "So the boy can get the care he needs."

But we're the care he needs, Emmeline thought. *He needs to be with his family!*

As though gravity itself had a part in Rocco's sentencing, Emmeline wobbled this way and that, and Dr. Takahashi, who had served as a character witness and specialist, leapt from his seat immediately behind her, to hold on to her elbow, gently steadying her. With just the slightest hunch forward, on the other side of Emmeline, Odysseus struggled to catch his breath.

"No!" River stood up and shouted at the judge as he finished pronouncing the sentence, a bit of a delayed reaction.

Emmeline hadn't wanted River and Roman to be subjected to the stress of the proceedings, but Odysseus said they needed to show that the entire family stood behind Rocco.

It likely hadn't helped matters that in front of the fair and honorable Judge Markman, Rocco had alternated between barely speaking, banging himself on the side of the head whenever he got too frustrated, and insisting that a ghost had committed the assault. River and Roman struggled to keep Rocco's fists down as he hit himself.

"Christmas did it!" Rocco shouted in moments of frustration throughout. "I'm good! I'm good!"

Afterward, as the Johnsons all poured out of the courtroom in shock, Dr. Takahashi had said to them, his eyes focused on Emmeline, "Please. If there's anything you all need . . . Or should you just need somebody to talk to, my door is open . . ."

═══

"WHAT ARE WE going to do about the interview?" River asked as they sat down to their third dinner without Rocco. The table was quiet, save for the sound of Roman occasionally coming up for air while scarfing down his sweet-and-sour pork from Sang's Inn. They'd eaten more takeout over the last month than ever before in their lives, Emmeline not much feeling like cooking lately. If it had been a normal meal, his mother would've yelled at Roman for his utter lack of manners at present, and Rocco would've covered his ears while whining at Roman to stop smacking, and his daddy would say he wasn't raising his boys in no barn, and

River would've said something smart-alecky, no doubt, but nothing about them was normal anymore.

"Are you fucking kidding me? That's what you care about right now?" Roman said. "The interview?"

He had never despised his little brother more.

"But it's supposed to be tomorrow," River whispered.

Odysseus interjected, "We'll figure it out. It'll happen."

Emmeline excused herself from the table.

It had been a very long time since Roman could remember a house this quiet.

Late at night, he snuck into the garage, where his father kept the beers. He drank until he could no longer feel where he ended and the rest of the world began. River and Odysseus saw him curled up in the fetal position on the lifting bench when they came down for Odysseus's morning routine. Roman had cramps in his legs from where his limbs had awkwardly dangled off the bench.

"It's the morning, son. Get up."

He struggled to get to his feet.

"Please don't tell Mama," Roman said.

Odysseus nodded. River looked at him wide-eyed.

Roman's back still ached a bit from where he'd been thrown and forced to the ground. Where he'd been pressed up against the hard tile as the officer dug into him as though the man's body was a pestle, and Roman a mortar, bits of Roman ground clean off.

═══

AT SCHOOL, MILTON kept trying to talk to River in the halls, and for weeks, he ignored him. Once, as River walked away from him, Milton grabbed his arm, and River turned around and punched him. River had never seriously punched anyone in his life. Not even his brothers. As Milton crumpled to the ground, they were both taken aback, stunned.

"Fight!" one of the other kids yelled.

Instead, River reached out a hand and pulled Milton up. Milton looked up at him with those big, searching eyes of his, glasses slightly askance. He straightened himself.

"Who are you?" Milton said, loud enough for everyone around them to hear. River felt the tears welling up in his eyes, but promptly pushed them back down. He couldn't afford to have anybody see him cry, not now.

Who was he? River Johnson, lead singer of the Johnson Three, brother of Rocco and Roman, except now Rocco was gone, and his father, mother, and Roman might as well have been.

When he walked down the halls, he was either that kid on the radio (which meant that people hated him because they thought he thought he was better than them), or the brother of that kid who nearly killed Wayne Smith (which meant that people hated him because his brother was almost a murderer). Whatever the case, River was no longer a person, exactly, but a story.

He would be lying if he didn't admit that for a brief moment, before their world got turned inside out like Christmas's gizzards, he'd wondered if school would be easier with Rocco gone. He'd resented Rocco sometimes, always needing to be his keeper. They were babies together, and sometimes mistaken for twins. It'd made it that much more noticeable when Rocco didn't hit milestones River already had. His mother had said, at first, River made enough noise for the both of them. Then finally, "Maybe we should take Rocco to a doctor."

River had held Rocco's hand as they went to school well into the fifth grade, when all the other boys had stopped holding their mothers' hands, much less their siblings' hand. Whenever Rocco had outbursts at their old school, River had been called to the principal's office. It happened over and over, and he soon knew the drill before the school nurse even said it. "Yeah, I know. Calm my brother down."

River didn't mind it too much because he got to get out of class for a bit, and Rocco's teacher often gave him a licorice or a peppermint for his troubles.

Emmeline was furious when she found out and insisted to the principal that River needed to be in class.

But not long after that, the teacher had hit Rocco with her hand. Then put him in the corner. Followed by hitting him with rulers, then even an old paddle. Nothing had worked, the teacher whined to River when he'd arrived, as though he were the adult and not vice versa. At home, Emmeline pulled Rocco into her and when he winced, she discovered the bruises dark and deep blue across his body. That night River could hear his mother crying and his father trying to comfort her.

"Why didn't you say something, River?!" his mama had said.

River thought of the licorice Mrs. McCarthy had given him, sweet and twisted in his mouth, stomach too.

River tried to press on with practicing, though who the hell even knew if they were still a group without Rocco? Their song was topping charts across the nation. They were getting offers to go on tour! Meanwhile, at home, the Johnsons were firmly grounded, sweeping up the fragments of whatever remained of their former selves. Roman didn't even bother trying anymore. And on the rare occasion when he did, his voice was all over the place. Often, he stayed out all hours with Tad or whomever.

"Again?" River whispered.

Roman mumbled back, "Mind your business, Riv."

═

"I THINK I should be a solo act," River said to his father as they waited for both Roman and his mother to come home. It had been a little over a week since Rocco was taken from them. Mr. X wanted River to attend a showcase with a bunch of other acts for the record company. Roman was unreliable. His voice wasn't the same. He didn't even want to be there. Never had. River made the case, feeling a bit of disgust with himself in the pit of his stomach.

Odysseus quickly agreed.

Glassy-eyed, stinking of drink and Lord knows what else, Roman fumbled with his shoes at the entryway. Their father was the one to broach the subject as Roman stood wobbling before them guiltily.

"Roman, you're out," Odysseus said, uncharacteristically blunt. "It's best if River is a solo act from here on out."

River's whole body tensed. Roman's face passed through a series of microexpressions as he drunkenly digested what exactly their father meant.

"Judas! You fuck!" Roman yelled at River.

"Don't go cursing at your brother like that. He didn't do anything wrong," their father snapped. He ran his hand over the top of his fro. River only knew him to do this when he was nervous.

But River had done something wrong, hadn't he? River had forced it out into the open. Had actually spoken it into being. Their father would never have been the one to kick his brother out, no matter how many times Roman screwed things up. Odysseus was too loyal, too much of a family man, and River and Roman both knew it.

"Et tu, Brute?" Roman yelled at River, again. River didn't know what the hell that meant. He wondered if maybe Roman might be taking Catholic school a little too seriously, and clearly, given the state of his inebriation, not seriously enough.

"Anyway, you can't kick me out. I quit!" Roman slurred.

"You can't just say you quit!" River snapped.

"I can. And I do." Roman took a deep bow before pitching forward and tumbling over the coffee table.

Just then, their mama opened the door.

River looked over at the clock. It was nearly eleven at night. Where could his mama possibly have been? Emmeline froze at the sight of all of them.

"Mama! They just kicked me out of the band," Roman said from the floor.

"See! You didn't quit!" River said, even though he knew he shouldn't pour salt in the wound.

"Unbelievable." Emmeline shook her head at Odysseus and her boys before heading upstairs.

"That's all you have to say?" Odysseus shouted up. River thought things had been tense between his parents ever since what happened with Rocco. Maybe even ever since they moved to California.

"Yeah! That's all you have to say?" Roman repeated, then laughed maniacally. The air around him smelled like layers of vice that made River's stomach turn.

═══

IN THE MORNING, Roman glanced at his brother one last time in the door and remembered when River was chubby and squirming and Roman had carried him everywhere, like River was his. He could hear his father in the garage lifting, grunting, preparing his body for the day. Roman walked into the garage and stood over Odysseus, spotting him.

He placed his hands under the weight of his father's barbell, bracing for a crash, waiting for it all to come tumbling down. Odysseus smiled up at his son.

"Good man," he said to Roman, and lifted just a bit higher. His father seemed to be trying to be nicer to him over the last few days. Mr. X had booked River on a tour. They were planning television interviews to bank on the success of the hit single. The single that was the Johnson Three's first hit single, not just River's. Hell, Rocco's voice was even the fucking lead on the track, not River's! How quickly Roman had become irrelevant in his own family, he thought. Poor Rocco too.

After breakfast, Roman walked to the recruiting office on Main Street. A lone protester stood outside holding a sign. He wasn't quite a hippie, didn't have the long hair, or youth, that had come to signify the counterculture. In fact, he looked almost old enough to be somebody's father. Maybe he was.

It was too early for most of the other protesters. Too early for even the recruiters themselves.

"Aren't you kinda old to be doing this?" Roman said to him.

"Who says there's an age to doing what's right?" the man replied.

"Is your son in Vietnam?" Roman asked.

"What? No. How old do you think I am?" the not-hippie replied.

Honestly, all people above a certain age kinda looked the same to Roman. Never mind that the man had that leathery sienna skin white folks got after spending too much time in the sun, which made it even harder to tell if he was twenty-five or forty.

After arguing about the war, and exchanging names, Roman and Gilbert the Protester spent the last ten minutes before the recruiting office opened chatting about the Dodgers.

"You can call me Gil for short," the man said, though Roman hadn't intended to call him anything at all.

Suddenly, they both startled at the sound of a shrill series of squawks in the trees. Roman looked up just in time to see several brightly colored blue-and-green birds pour out, the telltale red above their beaks.

"Parrots!" the not-quite-hippie yelled excitedly. "Look!"

"What the fuck? There's parrots in L.A.?" Roman asked.

"We have everything here!"

Roman and Gilbert both stared up into the sky appreciatively until the parrots flew off to whatever was next, and the recruiters approached to start their day.

"Baby killers!" Gilbert suddenly angrily yelled at the men as they unlocked the door, interrupting their short-lived idyll.

"Hey, Gil," the younger looking of the two recruiters said. He was dark and slight and looked a bit like a soap star, save for a deeply pockmarked nose.

"Don't do it!" Gil pleaded with Roman. "They're just sending boys like you to die. The U.S. government doesn't care about your life."

"Who said I care about my life?" Roman shrugged. He immediately regretted how melodramatic it sounded, but what was war if not dramatic?

Still, Roman lingered next to Gil, waiting for a sign. If the parrots returned, he would go back home. If not, he would march right in and sign on the dotted line to serve his country. Was it even a dotted line?

Roman waited five minutes, then ten, then fifteen, all while Gil chatted his ear off and occasionally interjected some fact or another about why the Vietnam War was deeply wrong. The parrots did not return.

As the recruiters handed him the paperwork, it only then occurred to Roman that he had never been a good liar. What if they saw through him? What if they called his parents? He lied just enough, or maybe the recruiters were just that desperate to believe he was of age. Everybody had secrets. Besides, most white people couldn't tell how old Black people were anyway, he reminded himself.

"You sure?" The man's name tag read Jimenez. He didn't seem that much older than Roman. Roman couldn't help but stare at the incongruent face—beautiful dark, sculpted features. The man's clogged nose was so red his pockmarks looked like canyons. It reminded Roman of the landscape they'd driven through on their way out west.

Roman nodded.

"Good man," the white one said. He was a smudge of a person, his only distinguishing characteristic being that he was definitely old enough to be Roman's father.

"Stay alive, kid," Gilbert said mournfully as Roman stepped out of the office and walked past two more protesters who alternately sipped their morning coffee and held up signs encouraging passersby to honk for peace.

═══

STUPID ROMAN HAD lost his damn mind and enlisted. River heard his parents and Roman fighting deep into the night.

"We can undo this, can't we?" his mother begged his father. "Call somebody. Anybody. Maybe Wexler knows somebody? Don't you know anybody from your army days?"

"I want to go," Roman shouted.

"You're not going! You're not!" Emmeline screamed and sobbed, and River could hear her unraveling.

It was to be only a matter of weeks before Roman would leave for basic, then something called AIT, then off to war.

In not even half a year, his brother would be in the jungle shooting and getting shot at. His brother could be like poor Norman Wiggins, who'd lived across the street from them their whole lives back home, until one day he was drafted, and next thing you know, the Johnsons were walking over a condolence casserole to his zombie of a mama. How stupid could Roman be? After enlisting, Roman was around even less than before. He barely spoke to River, and most conversations with their parents devolved into an angry verbal volleying that left their mother in tears. River hated Roman for making their mother cry. After a particularly awful fight, their father threatened to knock Roman out if he spoke to his mother like that again.

"Go ahead," Roman had drunkenly slurred.

"You know what? I'm glad you're leaving," River said late at night as Roman lay in bed, staring up at the ceiling.

"Of course you are. With me and Rocco gone you get all the attention to yourself, just like you've always wanted," Roman spat, and rolled over to face the wall.

During the day, River'd mostly been able to keep himself busy with practicing, but at night, he often found himself awake, desperately willing himself not to think about the day of Rocco's arrest. To forget the look on his mother's face as she tried to shield Rocco from the officers with her body. To forget what it had felt like to see his usually impervious father look helpless. To forget the thud Roman's body had made when the officer pushed him out of the way to get to Emmeline and Rocco. To forget how Rocco'd called out their names before being thrown in the police car. How the neighbors stood watching as though they were all just a bit of television, even after the police car had disappeared around the corner. River Johnson would have nightmares about Rocco's arrest in the weeks, months, and even years to come.

He deeply wished he could talk to Milton. Drunk Linda often drank until it was like she wasn't there. Or else she was like a hurricane, Milton said. He had learned to be quiet around her when he got home from school, until he figured out which mood she was in. Milton might understand.

River shouldn't have hit Milton. His face grew hot thinking about being near the boy; around Milton, he felt like the pluck of a string reverberated through his whole body. He thought of biking to Milton's house and apologizing that very minute.

But instead of going to Milton's, River felt himself hardening a little. He felt like one of the Easter jelly beans Mr. Sperling, their math teacher, had set out for the class even though it was still winter.

He didn't need friends. He didn't need anyone, really. All he needed was to dance, to sing, and a welcoming crowd.

He was going to be famous now, wasn't he?

PART TWO

1970–1972

CHAPTER SEVENTEEN

A FAMILY HAD WRAPPED THEMSELVES AROUND MY GIZZARDS, OR AT least they would've, had I still had my gizzards inside. I had woken up to pancakes and bickering and fallen asleep to brotherly secrets. I had loved more than I knew I could, more than anyone I had loved when alive. Except for Mama, whom I can't much remember these days. Over the years, Mama has faded away to pieces of a life, a pair of weary eyes, a smile with two back teeth missing, a tattered skirt hem that she re-hemmed so that it grew shorter and shorter still, and a pair of callused feet that I hated to rub, broken down and hardened as they were, not so much feet but cragged rocks.

"I don't want to!" I argued, and my mama would thwap me with her hand or whatever was nearby. Then I would pout while I continued the foot rub and she would groan until her groans gave way to song, and eventually I'd stop pouting and join in. Hard feet. Soft notes. This was what I'd known of love before the Johnsons.

Ms. Emmeline did not have hard feet. Everything about her was soft. Her smile, skin, hair. In her love was a cushion, a pillow, a bag of feathers, a cloud, kind words and knowledge and laughter. Which made it that much worse when I found myself falling out, of home, of brotherhood, of song.

I'm very stupid for a prodigy. I should've known nothing could stay soft for long.

When I saw that boy Wayne with Rocco, I saw only the man who'd tried to hurt Ms. Emmeline, the red-faced men who'd hurt me, the men I'd watched hurt Becky. I made a promise to myself then to never be a bystander again, to never watch anybody else's pain and do nothing. Becky didn't know of my promise, but it was for her nonetheless. Plus, I only meant to protect Rocco. Rocco, who wouldn't hurt a soul, not even a bug. Why, when Roman accidentally killed a snail once, Rocco had cried for an hour, until Emmeline convinced him that Roman had just hastened the snail's journey to heaven and its wonders.

"But what about Christmas?" Rocco had asked.

Yes, what about me? I thought. Perhaps Roman should kick and crack me open and send me to whatever was beyond, to Mama, to love.

But that's exactly what had happened, wasn't it? I had been spilled soft among the hard wood only to come to in the same place I'd been left. It was to there I decided to return when Odysseus cast me out. I wandered along roads, stowed away in trucks, and wandered some more until I eventually found myself back in the forest that begat me.

I was looking for Becky. I selfishly hoped she was still there, but also, for her sake, I hoped that she was still happy with the girls who had taken her home with them a few years before. Or maybe it had been decades? I can't remember time much anymore. It was as though the numbers on a clock had faded away until all that was left of time was a circle, a wheel, a merry-go-round.

There were new faces in the forest. A teenager who had been in a hunting accident.

"Mistaken for a deer and shot clean through by his own grandfather!" one of the rabbits, Gerta the Eighteenth, told me. Gerta the Eighteenth came from a great line of gossips. I knew her great-great-grandmother, Gerta the Fourteenth, and it was a marvel she'd had time to make so many lives, so fixated was she on the deaths of others. Gerta the Eighteenth told me to stay away from Tom—that was the teenager's name. Tom was not only very sullen but also quite racist.

"Such an unpleasant boy," Gerta said, "you know he killed Opal before he himself died? Remember Opal? Poor sweet, dumb girl. She was meant to be paired off with Randy. A fine stag indeed. If I were a deer . . . ooh. Anyhoo, Randy was quite out of her league, I always thought. Really, it was only a matter of time before a hunter got her, or a car."

"Have you seen Becky?" I finally asked Gerta once she'd stopped talking long enough to take a big gulping breath.

"The brat?" Gerta said.

It was uncharitable but also a little bit true. More than a little bit.

"Yeah," I said.

"What do you want with her?" Gerta said.

"She's my friend," I said.

"That girl doesn't have any friends. She came back, you know. Nobody wanted her anymore."

I winced.

I found Becky singing to herself and circling around a tree as though it were a maypole. She just barely glanced up at me, as though I'd been there all along, as though it hadn't been years or decades even since we were both in this place together. How many childhoods had it been?

"What happened?" I finally worked up the courage to speak.

"They grew up," Becky said. "Didn't want me around no more. Found a new set of girls and they grew up too. Keeps happening."

I sat down on a large mushroom next to her. I imagined that if I could still feel it, it would be soft against my skin. If I concentrated hard enough, I could feel something just barely under me. The mushroom swayed almost imperceptibly.

"Discarded me like an old rag doll when they got old enough! Told me I need to find somebody my own age to play with. Said it like they were doing me a favor.

"What happened with you?" She stopped to look at me. "You look in a bad sort of way. Even worse than usual . . ."

"I did something really bad," I said. "I didn't mean to. It was an accident."

But was it?

Becky considered me. "Did you kill somebody?"

I couldn't bear to say it aloud. And yet I'd done something even worse somehow; I'd broken a family.

"It's OK if you did. I won't judge you," Becky continued. "I did too once. On accident. The last girl wanted me to scare her ex-boyfriend and his new girlfriend. She was mad 'cause he cheated on her. So dumb. Who cares about boys like that? She was fun when she was little, but then when she got older, she kept wanting me to do things for her. Really mean things. And I did them because I thought she loved me. She said we were sisters."

The new teenager, Tom, strode over to the two of us, glowering. It was immediately apparent why everyone thought him unpleasant.

"What are you doing talking to this nigger?"

"We're friends . . . you'd have one too if you weren't such an asshole to everyone," Becky said.

"Your kind don't belong here," Tom said to me. His head flapped in the back where his brains had spilled out. Not that Tom ever had much to begin with, I figured.

"Belong here as much as anywhere, I reckon," I said.

"Tom. We're talking. Can you go away?" Becky and I were little children, but also we had been around for some time. Tom couldn't scare us; we'd seen too much. Tom looked at her in disbelief.

Becky turned her back to Tom and continued circling the tree in the other direction.

"Anyway, I scared the ex on a dark road and they lost control and the car swerved into a tree. My best friend ran away, but I stuck around to apologize. I felt just awful. The other girl started crying so hard when she realized she was dead. Turns out she didn't even know the boy had a girlfriend. She had this big hole in her chest where she'd been broken. I stayed with her awhile until she got used to it . . . being like this. She was actually really nice."

"I killed a boy. He kept hurting my brother. So I slammed him against metal until he broke."

I heard myself cry out just then, a sound unlike anything I'd ever made before. "I don't want to be a murderer."

Becky stopped circling the tree, sat down next to me on the giant mushroom. I felt all the sorrow well up somewhere from deep within. Enough for hours or maybe even days of sadness. We lost track of time in our tears. The animals did their best to comfort us a bit, but they had their own lives to attend to, food to catch, chicks to hatch, mates to seek, the business of life itself.

"Jesus, you two," Tom muttered.

It'd been a long time since I was around another child as desperate as me to love and live. That the forest was teeming with life all around us was usually a comfort, but at the moment it felt cruel.

"Shut the fuck up!" Tom yelled.

But eventually, he blubbered loudest of us all.

CHAPTER EIGHTEEN

FOR SIXTY DAYS, EMMELINE COULDN'T SPEAK TO OR VISIT ONE SON, and couldn't bear to look at another.

Whenever River and Emmeline found themselves in a room together, her son would stare at her pleadingly until she looked over at him.

"I'm sorry, Mama. Please forgive me."

"There's nothing to forgive." Emmeline would pat his hand and, after the appropriate amount of time, between five to ten minutes, remove herself from his company.

If she were honest, she resented River, only just a little less than she resented her husband, she confessed to Dr. Takahashi after showing up to his office unannounced, the day Roman left for basic, with a pie that she hardly remembered baking.

"Hello, Mrs. Johnson." He'd smiled at her. "What a lovely surprise!"

"I just wanted to say thank you for everything you did to try and help Rocco."

She extended what apparently was a blueberry pie. When had she purchased the ingredients?

"You didn't have to do that," Dr. Takahashi said. "I wish I could've done more . . ."

And he genuinely looked like he meant it. She remembered how gently he'd steadied her in the aftermath of the verdict when every piece of her had broken, like a glass of water carelessly placed in the freezer.

"I feel like I'm coming apart," she'd blurted, before spilling all the bile that threatened to overtake her whole body, that she had only narrowly managed to keep in.

When she heard River's beautiful voice, she wanted to yell at the top of her lungs. She carried an anger inside her she hadn't felt since her time as a child in the hospital, convalescing.

"Shut up. Shut up. Shut up," she'd whisper at River's closed door.

How deeply unfair to have her family picked off one by one, as though her boys were unripened fruit plucked by a vengeful farmhand. Christmas, then Rocco, and now Roman too! She had failed them. How often she found herself going over the details of the day they came for Rocco in her head, and what, if anything, she could've done, or said, differently, to provoke a different outcome.

And Odysseus. She felt herself recoil every time her husband went to touch her. He had let them take her boy, their son, without even throwing a punch. At random moments, when he washed his car, or spoke to River about his upcoming shows, she glared unabashedly and waited for her husband to look over, wanting him to see her disdain. What kind of man had she married?

Plus, she was so very lonely. Hadn't made any real friends in California just yet, other than Beth. And now, with everything that had happened, she was a pariah among the other mothers at River's school. Emmeline couldn't bear to be in that house, in her neighborhood, any longer. The walls, with their framed drawings and varying awkward family portraits, pressed in on her. She found herself actually walking sideways down the halls, arms raised like a goal post, or in surrender.

There was a blank spot on the wall where the picture of the boys at Coney Island had been. When had it been moved? By whom?

After she spilled her insides to Rocco's therapist, she stood there awkwardly realizing that they were in fact still in the reception area and surely she must've interrupted him as he was out to lunch, or on his way home for the day.

"I . . . I don't treat adults," Dr. Takahashi said after a long pause.

"Of course. I'm . . . I think I'm just very tired," Emmeline said, then upon realizing that his new receptionist was not at her post. "Wait, where's your receptionist?"

"Rachel's out to lunch, I think?" Dr. Takahashi chuckled. "Actually, she's often out of the office when I'm between patients."

"And you still pay her for that?" Emmeline asked.

"She's a Caltech kid. I figure she's probably off doing homework, figuring out how to cure cancer, or blow up the world, or something."

"On your dime." Emmeline laughed.

"As long as she puts my name among her benefactors," he said with a laugh.

"Or doesn't mention it during the tribunal," Emmeline retorted. Was that too far? She was unsure of herself while talking to this man. Talking to anyone these days really. Somewhere there had been a total breakdown between what she thought she knew of her world, and what was. How, then, to even carry on a conversation?

"Well . . . I'm . . . I should get going. I'm sorry, I don't know what's come over me," Emmeline stammered.

He paused for a moment. "You've been through a lot, Mrs. Johnson. It's OK to feel, and be, fragile right now."

She nodded.

"I can't wait to try this! I'm sure it's delicious." He gestured at the blueberry pie.

"To be honest. I don't really remember even making it. Hopefully I didn't accidentally use salt instead of sugar, or something ridiculous."

She turned toward the door.

"Say, would you like to accompany me on my walk?" Dr. Takahashi said. "I find it helps me clear my head, instead of sitting down to eat."

"You're not supposed to eat standing up! They say it's terrible for you," Emmeline admonished.

"They're probably right." Dr. Takahashi laughed. "Shall we?"

THEY WALKED UNDER the shade of the trees on California Avenue, cars whizzing past. The doctor's stride was long, his pace quick, and Emmeline struggled to keep up in her heels.

"Want a bite?" He offered her the PB&J in hand.

"Maybe a little, if you don't mind," she said.

"If I minded, I wouldn't have offered." He smiled.

There was something both intimate and disgusting about sharing a sandwich, she thought. Much less such a mushy one.

"Rocky hates mushy things," she said.

"I remember," he said quietly. "How is he adjusting to the facility?"

"They won't let us speak to him for the first thirty days and we can't visit for another thirty," she replied. "It's awful. He must feel like not only did everyone in his life fail him, now we've gone and abandoned him."

At the crosswalk, Emmeline thought about stepping into the street. How much easier it would be not to feel at this moment. To not even have to bother with the business of breathing.

As though he could hear her thoughts, Dr. Takahashi put a hand gently on her shoulder.

"Careful. Not yet," he said, pointing to the flashing red DON'T WALK. "Rocco knows how much you love him."

After what felt like an eternity, the green light across from them flashed WALK. A lady walked past and glanced over at the two of them. Did Emmeline know her? Was it somebody connected to River? A fan? Or perhaps somebody who had been at school with the boys? Who knew how much she'd lost? Or perhaps who blamed her for raising a boy who could paralyze another? She offered a timid smile and tried to keep her head held high.

"I know so much about your boys, Mrs. Johnson, but tell me something about you," Dr. Takahashi said.

"Not much to tell," she said.

"That can't possibly be true," he said. "Plus, I have another sandwich to eat. Entertain me for a few more blocks. What were you like as a child?"

She told Dr. Takahashi about her time at St. Joseph's, about Bettina in her iron lung. She told him about wandering the corridors and hearing war spill out from under the doors. She told him things she had never told anybody else, not even Odie. About the time when it snowed and they all made a snowman. The groundskeeper said he didn't want to see no white man every day, so they'd declared the snowman a Negro.

"Why, Joe, he's just light skinned-ed!" they'd joked.

Dr. Takahashi laughed and listened.

"That sounds incredibly lonely for a little girl," he said.

"Sometimes," Emmeline said. "It's weird being lonely with so many people around though, isn't it?"

"I don't think that's weird at all. We were surrounded by kids, adults, people who had been our neighbors, and people who were total strangers, at first. Still, I was often lonely."

"Those are lonely circumstances," Emmeline offered. "Were you at Manzanar?"

"Santa Anita first. Then Manzanar," he finally said. "When I was little, I was mad at my parents for not fighting more when they came to take us. For not fighting enough when we came back. There's this phrase my parents always used, *Shikata ga nai.* I hated it then. But all of us made it out alive. Not every family can say that."

"Where did you live . . . before?"

"Fish Harbor, Terminal Island. My father was a fisherman."

"I'm still learning Los Angeles."

"It's not there anymore," Dr. Takahashi said, almost abruptly. "At least, not as it was. They razed our neighborhood after . . ."

Then, it was like he'd turned something in himself off.

They only made it several blocks more before her feet began to go numb. Dr. Takahashi noticed her slowing down.

"Forgive me, Mrs. Johnson, I didn't even think about your footwear! Your feet must be killing you."

"A bit," Emmeline said, not wanting to complain. "And please, call me Emmeline!"

"It's not the nicest place for a lady these days," he said, gesturing around them at Old Town's badly worn edges, its not-so-urban blight. "It used to be much better."

"I'm not easily scared, Dr. Takahashi," Emmeline said. And it was true. She and Nurse Clarabel had not yet headed north when several sharecroppers were lynched miles away from their sanitarium. Everyone (except for Bettina and 'em in the iron lung) had huddled together, lanterns low, listening to the radio and jumping up at intervals to double-check that it was the branches cracking in the wind and nothing more. The groundskeeper, Bettina's daddy, and a few of the other healthy men took up arms, keeping watch through the night, shotguns and aging pistols at the ready for the Klan. The grown-ups whispered about all the souls lost in '19. And the very oldest of them, Blind Sally, moaned as she folded and unfolded her gnarled hands, repeating the story about her mama who just barely escaped those Irish burning down the Colored Orphan Asylum in New York in '63.

No, a few vacant storefronts sheltering the rank bodies of the down-and-out did not frighten Emmeline, not one bit.

"Next time bring sneakers," Dr. Takahashi said.

"Next time?" she said wryly. "I thought you don't treat adults."

"I'm not." The doctor smiled. "We're just going for a walk."

CHAPTER NINETEEN

AS THEY PASSED THROUGH CAMARILLO, EMMELINE LOOKED OUT THE window and saw the brown bodies stooped for miles—men, women, and children—fieldworkers, bent like sharecroppers picking cotton. Farther down the road, women in big straw hats stood under the sun and sold strawberries by the carton. On an overturned wooden crate beside them, a little boy read a picture book.

"It's way too hot for them to be out there like that," Emmeline said with a frown. She had been fanning herself ever since they'd followed the freeway slightly inland, and away from the ocean breeze.

"It's where the work is," Odysseus said with a shrug. Emmeline couldn't tell if it was a shrug of defeat or apathy, but either way she didn't like it. Though she didn't particularly like much about her husband at the moment.

"I thought they just signed a contract or something to make things better?" She squinted, trying to remember the particulars.

"The work is still the work," Odysseus said.

She glared at him even though he hadn't said anything wrong, exactly. It was just how dispassionate he seemed to be about everything and everyone except for River these days. Had he always been like this? Or was this some newer version of her husband after what happened with Rocco, after Christmas?

She looked over at the little boy. His dark eyes soaked up each page as he kicked his little legs against the wooden crate. On his right knee, a strawberry of scraped flesh where he must've had a recent hard fall. His left shoelace was untied. He reminded her of her sons when they were little. Of Christmas. How desperately she wanted to go over there and tie the shoelace, to place a Band-Aid upon his knee, kiss his little forehead, and ask about the book. How very much she wanted to mother.

"My sons . . ." she whispered.

She felt herself an uncooked egg with cracks running through, as though at any moment, at the slightest movement, her membrane would burst and she would spill her contents in a gooey mess all about. She heard Aaron Takahashi's voice in her head saying on their most recent walk, *You don't have to be strong. It's OK to feel, Emmeline.* Feeling was the problem though, wasn't it? She felt entirely too much around the doctor.

"Let's get some for Rocco!"

═

THE FACILITY WAS not what it had appeared upon their first visit. Then, everything had been sparkling, or at least, presentable. Now it seemed, there was a layer of dust upon every surface, and around each corner one could play a surprise game of "urine, antiseptic, or both?"

At the visitor sign-in desk, an older blond nurse with bright-pink lipstick looked at the strawberries in Emmeline's hands. Rather than accentuating her mouth, the lipstick had the unfortunate effect of drawing more attention to the fading edges of the woman's perma-pursed lips.

"No outside food, I'm afraid."

"Oh, it's just strawberries! You want to try? We just got them fresh! My son loves them," Emmeline said.

"I'm sorry. It's just policy. For safety."

"Is there somewhere I can put them at least?"

"I'll keep them up here for you," the woman said. "You can get them on the way back."

"Do you have a fridge or somewhere to keep them fresh?" Emmeline asked.

The blonde openly rolled her eyes before reaching out for the would-be contraband.

"She was unpleasant," Emmeline whispered to Odie once they'd finished checking in and left the front desk.

"She's just doing her job, Em," Odie said. Em cut her eyes over at him, but he wasn't looking in her direction. Why couldn't he be on her side for this? For anything?

Emmeline smiled at several of the nurses as they passed. "Hello! I'm Rocco's mother."

"Hi," a young nurse said back brightly.

She hoped putting a name to a face would help. That maybe they would remember the friendly, nicely-dressed Negro lady, and thus give her son a little extra care.

Two portly nurses headed down the hallway. She would try again.

"Hi! I'm Rocco's . . ."

But before she could finish, an alarm sounded in the near distance.

"What do you want to bet it's Victor again?" one nurse said to the other as they rushed toward some emergency, practically shoving Emmeline and Odysseus out of the way.

═══

INSIDE THE VISITORS' room, a young lady giggled loudly as she played a game of Connect Four with a very frail older man who seemed to grow increasingly frustrated. Across from them, a teenage boy with hair all the way down past his bottom stood with his back against the wall, his eyes darting to and fro like a cornered creature as a woman tried to speak with him.

"Andrew, please!" she pleaded. "It's me. It's Mrs. Mary."

At yet another table, an angry whisper of a girl alternately chewed her hair and scribbled obscenities across a notepad, periodically lifting it up to show her parents whenever the father yelled, "Speak, dammit!"

"It's like a prison," Emmeline whispered to Odysseus. She found the whole place deeply unsettling.

A nurse, not too much older than Emmeline, light-skinned with a close-cropped afro and a bosom so ample it was a miracle she didn't topple over from the weight of it, pushed Rocco into the room in a wheelchair.

Emmeline leapt up. "Why is my son in a wheelchair?"

"Look, Rocco. Your parents are here to see you!" the nurse tried to say brightly.

Rocco refused to look up at them.

"Don't worry, Mrs. Johnson. The wheelchair is just because he's been a little weak recently. He hasn't been eating as much as he needs to, but we started him on an IV yesterday and he's already getting stronger."

"An IV?" Emmeline repeated incredulously. "Rocco, baby, you need to eat! What are you feeding him? He doesn't like mushy foods."

"Did you give the intake folks a list of his dietary needs?" the nurse replied.

"He's not allergic. He just . . . he's very sensitive to certain foods."

"We can go over that before you leave, and I'll make sure to make note of it on his chart."

"Is he medicated?" Odysseus asked, trying to make eye contact with his son.

"It's been a tough adjustment, but he's making progress! Aren't you, Rocco?"

Rocco said nothing and stared right through the nurse.

"Let me leave you guys to have some private time, but if you need me, I'll be just over there!" The nurse pointed to a spot along the wall where two other nurses sat on a bench surveying the scene.

The next hour proceeded horribly as Emmeline and Odysseus both tried to reach their son from whatever unreachable place he had sunken into. Rocco stared around the room and up at the ceiling, everywhere except in the vicinity of his parents, who sat across from him, willing him to acknowledge them in some way, shape, or form.

"They wouldn't allow us here for the first sixty days, baby. We would've come sooner," Emmeline said and reached for Rocco's hand.

Still nothing.

"Your brother joined the army," Odysseus said. "He's at basic now before he heads to Vietnam. He sends his love."

Odysseus was lying. Roman hadn't so much as phoned them since he left. Unless he'd phoned the shop, which Emmeline highly doubted.

"I don't think that's gonna cheer him up, Odie."

"River's single's doing really well. Do they play music for you in here?"

Odysseus beckoned the nurse over.

"Is something wrong?" she said.

"Do you play music for them in here?"

"Sometimes! But we have the TV on usually. The radio tends to lead to more arguments. We don't have it going as often."

"What are you offering my son by way of recreation?" Odysseus said.

"Rocco hasn't been able to participate in some of the group activities just yet. But I'm sure he'll get to enjoy them soon!"

Just then, Rocco hummed River's single. But rather than being in any way reassuring, it sent chills down Emmeline's spine.

She looked around the room at the other visitors begging for connection. Was this how it was going to be from here on out?

"I thought this was supposed to be better for him than prison," Emmeline said.

"I'm sure prison's worse, Emmie," Odysseus said gently.

"He wasn't even the one who hurt the boy!" Emmeline said. "He doesn't belong here!"

The nurse patted her back and reached over to grab a tissue.

"It'll get easier, Mrs. Johnson. You'll see," she said.

Emmeline thought she saw her husband glance at the woman's bosom. Now? Really? Not that she herself had any leg to stand on, but still. She kicked him under the table.

"What are the other kids in here for? Are they violent?" Emmeline asked.

"We're not at liberty to disclose," the nurse said in a practiced tone. But leaning close to Emmeline, she quickly code-switched: "But . . . mother to mother . . . Some of these kids ain't right. Not one bit."

"Can you look out for my boy?" Emmie begged.

"I'll try. It's . . . it's hard in here," the nurse said.

"*Yes or no, no or yes!*" Rocco's voice suddenly rang out. "*Yes or no, no or yes!*"

Somehow it was even worse than his silence.

The drive home was quiet. The sun set, a cracked egg, over the ocean. Emmeline could find no beauty in it. The strawberry fields were dark. The field hands gone. As they drew closer to L.A. County, Odysseus turned on the radio. They heard River's song twice before Emmeline turned the radio back off.

"We forgot to get the strawberries," she said.

═══

AS SOON AS they walked through the door, the phone *brrrnged* in greeting.

"Whoever it is, they can call again tomorrow," Emmeline said, taking off her shoes and rolling down her tights, letting her flesh free.

"River?" she shouted through the house.

"He had a late rehearsal for the tour today," Odysseus said.

"Of course . . ." Emmeline sat down on the couch and began to rub her feet.

Odysseus sat down next to her and brought her leg onto his lap. "Lemme help you."

Momentarily, she allowed herself to be tended to. To remember that she had loved this man and promised to cherish him until her dying breath. Had. Were they past tense? Not yet. Did she even believe in divorce? Beth was newly divorced and she seemed happier than ever. Emmeline tried not to think of all the ways she resented Odysseus. How he had let the cops take Rocco away without a fight. How he'd not tried to stop Roman when he knew the ills of war. How he had been the one to bring them to California, breaking them in the process. How he had driven away a poor little motherless dead boy in his anger. How her walks with Dr. Aaron Takahashi made her feet callused and her heart raw with want.

The two of them had discovered many things in common on their walks, but largely an appreciation for beauty. Art. Flowers. People. Aaron Takahashi managed to find the beauty in most folks in spite of, or maybe because of, his childhood internment. And for some reason, he thought Emmeline was just about the funniest person ever. The quotidian observations that would elicit a mere grunt or chuckle from Odysseus, Dr. Takahashi found fascinating.

"You're really smart," he said to her.

"Please don't sound so surprised by that, Dr. Takahashi," she'd said with a laugh.

"*You coulda been anything that you wanted to and I can tell . . .*" he sang at her. He had a lovely, if thin, voice, and it momentarily brought her back to her babies practicing the song in their backyard. She pushed away the pang as he twirled her around on the sidewalk.

"Except for president." She laughed.

"Well, that makes two of us." He chuckled.

They had been talking about the recent shoot-out between the Panthers and LAPD and whether or not the FBI was behind those dead UCLA boys earlier in the year, not to mention Malcolm and Martin. Aaron was prone to believing the occasional government conspiracy theory, but mostly because if they could do what they did to his family that easily, what couldn't they do?

He was passionate and irreverent and a little bit crazy, and around him she felt free. Even better, she felt fun.

They'd kissed. Just once. Near Miller Alley.

At a moment of silence in an otherwise very impassioned conversation, Emmeline had been the one to make the move, surprising even herself. She'd pressed the doctor against the brick wall so that they were pelvis-to-pelvis, heart-to-heart.

"You've got me," he whispered jokingly, his hands raised in surrender.

How that short, stolen kiss had felt more erotic than anything she could remember in her eighteen years of marriage! She found herself going over and over the details of that moment as she washed the dishes, picked River's clothes off the floor. The exact feeling of his tongue in her mouth, fatter than her husband's, and more voracious. His hands at her hips. The sweat from their walk at his armpits. The dampness of his forehead as he'd rested it on hers afterward. How wet their want.

She should have felt more ashamed of herself; instead she simply felt more.

"Emmie, you're so far away these days," Odie said, rubbing the ball of her right foot. "I know it's been rough," he continued. "It'll get better. It has to. We'll get Rocco out soon as we can."

"This isn't working."

Odysseus leaned in to put more pressure into it.

"Odie, listen. Do you hear what I'm saying?"

He lifted his gaze to meet hers and said quietly, "I know. But I'm gonna fight for this family. I promise."

"Maybe that's the problem. I don't want to have to fight," she said.

The phone *brrrnged* again.

"I should get that," Odie said.

"We're in the middle of a conversation!"

"What if it's something for River?" He dropped her foot from his lap as he stood up. "Everything is raw now, but just give it time, Emmie. Give me time," he said, and kissed her on the forehead before rushing over to the phone in the kitchen.

"River's going on tour!" Odie exclaimed when he returned to the couch.

"Wow," she mustered, and realizing her lack of enthusiasm, added, "We'll have to take him out to dinner to celebrate." She knew she should be far more excited, but mostly she felt tired. What was Rocco doing now? Was he taking tonight's dinner in an IV? Was Roman scared? And Christmas? Where had the little boy gone? Had he found himself another mother? How deeply she missed her children. Even River, who should be coming home from rehearsal any minute now.

Emmeline drifted off, dreaming of strawberries. An hour later, the corner of her mouth puddled in drool, sleep in the corner of one eye, she arose feeling like Rip Van Winkle. She knew exactly what she needed to do.

CHAPTER TWENTY

THE ONLY REASON I SAW RIVER'S FIRST TELEVISION INTERVIEW IS BEcause Racist Tom was bored.

"I'm bored to death," Tom said, and laughed at his own joke.

The forest was quiet and the gossip uninteresting; many of the animals were consumed with the process of preparing themselves for winter. So Becky, Tom, and I decided to go into town.

I did not trust Tom as far as I could throw him, and did not generally enjoy his company, but that alone should tell you just how bored we were.

"He's only a little racist," Becky would say in his defense. "He's not that bad underneath it all."

It seemed to me that she was always making excuses for him. As though I were merely being inconvenienced every time he called me that most foul of words, or repeated some rude remarks of his father's regarding the relative worth of the Negro.

Main Street was a long road punctuated here and there by shops. A pharmacy. A laundromat. A Salvation Army store. A pawnshop filled with the lost items of a number of lost souls. An electronics store that sold Washers! Dryers! Radios!

And best of all, televisions!

The store had a number of televisions big and small so that screens covered the entire window. The biggest was also in color and very expensive indeed. As we approached, two very old Black men stood watching in matching tweed suits. Twins! They would be dead very soon and had one foot in our world already. One twin tipped his hat in my direction, the other ignored me for the television.

"Move out the way!" Tom said, but the old men refused. The approach of death meant not having to move off any damn sidewalk they pleased, one of them said triumphantly.

Tom huffed but didn't say anything further, although if he had, I might have bopped him one for speaking to elders like that.

Anyway, television was one of my favorite new things since being with the Johnsons! The marvels of a stage performance but for everyone to see everywhere! At first Roman had had to tell me that the figures on the screen were not always actually doing these things in real time.

"It's not a window," he said that first time, exasperated.

And yet wasn't it? A portal to some other world, some other experience, where you could bathe in the best soaps, ride horses into the sunset, and dance elegantly in the most dramatic of spaces. Well . . . not Black folks so much. But a few! I was especially fond of the show *Julia*, as I thought Diahann Carroll to be very beautiful and thought that I would be the happiest boy ever if she were my mother. Though I do recall Ms. Emmeline complaining about why did Ms. Carroll have to be such a super-Negro who was hardly Negro at all! And River was particularly annoyed that the Negroes on the show still called themselves colored now that we were Black and proud. You had to admit, it was hard to keep it all straight, I said, and River huffed. River was often huffing at me.

If I were still alive, I should very much like to have been a television star.

The idiot box, Odysseus called it. Well, an idiot I'd gladly be!

The old Black men stood watching an interview in color. Normally, I did not find these interview shows very interesting at all, as they were usually two old white people blabbing on about something or someone I didn't much care for or about. But today I saw why the dead men watched. There was a little Black boy onscreen, hair reaching skyward, bell-bottoms almost wide as the seat itself. My heart quickened. I knew that little Black boy and loved him as my brother.

"River!" I whooped. "Hot dog! It's River!"

"Shh!" the old twins said.

"We have a real treat for you tonight, ladies and gentlemen. It's my pleasure to introduce to you, River Johnson!"

River walked across the stage. He smiled and waved at the crowd before sitting down on the chair next to the white man's desk. I could tell he was a bit nervous.

"So, River, what's it like being famous?"

"You would know better than me, sir."

The audience laughed. The old men did too.

"Are you still in school. Do you homeschool?"

"I go to school like any old kid."

"A school with famous people?"

River giggled. "No sir."

"What's your favorite subject?"

"Art, I suppose. I like history but I'm terrible with remembering dates."

"Me too. I can't remember if my date's name is Rita, or Alice, or Mary . . ."

The audience laughed.

"River, let's get right down to it. You're about to go on a fifteen-city tour and, I'm told, you're becoming quite the heartthrob! A bunch of teenage girls would be very angry at me if I had you right here and didn't ask this next question: Do you have a girlfriend?"

River blushed. "Oh, I don't have time for a girlfriend, sir."

"So. There's not a special somebody?"

"No sir."

"Anybody you have a crush on?"

"I couldn't possibly say that on national television, sir."

The audience laughed again. River was very good at being on television. The crowd was eating him right up!

"If you could date any celebrity, who would it be?"

"I don't know. They're all so lovely."

"You're very diplomatic, kid."

Again, the audience laughed.

"Who do you draw from artistically?"

"James Brown. Sammy Davis Jr."

"Is it true you started off in a group with your brothers?"

"Yes sir. The Johnson Three."

"And what happened to that? You give 'em the boot?"

The audience laughed. I gasped. River didn't answer. He appeared to look somewhere behind him off-camera. Probably at Odysseus, I supposed. Or perhaps Ms. Emmeline.

How very much I missed her. How very much I missed them all!

“When you sing, who do you do it for? White people? Black people? Who do you imagine as your audience?”

What kind of a stupid question is that? I thought.

“I . . . I just wanna sing for anyone who’s listening.”

“And what would you do if you weren’t a musician?”

“I’d be an astronaut, sir.”

“Well, we’re happy to have you here on Earth with us for the moment. And now we’re going to hear River play a hit single from his certified platinum eponymous debut album. Boy, say that ten times fast! River Johnson, everyone!”

River walked over to the stage and began to sing a song about passing a note asking a girl in school if she likes you during class called “Check It.”

All the kids in the audience sang along loudly when it got to this part of the chorus.

Before the bell rings, check it no, or check yes, please oh please don’t make me guess.
Girl, won’t you please put me out of my misery,
I got it so bad can’t you see,
Won’t you please check it yes or no, no or yes! Check it yes for me.

Watching River bopping around the stage, I would most definitely have checked yes.

“I gotta go,” I said to Tom and Becky.

“To do what?”

“I gotta see Rocco.”

CHAPTER TWENTY-ONE

THE TOUR WAS MOSTLY FULL OF PEOPLE TWICE RIVER'S AGE. THERE were three female singers, cousins with their wigs styled in loose curls who cooed and shook, and everybody squealed. Every time they came off the stage, his favorite one, Marva, blew him a kiss. There was a man who hot-combed his hair and played guitar so hard that every night River was sure he was going to break it. When he got offstage, his hair had grown sky-high, with the hair closest to his scalp reverting to tiny kinks and coils. His hair seemed to straddle two worlds, two audiences. This man never acknowledged River at all but instead dove into the arms of the white girl groupies who awaited him by the dozens after his set. A white brother-and-sister duo sang downbeat songs about love and loss, and River thought it must be very weird to sing every night to your own brother about such things. River had never missed a woman, but he missed his brothers dearly. Sometimes, when the blond girl with her flipped hair sang into the microphone about losing her love, he imagined himself up there singing with Rocco, Roman, and even Christmas.

What would Christmas make of all of this? He too had been on tour once upon a time. Away from all the things and people he'd known before. The siblings had one another and the cousins, too—was this what he had lost in going solo? He wished he could talk to somebody who knew both how lonely and exhilarating it all was. If he weren't so angry at her, maybe River could've called his mother.

For two whole days, just right after they got the news he was going on tour, River and his father had combed the streets of California looking for his mother. They had driven up and down and all around Pasadena, branching out even into Altadena, Arcadia, San Marino, Monrovia, Sierra Madre, then to South Pas as the moon grew brighter and the streets quieter. River wasn't sure if they were supposed to be looking for her exactly, or just passing time until she appeared back home, having worried them both sick enough. He'd come home from rehearsal to see his father on the bottom step, staring at the front door.

"Your mama's blowing off some steam. She'll be back," Odysseus said.

"What did you do?" River said. But he knew the answer. He had seen the way his mother looked at them both these days. How she seemed to recoil at River's voice, his father's touch. When she returned several days later, like nothing had happened, they had gone out to dinner to celebrate his single hitting number one. It had felt obligatory, perhaps almost funereal. His mother had been silent nearly the entire dinner.

"Congratulations, baby," she said perfunctorily. "We're so proud of you."

Now River was glad to be on tour with all these girls yelling at him nightly to "Sing 'Check It'!" He didn't want to be in that house with just his parents and everything every Johnson had left unsaid. He never called home. Instead, home became the four walls of the cramped tour bus. That would do for now.

As the months went on, buoyed by sales, the buses grew more comfortable. He outgrew the costumes his father had sewn, until finally, on their day off, after three months on the road, Marva took him to a department store to buy new pants—jeans with the biggest bell-bottoms he'd ever worn. The legs swished against each other as he walked, announcing him to anybody nearby.

"It's funkier, don't you think?" she said, and he nodded.

River learned which beers he liked. On the rare occasion that he smoked, he knew he liked menthols 'cause they didn't burn as much, even if some of the roadies called them his baby cigarettes. He smoked grass as the pretty brown singers lay across his lap and told him about their arguments with their boyfriends. One even had a secret husband, though she was thinking of divorcing him soon.

The white siblings commiserated on what an absolute shit their father was. Often he called and yelled at them about everything they should be doing better, a long-distance stage parent. And afterward they would get drunk and argue bitterly in front of everyone as though all of that "yes sir" and "no sir" were a poison through the veins that had to be expelled somehow, and at someone, and who better than blood?

Whenever he called home, River allowed himself to be lectured by Odysseus on what he should and shouldn't be doing, but after a while, he stopped. Everything his father said felt theoretical and removed from the practicalities of life on the road. Besides, it was his mother's voice he most wanted to hear, and she rarely picked up the phone these days. On the few times his parents managed to call him, once River started talking about the tour, his mother had hardly seemed to listen at all.

Outside of Memphis, on a particularly hot night where they batted away mosquitoes and belligerent fans alike, and nobody quite played their best, somebody drunkenly decided they should do a day trip to the Great Smoky Mountains for a little morale boost. River wasn't too sure about the idea of several Black folks going deep into the woods, especially in a part of the country where there were so many Confederate flags with their angry blue bars. But one of the roadies, who had grown up not too far away, promised it would be beautiful, and after months of looking at nothing but one another and either the inside of the bus or the inside of a venue, everybody wanted a little bit of beauty.

"I don't have the right sort of shoes for this sort of thing," the lead singer of the trio complained.

"Just borrow my Keds," her bandmate said. The two of them were cousins, except the lead singer's father was white and the fathers of the other two were Puerto Rican, so they placed her front and center, even though she wasn't the best singer of the three, just lighter-skinned.

"That's just how the world works," Marva said sadly when River asked why she wasn't lead.

"That's not fair," River said, feeling like a baby even as he did. He was old enough to know that fairness was only for the few. How else to explain how he was here and not his brothers? Or why Christmas had died before he'd even lived?

The mountains were indeed great. River found himself leaning down to inspect the various insects and creepy-crawlies to be found. The guitarist lit a joint and shared it with the white boy and girl. They sang as they walked through the woods. River, the white girl, and Marva had the best voices. Everyone else filled in the space around them.

"Look!" the white girl stopped singing to whisper.

A stag reigned majestically over a clearing.

"Bambi!" River joked, and immediately felt embarrassed. It was a baby joke, and not a good one at that.

The white girl fainted. Not out of awe but because everybody knew she didn't eat, and everybody tried to slip her bits of food here and there. It wasn't about the food, not really, the cousin said knowingly. She wasn't that much older than River, but he thought her to be very wise and worldly.

The girl's brother slapped her a bit around the face until she came to.

"What happened?" she said.

"Maybe we should stop now," he said.

"My feet are starting to hurt," the lead singer said, and Marva rolled her eyes because she was walking in loafers since she'd lent her sneakers to her diva cousin.

The guitarist kept smoking and staring into the sky.

The night grew dark as they headed back to the roadie's van. Around them, lightning bugs blinked and buzzed. River didn't know how damn loud they were and said so.

"You ain't ever seen a lightning bug before?" Marva said.

"We don't got 'em in California, I don't think," River said.

"Feels like magic, don't it?" she said.

"Until one of them fuckers smacks you in the face, anyway," the white boy said. His sister was getting heavier as they walked, and he was getting cranky as all get-out. Nonetheless, everybody knew he wouldn't stop carrying her. River missed his brothers.

In the van, on the way back to the tour bus, River fell asleep against Marva. She smelled of vanilla and cocoa butter and sweat and dirt. He wanted to inhale her in, but he was not a creep.

"Girl . . . if he were only a few years older," he heard Marva whisper to the white girl who mmmhmed in agreement.

As they exited the roadie's van, making their way back to the tour bus, one of the white-girl groupies of the hot-combed guitarist came barreling toward them, seemingly out of nowhere, and slashed the guitarist across the face, just narrowly missing his neck. The trio began to shriek. The white boy dropped his sister. The white girl screamed, "Stop, stop, stop!" And the hot-combed guitarist stood there with blood dripping down his face and yelled at River, "Man, do something!"

River wasn't technically a man, not yet. And the guitarist hadn't so much as even acknowledged him before now. Still, out of some sort of misplaced race loyalty, or out of a desire to be seen as grown, or perhaps something self-destructive that ran through his veins, he grabbed the blond girl by the wrist and wrestled her to the ground. There, she stabbed him in his palm like a stigmata.

"Oh shit, you hurt the kid!" the white boy yelled. It was just enough to distract her so that River could get the upper hand and pin her down.

"I'm sorry," the groupie said, still squirming under River's weight, her hand still firmly holding on to the broken bottle.

"Crazy bitch!" the guitarist yelled.

"You said you would take me with you to the next city! You promised!"

Marva kicked at her with her loafers until the girl dropped the weapon.

Finally, the security guard rushed in and took over from River. He twisted the girl's arms behind her back and led her out of the room and into the night.

"Nigger, I love you!" she shouted at the guitar player. "I fucking love you!"

This was how River discovered that love and hate weren't far apart.

═

THEY DIDN'T GO to a hospital. Instead, River was stitched up by Marva, who had gone to nursing school for a semester.

"No use in going to a hospital. I got it," she said. She had him bite down on a rag as she poured alcohol over the wound and took out a small red sewing kit. River wanted to scream as the needle entered his flesh. Instead, he whimpered.

Marva sang, "*Don't worry, baby, everything will be all right.*"

He looked down her shirt at the cavern between her breasts and wondered what it would be like to touch them. He had never seen a woman naked up close before. Her needle pierced his skin again and again. Four times in total.

"You good?" she said.

River sighed and moaned dramatically. She leaned over and kissed him. Her mouth was soft. Softer than Milton's had been that time. He tried to slip his tongue into her mouth.

"Oh, you good, all right," she said, laughing. "Now, git!"

"You're a real one, River Johnson," the guitarist said when River ran into him in the hotel hall. "Didn't know you had it in you."

"I got a lot in me," River said, almost defiantly. It was the first time he'd addressed the man directly and one-on-one.

The man nodded as if to consider it.

"Don't let 'em take it from you," he said before ducking back into his room.

Before the guitarist could close the door, River peeked in and saw the bare long leg of the woman who'd stabbed him flung across the tossed sheets. The man caught him looking and shrugged, then closed the door.

"Take what?" River wondered aloud.

It was hard to get comfortable with his hand inflamed. He paced and he practiced, trying to exhaust himself. Finally, around three in the morning, he opened up the fridge, drank himself to sleep on hotel liquor, and dreamed of fireflies.

═══

RIVER SANG LOVE songs even though he'd never been in love.

He sang breakup songs even though he'd never broken up.

He sang of heartbreak and thought of Rocco, and Roman, and Christmas, and sometimes Milton.

He sang for his mother and his father.

He sang songs about dancing, songs with dances choreographed specifically for him at first, and then dances he choreographed himself.

He did not sing anything too political, per Mr. X's instructions. Part of his appeal was being as "All-American" as possible.

Girls older than him reached out their hands to touch him, kiss him. Full-grown women did it too. He grew scars from red and pink nails that accidentally scratched across and into his skin as they mobbed him, rabid love that felt like pain. He got used to his body no longer feeling like it was just his. He picked at the scabs before they could heal.

"They love you out there," his people whispered in his ear as they waited with him in the wings.

"We love you, River!" they said. Strangers screamed his name over and over till they were hoarse. He soaked it all up and reminded himself this was everything he'd worked for.

Fans fainted in front of him. Named their pets after him.

He sang for them.

He sang in languages he didn't understand, a vocal coach breaking and building each foreign word into parts and putting them back again, phonetically, until it sounded seamless and would make the appropriate amount of money.

He grew several inches and hair on his chest and elsewhere in just a matter of months.

He grew more confident with interviewers, making jokes and knowing how to command an audience from any one of three leather guest chairs. It eventually got a little less hard to fake being easygoing.

He sat in makeup chairs, got powdered up in shades too light, his fro inexpertly picked out by white professionals hired by the label. After all that fussing, he jumped into the air and smiled an all-American smile for half days while photographers shot for all his best angles. Then he posed for photo shoots with his leg up on chairs and stoops of various heights, with different props including, inexplicably, a basketball, even though River couldn't play b-ball to save his life. He iced his knee afterward and wished he could ice down his jaw muscles, all that jumping and smiling and posing just-so was harder than it looked.

He signed big, bright pictures of himself on posters and promo photos and stickers and album covers with markers and pens that quickly ran out of ink.

He signed checks to accountants and lawyers and PR people his father hired, and eventually what was left went over to Odysseus for safekeeping.

A woman licked his face as he took a picture with her.

An executive grabbed his butt at a party in the Hills, where only moments before he'd marveled at Los Angeles at dark, all those twinkling lights, all those dreams, and somehow here was he at the very top, and still only a teenager. The man who grabbed his butt did so as River stood poolside nursing a soda, needing just a moment to himself. When he complained, another exec said, "Oh, Phil just does that. You know how it is."

River stopped complaining. He left that party with two mosquito bites that didn't go away for weeks.

He sang a song filled with innuendo about losing one's virginity. He hadn't yet.

He even sang a song about a pet parakeet for a movie about a parakeet that goes on a murderous rampage. It was a huge hit.

Sometimes, when he performed, grown folks cried.

"How is this kid so soulful for his age?" people would comment about him to their TV audiences like he wasn't even there.

CHAPTER TWENTY-TWO

SOMETHING SINISTER CRAWLED JUST UNDER THE SKIN OF THE PLACE, ready to break through at any moment.

"I don't belong here," Rocco mumbled to himself.

"Me neither!" said a boy named Chad seated beside him at breakfast. Chad was sallow with wavy long brown hair that looked like it had been scavenged and placed atop his head, and a prominent pimple on his right eyebrow seemingly in perpetuity.

Chad decided that because they both didn't belong there, they should be friends.

"These people are crazy," Chad leaned in to Rocco and whispered.

"I want to eat alone," Rocco said.

"Nobody wants to eat alone," Chad said. He smacked loudly as he chewed.

"I do," Rocco said. He had only recently started both talking and eating on his own again. The IV feeds were painful. He had small veins, and many of the attendants weren't phlebotomists. They jabbed and poked with no regard for how many tries it took.

"We're going to have to install a port if you keep this up," the kindest nurse had told him.

In the mirror, Rocco could still count the bones in his chest. He had tried to waste himself away, to make himself disappear, but his body kept on, defiant. The first meal he'd eaten in the cafeteria, he'd thrown up all over himself.

At her last visit, his mother had snuck in strawberries from a pouch sewn onto her person. Either the guards overlooked it or perhaps, now that River was getting more and more famous, they didn't care.

"I had your father sew a secret hiding spot." His mother smiled conspiratorially. "Eat, baby."

"This is contraband," Rocco said flatly.

"When you were a baby and just learning to eat, strawberries were your very favorite food," Emmeline said.

"I'm not supposed to have those." Rocco grew agitated.

"It's OK to not follow the rules sometimes. You need to eat something," Emmeline whispered. "They're fresh."

He'd spent the rest of the day wondering if the guards had seen him eat the strawberries. If they could see any hints of red on his tongue or seeds stuck between his teeth? If he might get in trouble for it? Or worse yet, if one of the other boys found out about the strawberries and held them over his head as leverage, and for what? His mother didn't understand how something so sweet could quickly go sour in a place like this.

Next to him, Chad slurped his Jell-O cup, loudly. Rocco felt every bone in his body tense up but said nothing. He had already learned weeks before that it could be dangerous to speak out in this place.

"You've got a nice rack," a boy named Victor said to the nurse watching over the lunchroom. "I would suck on those."

Rocco wrinkled his nose in disgust but said nothing. Victor had dark wavy hair and a jaw that looked capable of masticating steel, not to mention muscles like a bodybuilder. Still, he couldn't even grow a faint mustache yet. His stocky legs remained smooth and hairless.

"You're fat. I wouldn't fuck you," Victor said to one of the student nurses as she bent over to feed one of the boys who wasn't mobile.

"That's very rude," Rocco said. "And mean. You shouldn't say those things."

Victor looked over at Rocco and, having decided he was no threat, kept on.

"I would put it in your butt so I don't have to see your ugly face," he said to the student nurse, who looked on the verge of tears.

"Stop it!" Rocco said.

Victor leaned over to him and said quietly, "I will kill you if you tell me what to do ever again."

Rocco wasn't sure if it was an idle threat, but he didn't want to find out. Victor had already beaten up one of the male attendants, who had walked around with a black eye and a busted lip for weeks. It was rumored that Victor was in the facility for killing his grandmother. (Though the rumors in this place had a habit of growing legs and feet until mere boys became the subject of the tallest tales. Heroes or villains, each one of them, instead of bored children finding ways to fill near-empty days.)

At least, to Rocco's knowledge, Chad had done nothing of the sort. He let Chad sit next to him, even as his whole body bristled as he listened to Chad chew and chew and swallow loudly.

"See you later," Chad said after slurping the last of a fruit cup.

═══

WHEN HE HEARD the stirring in his room later that night, Rocco thought maybe it was Chad. Had he told Chad which room was his? They were supposed to be supervised at all times, and it was well past lights-out. But where there was a will, there was a way in this place.

"Please go away. I'm sleeping," Rocco said. He desperately hoped nobody had found out about the strawberries, or that it wasn't Victor come to kill him.

"Silly, you wouldn't be talking to me if you were sleeping," the voice said.

Rocco sat up. He would know that voice anywhere.

"Christmas?"

The little ghost sat down at the foot of his bed. He remained remarkably unchanged, though Rocco didn't know what he had expected. The dead didn't exactly experience growth spurts. Rocco himself had grown an inch and a half, even with his attempts at starvation.

"I saw River on television," Christmas said.

"River is famous now," Rocco said, matter-of-factly. "How did you find me?"

"I snuck into your house a while ago when Ms. Emmeline went out. A card for this place is pinned to the fridge," Christmas said. "She looks so sad."

Rocco's poor mama. He imagined her in their empty house, lonely and bored while his father worked and worked, and somewhere out in the world, Roman fought and River sang. What did a mama do when there was nobody left to be a mama to?

"I can get you out of here," Christmas said.

"You're the reason I'm here," Rocco snapped.

"I can steal the keys," Christmas said.

"I'm not going anywhere with you," Rocco said.

A guard walked by his room. "Everything OK in there?"

"Yes," Rocco said. "Everything OK."

"I can fix this. I'll take you home," Christmas said.

"I don't have one," Rocco said, and felt it immediately to be true.

"Come with me," Christmas said.

"I don't want to see you!" Rocco felt his voice elevating.

"You can meet Becky and all the others in the forest," Christmas said.

"Leave me alone! I don't want to meet anybody. I don't care about your stinking forest!" Rocco yelled. "Go away. Go away. Go away."

"We're best friends," Christmas said. "Remember?"

"Remember? You destroyed my life!"

"I was trying to protect you!"

"I hate you! I never want to see you ever again!"

"I'm sorry," Christmas wailed loudly. His cries rattled the window in Rocco's room; the floor cracked underneath Rocco's feet. Even if he could rattle glass and crack concrete, Christmas really was just a little boy. Even littler than Rocco himself. Rocco had spoken too rashly in his anger. Even if he had every right. He should go with Christmas. Surely it was better than staying here.

"What's going on?" the security guard said, rapping on Rocco's door. "I'm coming in!"

"I'm fine!" Rocco shouted, just as the guard busted the door open.

The guard stepped in and looked around. "Who are you talking to?"

Rocco remained silent. Being entirely used to patients talking to folks who weren't there, the guard didn't press further.

"Go to sleep," the guard said, taking one last glance around the room before heading back into the hallway.

"Fine. I'll come with you," Rocco said once he heard the man's footsteps well down the hallway. "Christmas?"

But Christmas was gone.

═

THE NEXT DAY at breakfast, Chad once again plopped down beside him.

"Good morning," Chad said.

Rocco grunted in response. He hadn't slept all night. Every sound he thought he heard was Christmas. And when he wasn't hearing things, he mulled over his friendship with the little ghost. Christmas had only ever tried to help, hadn't he? And yet, Rocco was still very angry at him. At his family. At the world.

"You're upset?" Chad asked. Rocco tried not to stare at a bit of yogurt smeared in the corner of Chad's mouth.

Yes, Rocco thought, not speaking.

"I got something to cheer you up! Do you know anything about medieval torture? They had all kinds of weird, cool ways to punish people back then. It's insane," Chad said. Chad himself could definitely pass for a medieval peasant, at least as far as what Rocco knew of medieval peasants, which admittedly wasn't much, though that would soon change. "Do you want to hear my favorites?"

Victor eyed him from across the room and pantomimed throat-slitting. Maybe it was good to have Chad next to him. At least he wasn't alone. Not exactly.

"My favorite was when they would draw and quarter somebody. You know what that means?"

Rocco didn't. Chad went on to describe the medieval punishment in excruciating detail. Rocco imagined his limbs torn and his very own guts being spilled about the table before him, all the important pieces of himself wrested away.

CHAPTER TWENTY-THREE

FROM THE HELICOPTER, ROMAN PEERED OUT THE WINDOW AT THE lush forest below, green as far as he could see. Rivers, tributaries, lakes like veins all leading to a beating heart, until the countryside opened up and he saw people dotting the paddies, stooped as they were in the photos he'd seen of slaves. Still, it was the most beautiful place he'd ever seen. The ocean salt in his nose, on his tongue, the humidity itself bore down until his uniform pits were soaked within minutes of them landing. The last time Roman had been to the beach was the weekend before Rocco's incident, about four months ago now, when he and Tad had gone for a quick joyride along the coast in Mr. X's car. This beach was definitely not that beach, but it reminded him of the time before, when the future was something to be forged together with his brothers, a chord. Not a solitary Roman on a beautiful Vietnamese beach getting berated by a Southern mouth-breather named Red, a flat note that reeked of beer.

"Sir, yessir!" he said.

He wished he could salute the ocean, the trees, the night stars and pledge allegiance not to the Stars and Stripes but simply to the actual stars in the inky sky.

It's not that he hadn't expected the racism. He had. He hadn't prepared himself for how it would make him feel. His parents had always told him to be strong, to carry himself with pride, but he found it hard to stand up tall with all his gear and four hundred years of bullshit on his back. Every time he walked by the Confederate flag on yet another corner of the barracks, it was not the Vietcong he wanted to fight but his own countrymen. Apparently, before he'd arrived, after King's assassination, a bunch of the white soldiers had paraded around in hoods. He wanted to burn the whole thing down with them in it.

Plus, they picked fights. Taunted him and the other Black soldiers. Handed out infractions for their hair, for Black-power symbols. Roman didn't even have any himself, but soon he wanted them. He thought of what Mr. X had said about him, Rocco, and River, examining them as though they were horses, or slaves at auction. "They're good boys, well spoken, not too Black. Audiences will love them! They're perfect!"

Here, Roman was Black-ass Black. Here, he would be a raised fist. They wanted to give out infractions for pride? Fuck that. He grew his hair out and dared, and waited.

He'd regretted his choice to enlist almost immediately, but even more acutely the first time he saw a kid his own age, face almost as brown as his own. He couldn't tell if the kid looked at him with contempt, or curiosity, or superiority, or all of the above. The kid was their translator and his name was Tuyet. Most people just called him the Kid, or Tutu.

The Kid spoke English and French, having been educated at Catholic school by those who remained of their former colonizers. Roman and the Kid had Catholic school in common. Sometimes, Roman still rolled the Hail Mary around in his head. Especially in those early days in Vietnam. The words were like a security blanket, if one ridden with bullet holes. The Kid was well-read and always had a book in hand. He kept all Americans at a distance. Roman saw the way the Kid looked at the soldiers when he thought nobody was looking. The way older Black folks looked at white folks after they walked away, when their faces could relax and just be.

He missed Mama and Daddy and Christmas and his brothers. If Christmas could be anywhere, why not here with them, with him? Lonely, in the middle of all these people, in this beautiful country, where they had to carefully watch all their steps—though maybe that wasn't so different from back home, not really, not at all. Christmas was a testament to that.

Before he'd left, Roman snatched the photo of them on the roller coaster at Coney Island off the wall in the hallway. He wondered if his mother or father had noticed the empty hanging nail. He'd left the frame in his bedroom where River would probably find it if he crawled up in Roman's bed like he had in the days since Rocco left. Late at night, when Roman couldn't sleep, he often took the photo out and stared at it. River's mouth was wide open as though he were about to say something.

Rocco was grinning. He thought, even in the faint glimmer of light that shouldn't have been there, that next to Rocco he could see something of Christmas. Was that the last time they'd all been happy? He wondered.

One day, when there were no Vietcong with which to engage, and they all sat waiting, fighting off both dengue and boredom, Roman saw the Kid reading *Siddhartha* by Hesse.

"We were supposed to read that in school," Roman said by way of introduction.

"Did you like it?" the Kid asked. His voice sounded as though it were still going through puberty.

"I didn't get around to it. Came here instead," Roman said.

"Then I guess you won't be enlightened," the Kid said, and laughed hard at his own joke.

"Suppose not." Roman laughed.

Roman hadn't been much for reading when it was required, but now that he'd dropped out and instead dropped himself in the middle of a war, he couldn't get enough of it. How much more fun it was to read when a teacher wasn't standing at the front of the class telling you what and how to think. When a book came to life inside you and took over, like a parasite, helping you to remember, or, if you were very lucky, to forget.

The Kid lent him his copy when he was done. Roman didn't dig it all that much, but maybe one day he would.

In return, he lent the Kid his copy of *Black Money.*

Thus, it was established they were friends.

Nixon had already begun reducing troops. The troops who were left were mostly demoralized. Roman's unit would sometimes sit up in the countryside and radio in false coordinates and reports away from Red's watchful eye. When they did, Roman and the Kid would sit and smoke Mary Jane and read, the only two members of their wartime book club.

Together, they read everything they could get their hands on in paperback, *Madame Bovary, The Stranger,* and *The Amboy Dukes*. The Kid loaned him his brand-new copy of *Slaughterhouse-Five,* which Roman started but couldn't stomach. It was all too close. Instead, he read *Tropic of Cancer* and thought of Tania while quickly rubbing one out when he was supposed to be cleaning the latrines. They read *The Catcher in the Rye* and both agreed Holden was a whiny twat. The Kid loved *To Kill a*

Mockingbird and kept trying to foist his dog-eared copy on Roman, but he refused to read it on principle. Roman didn't need some Southern white woman telling him how wretched Negro oppression was, however well intentioned she may or may not have been.

Often, Roman used the Coney Island family photo as a bookmark. Between the characters and his brothers, he felt just a little less alone.

Several of the men in his unit were often high on heroin, but even in war, Roman was much too afraid of his parents to touch the stuff. He couldn't very well come home a junkie. Alcohol, on the other hand, there was a simple beauty in the bottle.

Banjo Brian played the ukulele, badly, making up simple songs to dirty limericks. They all called him Banjo Brian 'cause it was alliterative, but mostly because whoever had given him the moniker didn't know the difference between the banjo and the ukulele. Banjo Brian was good-natured enough that he didn't correct them. Somebody or another, drunk and in a particularly foul mood, was always threatening to smack Brian upside the head with the thing. Still, he played. Until that one day, anyway. That day, shots rang out, Brian stopped mid-note and slumped to the ground.

"Incoming!" Red yelled.

What followed was the banality of war. Shots fired. Shots returned. Kill or be killed. A ringing in the ears. Bile on the floor. They crawled along the ground, running where and when they could find cover.

When all was said and done, the Kid lay out on the ground, his innards around him. Roman would not leave him there. Not like this. There was no sense to this war. No honor in any of it. What would it be like to be here not with a gun but with a camera? To take in all the beauty and the sounds at night. Instead of preparing to lug his friend's body through a forest. They had been friends, right?

"Johnson. I know you're upset. We all are. But we gotta carry Brian. He's still breathing. We can't carry both of them," Red said. "It'll slow us down too much."

The Kid was getting heavier. More dead. Roman was strong but not that strong. He was a man but not quite. Not strong enough to carry another almost-man alone for hours. In some more honorable version of this war, his fellow soldiers would chip in and they would take turns carrying both Brian and the Kid. Roman stumbled under his weight.

"Leave him!"

"Don't leave me." Roman thought he heard the Kid's voice.

"But his parents won't know where he is," Roman said.

"They won't know anyway."

Roman didn't know where the Kid lived, where he was from. The blood-spattered ID papers in his front pocket partially obscured the name of a town nobody knew. How did nobody know where the Kid came from?

He thought he heard the Kid say, "It's only a day or two away."

"Why does only Brian's life matter? Why not Tuyet?" Roman screamed.

"Who the fuck is TWO-Yet?" Red asked.

"The Kid," PFC Chang mumbled.

Like Roman, Chang tried to stay unnoticed by the rest, lest it devolve into filth about sideways slits and dog-eating, being a double agent (even though Chang was from Oakland, like his parents before him), all manner of horrifying "jokes." For the most part, Chang succeeded in only blowing up at them occasionally.

"I always knew Red was a fucking asshole," the Kid said, and Roman laughed. The Kid was somewhere between life and death. Not a full-fledged ghost like Christmas, not yet. Somehow, he was still tethered to his body. For just a bit longer, at least.

"What the hell is so funny, Johnson?"

"Nothing. None of it, sir. All of it."

"Have you lost your damn mind?"

He had. Roman kept laughing in spite of himself. How horrible it all was. How stupid he'd been. He kept laughing until Red punched him in the face.

"Get it together, Johnson!"

Being punched by a grown man was very different from any of the schoolyard scraps or brotherly brawls Roman had previously gotten into. He touched his eye to make sure it was still in its socket, drawing back when he saw blood. Until he realized it was dry, and remembered that the blood belonged not to himself but to the Kid.

"I'm so sorry. I can't anymore," he whispered to the Kid.

"Fuck you, Roman!" the Kid kicked at him. It hurt. The Kid was fully dead now. Dead enough to have ghost legs with which to swiftly kick Roman. "Take me home. You fuckers owe me that much. Take me home!"

Roman cried as he placed the Kid's body gently on the ground.

There was a watch he must've been given by another soldier or bartered something for, plus a few dollars he'd had on him. The dead had no need for money, and if Roman didn't take it somebody else would. He threw his jacket over the open hole in the Kid's body.

The Kid began to cuss them all out in Vietnamese, French, and English, whichever language felt most effectively angry word by word. "You can't get me killed and then take all my shit. What. The. Fuck."

He kept yelling. The wind beat through the trees and the rain began to fall around them, stinging their faces, the water hitting their skin like a swarm of bees.

"Roman, the fuck are you doing, we gotta go!" PFC Chang whispered as Roman grabbed the Kid's copy of *Tropic of Cancer*.

"Leave it, you horny fuck!" the Kid whimpered. Roman put it back. Then, he took another one out of his bag. *Siddhartha*.

Perhaps now was as good a time as any to find enlightenment.

"Food. I need food too."

Roman took out a granola bar. Tried to surreptitiously put it in the Kid's pocket.

"I'm sorry. Did I just see you put food on a dead body, boy?" Red yelled.

"Roman's lost his goddamn mind."

He then did something that surprised himself; he said a prayer. Not to God. Not a Hail Mary. But to Christmas. "Watch over him, if you can, wherever you are."

To the Kid he said, "I'm sorry. I'm so sorry."

That was the day he decided to desert.

═══

SOUL ALLEY WAS where he landed. There was fried chicken and red beans that tasted like the South, made by Vietnamese hands. There was Coltrane and the Jackson 5 and cover bands that sang songs from home. At the nightclubs, the soldiers danced and laughed and were able to forget that even in war they were colored. White men didn't usually come around, and even the ones who did had been vetted. "He's all right," somebody would say. "He cool."

The girls would sit, or stand, or sway or drink, their eyes shimmering or near glossy with tears, or dead. The men danced with them like it was not a transaction. Like each hip gyration wasn't an exchange, or a promise. Under some haphazardly strewn Christmas lights, as a plastic Santa stood watch, Roman danced with one girl who told him her name was Tran. She had a fake flower tucked behind her ear and looked at him in a way that was both expectant and weary. She reminded him a bit of one of his schoolmates.

"Merry Christmas," she said as the lights flashed red and green across her face.

And then, over the speakers, he heard his brother's voice. He'd know it anywhere. Even in this godforsaken place. Somewhere in the jungle, likely during the ambush, he'd lost the photo of them all together at Coney Island, faces lit up, preparing to launch skyward. That loss hurt much more than all the mosquito bites, all the jungle rot.

Roman grabbed the Vietnamese girl tighter. He harmonized with his brother and began to cry. She kept dancing as if she were used to men crying on her pale shoulder. She didn't comfort him, but neither did she wipe his tears from her skin. They finished the song this way. He wasn't even embarrassed until the next song came on, a fast one, where everyone else began to dance and thrash and he couldn't stop crying.

He excused himself and drank until he couldn't think. Until he was just a series of pulses and impulses, until he was passed out drunk on the floor and the old man picked him up and took him inside.

"First holidays away from the family are the hardest," he said. "If you got 'em . . . people that is."

"I do," Roman mumbled.

The old man was a known deserter who crafted the stuff of magic. There was a tailor in town who made suits as cool as the ones back home. Stuff that made you look like a real cool cat at the clubs. The old man wasn't that old at all, but he'd been there as long as the longest of them and had a few grays—that was old enough.

The old man taught Roman how to create instead of destroy. To stitch. Roman thought of when he'd watched Odysseus make their costumes late into the night. Each press of the pedal made him homesick and also made him feel closer to his father. He found the rhythm therein and hummed. Why had he been so angry at Odysseus again? What was his mother doing? River? Rocco? He hadn't sent them any letters from this place. He was afraid of getting caught as a deserter. He sewed and he ripped things apart and put things back together piece by piece. If every time he closed his eyes was a nightmare, each suit was a series of daydreams. It wasn't music, but it was art, and it was his. He thought often of the Kid.

The Kid's watch had come in handy. It bought him food and shelter and occasionally info, but most important it bought him time.

He was packing up the shop one day when he felt a tingle across the back of his neck.

"Christmas?" he said.

"What?" the voice said.

He turned around and found himself face-to-face with the Kid.

"How did you find me?" Roman asked.

"I asked around," the Kid said. Roman wasn't sure if he was joking or not.

"Hey, do you know somebody by the name of Christmas? He's dead too—or . . . like you, I mean."

The Kid laughed at him and ran his fingers across a hat on a wooden mount. "We don't all know each other, you know."

"Why are you here?"

"I'm bored. I read the books you left me. I need to get more."

"Why do you need me for that?"

"I don't. It's just a statement . . . but I'm not a thief. I know you Americans all think we are."

"I never said that."

"You're a thief," the Kid said lackadaisically, and Roman couldn't argue with him because war had made it true.

That's how Roman found himself buying books for a ghost with his money from fancy suits. It was the very least he could do for the Kid. The problem was that the bookstore was not in Soul Alley, and to buy a book for the Kid meant venturing out of the safety of its borders.

For Dostoevsky, he held his breath for what felt like thirty whole minutes; he was scared shitless of getting caught by a higher-up. There were too many men in this bookstore. Too many variables. He hadn't given much thought to desertion, what would happen to him, he just knew that after seeing the Kid die, he didn't want to see any more kids die, or anyone else for that matter. What did he care if the Vietnamese wanted to be communist or not? *The Idiot.* They were all idiots. This war was idiotic.

"Here's your book," he said to the Kid, who read it in three days.

"I would like to read *Go Tell It on the Mountain* next . . ." the Kid said. "By Baldwin."

Roman stared blankly back at him.

The Kid looked at him. "James Baldwin? The Negro."

"I know who wrote *Go Tell It on the Mountain,* asshole," Roman said. He didn't, but the Kid really didn't need to be so smug.

They spent their days like this in the shop, with Roman sewing and the old man tending to customers and the Kid reading, and Roman couldn't help but picture that maybe this is what life might have been like if he'd just stayed home. It could've been him and Christmas and his father, quietly working and reading to the sound of machines bringing fragments together until the garments were not just thoughts but whole sentences, poems, even. Some romantic and soft. Some brash and loud, punctuated by a feather or a square of silk. Often, he forgot entirely why he'd run away in the first place.

═

UNFORTUNATELY, IT TURNED out that the usual store didn't have *Bleak House,* but there was another store that he might try. Not too far. It wasn't a bookstore, per se, but the owner sold American things. Sometimes those things were books or magazines. Never mind that *Bleak House* was British.

This is how they found him eventually.

After, he'd wonder if the Kid meant for him to get caught, if the books were merely a reason to get him farther and farther away from some sort of safety zone. A kind of retaliation meant to return Roman to the forces of American imperialism. But why? He had genuinely liked the Kid and the Kid seemed to genuinely like him. Yes, Roman had technically stolen his watch and not returned his body to his family, but they'd already discussed that and made peace with each other. Or so he'd thought.

"You're a thief," the Kid had said.

"You're a deserter," the military courts said.

CHAPTER TWENTY-FOUR

1971

ODYSSEUS STEAMED WOOL HATS AND REMEMBERED THE SMELL OF death. How it clung to his organs for years. He had been even younger than Roman then.

He wondered if by now Roman had seen his first dead body. If he had already seen combat. If they had him on combat duty at all. Odysseus had been a year younger than Roman when he too lied about his age (like father, like son!) and enlisted, ready to do his part, and to escape both a house and a man who had fallen apart after his mother's death.

Their journey to Europe had been in the bowels of the ship, which is where he'd met Willie Shipp. The two of them chatted as the seas tossed them about, and around them other colored soldiers lost their guts in sloppy buckets. Willie's mama was a cousin of Odysseus's aunt Sue's husband, which they discovered in a conversation that untangled and drew together the stuff of family like a game of cat's cradle. In any case, Willie was his people's people. Above deck, the white soldiers could be heard moving more freely about.

"They got us down here like slaves," Lonnie B. grumbled. He and Lonnie W. hated each other from the start. It was no surprise to anyone when, upon disembarking, Lonnie B. knocked Lonnie W. out over a shady card game. Odysseus never did get his full surname.

"You expected different?" Parker said. Parker was from Alabama and had just narrowly escaped a lynching the day before he enlisted.

But the truth was that they had. That they continued to expect more even as they made their way to the shore and into segregated quarters. That they were eager to do their part as they made their way through the Dutch countryside. They expected different even up until that October, when they were led to the field that smelled of death and told that this is how they were to serve their countries.

There, the dead white boys were lined up row by row. Willie and Odysseus looked down and saw holes, whole parts of bodies and faces missing, a human subtracted. Lonnie B. had seen death like this as a boy in Rosewood and he looked on stone-faced but not nearly as rattled as the rest of them. As the littlest of them all, Odysseus told himself to just breathe. Except, he couldn't even do that, due to the smell. He thought he heard the rattle of bones, only to look down and see his own knees knocking. Behind him, a grown man whimpered.

They were given instructions, six by six.

"Dig, boys," the white officer said.

They dug in the rain day after day, fighting against mud, and wind, and parts of bodies that wouldn't stay buried. When the snow hit, they used blowtorches or picks to find and fight the earth. Holding cotton to their noses and mouths, all those Black soldiers tried not to gag.

Odysseus felt a numbness begin to creep in. On the third day, it started in his toes until it spread quickly throughout. At dusk they played taps while covered in other men's blood. Odysseus dreamt of placing dog tags in frozen mouths, of burying in human fractions.

One night, after a particularly long day, Willie came over to share a sip of whiskey and chat about home. Then he confessed that he had a girlfriend in town, Hilde. Willie wanted to marry her and bring her back with him to North Carolina. Willie's mama would flip. Hilde was white as they came, with ice-blond hair and the bluest of eyes. When he finally did see her, Odysseus himself thought the woman was so pale as to look almost featureless. Like she herself had been crafted of ice and snow. Odysseus preferred his women warm as earth itself, as hearth, as home. Nobody would ever accuse Odysseus of being color-struck. Still, Willie Shipp said pale-ass Hilde was worth getting yelled at by his mama. They'd come to love each other, eventually.

"Don't matter, they won't let you," Marcus from Selma said.

"Shut up, man," Odysseus said. He had grown fond of Marcus, but he could be such a killjoy.

"Nah, he's right. Ain't the Danes you gotta worry about. If you can't do it legally in the States, the army won't sign off."

"They don't want us touching any of them until they're dead," Lonnie B. said, and laughed.

"Ain't that the truth," dimwitted JoeBoy said.

Odysseus didn't feel the tears well up, didn't know he'd been crying until Willie gently passed him his kerchief. He felt it seize through him, and he looked around to see he wasn't the only one.

A few days later, Willie Shipp got blood poisoning. A hazard of touching bodies.

"If I die, make sure they give my money to Hilde," Willie said before they carted him off somewhere. "We family, Odysseus! You better see to it that they give everything to my girl."

Odysseus never found out if Hilde got the money or not.

After, he had not wanted to return to New York, except that he'd met a girl. At first, he smiled and laughed and did all the things one expected of a man gone courting, but soon he couldn't even leave bed, and she held him in her arms for what seemed like days. He knew he was different after the war, hollow, numb. Knew that he had tucked some huge piece of himself away, or perhaps it was gone entirely. Shell shock, he heard people whisper about him, and some didn't even bother with the whisper. Still, Emmeline loved him with her whole heart, and he tried as hard as he could to give her as much of him as was still there.

They wed at a courthouse on a snowy day. Emmeline caught flakes on her tongue and some were sprinkled about her bouquet.

"Let's go west," he said as they ate pastrami from the kosher deli around the corner, not ten minutes into their married life.

"Why not?" Emmeline said, because she had no people to anchor her either. And so, together they floated. They only wound up getting as far as the Midwest, but no matter.

He didn't feel himself begin to thaw until that fateful day when that first baby opened his mouth and screamed. Something inside of him let go, reborn. He bawled as he held Roman close to his cheek and felt the life surge through his new son. His son! Somehow, he and Emmie had made an actual person! He counted all the newborn's fingers and toes and prayed for a future in which the boy was always safe.

Emmeline had been patient with him then. So patient. He had done everything he could to get better, to be better. He willed himself not to be angry with her. Tried to remember everything she'd done, how she had held him at night even as she was exhausted from a baby who wouldn't sleep, sore from breastfeeding a colicky infant with a shallow latch. Emmeline was a woman who knew war in her own small way, having gone through years of her young life as a crippled colored orphan, abandoned by the only family she'd had left. His wife was herself a survivor.

Odie drove to McAvoy's on his lunch break. He needed a distraction.

As Odysseus sat down in the leather chairs across from the man, he looked out at the fake ship mast.

McAvoy raised his eyebrows but said nothing. Then: "Have you heard from your son yet?"

"No. But you know how that goes," Odysseus said.

McAvoy too had known war as a guard in the Orkney Islands in Scotland, where they'd taken the Italian POWs from North Africa. Initially things had been tense between the guards and the POWs, but eventually he'd spoken fondly of the shows the Italians had put on to entertain each other, or about playing soccer against them.

"Even learned a little bit of Italian!" McAvoy had said. "Only thing I still remember is Vaffanculo a chi t'e morto."

"And what's that mean?" Odysseus asked.

"'Fuck the souls of your dead family.'" McAvoy laughed.

"Well damn." Odysseus started laughing alongside him.

McAvoy's war was not Odysseus's war. The Nazi POWs held by the Americans sat among the white prisoners, used the latrines designated for them, had even been allowed to walk freely among them while the Black soldiers had themselves been guarded by their fellow armed white soldiers. When entertainers came to visit, the Germans had been allowed to sit in front of the Negroes.

"Nothing about America makes sense," McAvoy said when Odysseus told him. "And yet here we both are."

Odysseus would normally have never spoken as openly about his version of that war, but he felt as though he could be more open with a white person who wasn't born here, whose heart and mind were not yet in the belly of that old American peculiarity.

"Well, didn't much have a choice in the matter, now, did I?" Odysseus said. He added a chuckle to make McAvoy feel more comfortable, and then immediately hated himself for doing so.

"Suppose you didn't," McAvoy said. "How's the wife?"

"She's left me," Odysseus blurted out, surprising himself. McAvoy was the closest thing he had to a friend in California. His life revolved around the shop and his family; who had time for making friends?

"When?" McAvoy looked a little peaked himself, but Odie figured he oughtn't project his own misery onto others.

"This morning," Odysseus said, sinking his head into his hands. He felt like a walking scab. Like the men whose bodies had been blistered and burned before he and his fellow soldiers had buried them.

That very morning Emmeline had made them both breakfast and then sat down across from him to eat it. He should have realized something was off by how soberly she held her spoon. The whole damn breakfast was practically funereal, in retrospect. An extra side of bacon. Fresh-squeezed orange juice. Sliced peaches next to his usual grits.

"What's the occasion?" he said as he stuffed the perfectly crisped bacon into his mouth.

"I . . . I've been telling you I wasn't happy for a while now, Odie," she started off slowly.

He hadn't heard most of what she said after that, could hardly believe it even now. He felt as though he'd been dropped into some maudlin movie as he pleaded and said they'd been through too much together to give up now and she cried and said it was too late and then finally he slammed his dish to the floor and the peaches with it.

"Dammit, Emmeline!"

Finally, he looked around at the mess he'd made.

"You know where the broom is," she said calmly, coldly, before walking upstairs. Then he picked up the broken plateware mostly by hand, because he did not, in fact, remember where the broom was.

When she reemerged minutes later at the top of the stairs holding the forest-green Travel Smart suitcase, he felt like one of the soda pops Roman would shake as a prank before telling River to open it. The room spun around them, closing in tighter. Then Odysseus said something he probably shouldn't have.

"That's my suitcase!" he said as she walked past.

"Is it?" Emmeline said, letting the door slam behind her on her way out.

McAvoy looked at him carefully. "There somebody else?"

"I don't know." Odysseus felt himself crumble. "I think, maybe? She's not been herself these past six months."

McAvoy pulled a glass from the bar cart behind him and placed it in front of Odysseus. With a generous pour, he filled the glass and said, "Drink. And when you're done feeling sorry for yourself, go on and get her back."

Where was Emmeline now? How desperately he missed her. Missed their beautiful little family.

Everything had changed once the little pick came into their lives with the past hanging from him like those soldiers Odysseus had buried. This is why he hadn't wanted to pick up little Christmas in the woods. He hadn't wanted the stench of death anywhere near his children. They would be famous. So famous that they nearly transcended race itself.

Like Nat King Cole or Sammy Davis Jr.! They could be safe! He would've begged, borrowed, or stolen a million times over to make it so.

CHAPTER TWENTY-FIVE

AFTER MY FAILED VISIT WITH ROCCO, I SANK INTO A MOST SEVERE MELancholy, as though somebody had tied an anchor to my very soul and thrown me into the deepest fathoms of the ocean.

"You're awfully quiet these days," Tom said.

I shrugged. Normally arguing with stupid ole Tom was at least a way to pass the time, but I wasn't in the mood. Across from us, Becky hummed the songs River had performed on television. She had been humming them nonstop ever since, as though she'd never heard another song before in her life!

"I could've watched him all day!" Becky said. "Couldn't you?"

I had, in fact, watched River, Rocco, and Roman all day. Had heard them miss notes, and curse, and fart, and yell up and down stairs. Had heard their shrieks of joy and the occasional set of tears when they thought nobody was listening. I'd loved watching them grow up, even if growing up was very hard it seemed. Adults made it harder, far as I could tell.

I curled across a bed of moss in our forest. A spindly fawn wobbled over to me and shouted right in my face, "Hi!"

Babies of all species have no regard for personal space.

"Hi," I mumbled back.

"Don't even bother with him," Tom said to the fawn. "He's in a mood."

"I am not!" I said. Even though I most definitely was.

"Why are you in a mood?" the fawn said and curled up on the moss next to me. If I concentrated very hard, I might almost smell the mother's milk on his breath.

"Because," I said.

"Because, why?" he said.

The fawn had been alive for only two or three weeks, I guessed. I couldn't very well tell him *Because the world is awful and adults are awful and nothing is fair and I'm sick of being dead.* That's not the kind of thing you tell a little baby creature, now, is it?

This is what I should tell him: That I've learned that you can't trust adults, no matter how much you want to, no matter how much they want to believe themselves. The adults in my life were always making promises and breaking them. Even beautiful, kind Ms. Emmeline broke her promise to keep me safe. And before her, Mr. Farraday, and before that, Mr. Powell, who had promised that I would never go to an orphanage. But he couldn't keep his promise on account of him going to jail. It wasn't his fault. Not really.

I don't remember much of my time at the orphanage. I wasn't there very long, and it was many moons ago. Perhaps my brain has emptied itself of my time there, because I was so miserable. Some of the other orphans took comfort in the *Little Orphan Annie* comic strip.

"See!" they said. "One day!"

But I knew there was no Daddy Warbucks for a little Black boy such as myself. No Sandy neither. There was, however, a concert in which we were expected to perform for the white benefactors who donated to the place and kept it running.

It was there, as I sang "Little Pal," that I first locked eyes with Mr. Farraday. At the orphanage, it had become known that I was something of a talent, and they decided they should put me front and center when the white people came. "Little Pal" and "Sonny Boy" always made our donors tear up, and when they teared up, they were more likely to reach into their pockets, so I put my enthusiasm into every last bit of song. Plus, if I did a good job, I had been promised cakes, and maybe even a new toy of my very own.

"*So till we meet again, heaven knows where or when . . .*" I sang with my most pitiful face. I even squeezed out a few tears. Real ones, because I found myself thinking about Mr. Powell and Moses and how dearly I missed them both.

I guess I did well enough that Mr. Farraday decided to talk to the matrons afterward about adopting me, which I found curious, since as I said, there weren't no Daddy Warbucks for a boy like me, never mind that my time with the white man at Mr. Powell's store, and life itself, had me afraid of what white men might do.

"Are you happy to have a home now?" Mr. Farraday said after I was told to fetch my things and say goodbye to my friends. I don't remember any of them now, but I suppose I must've had some.

"Yessir," I said, though I wasn't really all that excited, to be honest.

Mr. Farraday then told me he collected all kinds of different people, as though we were specimens, for his traveling revue. In another life, he had been an opera singer and performed all over Europe. I'm not sure that was actually true or if he was just putting on airs, since I never did hear Mr. Farraday sing a lick. But he drank all the time and smoked even more, and that'll make mush of any voice, good or bad, you do it long enough.

Anyway, this is how I came to know my next family of sorts.

We were none of us freaks, but Mr. Farraday tried to argue that "freak show" would attract more attention than if we had simply labeled ourselves a traveling revue. But apparently the other acts refused to perform if we were freaks. So, our traveling revue consisted of the Two-Headed Lady, Fanny's burlesque act, Dottie the elephant (and her trainer, Joe), Peter, who swallowed swords or ate fire, depending on his mood, and the final act, the one that brought even more people than Dottie or Fanny—me! The Pickaninny Prodigy, Christmas Jones.

Mr. Farraday taught me everything he thought I needed to know about working a crowd, including how to rub cork on my face. "For a bit of drama," he said.

"What drama?" I said.

═══

TOGETHER, WE TRAVELED the countryside, performing in tents, or under the stars, as local vendors sold peanuts or cotton candy or fortunes or moonshine. The Two-Headed Lady, who was actually two ladies in one, Liza and Elizabeth, were the kindest people I'd ever met.

"Aren't Liza and Elizabeth the same name?" you might ask.

I didn't name them!

Liza and Elizabeth were connected at the torso and always wore hand-made silk or taffeta dresses that they labored over carefully, seamlessly working the pieces of fabric in tandem. At first, Mr. Farraday wanted them to appear onstage in their bloomers and do a little striptease, but Liza and Elizabeth put their foot down. They would be on display, as per the contract their parents had signed when they were still little girls, but they would not do any sort of burlesque. If it were anybody else except for them, Mr. Farraday would've beaten them into submission, but he had a soft spot for Liza, having practically raised the girls. Not so much for Elizabeth, who was gloriously ill-tempered with everyone else, and prone to biting when provoked, but gentle as a lamb with me. Instead of making Liza bawl or Elizabeth brawl, Mr. Farraday brought in Fanny, a Brit, who gleefully shook her shapely bits with abandon.

After the shows, I would cuddle up with Liza and Elizabeth, who would stroke my head and sing me lullabies. Although occasionally they would kick me out so that Peter might play a game with Elizabeth, and sometimes even Fanny would join in their game too. I would beg to stay, but they would say this was special grown-up playtime. Then I would pout, because I had no children to play with.

It was then that I would head to Mr. Farraday, and he would put on the Victrola to drown out the mirth coming from Elizabeth and Liza's tent. The two of us would spend hours listening to music under the stars. This is how I came to know all the lyrics to not only all of Mr. Farraday's favorite pickaninny songs but also to *La Traviata,* which became my favorite album ever!

I would sing along in perfect mimicry of the Italian, and Mr. Farraday taught me all the words. Or at least the overall idea.

"Can I perform something from *La Traviata*?" I asked the next time we had a show.

"No. You better stick with the usual. Folks around here wanna see a pickaninny prodigy, not opera."

"Why can't I do both?"

"Maybe in a few months?" he said.

"Fine," I huffed.

I continued on with my act as usual. I tired of the same old songs, but to make things a little more lively I made up all kinds of new dance moves to accompany them. My feet went very, very fast. Sometimes crowds would gasp audibly at my footwork.

"He's gonna fall and crack his skull right open!" the women would exclaim.

But once they realized I would not, everyone would start clapping loudly for me before my number was even finished!

My footwork became so renowned that a man from the pictures came over to Mr. Farraday one day after one of my performances.

"I'd like to put the boy in the talkies," the man said.

"I'm afraid that's an awful lot of travel and lost wages for the whole revue," Mr. Farraday said, gesturing around to all of us.

"I think we can make it worth your while," he said. "The boy's something special."

"That he is," Mr. Farraday said, and Liza and Elizabeth squeezed me tight with delight.

"You're gonna be a star!" Liza whispered.

We all took a detour to Hollywoodland together. And this is the story I told you before, about that moppet of a girl with the little ringlets, and the studio, and the orange groves. What I didn't tell you was that not too much longer after that, when we were back on the road with our revue, we came across the movie poster while we were in Alabama.

"Oh, we have to go see it!" Fanny said. Everyone agreed, and on one of the very few nights in which we weren't performing, we all went to the pictures.

The theater had very plush red velvet seats in the main section, where Mr. Farraday, Fanny, and Peter sat, but I had to go upstairs to the colored section, where the chairs were hard and wooden. The elephant trainer stayed behind with our elephant, Dottie. Liza and Elizabeth accompanied me upstairs, even though they were white and could sit in any chair they liked. Though the benches were likely more comfortable for them. They didn't stand out that much though; there were plenty of Black women who looked like white women upstairs, but not any with two heads!

After a great deal of waiting through a bunch of boring story stuff, I finally saw myself up on the screen!

"It's me!" I shouted and stood right up. Liza and Elizabeth clapped loudly and said, "That's our boy!" Everyone around us looked over at me and then back to the screen and then back again.

"That's him!" I heard a girl whisper to her mother.

"Shh!" her mother said. "No talking!"

Wouldn't you know it? For all of that work I had to do in California, didn't more than two minutes make it on the screen. Maybe three. Still, I was happy as a clam as I sat up in the balcony with all the other coloreds watching myself sing and dance. Now, you might think I was living high upon the hog, being in the pictures and everything, but I never did see a red cent from that movie! Mr. Farraday insisted that, as my guardian, he would watch over my funds for me and make sure they were properly invested. He sure did increase the price of our show because of my two or three minutes on the big screen, though. And whenever I asked about my money, he'd let me have all the Tootsie Pops I wanted.

OH TO SIT in a big theater and listen as everyone oohed and aahed over you up onscreen all big as a giant and them just little bitty ants! Onscreen, or onstage, a little colored boy could be bigger than life and time itself, even if at that very moment he was smelling somebody's hot breath up in the peanut gallery. How I wished I could've been in all the talkies, in all the theaters, on all the stages of the world! Maybe I would've been, even, if there had been more time.

CHAPTER TWENTY-SIX

FOR THE PAST SEVENTEEN YEARS OF HER LIFE THERE HAD BEEN DIAPERS to change, boo-boos to kiss, shopping to do, field trips to attend. Emmeline had spent much of her adult life anticipating, or meeting, the needs of her little men. How strange now to be bored. To think, not of what needed to be done but simply just to have time to ponder. She didn't like it. There was too much she'd pushed away that rode in with the quiet.

She was over her phantom marriage, but the boys were still very much of her flesh—Roman, Rocco, River, and even Christmas, firmly tucked inside each chamber of her heart itself. She told River as much as the two of them sat in the backyard and looked up into the stars one night Odie was at the store late and River just returned from his tour.

"I can't do this anymore, Riv." As soon as she said it, she knew it to be true.

"Do what?" her son asked.

"I love you boys more than anything, OK?" she said.

"What are you even talking about?" River asked.

"I think . . . I'm leaving your father," she said. "I want you to know before I tell him."

River looked over at her for a long, long, long time, then back up at the stars.

"Do you want to talk about it?" she said.

"Everyone leaves," he said, and leaned farther back onto his elbows. "I left too for a while, I guess."

What had the past year done to her happy, shining boy?

"You had to do that, River," she said gently. "None of this is your fault, OK? None of it."

But before he could speak, they heard the heavy door slam at the front of the house.

"I'm home!" Odie shouted.

AND SO, HALF a year into her walks with Aaron Takahashi, Emmeline wound up on Beth's doorstep and said in a great rush, "I've left my husband."

Beth had looked her up and down and simply said, "Whiskey or wine?"

"Whiskey. I think," Emmeline said.

"Oh dear. You really mean it," Beth said.

"Do people just casually leave their husbands?" Emmeline asked.

"I had a friend who left hers once a month." Beth laughed. "On a Friday, she'd come over here, bags packed, and sit and tell me everything she hated about her husband, and her kids, and her life, and what she could've been, or who she could've married. By Monday, she would be back in time to make them all a pancake breakfast."

"Sounds exhausting."

"She did leave him eventually," Beth said as she poured Emmeline a stiff one. "For a woman she went to college with. Officially, they're roommates, of course. But you know . . ."

"How very modern," Emmeline murmured.

"I think I've somehow become *the* confidante for friends who want to leave their husbands," Beth said with a laugh. "Since it worked out so well for me."

It had, in fact actually worked out pretty well for her. Beth and her ex-husband, Glenn, shared custody of Edie every other week. Divorce was practically unheard-of, but this, this was something else entirely. Beth was a part-time mother. But who was Emmeline to judge this woman who had been so kind to her?

On Beth's burnt-orange velvet couch, out it had all come. All about Aaron Takahashi and their peripatetic courtship.

"You must think I'm pathetic," Emmeline said when she was done.

Beth grabbed her hand. "I think you're very brave to try to seek happiness in the middle of everything you've been through."

"Not brave. Stupid. I didn't think any of this through. Where am I gonna stay? What am I going to do for money?" Emmeline said. "I haven't had a job in over sixteen years."

"Nonsense. You stay here as long as you need. You can have the guest room. I still have to clear up some of the stuff that we've been storing in there. But you can sleep with me in my room tonight, if you like."

"I couldn't possibly impose on you like that!"

"It'll be like a slumber party."

"I never went to one of those growing up," Emmeline admitted.

"Neither did I. All the better," Beth had said. "We'll paint each other's nails and tell ghost stories."

Emmeline thought briefly of the little ghost who'd briefly been her son. What was Christmas doing? Was he with people who loved him? Or had he maybe, hopefully, gone on to whatever came next? She thought of dead Bettina sitting with her daddy until all the gossips began to think the good doctor was crazy. And then she thought of her parents. Why had Emmeline's parents never found her worthy of haunting? She had been so young when they'd died. Didn't they think that maybe she needed tending to? Watching over? When they'd left her, they'd just . . . gone. If Emmeline were to ever die, she would never leave her kids like that.

Then again, isn't that exactly what she'd just done?

Hers weren't the kind of ghost stories Beth wanted to hear. Of that she was sure.

That night, with curlers and face cream as their shared uniform, Emmeline and Beth sat next to each other in bed and watched *The Flip Wilson Show,* which Emmeline had never watched with Odie because he thought the whole thing stupid and demeaning. Emmeline found it stupid too, but a soothing kind of stupid.

═══

AARON TAKAHASHI'S OFFICE was walking distance from Beth's house. A long walk, but doable. Emmeline decided to walk there while Beth's girl, Carlotta, cleaned the space, awkward as it was to sit around doing nothing while another Negro woman got on her hands and knees to clean a white woman's baseboards.

"Hi, Mrs. Johnson! Do you have an appointment?" Rachel said when Emmeline arrived. The frazzled girl rummaged through the stuff on her desk. "Did I forget to write it down? I've been so caught up in my dissertation."

"Oh no, I just came by to say hi!" Emmeline said. Did Rachel know of whatever it was between her and the doctor? She was infrequently at her post.

"He has patients back-to-back this afternoon, I'm afraid." Rachel frowned, checking the calendar in front of her.

"Oh, never mind then! Just tell him I said hi!" Emmeline said.

The truth was that she wasn't sure what to say to Aaron anyway. The day after she'd left Odysseus, she'd called Aaron up and breathlessly said, "I did it. I left him."

He'd paused for a very long time on the other end. "Are you sure that's what you want?"

"Is it not what you want?"

Another long pause. "It's a big step."

"Right."

"I mean. I want you. I love you. But . . ."

"But what?"

"I want you to be ready is all," he said. "It's a big step."

"You said that already."

She'd ruminated all night about those three words. It was the very first time he'd said I love you. Well, four words really: *I. Love. You. But.* This is what she'd left her home for. And now, several days later, here she waited, feeling rather like an idiot, across from his assistant, who politely struggled to assist. The girl would clearly much rather be tinkering around in some lab, or in her own head, at the very least.

Maybe it was for the best that Aaron was occupied at the moment, Emmeline thought. She might actually scream if he repeated "It's a big step" one more time.

"What's your dissertation on?" Emmeline asked.

"Oh, it's dry." Rachel laughed.

"You should be extremely proud of yourself."

"My mother's just livid I've not yet married. Mothers, right?"

Emmeline forced a laugh.

"What are you going to do with the PhD when you're done?"

"I'm not sure yet. But I've been thinking and maybe it's OK just to know things?"

"That's a lovely way to look at it," Emmeline said before heading out the door.

═══

THE NEXT DAY, Emmeline called the office again. This time it was Aaron who picked up the phone.

"Can we talk?" she asked.

"Isn't that what we're doing now?" Aaron said. She couldn't tell if he meant it earnestly or not.

For a man whose job it was to be sensitive about feelings, he was really shitty at them sometimes. Maybe he could only handle emotions when they came from children.

"I'm at my friend Beth's," she said, then clarified. "Edie's mom."

"Yes, I know who Beth is." He took a deep inhale. "Are you OK?"

She paused before repeating his words back at him. "It's a big step."

"I'm sorry. I didn't know what to say in the moment, Emmie," he said. "I just don't want to be that guy, you know?"

She could picture him running a hand through his inky curls.

"Look, I didn't leave my husband for you. If that's what you're afraid of," she said. "I . . . I just needed to breathe for a minute."

"Breathing is good," he said, after what felt like an eternity.

"Did you mean it?" she said. "What you said?"

She didn't dare repeat the words themselves.

"I don't say anything I don't mean," he said softly.

═══

A DAY LATER, on their afternoon walk, Aaron stopped in the middle of the sidewalk and fumbled with something in his pocket. Good God, he wasn't going to propose, was he? She wasn't even divorced. Not yet. And surely he wouldn't do so atop the purple slush of a denuded jacaranda tree while traffic whizzed past. Is that what she wanted? Did she want a whole new life? Or had she merely just wanted her old one, but better? She hadn't thought any of this through. Not really.

Then the doctor turned up the walkway of a light-gray American Foursquare. Roses lined the concrete path up to the front, but the doctor wasn't heading toward the front door.

"Where are you going?" she asked.

Aaron smiled. "I want to show you something."

He headed down a series of hexagonal stepping stones toward a cracked wooden fence.

"I don't think we should go back there," Emmeline said. She was not in the habit of sneaking into places. Much less in neighborhoods where there hadn't been a face that looked like hers in at least fifteen minutes. Far as she could tell, fifteen minutes of walking in Los Angeles often felt like gathering stamps on a passport, so vastly different were some neighborhoods from others.

"I promise you it's worth it," Aaron said.

He twisted something behind the fence, unlatched near where the faded wood had split, and held it open for her.

"I'm not trying to go to jail for whatever this is, Aaron," she said sternly, feeling a bit like a dog pulling against a leash.

"Way to ruin a surprise." He laughed. "Don't worry. It's mine. This is my house."

She felt suddenly very shy as she stepped through the worn gate into a series of impeccably tended hedges, a labyrinth. They had never ventured into each other's private spaces before. This was another step. And how beautiful it was. Lavandula, hydrangea, lavender cotton, bee balm, an overabundance of perennials in Technicolor, with hostas and various foliage throughout. A winding stone path through them all led to a simple bench under a pergola, next to a raised concrete bed.

"Wow" was all she could get out.

He laughed. "My mother started with a few plants here and there. My parents lived with me for a little while, but when my sister got married and had the kids, my parents wanted to live with the grandkids. I didn't want to just let everything die after she'd worked so hard on it. And anyway, it calms me down at the end of a long day. My days can be stressful sometimes. Like any job. But . . . other people's emotions get so heavy and here, I feel light."

Emmeline had never met a man who gardened before. Unless it was as a profession.

"I'm rambling," he said. "I'm nervous."

She looked at Aaron in wonder, for here was a man who made things grow, not for money but just because he wanted to.

Where did you come from? she thought, feeling herself bloom.

"Look," he said at a near whisper, pointing at a section of the garden. There, across from the birdbath, next to the pergola, monarchs fluttered from rose to rose, their petals bent almost imperceptibly before the butterflies took off again.

Emmeline thought of her dear, sweet Rocco, and how much he would love this place. She buried her face in Aaron's chest as though she were a mole, digging deeper and deeper still. How far could she go and not feel herself anymore? It would've brought her to tears except that she had cried so much over the last few months that she felt wrung clean out. Emmeline needed tending.

Aaron grabbed her hand and placed something hard and metal inside.

"Not to move in. I'm not trying to scare you, or force you. But you can stay whenever you want," he said. "So you can have a break when you need to. You don't have to even go inside. You can just sit out here. If you want."

The key felt heavy in Emmeline's hand. What would it mean to have it? To use it?

"I promise the rest of the house isn't nearly as spectacular." He laughed. "I spend all my free time out here."

"Wow," she repeated, feeling a bit like an idiot. "I . . . I promise I know other words. It's just . . ."

"It's yours," Aaron Takahashi said, and held his hand over the key in hers. "I'm yours."

CHAPTER TWENTY-SEVEN

ROCCO WASN'T SURE HOW MUCH MORE HE COULD TAKE OF CHAD'S MEdieval torture tales when he just wanted to eat his gruel in peace. At least there was no more Victor to contend with. Victor'd beaten one of the guards such that, days later, while following the path of a roly-poly that had somehow made its way indoors along the baseboards of the cafeteria, Rocco had found one of the man's teeth. This time, the state decided to try Victor as an adult.

He wasn't expecting a visit from his little brother.

The first visit, or at least what he'd thought was the first, Rocco was in the rec room playing chess against himself when River appeared across from him. Rocco thought he was seeing a ghost. His brother had grown taller since he'd seen him last. Although, he supposed, so had he. River approached him tentatively, as though Rocco were a wild creature. As though he had done what they both knew he hadn't.

Rocco had called out for his brother over and over that calamitous day with Christmas and Wayne in the hallway. River had been smiling when he turned the corner, his arm slung across his friend Milton, before they saw Wayne's crumpled body on the floor. Rocco remembered just how supremely happy River had looked in that moment before his face fell.

As he approached Rocco and the chess set, River looked to be on the verge of tears. He walked around the table and knelt down beside Rocco, knocking over a knight.

Then River wrapped his arms around Rocco and held him for as long as Rocco could possibly stand. He briefly wondered if River might want to see the guard's tooth.

═══

TURNS OUT RIVER had visited even earlier, during his tour, but Rocco had not seen him. It had been just after the first bit of electroshock therapy, when he was neither here nor there or anywhere at all. The nurses had told River that Rocco might not be himself for a few days. Apparently, his brother had sat across from him and waited for a Rocco who never came.

"You told me to go away," River said. He turned his head so Rocco couldn't see his eyes shining, the tears at their corners, but Rocco saw them all the same.

I don't remember that, Rocco thought, but the words were still difficult coming up his throat; the journey to his tongue felt downright interminable.

River glanced around at the guards posted by the door to the rec room.

"Let's get out of here," River said.

River being River, he had convinced the head nurse and guards to let him take Rocco out for the day. He told them he was on tour and would only be in town for the night, that it had been so long since he'd last seen his baby brother. He was famous enough now that several of them recognized him immediately and sang his most recent hit single at him. Rocco's brother smiled and sang it along with them. River's voice had deepened even more since the single's release. It was not his real smile.

Rocco had seen the sleepy college town surrounding the hospital only in bits and pieces when the hospital arranged a few tightly supervised outings for the residents. Rocco and River walked along the main drag as River tried to decide on a restaurant.

"Nothing too mushy, right, Rocco?" River said. "What are you in the mood for?"

Rocco shrugged.

They stopped in front of a Cajun place.

"I think my manager said this place is supposed to be good?" River said.

He passed Rocco a menu. It was when Rocco reached for it that River noticed the bruises on Rocco's arms.

"Who did this to you?!" River said. "Have Mom and Dad seen this?"

Again, Rocco shrugged. He had learned to go outside of himself whenever these things happened. It was almost as though he himself were a ghost, floating over the scene, watching a life that wasn't his.

"This is my fault, all of it," River said.

Rocco's brain was foggy. He was always so tired.

"I'm sorry." His brother looked to be on the verge of tears.

River held Rocco close. People passing by on the street stared at the two of them, and then again, as they looked to see if River was who they thought he was. A girl approached them asking for his autograph.

"Please, not now," River said to her.

"Jerk!" she mumbled as she walked away.

"We gotta find a payphone."

It was then that Rocco noticed a trail of girls following at a slight distance.

"Yes, hi, uh . . . Mrs. . . . Hi Beth, may I speak to my mama please? This is River Johnson."

Emmeline answered. Rocco could hear his mother's excitement through the phone.

"Hi. Um . . . I'm here with Rocco."

A pause. Rocco strained to hear his mother's response.

"I hadn't planned on it. Just had some downtime . . ."

His mother had left their father and moved in with a friend of hers. She'd been living there for a little over a month. He knew that things were weird whenever his parents came to visit, but Rocco always thought he was to blame, his tongue and head thick with shock and meds. It never occurred to him that whatever heaviness was in their silence might also be between them. Since when did his mother have friends he didn't know? River seemed to be holding something back.

"I just wanted you to know that I'm getting Rocco out of here. I'm not taking him back to that place."

River pulled the phone to his other ear so that Rocco could no longer hear them easily.

"He's not himself. I don't know what they have him on, but it's not good. Here, you wanna talk to him?"

And then Rocco heard his mother's voice on the phone.

"Hi baby. Is what River's saying true? Are they not treating you right?

Last week, Nurse Tina said you seemed to be doing better when we talked."

His mother and father had made it a point to talk to the staff whenever they visited, seemingly believing that if they just made their presence known, Rocco would receive better care. Never mind that in the eyes of most of the attendants, Rocco was just a half step up from prisoner.

"Please, Rocco, will you talk to your mama?" Emmeline said.

He could hear his mother choking up on the other end.

"OK," she said before Rocco handed the phone back to River.

River searched his pockets for more quarters.

"Shit. We're gonna get cut off soon . . . You got any quarters?" he asked Rocco, who shook his head no.

"OK, I'm gonna take him to my hotel. He's with me. He'll be safe."

Rocco looked out of the cramped phonebooth to see a small crowd had gathered around them. Fans.

"Fuck," River said. "OK, Rocco, we have to move very quickly. When I say run, you run."

Rocco nodded. He stepped out the phonebooth first as the crowd pushed in closer. Then River followed behind him.

"River! River!" they shouted.

River waved to the crowd and leaned in. Rocco could feel his brother's breath against his ear.

"Run!"

They pushed through the crowd of screaming fans and ran as the mostly teenage girls nipped at their tails. He and his brother ran through alleys and up tiny backstreets until they'd lost most of them. Still, they kept running. Rocco tilted back his head and laughed as the wind hit his face. It was the first time in forever he'd felt almost free.

═══

RIVER'S HOTEL ROOM was the nicest Rocco had ever been in. He ran his fingertips along the glass table, along the velvet chair. It was the softest chair he'd ever felt.

"We'll get your things somehow," River said. "Or I'll get you new things."

Rocco nodded.

He saw on River's skin scratch marks that crisscrossed the surface, like something feral had attacked his brother. He pointed at them and River looked down.

"The girls do that sometimes. It's their nails. Fans." River shrugged.

There was a knock on the door, and Rocco felt himself tense up.

River's newest tour manager was a stout white man with nose hairs in desperate need of trimming.

"Riv, the sound check is in thirty minutes, and I have you scheduled for a meet-and-greet right after . . ."

The man paused when he glanced up and saw Rocco.

"Hi . . . Rocco?" he said.

Why did everybody know his name?

"We're gonna have to cancel the show tonight," Riv said. Rocco thought his brother sounded slightly afraid of this man.

"You can't," the man said.

"Come up with something," River said.

"That's thousands of dollars. The venue is sold out. You don't want to piss them off."

River glanced over at Rocco. "I have a family matter."

"Great. I'll take care of it. That's what I'm here for."

"No. I need to handle it myself."

"It's bad press."

"I've never canceled a show before. Not even when I should've."

"You don't show this late, it's a big deal."

"Just tell them exhaustion or some shit. I don't fucking care. I'm River Johnson and my brother needs me. Handle it, Jerry."

Rocco had never heard his brother speak to anyone like that before. His brother had always been shy and eager to please. Where had that River gone? Is this what being famous was? Still, Rocco felt the most immense swelling in his heart. Pride.

The man grumbled and let the door slam behind.

"Let's order room service," River said.

Together they lay out on the bed and River ordered anything and everything from the menu. They split a sundae with extra cherries, and River told Rocco all about his adventures on the road, including his time with the very famous guitarist who had just been found dead earlier that week in his girlfriend's apartment in Lisbon.

"He was wild," River said, and stared off into space somewhere. "I didn't like him. But he was good. Really fucking good. Even if he was a huge asshole."

Rocco imagined what the man might have been like. What it would have been like to be on the road as part of the Johnson Three. Who would Rocco have been as a famous person?

The phone rang, and River took the call in the other room. Rocco strained to make out words, but the world was muffled, the wall between them swallowed the sound and digested it into nonsense.

"Fucking Jerry," River spat as he emerged. River cursed more like a grown-up now.

River wrapped his arms around him and Rocco let him hold him longer than anyone had in a while. He thought of how the attendant at the facility had restrained him before each time they took him to that place and shocked his system, but tried to put it out of his head. He was safe here.

In the morning, Rocco woke up around the time he normally received his morning meds. Next to him, River snored as though he were choking on sleep itself.

Rocco went into the living-room area and turned on the television. Saturday-morning cartoons! He hadn't seen these in forever. At the facility, they usually just left the radio in the rec room on all morning and made them listen to something awful boring like Pat Boone.

After about half an hour of Rocco flipping back and forth between CBS, ABC, and NBC, River joined him.

"I haven't slept that well in forever," River said, and sat down next to Rocco on the couch. He handed Rocco a cup of freshly brewed hotel coffee.

"Don't tell Mom." River laughed. Their mother was convinced coffee would stunt your growth, and that was just one of a number of other maladies that could befall them from drinking it.

Emmeline would be driving up about now, and together they would figure out what happened next. The world felt less blurry around the edges, colors brighter.

"You just speak when you're ready," River said gently, patting Rocco's hand.

Then the brothers laughed as the coyote chased the roadrunner off a cliff.

CHAPTER TWENTY-EIGHT

IT WAS AS THOUGH ODYSSEUS HAD GONE IN FOR SURGERY TO REMOVE A spleen and instead they'd removed his heart, his very lungs, and simply left them on ice, forgetting to sew him back up again. That's how he felt moving through a world with no Emmeline in it. Or like the little dead pick with his guts spilling out and into his hands from time to time.

A new kid, Bill Withers, had come out with an album *Just As I Am,* which seemed to speak to Odie's very soul. He played the record over and over at the store, at home, until the grooves wore down as though he'd owned it for years instead of merely weeks.

"Jesus, Dad. Not Bill again!" River shouted from his room.

River had been back from his tour nearly as long as he'd been on it. Still, he'd changed so much since his return. Odysseus had no idea how to deal with him at the moment, brooding and sulky, but with the power of a child who made more money, and had seen more of the country, or maybe just more, even, than most of the adults around him. What the boy needed was his mother.

"Maybe instead of being all mopey-dopey, you should actually do something," River said as they both sat in front of the television with a meatloaf TV dinner, watching *The French Chef.*

Onscreen, Julia Child diced onion.

Odysseus thought about what McAvoy had said, last he'd spoken to him.

"What do you think your mom would like? Anything she's been mentioning that she wants or . . ." He trailed off as River raised an eyebrow at him. "We've got to win her back."

"We?" River said.

"Don't you want your mother home?" Odysseus said.

"If she wanted to be home, she'd be here."

Emmeline wasn't a woman who could be brought back by a fancy ring or promises of a vacation somewhere exotic. She wasn't a woman who especially cared about stuff. But what did Emmeline care about more than anything in the world? Her boys! That was it! She'd ignore a request from Odie, but she'd never ignore a request from one of the boys.

"I've got it. Maybe you could say that you'd like us to have a family dinner. Or even that you want us to start having family dinners once a week!" Odysseus said. "Tell her that you've really missed having time all together since so much of this year was spent touring."

"But we're not all together." River sighed and twisted his mouth. "Plus, that's diabolical, Dad. Using me to get to Mom."

"But it might work, right?" Odie said.

River shrugged yet again, ever the teenager, and headed to the phone in the kitchen. When Odie went to follow his son into the kitchen, River held out his hand to stop him.

"Privacy, please," River said.

What felt like a whole hour later, but was probably less than ten minutes, River returned.

"She says we can start doing this dinner thing next Friday."

Odysseus lifted his son off his feet and into the air as he had when the boys were little. River felt stolid. Somewhere between boy and man. How much time had passed since the last time he'd lifted his son up in the air? Odysseus had the horrible sinking feeling that this was the very last time he would be able to do this and gripped on to River tightly, pushing back tears.

"Calm down, old man," River said. "Also, you can't invite her here and make her make dinner for us. You should probably figure that out."

The very next day, Odysseus went to Vroman's on Colorado. He paced up and down the aisle in the cookbook section picking up titles and placing them back on the neat shelves. He needed to make his wife something fancy, but something that he wouldn't mess up. What was the right recipe to stitch a family back together? To bring a marriage back from the brink? Did it involve tomato? Cardamom? Leeks? Definitely not leeks.

He and River had mindlessly watched Julia Child cook so many times, and yet Odysseus hadn't the foggiest idea how to actually do any of it himself. He settled on *Mastering the Art of French Cooking*. It was popular for a reason, right? Julia seemed like she knew what the fuck she was doing.

When he got home, he plopped the behemoth of a book down on the kitchen table. River leaned over and flipped through the pages.

"These look kinda complicated," he said.

"We'll do it together," Odysseus said hopefully.

River didn't look up from flipping the pages. "Again with the 'we' shit."

Still, River kept turning intently, a young man on a mission.

"This," River said, and pointed to the coq au vin. "This is the one."

That Thursday they went to Fedco and picked up all the ingredients. He and River had never actually been in a grocery store together; shopping had always been Emmeline's purview. As River stood up on the shopping cart and scooted down half an aisle before nearly crashing into a cereal display, Odysseus could picture River as the little boy he once was.

"My goodness, is that—?" Shoppers looked over at River and Odysseus. A few began to follow them, crowding the edges of the aisles, hoping to get a peek.

River and Odysseus hurried through the rest of their shopping, throwing things into the cart as teenage girls around them swooned and swooped.

"How the hell did they find out we were here?" River asked. "Shit, we gotta go."

As they exited, approaching paparazzi took photos of the two of them. River scowled and shielded his face with the grocery bag.

"Smile," Odysseus said. "Make sure you smile at them, son!"

River lowered the bag and waved at the camera before ducking into the car.

"Sorry," River mumbled.

"Ain't got nothing to apologize for," Odie said. "You looked good. I'll bet those photos end up in a magazine, don't you think?"

River sighed. "Who do you think called them?"

"I'll go back out tomorrow," Odie said.

THE NEXT DAY, he decided to swing by McAvoy's before picking up the last few ingredients, excited to share his plan to win Emmeline back and maybe get some advice before he gave McAvoy the final payment. But instead of the formidable tiny man who'd become a friend, he found a larger, duller version. McAvoy but Americanized, supersized. If McAvoy, as an outsider, had found some kinship with other immigrants, and occasionally even the Blacks, his son's body language told Odysseus that he felt no such kinship at all. This man didn't seem as though he would, or could, find kindship with anyone, or anything.

"You must be Odysseus," the man said.

"Indeed," he said, and stuck out his hand. He found it rude, though not particularly surprising, that the younger man hadn't addressed him as Mr. Johnson. The younger McAvoy glanced at Odysseus's hand before motioning at him to sit.

Odysseus said, "Where is your father?"

"He's been hospitalized," the son said.

Odysseus waited for more information, but none was forthcoming.

"Which hospital? Is it serious? I'd love to visit . . . or send flowers—" Odysseus started before the boy interrupted.

"Thank you, but that won't be necessary. I believe you owe my father a last payment, correct?" The son raised a ledger up close to his face and then back down again. Odysseus had never seen it before.

"I'll come by again when your father returns," Odie said.

A pained look flickered across the boy's face. "My father will be taking time away from all business for the foreseeable future."

The Scot was the first and only friend Odie had in this place. The only adult to whom he spoke on a regular basis other than his wife, or River's people. Odysseus hadn't realized how much he'd looked forward to their conversations until now. As ever, how quickly life turned.

"Well." Odie dug into his wallet for the remaining amount. "I guess this is it then."

"I guess it is," the man said.

"Tell your father to call me when he's feeling a little better," Odie said hopefully.

═

HE WAS SO deep in thought about what could have possibly befallen the elder McAvoy that he nearly missed seeing his wife among the apples. He went to the Alpha Beta on Los Robles thinking maybe it might be best to avoid returning to Fedco for the foreseeable future. He had not expected to see Emmeline and Dr. Takahashi pushing along a grocery cart naturally as could be, as though the two of them had always been. As though Odie and the boys didn't exist at all. The doctor briefly rested his hand on the small of Emmeline's back. She didn't pull away. So, it was him then, was it?

He wanted to yell at her, to disembowel him, to cry amid the overripe tomatoes. All three all at once. How could she disrespect and dismiss their whole lives together to date, and in the middle of Alpha Beta, no less? How could she look so radiantly at somebody who wasn't him? Rather than do or say anything at all, he abandoned his grocery cart mid-aisle and returned to the Caddy, where he yelled at the top of his lungs for a good minute before turning the ignition and driving home.

"Where is everything?" River said as Odysseus entered the kitchen. He looked over at him from the marble island where River sat, hands sticky and surrounded by ingredients. "We can't exactly make coq au vin without the vin."

"Dinner's canceled," Odie said.

"What? Why?" River stood up and followed Odie around the house. "What happened? Is Mom OK?"

"She's fine," Odie said bitterly. "I'm canceling."

"You can't just do that. I already parbroiled the bacon!"

"I don't give a shit about the bacon right now, Riv."

"I'm not canceling dinner. Mom and I can just have it then," River said. "You can just stay upstairs, or go out, or whatever."

He began defiantly chopping onions. The boy had already come dangerously close to losing a finger on tour; he wouldn't lose one over this nonsense with Emmeline. Odysseus snatched the knife from River's hand, slicing himself in the process.

"Last I checked, I'm still the parent, River." He winced as the blood began to trickle down his palm like some French cooking–induced stigmata. "Me. And I just said dinner is canceled."

"You're such an asshole!" River yelled.

"Oh well. At least I'm the asshole who's still here!" Odie yelled back as he climbed the stairs to his room.

It was a B-side kind of night. Once upstairs, Odysseus placed the needle on the record. Bill's plaintive baritone almost swallowed up the sounds of River angrily slamming the kitchen-cabinet doors downstairs. Almost.

CHAPTER TWENTY-NINE

"I WANNA BUY A CAR," RIVER SAID AS HE AND ODYSSEUS SAT WATCHING *CBS Evening News with Walter Cronkite.*

Now that he was almost legal to drive, he imagined himself flying through San Francisco in his very own green Mustang like Steve McQueen in *Bullitt*. Or perhaps one of those Mini Coopers like in *The Italian Job*. He would get away from his asshole father, then he would pick Rocco up and take him for a drive up the coast as they both sang along to the radio at full blast.

He'd had his fancy lawyers file a motion to get Rocco moved from that horrible facility and placed somewhere more suitable. A car would mean he could visit his big brother whenever he wanted, without paparazzi, or even his parents' knowing. River still felt the immense weight of what had happened to Rocco, what might have been with the Johnson Three had he not been in that bathroom with Milton a few seconds too long. The guilt hung and River embellished it with everything he'd ever done wrong as a brother, as a son, as a person. It draped across his shoulders like a heavy cape, or one of Odysseus's old barbells, even as he danced across the stage looking weightless.

"I think we'd need to talk to your mother about that," Odysseus said.

"Why? She didn't make the money, I did. And besides, she's not even here . . ."

Emmeline still hadn't returned home. After their failed attempt at family dinner, she'd taken to calling at eight P.M. several times a week to check in with him. Sometimes, River answered. Other times, he told his father to tell her he was in the studio. Why should his mother get to have her cake and eat it too? As far as River was concerned, she hadn't just left his father, she'd abandoned him as well. She'd forfeited the right to hear about his life the moment she stepped outside that door with her suitcase and let it close behind her.

"You don't even know how to drive, River," Odysseus said.

"I can learn easy enough."

"I don't think it's safe for you to be out there like that. What if the police stop you? You know how corrupt LAPD is. And what about crazed fans?"

"Even normal kids get cars for their sixteenth birthdays!" River whined.

"I don't see no normal kids around here, do you?" his father said. "Besides. Rocco's new place is significantly more expensive. I think we should hold off on any big purchases for now."

"Can't I afford both?"

"Drop it," his father said.

LATER THAT NIGHT, River tried not to make so much as a peep while he passed Odysseus snoring loud enough to wake the dead in his parents' bedroom. He slid down the banister instead of using the squeaky stairs, as he had seen Roman do on several occasions before he left for Vietnam. Then River crept into the study, where he knew his father kept files with all of River's expenses. Under the box of paper clips in Odysseus's desk was the key to the mahogany filing cabinet. He tiptoed toward the back corner of the study, where the cabinet stood against the wall. Sneaking was OK if he was just looking at his own money, right?

River fingered through the accordion files full of ledgers, numbers upon numbers written in his father's absurdly neat penmanship. Graph papers full of addition and subtraction. Contracts that River had signed and Odysseus had filed away. His eyes widened when he saw just how much he had taken in over the last year. Enough for an Aston Martin, a new house, and then some. Rocco's new facility was definitely more expensive, but not outrageously so. And especially as his father still had the store, and that business at the store had definitely picked up. People really wanted to do business with River Johnson's father. River was no math wiz, but as he continued to pore over the documents, something didn't add up. Huge sums of money were being paid to somebody, or something, named McAvoy. River didn't know of anybody named McAvoy on his team.

In the early morning, after hours of staying awake, staring at the ceiling, wondering what to do, he heard his father go to the garage to work out. River followed behind him. He waited until Odysseus began to do his chest presses, when, under all that weight, his father could not easily wriggle away.

"What or who is McAvoy?" River said.

"What are you talking about?" Odysseus said.

"I apparently made big payments to somebody or something called McAvoy every few months?"

"Who told you that?"

"I went through my expenses, since you said we couldn't afford a car."

"I never said you couldn't. I said I didn't think it would be smart. I don't want you to end up a spoiled brat. And you're not supposed to be going through my stuff."

"They're my contracts!"

Odysseus sighed very, very deeply. "When I moved here, nobody would lend to me. Not enough for what I needed, for the business, or this house. I found a way."

"And that way involves my money how?" River said.

"I had to pay the man back."

"You stole from me!"

Even after uttering it aloud, he still hoped somehow it wasn't true.

"You boys got things loads of Negro children could only dream of. Everything—moving out to California, uprooting our lives back home, borrowing from McAvoy—all of it was for you! For this family!"

River yelled, gesturing around himself at their now oh-so-quiet home. "This isn't a fucking family!"

Your adults were supposed to protect you at all costs, and here River was with one parent who'd groomed him to be his personal cash cow and another who'd thought nothing of abandoning him for whatever, or whomever, River was afraid to ask.

Where the fuck had his childhood gone?

═

HE FIRED HIS father. And several days later, on his sixteenth birthday, he bought himself an Aston Martin. He'd failed his first driving test; the proctor clearly wanted to make a point that he wouldn't make any concessions just because River was a celebrity. Whatever, he'd figure it all out eventually. The record label had offered to throw him a birthday party at a club in Hollywood, but when River said he'd rather do something at home, the label suggested inviting a bunch of up-and-coming teen acts that the label wanted to promote, those who could use a bit of publicity, and the people who worked for all of them. A sixteenth birthday party at a family home would look charming! So down-to-earth! Rocco had been granted leave for the day to celebrate. They didn't often grant leave to patients who had just moved in, the director of the program said. But then again, Rocco wasn't most patients, was he?

"How is it going?" River asked Rocco, who sat in the corner quietly taking everything and everyone in as the party got under way.

Did his brother look around the room at everyone gathered and think, *This could all have been mine*? Or was that just River's guilt?

"Good," Rocco said.

"Are you having fun?"

Rocco sighed. "Mama has spoken only sixteen words to Daddy. You've spoken thirty-one to me."

"You're counting them?"

"There's too much space in our sentences," Rocco said. "And everybody acts like Roman doesn't even exist."

River felt the deepest pang of guilt that his brother was at actual war while he celebrated his birthday with teenyboppers. That maybe this could have been Roman's too. That he could've been safe. That for just a few months, for River's birthday, they could've been once more the Johnson Three.

Instead of saying all of that, River said, "How do you like the new place?"

"It's OK," Rocco said.

But before River could ask him for more details, one of the guests invited by the record label, another teen act whose own record had soared a year or two earlier as part of a quintet modeled after the Temptations, plopped down next to him. What was his name again? Was it Bobby? Or maybe Cornelius? He'd met so many people over the last year, it was hard keeping everyone straight.

"You buy yourself a house yet?" Bobby Cornelius said. "You gotta get property. Invest and grow your earnings. That's how white folks get rich. You don't want to be one of them little niggas who burns through all their shit and then wonders where it all went when you're all old and not cute anymore."

"Damn," River said. "Can I at least blow out my birthday candles first?"

Bobby Cornelius laughed. "Gotta get it while the gettin's good."

I'm still a kid, River thought. I don't know a damn thing about investing or earnings. Or how to take care of a house. That was what parents were supposed to be for. Plus, he knew it was irrational, but he just couldn't shake the uneasy feeling that once he bought a house of his very own, there would be no more going home ever again.

"River has a house," Rocco said quite firmly to Bobby Cornelius, who didn't hear him, as he was already on to schmoozing the next party guest.

It was as River wiped birthday-cake frosting from his mouth that he spotted Milton across the room looking vaguely uncomfortable. The girl next to him had a face from a lifetime ago, when River was a just another kid in a school. River glanced down and noticed the girl's arm wrapped through Milton's. Why was he here?

"Surprise!" Emmeline whispered, catching River unawares. River startled at his mother's voice and promptly dropped his piece of cake all over his new red leather pants. "I thought it would be nice to see a familiar face."

"What are you doing here?" he demanded.

"I'm your mother," she said, as though it were obvious.

She waved at Milton, who practically bounded over to where River stood, and the girl quickly followed behind him.

"It's good to see you again, Milton!"

"You too, Mrs. Johnson. I'm sorry I'm late." Milton went in to hug Emmeline.

"I'll leave you boys to catch up." Emmeline scurried away.

Was the girl's name Holly? Or maybe Phoebe? Either way, River felt something stir inside of him that he immediately tucked somewhere into the deepest recesses of himself. Whatever had happened with Milton had become a locked box inside a locked box tucked behind the rib he had broken during one of the last fights he'd had at school before being pulled out, which still ached on rainy days. But why did the sight of this random girl make River feel vaguely sick to his stomach?

"Hi, Riv!" Milton said, as though it'd been mere days since they'd seen each other last.

"I'm Holly," the girl said.

"Holly's a huge fan!" Milton said. "Not that I'm not, of course . . ."

"Of course," River said.

"She has all the lyrics to your songs memorized. The whole album. Even the liner notes. Like some sort of River Johnson savant!" Milton laughed.

"OK you're embarrassing me." Holly giggled. "I'm not that bad. I swear."

Holly was more Gidget than Marcia Brady, but she was cute. Her cat-eye glasses hadn't been fashionable in quite some time, but they worked for her, he supposed. She had very kind eyes and the apparent temperament of a golden retriever. It was irrational to dislike her, but River did.

"This is quite the party," Milton said, gazing around the room.

"We made something for you!" Holly said.

"We?" River said.

"Holly's my girlfriend," Milton said.

"Cool," River said with a feigned insouciance.

"Pardon me," Holly said. "Where's the powder room?"

River pointed her in the direction of the guest bath.

In the girl's absence, he and Milton stared at each other. Milton was taller than River now. Still lean, but with muscle threatening to emerge from under his skin's surface. The braces had left his teeth straight, even if he still did have that slight overbite. His glasses were still thick as ever, and yet he looked good in them. Smart. Like he might grow up to be somebody who solved the world's problems. His shaggy hair fell across his face like some sort of nerd heartthrob.

"She's incredible. You know she speaks three languages?!" Milton said, breaking the silence.

"Lots of people do."

"And she's the head of the Science Olympiad team!"

River stared ahead at his newly platinum album on the wall.

Rocco walked over to them from his previous perch, sitting on the fireplace, watching.

"Hi, Rocco!" Milton said brightly. "I haven't seen you since . . . in forever!"

Since the incident. Since their family and their lives were cracked open. All because of Milton, River thought. Because of the two of them. What might the Johnson boys' lives have been if he had been at that locker to meet Rocco when he was supposed to be? He felt the weight of his anger, his shame, barreling toward them. He was so very angry. At Emmeline. At Odysseus. At Roman. At Milton. At himself.

"Hello, Milton Bradley," Rocco said.

"You having fun?" River asked.

"Everything is too-too," Rocco said.

"It is a lot, isn't it?" Milton said.

Rocco nodded. "I'm going upstairs."

"But you're only here for a few more hours?" River said. Rocco was to return to his new facility later on that evening, per their agreement.

Rocco shrugged.

"Bye, Milton Bradley," Rocco said, and disappeared up the stairs.

"Your mom told me Roman's in Vietnam. Do you get to speak to him ever?"

The truth was that River couldn't remember the last time he'd spoken with his older brother. River hadn't reached out. But neither had Roman. River wasn't sure he'd know what to say.

"I mean. It's kinda long-distance," River said sarcastically.

Milton too looked over at the album. "This is incredible, Riv. Really."

"Mmm-hmm," River said.

"Look, if you didn't want me to come, why did you invite me?" Milton said after a protracted silence.

"I just think it's kinda shitty that you'd come to my party just to score points with your girlfriend."

"What? What are you talking about? I wanted to see you," Milton said quietly.

Holly rejoined them. "Oh my God did I just see the Artful Dodger?"

She looked in the direction of where the British actor stood talking to another young actor.

"Let's go," Milton said.

"But we just got here?" Holly said.

"And I didn't invite you. My mother did," River said.

"Fuck you, River," Milton said.

"Who's that white boy, and what's he so angry about?" Bobby Cornelius said as he snuck up behind River and offered up a drink from the very recently spiked punch bowl.

"Nobody. And he's just mad that his girlfriend wants to suck my dick," River said loudly enough for Milton to hear, and laughed. It was both the crudest and cruelest thing he'd ever said. He regretted it instantly. Holly looked back at him like she'd been punched in the face.

Emmeline looked at him aghast.

"Party's over!" Emmeline yelled above the crowd in the living room. "Everybody out."

"This isn't your house anymore," River said snidely.

"I forgot. We have to sing 'Happy Birthday,'" Rocco said, descending the staircase. "Then I can go back home."

"This is your home, Rocco," Emmeline said gently. River tried desperately to ignore the devastation on his mother's face at that moment.

Odysseus said nothing, having moved through the party most of the afternoon like he wasn't even there.

In front of an enormous sheet cake in the backyard, some of the best acts in the country wished River a happy birthday, all of them trying to out-sing, to outshine one another on the song that felled even the most seasoned of voices.

Still, the only voice River could hear was Rocco's. Even now, he could pick his brother's voice out in a crowd of talent. A little deeper than he remembered, but still so tonally perfect. So beautiful. Better than his own. How long had it been since they'd sung together? He closed his eyes and concentrated until it was only the two of them.

"*Happy birthday to me.*" He harmonized with Rocco.

"Blow out the candles, River!"

"What did you wish for?"

"World peace," River said, and headed through the celebrants toward the front yard.

Inside the quiet of his new Aston Martin Volante, he sank into the caramel leather and opened the box Milton and Holly had brought with them.

It was a small golden starfish paperweight. "Starfish" wasn't one of his singles, but it was River's favorite song on the whole album. Somehow Milton had known. Holly too.

At the bottom of the sea, little old broken me,
At the bottom of the sea, little old broken you
One two three four five
Let's both grow back, brand-new
One two three four five
With you I'm most alive

Engraved at the bottom of the paperweight was simply, "*At the bottom of the sea . . .*" What kind of teenagers gifted another teenager a paperweight? River laughed to himself. It was perfect.

It was too late to go after them. River had been too awful. He was too embarrassed. Besides, he didn't deserve them or anyone else anyway.

He leaned his head against the supple steering wheel.

"Too-too," he said to nobody at all.

CHAPTER THIRTY

ODYSSEUS HAD TAKEN FROM HIS BOY, IT WAS TRUE. BUT HE'D ONLY meant it to be a temporary thing.

He hadn't told Emmeline and the boys about the KKK card taped to a rock that had smashed the front window that night the boys had been recording at the studio with Mr. X. He hadn't told her of all the months of no customers when he'd first opened, or those who would come in seemingly just to gawk at him like an animal. He didn't tell them about how hard it had been to secure that store in the first place, how the landlord had initially not wanted to rent to him for fear it would affect the other businesses. How he had to tell the landlord that he'd served in the war before the landlord would even consider it.

He didn't tell them how he'd had the cops called on him one night because a passerby thought he'd broken in. He didn't tell them about the gun he kept under the register after the window had been smashed. Or the bat in the back. He didn't tell them how the girl he'd briefly hired for the front desk had stolen from him and taken off. He didn't tell them how, in order to start fresh in California, he'd had to go dirty. McAvoy had charged an insane amount of interest on the loan, for the house, the business, and then again for Rocco's bail. It had grown legs and arms and teeth and threatened to bite.

He didn't tell them about what it had been like for him in the war. Or how it had been to come home. He didn't tell them how tired he always was. Or how exhausting the constant pressure of being perfectly palatable, professional, nonthreatening. He didn't tell them how he'd considered moving them all to South Central or the Valley. Hell, even a few miles north. But that he loved the house's proximity to the shop, and the San Gabriel Mountains that he could see from his window. How beautiful Mt. Wilson was on chilly mornings, snowcapped, majestic, and right there.

He didn't tell them how he moved them here 'cause he wanted more, the most for all of them. He didn't tell them how the lessons and the private school and the house and all of it added up to more than he could handle alone. He didn't tell them how he wanted Emmeline to be a stay-at-home mom like all the other moms on the block, because wasn't that a luxury for a Black woman? And didn't his beautiful wife deserve that luxury? To be pampered like all the white women around them?

He didn't tell them that he'd suffered a minor heart attack earlier this year. That the girl at the ice-cream shop next door had called for help and that the ambulance drivers seemed surprised he was a Negro. That the doctor said he needed to take a break. That his scans looked like he'd had another small heart attack before. That they'd wanted to admit him overnight, but he wanted to come home.

He didn't tell them how much guilt he felt for what happened to Rocco. That it wouldn't have happened if he hadn't split the boys into different schools.

He didn't tell them the guilt he felt over exiling Christmas out there all alone, when everybody knew all that boy ever wanted was love. He didn't tell them that Christmas's presence made him remember things he'd tried very hard to forget.

So yes, he didn't tell them that he'd needed money, that he'd taken it, that it had gotten briefly out of hand, and that he'd fixed it. But there were many things he didn't tell them.

═

ULTIMATELY, HE DID finally tell Emmie something as the two of them cleaned up after River's birthday party. River had wanted to pay somebody to do it, but Odysseus said he could, and surprisingly enough Emmeline offered to stay and help. River had snuck off somewhere into the night with Rocco in his new car before it was time to bring Rocco back to the facility.

"Suppose we should have seen that coming," Emmeline said after they'd tried and failed to track their sons down. She bent over to collect a beer bottle left buried and half-drunk in between the couch cushions.

Emmie opened her mouth like she was going to say something and then shut it firmly again. What had that mouth done to that doctor? How had that man touched his wife? Or worse yet, did they share secrets and talk for hours? Did she love him? There would be time to ask her that later, if at all. Maybe when they were older and happier and could look back at this as just some awful time that happened to another younger, more foolish, version of themselves. He couldn't, wouldn't, ask any of that now. Now there was only one thing.

He knelt down in front of her, and grabbed her around the legs as though he were a small child. He rested his head on her thighs. How he missed the way his wife smelled of cocoa butter and Diorissimo. He felt the longing rise up in him. He gently pushed his hands up slowly under her slip, touching the warmth of her thighs.

"Odie, the boys . . ." she murmured.

But she didn't push him away as he lifted the garment higher and higher. Until finally, he walked her over to the couch, gently resting her on its arm, as he pushed her seamed tights downward, her lacy panties to the side so he could taste her. Then Emmie herself frantically pulled both the tights and her underwear down and kicked them off around her ankles. His wife moaned against his mouth, pushed his head closer toward her.

"Oh!" she called out, shuddering against him as he took in as much of her as he could.

And then, a few silent aftershocks. Emmie stood up and quickly grabbed everything off the floor, as though the two of them were a young couple barely known to each other. As though he had not watched her birth the first of their boys at home. Roman crowned before they could even finish gathering up the items meant for the hospital bag when it was closer to her due date. Odie hadn't been prepared for the sheer amount of fluids involved, her waters gushing, running down those same beautiful thighs, how much she'd thrown up while pushing, the bloody mess of the placenta itself flopping to the floor. How messy life was, even in those very first few moments. And with a few subdued whimpers, there he was! Roman!

"I don't remember life before this," she'd said then as they leaned their heads together and stared down in wonder at their baby, his fine newborn hair plastered to his head in a bloody mess. "I mean, obviously I do, but also I don't. Everything else feels very far away and unimportant now, doesn't it?"

At that Roman had opened his eyes, only briefly, and they'd seen him and he, them.

And now how very far away all of that felt. How far away they'd felt from having once been us.

"You think this is what River wished for when he blew out his candles?" Odie tried to joke with his wife. "You and me. Together, I mean."

"I highly, highly doubt that." Emmeline laughed heartily before her face fell suddenly. "I . . . I have to go."

She quickly turned her back to him as she lifted her undergarments up and over her ample bottom. Odysseus felt another wave of desire crest, but he said and did nothing except get up off his knees and reach out a hand to help steady her as she slipped her heels back on.

He leaned in to kiss her and she dodged him, placing her hand up to block her face as though they were in a boxing ring.

And then she left. Odysseus walked back over to the couch and sat down, still smelling of her. He couldn't bring himself to wash her away just yet.

He could wait. He would.

CHAPTER THIRTY-ONE

EMMELINE HADN'T EXACTLY MEANT TO TRY LSD, AND SHE CERTAINLY hadn't meant to have an affair, but both had happened, and there wasn't much she could do about it now.

Now the floor rolled under them. She giggled and swayed. Her life was in shambles. She was in love. Maybe.

Aaron's dark curls stuck to the back of his neck. His shirt had been unbuttoned and his tie cast aside hours ago. His eyes weren't as glassy, but the both of them sprawled immobilized across the faux bearskin rug.

"Rawr," Emmeline said, looking at the bear. If you came across a bear in the woods you were supposed to make yourself larger. It was quite the opposite of everything she'd been told as a woman, and a Black one at that.

"You OK?" he said, stretching out his fingertips to hers.

"I can't believe Odie stole from our child," she said. "What kind of man does that?"

"I don't really want to talk about him right now, Em," Aaron said, not-quite-gently.

"Right," she said. "Of course."

She hadn't told Aaron about what happened after River's birthday party several weeks prior. What she and Odysseus had done together. She hadn't been able to put it out of her mind since.

"Come home," Odysseus had said. But where was that exactly?

Beth had Edie for the weekend and she and her ex-husband were going to attempt to do something together as a family, for Edie's sake.

"Dr. Takahashi said it might be good for her to see us together and getting along," Beth said.

"That sounds smart," Emmeline said. Aaron was nothing if not smart.

"Does he talk about us with you?" Beth said, suddenly shy.

"No. Never. He's a professional!" Emmeline said.

"Right. Except for the whole you-two thing . . ." Beth said, and laughed.

Emmeline felt herself grow hot in the face.

"Oh honey." Beth reached over and held her hand. "I don't judge. Not you."

"I know." Emmeline forced a laugh. She hadn't told Beth about the afternoon with Odysseus either. Though Odie was still her husband technically. Whatever he was, she had barely processed that moment herself; she didn't want to share whatever that had been with anyone else.

"Let's go somewhere." She'd called Aaron from Beth's. "It's a long weekend!"

"Our first vacation?" Aaron joked. "Where do you want to go?"

"I don't actually know much about where people like to vacation in California," she admitted.

"I have just the place," Aaron said.

Halfway up Big Bear Mountain, Aaron had to stop so they could put on snow chains. He knelt before the car with the chains, in the gravel, like some kind of penitent. The cars whizzed by them, taking the curves entirely too fast, and Emmeline briefly thought about stepping in front of a white Cadillac with a blond couple inside.

Across from them, as Aaron wrangled the chains, little cherubic children made a rudimentary snowman and their older sibling made a big snow dick until their father finished putting the chains on their station wagon, saw it, and knocked the teenager about the head.

They'd stopped for liquor, food, and firewood at the kind of folksy wooden structure labeled a "country store." The young bed-headed cashier had followed the two of them around like they were sheep in need of herding.

"We have a special on those!" he said when Emmeline picked up a pair of mittens.

"Thanks, but I'm just looking." Emmeline smiled and put them back.

"Don't forget some salt for your driveway!" the cashier hollered at Aaron. "Never can have too much this time of year."

Aaron nodded. "Thanks, man. Appreciate it."

"You'll need better shoes up here," the cashier said, looking down at Emmeline's heels. "Unless your husband's planning on carrying you everywhere."

Emmeline looked over at Aaron, who gazed back at her adoringly. Neither of them bothered correcting the cashier. She felt a flush of utter delight in her heart and her nethers at the idea of this man as permanently hers, then, inexplicably, a bit of dread. She did everything in her power to push her actual husband to the very furthest reaches of her mind.

"That's exactly what I'll do," Aaron said, swooping her up into his arms and kissing her dizzy. It was the first time they'd done so in public.

"Honeymooners?" the cashier said.

"Something like that," Aaron said. He grabbed up the mittens she'd been looking at and added them to the pile.

"Power to the people," the cashier said, raising a fist as they exited the store, and it took everything in them not to burst out laughing.

"Hey, wait!" The cashier jogged up to the car as they were about to pull back onto the road. "Want some shit that'll blow your mind?"

═══

THAT WAS HOW they wound up frozen on the floor holding hands, Aaron's pale fingers wrapped in hers. The cabin was a drafty A-frame with big windows that opened up to nature itself.

"Was this in the family?" she asked when they first arrived.

Aaron laughed. "Oh no, I bought this a few years ago. Just somewhere to hike and clear my head during the summer. I guess I ski a little too."

From the floor, Emmeline thought the trees outside looked like giants about to crush them. Aaron had put on a record, *Gal Costa.* A friend had introduced him to her.

"A female friend?" Emmeline asked.

Instead of actually answering, Aaron just smiled at her.

She fucking hated when he did that, but she didn't press. She was still married, after all. She had no standing here.

The Brazilian woman's voice was sexy and airy, like something out of a dream, until at the very end of the first song, the notes unexpectedly devolved into cacophony. Emmeline closed her eyes and allowed herself to be transported. The music the kids listened to was so cosmopolitan these days, twelve inches of vinyl stretching across thousands of miles, a 33 rpm plane ride. She wanted to be the kind of woman who handed a man like Aaron this disc and commanded, "Listen!"

They lay there forever, until there was just the static of the record player going in circles.

"We should stop that," Emmeline said.

"What?"

"Stop that!" Emmeline giggled and pointed at the record player.

"Not this," Aaron said.

"No. This is perfect," Emmeline said. Was it?

"I can't move," Aaron said. "Not yet."

The walls around them moved forward and backward as the floor rolled and Emmeline had the feeling of being on a boat, the ocean rolling as she steadied herself, and kept a firm grip on her colorful drink with an umbrella. If she dug deep into her earliest memories, the ones she locked away, the furthest pieces of herself, she remembered being on a fishing boat, the stink of guts and salt in her nostrils. She remembered her hands skimming the water, and watching dragonflies. Who had she been on that boat with? It was a good memory, she thought in the unearthing. Wasn't it? And yet . . .

Now she imagined herself in wide-leg linen pants blowing in the breeze, a scarf wrapped on her head, and big sunglasses, like all those glamorous photos of Jackie O with her new Greek shipping-magnate husband. Or perhaps on a yacht. Not that Aaron owned one.

"Have you ever been on a yacht?" Emmeline asked.

"What do I look like? A Rockefeller?" Aaron said, and they both burst out laughing. "I'm not the one with the superstar for a child."

The world had only just started to right itself when Aaron asked about Christmas.

"Tell me about Christmas. The child. Not the holiday."

"What?" Emmeline said, stunned.

"Rocco said Christmas was his best friend. He also said he was dead."

"Rocco is very imaginative."

Aaron tilted his head and bit his lip. "Emmie . . ."

She liked the way it came off his tongue. He always said her name like it meant something to him. Like she did. Something about him felt like home. Like she could tell him anything.

So, she did.

Emmeline told Aaron about Christmas and how he'd come to live with them, not to mention how he'd left.

Afterward he simply said, "Thank you for sharing that with me. I mean it."

"I'm not crazy, promise."

"We don't use that word. 'Crazy.' " He turned onto his side and leaned against his elbow. "My grandma used to tell us stories of the zashiki-warashi."

"What's that?"

"They're kind of like little ghost children. They stay with a family in the home and sometimes they're mischievous. In some stories, only children can see them. In others, only the members of one family. Depends on who's doing the telling. Your Christmas is like one of those."

"He's not particularly mischievous," Emmeline said.

"My grandmother said they had a zashiki-warashi in the school near their house before the war."

"Which war?"

"The first Sino–Japanese war, I think? I didn't ask . . . I was just a kid."

"Were the schoolchildren scared?"

"When they're in your house, or building, or whatever, they're thought to bring you good luck and prosperity. It's when they leave that things go south."

He rolled onto his back and stared up at the ceiling. "It's all just the stories people tell themselves to try to . . . process, I guess."

"Rocco didn't hurt that boy . . . It was Christmas. That's not just processing. He's real."

"I know, Em. I know."

The four-poster bed looked almost too grand for the room itself, which looked like the interiors of the Lincoln Logs her boys played with.

"Help me make the bed," Aaron said, stumbling as he gathered fresh linens from a wooden chest along the foot of it.

They had stayed up through the night, and the early morning crept in, cool slivers of light across the room.

That very first time with Aaron, how she felt herself suddenly grow very shy at the prospect of being in a bedroom with him. This was where she should say no and volunteer to sleep on the couch. This was where she should snap out of it and return to real life, she'd thought. Now she was silent as they worked together to stretch the edges of the fitted sheet under the mattress. The top sheet was crisp, as though it had been ironed before being placed in that chest. Who had ironed it?

It was dangerous, playing house with another man like this. Reckless.

Still, Aaron reached out his arms to her, and she rushed into them.

The first time they had sex had been both amazing and terrible. It took them forever to get into any sort of rhythm and when they finally did, when she was ready to absolutely explode with desire, he abruptly had to stop and run to the restroom, his pale ass scurrying comically across the room and down the hall. Amazing, because she wanted always to feel his skin on hers, to intertwine her legs with his and to turn and hear his voice.

Afterward, they lay there, heads wine-heavy, with their fingers interlaced, and she wanted nothing more than to keep holding his hand until their individual fingers fell away, faded into oblivion, and there was only the smoothness of touch, touching, having touched, all the tenses past, present, and future in their hands.

═

HOURS LATER, SHE woke up to use the restroom in the cabin, jolted awake by her bladder, as well by Aaron snoring next to her, an entirely jarring sound, like a wild animal being strangled. How could a man so small snore so loud? She still hadn't gotten used to it. She marveled at how blemish-free his skin was, how beautifully smooth the length of him was. She kissed the inside of his forearm, then got up out of the bed, gingerly, so as not to wake him, and walked down the hall.

How long it had been since she'd wandered around in any space naked as the day she was born! The boys were too grown for that sort of thing, and of course there was Christmas. You never could quite be sure when he might pop up beside or across from you. She missed the little boy more than she could bear to say aloud. If she had gotten used to her children out in the world, growing and pushing themselves away, Christmas had been a special gift. He needed her, wanted to be around her, saw her not just as the maker of sandwiches, embarrassing bestower of public kisses, payer of bills, perpetual report-card and field-trip signatory.

Emmeline looked at herself in the bathroom mirror. She was still mostly strong and soft in the right places. There was a small pouch at her stomach, with its topography of rivers and tributaries, where she had held all her dreams for her children, where they had smashed her bladder and torn her muscles from each other. For a year afterward, there was a slight canyon in their wake. Her stretch marks were faint now, thank God. She ran her hands over the breasts that were almost a full inch down from where they once had been, but formidable nonetheless. Her hips had widened, ass spread more with each kid, no matter how many miles she walked. With each child born, her body had fought to take up more space. A mama bear.

"Rawr," she said to herself in the mirror, and laughed.

It was snowing in small flurries. It was the first time she'd seen snow in ages, and she felt compelled to run outside, until she remembered she was butt-naked and it was quite cold. Instead, she ran to the bed, actually more like scuttled, because she was still quite hungover.

"Aaron!" she said, shaking him awake.

"Huh?" He blinked his eyes open, trying to pull her into focus.

"It's snowing!"

He pulled the curtains from the window behind the bed and the two of them looked out at the trees, and the snow, and the houses in the distance, like they were in their own personal snow globe. And wasn't that exactly what it felt like? Aaron shook her up and down until she remembered what was most beautiful about living.

"I've missed snow," Emmeline said wistfully. He pulled her down from the window, close to him, and kissed the back of her neck. The same spot he'd kissed the night before while making love to her from behind, the full weight of him on top of her. She could just barely breathe, and yet each breath felt like the deepest she'd taken in forever.

"You stay right here. I'm going to go make breakfast," he said before pulling on his boxers and heading out the bedroom door.

═══

"LOOK!" EMMELINE EXCITEDLY pointed out the window at a baby black bear playing in the snow. But why was it alone? The cub rolled around on the floor, and down the slight slope in thc yard. "Where's its mama?"

"She's probably around here somewhere," Aaron said gently.

She kept looking around for the mother to appear as the cub scampered up the slope, only to roll back down again.

"Should we go out and help it? What should we do?" Emmeline said with some distress.

"Let's not get mauled, Em," Aaron said. "She'll come. Eventually."

Would she though? In a quick flash, Emmeline saw her Roman out there in a foreign country all by himself. Rocco too was alone in a strange place; she quickly pushed him out of her mind. It hurt too much. And River. Poor River. She knew he blamed himself for everything, could see the weight of it on him, but maybe he sensed that she did too. Try hard as she did not to.

She found herself thinking about how her boys would love this place. Could picture them pelting one another with snowballs, making snow angels, even as Roman insisted they were too old for such things but did it anyway.

"The boys would love it here," she murmured.

Aaron nodded. They had an unspoken agreement not to talk about them, or it took you out of the fantasy. But what exactly was the fantasy, and why? Weren't the boys her little dreams? Just a little bit. Each boy a cloud, a drop of rain, a muddy footprint, a held note, her three boys and Christmas as a poem or a passed piece of paper: "Do you love me? Yes! And how!"

The phone call came just as they'd settled into a game of Scrabble by the fire. Aaron had gone to retrieve a bottle of wine, and the ringing had startled Emmeline from her fantasies. She waited for Aaron to pick it up, and when he didn't, she did.

"Hullo?" she said a little too forcefully, wondering who could have this number.

"Hello?" The voice on the other line sounded young and female and quite confused. "Dr. Takahashi?"

As Aaron barreled into the room with clean wineglasses and a bottle of some recent vintage, Emmeline pointed to the phone in her hand.

"It's for you," she said, covering the mouthpiece. Which seemed quite silly because of course it was; this was his cabin, nobody even knew she was here.

Aaron set the glasses down and brought the phone to his ear. It was his assistant, Rachel, the student who never seemed to be there, and yet here she was. Emmeline exhaled. She hadn't realized she was holding her breath. Aaron nodded and said OK many times, among other things. Then he hung up the phone and said, "Fuck."

"What's wrong?" Emmeline's heart dropped to her stomach. Had Odysseus come by looking for her? Was something wrong with one of her children, her house?

"A patient of mine just . . . she . . . had to go to the hospital last night," he said obliquely. Doctor-patient privilege, Emmeline supposed. She felt a deep and uncomfortable relief that it wasn't anything to do with her.

"Is she OK?" Emmeline asked. "Your patient?"

"I have to go," Aaron said. "She's in crisis. It's bad."

I'm in crisis, Emmeline thought, a rush of all the feelings she had been keeping at bay flooding over her. *What about me?*

She accidentally said it out loud. "What about me?"

Shit. Now she sounded like a selfish cow.

"I guess. I mean . . . we both have to go . . . I'm so sorry, Em."

"Of course!" she said.

Aaron put the fire out while she gathered her things. Not that there was much to gather. They walked through each room, double-checking everything before turning the light out. In the living room, she lingered on the two abandoned wineglasses, the bottle opener, and the full bottle. There was a chill in the air now that Aaron had powered the furnace down.

"Time to go home," Aaron said. "We'll do this another time, I promise."

He tilted her chin toward him and kissed her and she wrapped her arms around him not wanting to let go.

"I want you," she whispered.

"I'm right here."

A wolf howled in the distance. Suddenly, every part of her body felt immensely heavy. The two of them lingered in the doorway, neither wanting to be the one to close it.

CHAPTER THIRTY-TWO

JAIL IN VIETNAM WAS THE SAME AS JAIL IN THE USA. THERE WERE TOO many Black folks in there for dumb or questionable offenses, and too many white boys shown too much leniency for too long. Black men who were in for not trimming their hair, and white boys who were in for murder. In jail it was abundantly clear that whatever was supposed to have united them only existed when they were under attack, and even then, not always.

Roman recognized a guy or two he'd seen around Soul Alley. And another one he'd sold a suit to. They sat together along with the other Black dudes on one side of the yard, while the white men sat on the other. Those who were neither generally sat with the Black dudes. Black or brown barely made a difference to the white men. There were lots of Black men in solitary. And lots of white men who weren't, but should've been.

One of the white men they called Nose. He was a murderer.

"He's a murderer. Stay away," even the white men warned Roman.

"Lots of us are murderers. It's a war," Roman said.

"That one's different. Most of us are here out of some sort of duty, or because we got drafted, but for others, war is a free-for-all. They keep putting us in solitary while letting that motherfucker roam around."

Turns out they called him Nose 'cause he could sniff out fear, and also because it was rumored that he had cut off his victims' nose and ears. When he was arrested, he had a nose in his pocket.

"That's fucking barbaric," Roman said.

"That's Nose."

The Black men listened to the radio and spoke of the revolution. Yusuf was a Muslim convert, although Roman wasn't sure who had time for conversion in the middle of a war. Or maybe that's exactly why he converted. Yusuf always greeted Roman with "As-salamu alaikum." Or "Afternoon, Soul Brother!"

Roman learned to respond, "Wa-alaikum-salaam!"

Roman missed his actual brothers. In the middle of all these men, he felt the pang more acutely. Once, Nose got into a shoving match with Yusuf and the whole jail turned out as though it were the fight of the century. There weren't enough guards to break it up. And the biggest guard who was there looked as though he didn't want to; a fight was something to break up the monotony. Men on both sides of the racial divide jeered. How strange to root for a man who'd carried a nose in his pocket like a trophy. But that was the erotic pull of us-versus-them.

A few of the white boys were cool. Daren from Cincinnati. Nate from Missoula. Banks from somewhere and everywhere. They would sit with the Black men and play dominoes and sing along with Marvin Gaye.

The days blurred together and became more hopeless. Eventually Roman snapped. When Nose bumped into him and said, "Move, nigger!" to everyone's dismay, Roman yelled, "Shut the fuck up, psycho!"

If it weren't for Yusuf, Roman might have died right there. Nose gnashed his teeth and began to pummel Roman, ready to disembowel him and take Roman's nose as a prize. Roman lay on the ground ready to accept his fate.

Instead, Yusuf, praise Allah, lifted Nose off Roman and tossed him across the room. When Nose tried again to charge, Yusuf stopped him in his tracks with a shake of the head. Yusuf was the only person even a sociopath like Nose was afraid of, large as an oak was he.

Still, the fight landed Roman in solitary confinement. Even though the guards had seen it all unfold and had done nothing to stop any of it.

Silver City, as they called confinement, was merely a bunch of shipping containers with ridges like a potato chip. They were hot as hell and the lights bore down on them constantly, a never-ending shit summer. Roman slowly lost his mind. He thought of his parents and his brothers. He thought of Christmas and where he might be. He wondered how much of the Kid's body had decomposed. Roman spent several days wondering if perhaps he himself wasn't already dead. He badly wanted to be. He banged his head and boxed the wall until he cracked and bled. He ran into the wall and knocked himself clean out for who knows how long. Minutes? Hours? The blood had long crusted over when he came to. He cried and called out for ghosts.

And then, one day, as Roman busied himself counting the ants marching across his cell, a man he had never seen before opened his door.

"Come on, brotherman!"

But where was he going? He followed the man out through a sea of other released men.

In the yard, everyone was fighting. Soldiers were using anything possible they could get their hands on. Forks and knives from the mess hall. Hammers. Shovels. Picks. It had the feeling of inevitability. Savagery in black-versus-white.

What a weird thing to fight a race war in the middle of a foreign war. Those who were neither Black nor white mostly joined in with the Blacks, but some just stayed on the periphery, away.

In the chaos, the white men launched a coordinated attack on Yusuf. They jumped on him as though he were not man but beast. They hit and they hit and they hit. Roman ran toward his soul brother.

"Yusuf!" Roman called out. He picked up a nearby shovel from an injured man and smacked the white men away from his friend.

He didn't even have time to register the hit to the back of his own head, just the world around him spinning. This is it, he thought as the world around him went black.

When Roman came to, the Kid was hovering over him.

"Am I dead?" he asked. The Kid laughed and shrugged.

"They're sending you home," the Kid said.

Roman lifted his head and looked around him at the makeshift hospital, at all the soldiers wrapped like half-assed mummies, many of them either missing limbs or missing minds. How funny that in the aftermath, here in their hospital whites, bruised, battered, burned, and maimed, some of them quite literally skinless, they were fully integrated.

"Why are you here?" Roman asked the Kid. "You sold me out."

The Kid laughed and leaned in close to Roman, flicking him in the head. "I only did it 'cause you made a promise and didn't keep it."

He was right, but promises meant nothing in war, did they? Nothing meant anything. They were all nothing. Ideas fighting ideas, black and brown and yellow puppets, expendable proxies for powerful white men far away. Nothing about this war was cold for them.

"How did you find me?" Roman asked.

"I heard about the prison riot from others. Thought I'd come see for myself," the Kid said.

"What others?" Roman said.

"Dead people, you idiot," the Kid said. "We watch you guys sometimes."

"Like television?"

"Like life," the Kid said.

A long-haired nurse in fatigues walked over to Roman's bedside. "Hello, handsome! You're up."

It was falsely cheery, but she had kind eyes. She looked to be Native American, but that could just be the effect of the two long dark braids down her back. The nurse was missing part of her forefinger. What kind of woman could survive a place like this? The nurse caught him staring at her hand.

"Y'all aren't the only ones who get into trouble here." She smiled. "Take this."

He opened his mouth and received the water and the meds.

"I'll come check on you in a bit." The woman patted his hand gently. Roman watched the Kid watch her walk away.

"She has a nice ass," the Kid said. "Too bad you can't look at it from my angle."

"I heard that, kid!" the woman said over her shoulder. And Roman and the Kid burst out laughing together.

"Come home with me now? When I'm done here, I mean," Roman said. "My family can be your new home. In America."

"Fuck America. I need to find my own family," the Kid said.

Roman hoped for his sake they were still alive, but imagined it was equally likely the Kid's family were either dead or fled.

Every part of Roman's body ached.

"Anyway, I just wanted to say goodbye, Roman," the Kid said. "You're getting sent home any day now."

"I'm sorry," Roman said. "I'm really, really sorry for everything. You can keep all the books, by the way."

"I wasn't planning on giving them back" the Kid said with a laugh. He paused for a moment. "Hey . . . Me too. Sorry . . ."

"I really hope you find your family," Roman said.

"I've got time," the Kid said.

CHAPTER THIRTY-THREE

"YOU WEREN'T IN NO MOVIE!" RACIST TOM SHOUTED AT ME AS I REgaled Becky, Gerta the busybody and her babies, and anyone else who would listen about my short life. The inhabitants of the forest had crowded around, as I was apparently a very good storyteller indeed.

"I was too!" I shouted back at him. Tom stayed getting on my nerves and I ain't no liar.

"Don't go picking on that boy just 'cause you're jealous!" Lucretia, the whore, said.

I would never have called her a whore, her real name was Lucretia, but she insisted.

"Ain't no shame in it," Lucretia said. "I was a whore. And I was good. Now, the men who put me here? That's the shame!"

Lucretia was a very smart woman, and I think she probably could've ruled the world if she had been born later.

"Jealous of what?" Tom scoffed. "He's dead just the same as you and I."

Tom wasn't wrong; I was very dead. In fact, my death was just what I had been about to tell Becky about. Now, normally that would be a very depressing bedtime story indeed, but since Becky was herself also quite dead in the most wretched of ways, it wasn't so bad.

After Tom finally stopped his yapping, I started the story of my very tragic and untimely demise.

I had a bad feeling as we'd come into town and told Mr. Farraday I wasn't sure about this place. But I was just a little Black boy and Mr. Farraday was a grown man, plus the place had beautiful mountains all around it and a field full of poppies, which Mr. Farraday said were a sign of good luck.

"They are?" Becky asked.

"No. He lied."

The grown-ups were still mad at Mr. Farraday for not increasing their wages, but he assured them that at this performance we could command some of our biggest to date. I wasn't sure how that was supposed to work, but I knew it had something to do with me. I was to be the biggest draw for two reasons of which I was aware. Firstly, because *Amos 'n' Andy* was all the rage on the radio those days, and Mr. Farraday thought if I could play it up to the crowd ("be really Black" he said), a little of that love might rub off on us.

More important, nine boys in Alabama had just been accused of raping two white women on a train while hoboing, and Mr. Farraday thought the Southern audience might respond very well to "a good-natured little darkie who knew his place." In so doing, I could help my race, he said. And make lots of money when we passed the hat.

The crowd looked like our usual crowd. White men and women, some of whom dressed in their finest for the evening's entertainment, and some of whom looked like they'd just come from the fields with long beards and dirt still under their nails and in the creases of their necks. They laughed and roared and clapped at all the right times. Fanny was especially on that night, and the men up front got extra rowdy. Those in the crowd were only white because Fanny was half-naked, and weren't no coloreds allowed to pay money to see a white woman in next to nothing. And also because there were no coloreds allowed anywhere near their town after dark anyway. Excepting the entertainment.

Before I went on, Mr. Farraday squatted down to face me. "You gotta do your absolute best out there OK?"

"Yessir!" I said. I always did my best.

When I came on, I did my usual. I danced my acrobatic pickaninny dance. I sang my happy pickaninny songs. I performed with a watermelon grin and the lightest feet and the broadest of gestures. And between these songs I told the pickaninniest of jokes. The crowd roared and stomped and I could feel the energy surging through my limbs and lungs. When normally I would bid the crowd adieu and Mr. Farraday would come out to wrap up the show, instead I decided it was time. He had told me to do my very best, and so I would.

"I would like to present this very special audience with a very special treat." I stood up straight and closed my eyes. Tonight, I was going to sing my absolute best, just as Mr. Farraday'd told me to, for these white folks, yes, but also for those nine boys in Scottsboro, and for myself.

Maybe, in another language, they might see us as human.

I knew every last word to the opera and my very favorite part when Violetta sings *Amami, Alfredo! Love me, Alfredo . . . love me as much as I love you!*

I felt her words in my fingertips and toes. My voice could hit all of Violetta's notes with relative ease. That night, I sang with my whole heart and willed the crowd to receive my words. To love me as much as I loved them!

For the first few bars of the song, the crowd laughed heartily thinking it was all a joke. Then they grew silent, enraptured even.

"That was the word Ms. Elizabeth and Ms. Liza used," I said. "Enraptured."

You could hear the sound of the crowd collectively holding its breath, the drunks sweating out their whiskey, the ladies flapping their dainty handheld fans in the thick night air. When I finished, I stood straight up and took a deep bow. Half the crowd was euphoric and the other half booed.

"Who this little nigger think he is?" somebody shouted.

"I am Christmas Jones the Third," I replied. "Good night!"

After the show, Liza and Elizabeth gave me pecks on the cheeks. "That was fabulous!"

Fanny smushed me into her perspiring bosom. "Smashing!"

I fed Dottie a carrot, and her trainer had her bow to me. "Well done!"

Peter raised up both his swords in triumph.

"You must never do that again!" Mr. Farraday said, grabbing me up by my collar.

"Wasn't I good?"

"Christmas, these white people don't want to pay to watch a little nigger put on airs."

"I was singing!" I said.

"You let him call you a nigger?" Lucretia interjected.

"He didn't really mean it like that . . . I think," I said. "Please, don't interrupt."

Later, in the crowd, I saw a swish of taffeta and silk, like an upside-down rose, and I ran to hug Elizabeth and Liza. I gripped tightly around their hips, waiting to be comforted.

"I did well, right?" I pleaded, looking for just a little bit of love.

Only, it was not my two-headed lady. It was a one-headed lady and her very face was bright red. With drink, yes, but also, with total indignation.

"He's touching me!" she screamed, apoplectic. "The nigger child is touching me!"

"No. I didn't mean it, honest!" I said. "I thought you were my friends!"

The men around her charged into action, kicking and punching, beating me ferociously until Mr. Farraday and the others came running. The elephant trainer snapped at the men with his whip, Peter brandished his swords, and they scrambled off me.

"It was a mistake!" I cried, my eye already starting to swell from where the men had kicked it.

"He's just a boy!" Elizabeth yelled. "He didn't mean anything by it. I promise he'll be punished!"

"Damn right, he will!" a most belligerent man replied. He was so drunk he could hardly stand up.

When the commotion finally died down, Mr. Farraday instructed me to stay by the elephant trainer's side. He had a whip, and in his sleeping quarters he had a pistol for the towns where people got too close to them, or thought thieving was an option. Plus, Dottie could crush a man's skull if need be.

"You trained her to do that?" I'd asked the trainer.

"The trainer before me," the trainer said. "Dottie had some rough years."

"Didn't we all?" Fanny sighed.

They decided to sleep in a circle to keep a lookout for trouble.

"We're family!" Liza declared, and I saw Mr. Farraday swoon at his brave girl just a bit.

Late that night, I had to pee. I made my way outside of the circle, but not far. I thought I could be heard if I yelled for help. It wasn't close enough.

There were three men. The first man stuck a moonshine-soaked dirty cloth in my mouth, and as soon as I tried to scream, the moonshine burned bitter down my throat. They dragged me away from Liza and Elizabeth, away from Dottie, away from Fanny, away from Mr. Farraday, away from everything at all.

They tortured me and called it justice. They burned and slashed and cut away important pieces of me and I screamed louder than I'd sung, "Love me!"

Nobody could hear me.

I paused for dramatic effect, but I needn't have. Becky was now sound asleep, as were the little baby bunnies. The adults were silent. Lucretia crossed herself.

Tom sat across from me, wiping away tears. For somebody who was always trying to act all tough, he really was such a crybaby.

"We should find those men and kill them!" Tom said.

Most of them probably were still alive and moving through the world as though they hadn't killed a little boy in the most savage of ways. They were probably members of their local city council, or kindly grandfathers, according to their grandchildren, who were likely about my age by now. I didn't want to kill anybody though. All I'd ever really wanted was to be loved.

CHAPTER THIRTY-FOUR

"THEY WANT YOU ON A SUPER SUGAR CRISP BOX, RIV? ISN'T THAT great!" River's new manager, Arnie, said.

Arnie sat next to River at all of these meetings where loads of crusty old white men with limited-edition Rolexes and very important Rolodexes wined and dined him, trying to get him to endorse different products. River liked having Arnie there as a buffer between himself and these businessmen who he wasn't entirely certain would have been all that in favor of the Civil Rights Act but were all too ready to make money off a sixteen-year-old Black kid.

Arnie was the kind of white man who always looked a little red, whether from anger, drink, or pleasure, one couldn't be sure. His aviator glasses took up the whole airspace that was his face and gave character to an otherwise very forgettable visage. Arnie couldn't sing or play any instrument to save his life (not for want of trying), but he had a knack for recognizing talent, and the connections that came from going to a super-exclusive private school in Sherman Oaks. He had gone to business school to satisfy his parents, then dropped out to manage a number of acts. Mostly all those white folks who were a bit whiny for River's taste and did lots of psychedelics while playing plaintive guitar and sleeping together in the cabins around Lookout Mountain.

It was rumored that Arnie himself had slept with a few of his acts too. None of them female. But River didn't give that much credence as Arnie was unmarried, over the age thirty, and that tended to be the going rumor for single men of a certain age in the industry, even in these modern times. There were tales of pool parties full of beautiful men, powerful men cavorting in various states of undress and tucked out of sight in neo-Spanish mansions.

A friend had told River the rumors after River secretly put out feelers as to who might be a good manager to usher him into the next stage of his career. At least, that's the way he framed it. Not "I'm pissed that my father betrayed me and can't bear to look at him, much less have that fucker manage my money even a minute longer."

"I don't know, Riv," Ty said. Ty had been the assistant tour manager on River's very first tour with the now-infamous gone-too-soon guitar player. "Cargill's rumored to be a faggot. Like not even a little bit, like a huge one."

"What's the difference?" River asked.

Ty shrugged. "I'm just saying."

"Does he get shit done?" River asked.

"Yeah. But . . ." Ty trailed off.

That's how River found himself in Arnold Cargill's small, shabby office off Wilshire, only blocks away from Rodeo Drive. Rather than facing the hustle and bustle of Wilshire itself, all the moving and shaking that might be going on outside of its walls, the office faced onto a very small parking lot where several young men in ill-fitting suits looked to be commiserating while taking a smoke break. It did not inspire confidence.

"If I had any sense, I would've turned around and left immediately," River often joked in the meetings with Arnie that were to follow.

Arnie's secretary was a lithe, blond young man not too much older than River himself, who whispered before River could even open his mouth to announce himself, as though he knew River was deciding whether to stay, "It doesn't look like much, but don't let that fool you. He's very good, River Johnson. You're gonna love him."

The secretary winked, and River wasn't sure he'd caught the joke. Or was he the joke? He'd missed out so much on interacting with people his own age. It was as though they spoke a whole other language, knew references that he should, but didn't.

"Sorry, I didn't get your name?" River said.

"I wish it were something interesting like Ziggy, or River, but my parents have given me the truly boring name of Paul," the young man said with a sigh.

"Can't you change it? Doesn't everyone reinvent themselves here?" River said. He was accustomed to being surrounded by all kinds of people who had clearly shed their old skins and openly left them on the ground for estranged parents, abusive ex-lovers, and former bullies to collect, only to say to any sucker who would listen, "This once was mine."

"You didn't! Isn't River Johnson your given name?"

River nodded. It was weird how people he met knew so much more about River than he did about them. He hadn't introduced himself to somebody who did not know at least some crumb of his life cake in quite some time.

"Are you a musician too?" River asked.

"Oh God no," Paul said. "Can't sing, can't dance. I'm not bad-looking in person, but really only from certain angles on camera. I've made my peace with it."

"But you're young?" River said gently. "Maybe your face isn't done growing?"

Paul shrugged. "I'm older than you. I know things already. And one of the things I know is that I'm content just to do a little of this and a little of that. My father is one of the most ambitious people I've ever met. He's made truly obscene amounts of money, never mind that he already had oodles to begin with. And that guy is one of the most miserable fucks I've ever met."

Everyone River encountered was trying to be somebody—waiters were actors, valets had demos. This was a town of people lying in wait. How strange, then, to meet somebody content just to be! Still, it seemed to River such a privileged-white-kid thing to say. Money, not important?! Happiness looked different when you were colored. Money forced them to treat you like you were human. Sometimes, anyway. Odysseus had drilled this into his boys. Odysseus had never been a Communist, not because of any moral argument but because he figured he, and by extension, his boys, needed to live in what was, rather than what could be. But fuck his father. River guessed he and this skinny white boy had at least that sentiment in common.

In any case, Paul had been right about Arnie. River had hit it off with him instantly. Not because of anything that Arnie had said really, though he had said all the right things, but rather it was a feeling that River hadn't had in quite some time. With Arnie, and even with Paul the secretary, River felt almost . . . safe.

"Why are you here?" Arnie asked him before River had even sat down in the overstuffed couch across from him.

"My father stole from me," River said. He was surprised at how quickly it came out of his mouth.

"Anybody else know?" Arnie said.

"No."

"Do you want anybody to know?" Arnie said.

"No," River said.

"It's awful when you can't trust the people who are supposed to take care of you, isn't it? But that's family business, isn't it?" Arnie said in a measured tone. "We'll keep it out of the press."

"We? I haven't even decided whether or not this"—River gestured between the two of them—"if this is gonna work."

"You wouldn't have told me about your father otherwise," Arnie said.

He wasn't wrong.

"Look. The world is yours," Arnie said, clasping his fingers behind his head. "You tell me what you want, kid. You got it."

And what did River want? Rocco, Roman, and Christmas. A father who had not stolen from him. A mother who hadn't abandoned him without so much as a word of explanation. A friend. That might be nice.

Apart from that, River supposed the rest of the world would have to do.

Upon hearing through "the grapevine" (of course the loose lips belonged to Ty) that River was taking meetings with new management, Odysseus hadn't begged and pleaded with him not to let him go. And he certainly hadn't apologized profusely for embezzling.

"You gotta do what you gotta do, River," is all his father said.

At a party later that very same week, River had run into Marva, with whom he'd been on tour what felt like damn near a lifetime ago. When River told her he was looking to move out of his parents' house, she'd told him she was subletting her place in Whitley Heights while she went on a small solo tour, first stateside, then abroad.

"You can even hear concerts at the Bowl from the balcony!" she said. "Gotta climb a bunch of steps to get to it, but you're young! It's good exercise and the view's worth it."

Odysseus offered to help him move in, but River told him no need, wasn't much to move. His father had looked pained but said nothing. River might've said it out of spite, but it was the truth. When he opened the door to Marva's house, his for the next several months, River had his whole life in only two suitcases. Plus, a box full of records that he'd fetch from the car after catching his breath.

Within weeks of being hired, Arnie got to work securing new deals, of which the Super Sugar Crisp box was only the first. Riv's favorite cereal as little kid had been Post Count Off with the rocket on the box propelling into the Great Beyond and the numbers shooting into the future. He'd even saved the two box tops and got the posters.

"You can count on it!" he and Rocco would shout along with the commercial.

Mostly they had grown up eating Cream of Wheat. Odysseus did not want the boys to rot their teeth with cereal, though every so often Emmeline snuck a little something special into the week's grocery shopping. River took a special pleasure in the fact that his dad definitely wouldn't have approved of this particular sugary cereal.

Soon after the Super Sugar Crisp box, River was offered his own TV show. A musical revue.

For the musical revue, Arnie told River he would have to be on his A game. River still wasn't even a grown-up and yet they expected him to hold his own talking to other famous people, performing in skits with them, and Lord knows what else. It was a lot of responsibility for a kid.

"But if anyone's up for the challenge, it's you!" Arnie clapped him hard on the back. Arnie was often clapping him so hard on the back that it took River a second to catch his breath.

River desperately wished he had his brothers with him. That he could make his television-hosting debut as part of the family group Odysseus had envisioned all those years ago.

He hadn't known how lonely success would be.

"You gotta make sure you fucking wow them!" Arnie said as they brainstormed with the executives what the shape of his show would be. *The Judy Garland Show* only had twenty-six episodes, and Judy was a megastar. *The Sonny & Cher Comedy Hour* had only recently found its footing. A Saturday-morning cartoon might even be in the cards, given River's age, but they wanted a bigger audience than that for him. That said, most revues didn't stay on too long, according to Arnie.

River didn't have many dance moves of his very own, but he remembered those that Christmas had done for them in the backyard, the ones his brother had repeated and gotten ostracized for that day in the cafeteria. There was something there, if you modernized the dance just a bit. He'd suggested as much to his father.

"Why can't we do a modernized version of it?" River had asked that night, way back when. "The audience would love it."

"I don't want my son out there doing pick'ny moves," Odysseus had argued. "Your mother and I fought entirely too hard for you boys to be who you are. To be up there with dignity. I'll not have you out there cooning for white folks."

"How is it cooning? It's not like we're singing those Al Jolson songs, or in Blackface or whatever," River whined. "I just want to dance."

"Nobody's stopping you from dancing," Odysseus said. "Dance all you want!"

Now his daddy couldn't hardly tell River what to do, and River's act needed a bit of a refresh. Things were changing fast in music these days. In the world. He needed to stand out. To cement his place at the top. The new show *Soul Train* was full of great dancers; ordinary Black folks who were inventive, who buzzed with energy, who could get down with the very best of them. Who brought their joy, their verve, onto television screens and into homes across the nation. River needed to stand out in a crowd full of extraordinary ordinary people.

And so he choreographed a new dance routine for himself with several of the moves that Christmas had shown the Johnson Three—pickaninny, vaudeville, cakewalk, wherever else Christmas had gotten them from. There wasn't anything wrong with the dancing itself really, right? River took those old moves and shaped them into something new.

Finally, to cap it all off, River took the signature move, where Christmas shimmied and shook, got up on his tippy toes and leaned all the way back before finishing with a twirl. He practiced until it looked effortless. Until it looked like River, like Christmas before him, was floating.

"Fuck! That's it!" Arnie shouted.

Paul leapt up and down beside him, hands on his cheeks. "What did I just watch?"

And with that, River was ready for his television-hosting debut.

CHAPTER THIRTY-FIVE

THE BIRD STREETS WERE SO NAMED BECAUSE EACH WAS NAMED AFTER a kind of bird. Blue Jay Way. Skylark. Oriole. Nightingale. How delicate, how provincial for streets with such titans! Arnie's assistant, Paul, flew around their avian curves in a hand-me-down forest-green Du Pont. River had quickly learned that the very rich in Los Angeles loved playing at being merely a half rung and stroke of good fortune above middle class. Hand-me-down cars. Streets named after birds. Birds were democratic in the truest sense, flying over and shitting on rich and poor alike.

Paul knew everyone, and everyone knew Paul. Paul had decided he and River were going to be friends. And, not having any, River wasn't inclined to say no. It didn't take long before River was a fixture at all the parties.

"Is a thrasher a bird?" River asked. Normally, he'd be afraid to ask such a thing, lest he reveal his own ignorance, but Paul had a way of putting him at ease.

"I guess so! But I'm no ornithologist, darling," Paul said, and giggled as they pulled into their destination. "Oooh, would you look at that!"

At first, River thought Paul meant the house, which did seem large, but not all that impressive given that all you could really see from the street was the garage. Then he followed Paul's eyes to the floppy-haired valet. The valet, with his aquiline nose, leaned against a pillar waiting for them to exit the Du Pont, like a Greco-Roman statue who'd rather be attending a Vietnam protest. River expected the valet's eyes to widen, or some acknowledgment of who River was, seeing as how River was pretty famous now, last he checked. Instead, the valet nodded at them both, glanced at Paul's car, and upon taking Paul's keys said rather laconically, "Enjoy."

Inside, on a circular red velvet couch, a rock star whose greatest hits were behind him wrapped his sinewy arms around two girls, one dark, one light, who looked to be even younger than River. Across from him, the director of that summer's biggest blockbuster was in deep conversation with a freckled redhead who could've been his daughter. She rested her pink fingernails on the man's hairy arms, occasionally reaching up to twirl her small fingers through his graying hair.

Paul gestured in their direction. "So many of these fuckers like 'em young. And their parents just sign 'em over. If they ever had any to begin with. Lot of them are runaways."

River had the very self-pitying thought that it wasn't too dissimilar from how his parents had signed him over. But hadn't he sold himself as much as anything? He'd been so quick to kick Roman out at the earliest sign of trouble. But he'd been so very young then. He wondered if the girls felt the same. As though she'd read his mind, one of the girls caught his eye and smirked.

The girl wore a full-length mink coat and tattered jeans, her dark curls were cropped close to her head like a boy's. Her mouth took up most of the real estate on her face, but it was in definite competition with her eyes, which looked hungry. She and River were the only Black folks at the party, as far as he could tell. River immediately felt as though he'd known her for a very long time, but also that he should run far, far away. Grown women threw themselves at him now; River was not afraid of girls. But something about this girl unmoored him. River retreated to where he felt safest, the dance floor. They were playing his song.

What had once been the dead boy's was now River's signature move. And because Arnie advised it, River agreed to allow his likeness on all manner of "official" merchandise. On lunch boxes, T-shirts, on posters, on calendars, on anything and everything you could imagine, they printed the "teen sensation" in silhouette.

Flanked by the rich and famous, River danced as they tried to imitate Christmas's move alongside him. Even as he chuckled at his good fortune, he couldn't help but wonder, was it stealing? Christmas was very dead and couldn't much entertain a huge crowd, now, could he? And River had changed it just enough, hadn't he?

Poolside, their caftans swinging side to side, the actresses and muses danced, and River took his place alongside them. He twisted and twirled and snapped, and they clapped in delight and stomped their platforms slightly off-beat.

"Oh, but you're so handsome." They giggled as Los Angeles twinkled down below.

Everybody clapped as the song ended and there were those few glorious moments when River was punch-drunk on attention. When he finally came down, the Black girl in the mink was staring at him, some sort of fizzy drink with a cherry atop in hand, her rock star nowhere to be seen.

She disappeared inside and River went to follow her.

Back into the house, through a kitchen, and up one flight of stairs, he followed at what he hoped was a non-creepy distance until, finally, he caught up with her on a tiled balcony staring down at the crowd gathered below.

Upon having caught up with her, he didn't know what to say.

"Is Jonesie your boyfriend?" was the first thing he said. It was awful.

"We're friends," she said, back still turned, her face lifted to the stars.

"He's so old," River said. He knew he sounded petulant, but he couldn't help himself.

"He's nice," she said.

"Still . . ." River said. "Isn't it kinda creepy?"

"Nice to meet you too, River Johnson." She laughed and turned to him, leaning her elbows against the iron railing, which wobbled.

"Be careful," he said. "Sorry, I didn't catch your name?"

She smirked and River couldn't tell if she was being smug, or flirty, or if she was simply embarrassed by her teeth.

The girl had a gap in between her top two front teeth, bottom ones too, not quite big enough for a pencil but definitely for an angry kernel of popcorn. It was as though her teeth were pulling the curtains on themselves. Nobody had ever made her wear braces. Or perhaps they hadn't had the money to pay for them.

"I can look after myself, thank you very much," she said.

"I didn't mean to offend you," River said.

After chugging the last of her drink, leaving the maraschino cherry split on the rim, she placed the emptied glass onto the tiled balcony floor, where it joined a host of others. River thought briefly that she might try to kiss him. Instead, the girl raised herself up on her tiptoes and came the closest anyone else he'd ever met had come to executing Christmas's move. Then, wordlessly, River did it and she mirrored him, until finally they were dancing together and laughing. They were the youngest people at the party by far, and for once, with her, River felt like the kid he still was. He hadn't felt like a kid in such a long time.

"My muse!" The rock star appeared behind them, two sheets to the wind and another two drinks in hand. "I've been looking all over for you. I have somebody I want you to meet!"

White powder still circling one nostril, the man was unsteady on his feet. He quickly extended a drink to the girl, replacing the one she'd just set down, and River immediately had the urge to push him over the balcony.

"It's a school night!" River said to the man assertively, and both of them started to laugh. He felt like the biggest dork in the world.

"Good one, kid," the rock star said, and ushered her away.

Thinking it would be entirely too awkward to follow the two downstairs, instead River stayed up on the balcony looking out at the city below. He reached down to grab the maraschino from atop the girl's drink, and popped it into his mouth, sweet but with the lingering bitterness of spirits.

On the streets below, a drummer threw a drumstick at an unruly fan, a young woman got catcalled by horndogs cruising Sunset, and apartment-dwellers dreamed of what it might be to live just a mere three or four blocks skyward.

River went in search of Paul and finally found him smoking a cigarette up front with the Greco-Roman valet. "Hey, do you know anything about that girl?" River asked.

"What girl?" Paul said.

"Never mind," River said.

"We gotta get this kid to some better parties," Paul slurred. "Don't we?"

The valet concurred.

"He's not ready yet though, is he?" Paul said, and winked.

The valet demurred.

River wasn't sure what any of it meant other than that Paul was fucked up and definitely shouldn't drive them back.

CHAPTER THIRTY-SIX

A SLUG INCHED ITS WAY ACROSS THE DRYING EARTH AT EMMELINE'S knees. She watched the slow, slimy trail it carved, leaving some shimmering part of itself behind.

"Do you think maybe we could arrange for a dinner with the boys?" Aaron said as she pulled a dandelion rosette up by its scalp.

He continued as Emmeline batted away a particularly pesky gnat, "When Roman returns? I think it would be nice for us to get to know one another."

As a surprise, Aaron had purchased a pair of gardening clogs and gloves so she could join him. Except, Emmeline wasn't sure she actually enjoyed gardening herself. Rather, she just liked sitting next to him as he did the thing that he enjoyed, seeing how much pleasure he got from the growing, the seeding, the dirt underneath his nails, the life.

"I'm not sure that's a good idea," she responded.

"Em, what are we doing here?" He stood up and brushed the dirt off his pants.

She sighed. When they'd first started, being with Aaron had been like taking in a deep breath while swimming far from shore, something that made it so she could keep going. And now . . . how she missed home. The way Odie flopped his arm all heavy on her in the middle of the night, inching nearer, even as he was fast asleep. The way the boys stuck their feet in each other's faces and belched in each other's ears, followed by the most ridiculous boyhood giggles. Or the way River and Roman would patiently lie next to Rocco on the lawn, tiny little cups of sugar water in all of their hands as they held their breath and waited for Rocco's butterflies. Odie's mouth on hers had conjured up so many things.

She'd loved being his, being theirs. They were all scattered to the wind, but it wouldn't be forever. It couldn't be.

Still, she and Aaron might have been OK, had it not been for what had happened earlier that week in the garden.

Emmeline had stretched out on the wooden bench by the birdbath to soak up the sun. Around her, the blooming perennials beckoned for bees. She was lost in a copy of *The French Lieutenant's Woman* when she heard a voice call out.

"You!" An older white woman still in her rollers peeked over the fence. The woman's skin was near-translucent, pale and paper-thin, as though she hadn't left her house in years until just this very moment, just in time to pester Emmeline as she tried to get a little afternoon sun.

Emmeline looked around to make sure the woman was in fact referring to her.

"That's not your house!" the woman yelled, shrill. "You don't belong here!"

"I'm . . ." Emmeline paused and searched for the words. Was she Aaron's girlfriend? She was still married. What was she? "I'm with Aaron!"

Plus, she'd wanted to yell, *Do you know who you're talking to? Do you know who my son is?*

"I'm calling the police!" the woman yelled.

"I'm friends with Aaron Takahashi! The man who owns the house!" Emmeline said. "Call him. You'll see."

Still, she wasn't going to wait around for trouble. There was her safety to consider, never mind that River was famous enough it could make the news. Emmeline had taken her book and left through the side gate, gotten in her car and driven around, not knowing where to go, shaken.

"Joan's a busybody, but she's mostly harmless," Aaron had said when she'd unloaded the afternoon's goings-on upon his return from work.

"Not if the police had come while I was still there," Emmeline said. She found herself back in the kitchen with Odie and the boys, hearing the sickening thud of Roman's head slammed against the tile, Rocco's screams ripping through her body as the police officers had violently wrested her child from her. "Mama!"

"Do you want me to go talk to her?" Aaron said.

"I want you to want to go talk to her," she finally responded.

Earlier, in his sock drawer, she'd found a ring, a large emerald surrounded by diamonds on a simple gold band, and tried it on. Her fingers rarely fit normal rings. She played with the exquisite ring, making a tiny Hula-Hoop of it around her empty left index finger.

"This isn't fun anymore," she abruptly said to Aaron, taking off her gardening gloves and holding them by her side.

"Relationships aren't supposed to always be fun," he replied.

"Yes, but affairs are," she said, "aren't they?"

She regretted it immediately. He looked at her, then down at his chest as though there was an actual wound that needed to be stanched.

"You don't have to do this, Emmeline," he said quietly. "Not this way."

It was too late to turn back. She felt herself once more a little girl with some unknowable rot at the core of herself, orphaned and abandoned in St. Joseph's Sanitarium with her poor hobbled heart. She wanted to kick. To scream. But Emmeline was an adult now. And so, there were simply words.

"Who is that emerald for?" she asked. "Not me, I hope."

He shook his head. "Stop."

"I think I should go back home," Emmeline said.

"Is this because Roman is returning?" he asked.

"I'm not one of your patients," she said. "You don't treat adults, remember?"

She still hadn't told him about her encounter with Odie. But did she owe him that? Odie was her husband, after all. Even without that, there were many little things Aaron seemed to get mad at her for, ever since they'd returned from their brief vacation. How she responded to something he'd shared with her. The way she said "that's interesting," when she found something interesting and was turning it over in her mind before elaborating.

"If you don't find it interesting, you don't have to say that," he'd snap before she could even gather her thoughts.

How annoyed he seemed to be by things that Odie had never faulted her for. Had never even mentioned as faults. And how often Aaron seemed to talk not with, but at her. She was starting to feel their time together like a winter quilt come spring. Even Beth had noticed.

"You open that front door like it's the heaviest thing in the world after you're with him sometimes," Beth said after Emmeline came over after the fight about Aaron's neighbor. Across from Beth, Edie sat contently flipping through the pages of an illustrated book of fairy tales that Emmeline had bought her for her birthday.

"She's reading it!" Emmeline said excitedly.

"I think she's just flipping through the pictures." Beth had been ground down by the institute's failure thus far to help Edie find her words.

Emmeline could've sworn she heard the girl grunt in response.

"Maybe it's OK if it's over, honey?" Beth said softly to Emmeline.

The words rolled around in Emmeline's mind for a whole week until that fateful day in the garden.

"The ring belonged to my grandmother," Aaron said calmly.

She hated how his calm felt like condescension.

"You're just running away 'cause things are hard right now, Emmie."

"No, I'm not," she said, and placed the gardening gloves on the ground next to him.

She wasn't running away at all. Quite the opposite.

═══

ODYSSEUS STOOD ACROSS the street from the house on Mar Vista and tried to picture everything Emmeline might see. The ways it had changed since she'd last lived there. The shrubs had been cut back more than she usually would tell him to. He'd placed in a whole new lawn the other weekend after her call. Spent hours laying fertilizer, row after row of fresh green. He thought by now the smell of the dung might've abated. But how it lingered. Everything needed to be perfect.

He decided to move the flowerpots over closer to the stairs. They made more sense there. No longer were there little boys with careless limbs or wayward balls to threaten the begonias. It would be just them, Odie and Emmie. And, upon his return, Roman.

Roman they would have to deal with. Somehow. War would have changed him. Odie didn't know the details of why he'd been dishonorably discharged, but he could picture it well enough. Some things didn't change, not even abroad. Odysseus got that.

He tried not to let the resentment creep in. Tried not to think of where that man had touched Emmeline and how much she might have liked it. Tried even harder not to think of whether they'd exchanged secrets or,

God forbid, even spoken of Odysseus himself. Once, just once, he'd driven by the doctor's house. Had wanted to huff and puff and go up to the home and tear it shingle by shingle, barehanded, with Emmie and the doctor in it. Entertained thoughts of ringing the doorbell and punching the man square in the jaw, or the gut, of ripping him limb from limb, just as he'd thought nothing of ripping out Odysseus's very heart and claiming it as his own. Emmie was not a possession, he reminded himself. From entirely too young an age, his wife had belonged to nobody but herself.

Odysseus was hardly done taking the roast out of the oven, pouring the wine, when the doorbell rang.

"Hello," Emmeline said as Odie whisked open the door, potholders making floppy mitts of his sturdy hands.

"Let me help you." Odysseus lifted up the suitcases that she'd taken with her all those many months ago. She hesitated in the doorway.

"I don't know where to even begin," she said.

"We don't gotta talk about it right now, Emmie," Odie said. He lifted her face to his. "All that matters is that you're home. We got time. All the time. You know what I mean?"

"I do," Emmeline said, and stepped over the threshold. "Is that roast I smell?"

"I picked up a trick or two while you were away," Odie said.

"Oh, you did, did you?" Emmeline raised her eyebrows.

"Only in the kitchen," he said.

"We'll see," she said.

THAT NIGHT, EMMELINE got ready for bed in the bathroom. Went in wearing her day clothes and emerged wearing a nightie he didn't recall seeing before.

"That new?" he asked.

"I didn't have enough to wear at Beth's," she said defensively.

"Didn't mean nothing by it, Em," he said.

She reached for his hand across the bed and he took it, kissing her fingers, then her palm and bringing the back of her hand to rest momentarily on his cheek. Then he curled his body up next to her, feeling himself reborn.

She held her husband and tried not to think of the emerald ring in Aaron's drawer. Of the mama bear in the cabin. Of the garden at dusk. This was where she belonged, she was sure of it.

Still, in Aaron's garden, she remained, in some shimmering part.

CHAPTER THIRTY-SEVEN

NEARLY A MONTH AFTER EMMELINE'S RETURN, SHE AND ODYSSEUS ACcidentally bumped butts in the small Jack-and-Jill bathroom that connected the boys' rooms. On one side, Emmeline fastidiously scrubbed the sink, while on the other, Odysseus fastidiously scrubbed the toilet, both of them so wholly absorbed in the task of making sure everything was perfect for Rocco's and Roman's arrivals that they didn't realize they'd wandered into each other's provinces. Emmeline laughed as Odie turned and, this time, intentionally swatted at her behind with a yellow cleaning glove. He loved hearing his wife laugh. He loved that he made it happen.

They had spent the last several weeks in some liminal space between being little more than roommates and a return to the familiarity of domesticity. Occasionally, Odie felt the old resentments creep in. He'd wanted nothing more than for Emmeline to be home with them, and now that she was, sometimes he looked over at her while they were watching TV and thought, *How could you? How dare you!*

And then, she would cut her eyes as though she were able to read his very thoughts, before excusing herself for bed.

But increasingly there were fewer moments like that, and more glorious ones like this. Now Emmie took her gloves off, placed them on the sink, and wrapped her arms around his waist, pressing her cheek into his shoulder.

First they would pick up Rocco, the facility having granted him a furlough for the weekend to greet his big brother returned from war. Then they would go to LAX, where all of them, even River, would wait for Roman to return to them (though the logistics of how exactly their famous offspring would just stand and wait, un-accosted, in such a public place eluded them).

"Do you think he hates us, Odie?" she said.

"Which kid?" Odie said.

"Both? All?" She laughed ruefully.

"I can't imagine Rocco hating anyone," he said truthfully.

It was hard to imagine their Rocco having the capacity to store that kind of anger, much less directing it toward anyone. But the Rocco who would be coming home soon wasn't exactly the Rocco who had been, now, was he? Just as the Emmie who returned wasn't. And Roman certainly wouldn't be. River remained just outside their orbit, among the stars. The Johnson family felt like reanimated bits and bobs of what it had once been. Like Frankenstein's monster, he thought. Odie hadn't read the book, and when he and Emmie had gone to see the movie's reissue, just a year before Roman was born, they'd made out so intensely in the back of the theater that they'd been asked to leave before the halfway point. So maybe they weren't like the monster at all.

Around them, the bathroom smelled of bleach, noxious and overpowering from tub to toilet, sink to tiled floors.

"I think I'm starting to feel lightheaded." Emmie looked around at the newly pristine bathroom. "We might've gone a little overboard."

Still, she wrapped her arms around him tighter.

" 'Pepé Le Pew,' " Odysseus said, imitating Rocco.

She laughed and grew quiet.

"And Roman?" she said. "Do you think he hates us?"

"He chose to go," Odie said. "Didn't nobody want that for him but him."

His wife's silence was an ellipsis. All those years ago, Odie too had chosen to enlist, and yet . . . how many times had Emmeline felt him flail against his memories in his sleep, felt him freeze as he tried to remember what he did with his hands when they weren't digging the dead.

"I think he probably spent many months over there wanting exactly this. To be here. With us," Odie said, trying to assuage her.

After all this time, he still found himself unsure of what to say, terrified as he was that she might up and leave him yet again. Her chin was starting to dig into his back. It hurt like hell, but he didn't dare move.

CHAPTER THIRTY-EIGHT

"DISHONORABLY DISCHARGED MEANS THAT ROMAN DID SOMETHING wrong," Rocco said.

Already, Emmeline noticed, Rocco kicked the ground in front of him with increasingly greater intensity, clearly uncomfortable amid so many people. The little American flag Emmeline had brought for him to wave dangled at his side.

Rocco was scheduled to be released soon from the second facility to which River had brought him. Between being River Johnson's brother and his own good behavior, he would get out much earlier than his sentence, time served. Odysseus and Emmeline had to figure out where he was to go next, which meant the two of them had to actually really and truly speak with each other. Barring this, they came to an unspoken agreement that home was what would be best for Rocco, for the moment.

Across the way, several teenage girls tittered and held up a WELCOME HOME! banner. Who were they waiting for? A brother? Cousin? Fiancé? She and Odie had been newly affianced when they'd come back to each other for the first time.

Odysseus stood slightly off to the side, leather jacket draped across his arm, lost in thought. Ordinarily, Emmeline would've asked him what his brain was chewing on so loudly, but they weren't there again, not yet. Odie hadn't been one to talk much about his emotions to begin with, and certainly not now that something fundamental had been broken between them.

Once, during a fit when he was younger, Rocco had thrown a vase that belonged to Odie's late mother and Odie didn't say a word for damn near an hour. After Emmeline calmed Rocco and put all the boys to bed, she and Odie sat across from each other, picking up shards. Well into the night they'd super-glued, occasionally snapped at each other, and swapped stories about their day until finally, around two A.M., Odie had taken her hand gently and said, "It's OK. Let's go to bed."

Emmeline still had the half-broken vase in a bag in the garage, a small bag of shards in a Ziploc bag next to it. Just in case Odie decided he wanted them one day. She wasn't sure if one of them was the vase, or the vase was their marriage itself, or all of the above, but how she longed for the day Odie might grab her hand and say, "It's OK." For when he'd mean it.

Emmeline searched through the crowds for her baby boy and wondered what ghosts Roman'd brought back with him.

"River should be here by now," Odysseus said.

"He's probably just trying to find a way in without drawing too much attention to himself," she said.

River had insisted on greeting Roman upon his return with the rest of them. Had said it was important to him to be there, even as Emmeline had insisted maybe the commotion might be too much for his brothers. They had special entrances for accommodating the famous at LAX, River promised. Recently, he had moved into a new house across town. An income property, he'd said. Emmeline had yet to visit, had no idea about her youngest son's comings and goings anymore. This was the way he wanted it. And she supposed she deserved it, as for so long he'd had no idea about hers.

═══

"IS THAT THE plane?" Emmeline asked, watching one descend.

"I think so?" Odysseus responded. They still didn't have much to say to each other.

"Roman is on a Boeing 727. That's a Douglas DC-9; they're not even remotely the same." Rocco sighed.

A great roar went up as eager family members around them in the arrivals area pressed in closer.

"That is the wrong plane, people," Rocco repeated, exasperated.

But it wasn't the plane the crowd was getting excited about. It was River Johnson, Emmeline's son, in all his glory. The hat and sunglasses meant to shield him from attention only drew more of it. The paparazzi who always seemed to buzz around the airport swooped and snapped photographs.

"That's not a very good disguise," Rocco said.

A few feet from them, River signed the girls' WELCOME HOME! sign. Then he signed a few more autographs for the people crowded around him who saw that he was somebody and figured they should grab his sloppy signature for daughters, granddaughters, or resale.

In the commotion over River, the arrival of some of the actual returning soldiers had been lost. It wasn't until Roman appeared next to them that they'd realized his plane had landed.

"Welcome home," River said, bringing Roman in for a hug. Emmeline turned from the cameras.

"I was in Vietnam longer than I was ever in California," Roman said.

"Why do you smell like a liquor store?" Rocco said.

Roman pounded Rocco's fist and turned toward Emmeline. "Hi, Mom."

"My baby!" Emmeline started to cry as she pulled him in. How many nights had she spent praying for this moment! Every time she'd answered the phone, or heard the ring of a doorbell, how she'd feared uniformed officers like reapers with their scripted solemnity, saying, "We're sorry to inform you." She realized just how very long it had been since she could relax into a moment, her family safely by her side. She squeezed Roman tighter and smelled the spirits on Roman's breath, through his pores. How much had he had to drink on the plane?

"Dad," Roman said by way of greeting.

Immediately, Odysseus drew his son in close. Briefly, Roman relaxed into his father's body, letting himself be held. Odysseus clapped his son on the back a few times before releasing him.

"RoRo," River said.

Emmeline hadn't heard River call his brother that in some time.

"That hat looks stupid," Roman said.

"So's your face," River said.

"Can we get a photo of all of you together?" a photographer said. Somehow, Emmeline had briefly forgotten they were there.

"I don't know. This is such a private—" Emmeline started.

"Sure!" River interrupted. "Only if you cats promise to leave us alone afterward."

"Deal," the photographer said.

The Johnsons all turned toward the camera. River stood between Roman and Rocco, arms around them both, with his megawatt grin, and his body was decidedly angled away from both Emmeline and Odysseus. Emmeline could feel the gulf between them. Was the chasm visible to everyone else?

On the other side of Roman, Odysseus leaned in.

"I'm happy you're back," he said, just before the camera flashed. But audibly, as though he meant for everyone to hear. Emmeline briefly wondered if he had called the paparazzi himself, to make sure news of their family reunion drowned out the whispers that River Johnson had gotten new management because of his father's embezzlement.

"Great! One more!" the paparazzo said.

"My sons," Odysseus murmured.

"Please let go of me now," Rocco said.

═

AS THE JOHNSON family headed back to the car, passing all the airport newsstands with their last-minute pulp novels and travel comforts, Emmeline rushed over and snatched up a copy of *Jet,* then another.

"Look!" She beamed at River.

"Yeah. Look," Roman repeated mockingly.

Emmeline quickly grabbed up five copies, one for each of them. "You didn't tell me you were on *Jet* this month!"

River shrugged. He still didn't have much to say to her. Not that she blamed him. It would take time for him to trust her again. She could wait.

"That's you?" The elderly cashier scratched her bright-pink nose and looked down at the magazine and back up at River.

"My son!" Emmeline beamed. She felt River stiffen up next to her.

"You must be very proud," the cashier said.

Roman shifted his army-issue duffel bag from one shoulder to the other.

"I'm proud of all my kids," Emmeline quickly said.

"We're not famous. We're nobodies," Rocco said matter-of-factly.

Before Emmeline could correct him, before she could say that they were each of them her whole world, that she had loved all of them fiercely no matter where she, or they, were, Rocco turned to his brother and said, "So what did you do wrong?"

"Yeah, what did you do?" River said.

"We don't need to get into all of that now," Emmeline said.

"Congratulations," the cashier said. "That'll be three dollars and forty-two cents."

═

"WHERE ARE WE going?" Roman asked from the front seat, River having made a show of graciously offering him shotgun in the Caddy.

"I don't care about that shit anymore," Roman said.

River looked embarrassed for a moment before quickly fixing his face so that all that remained was a vaguely cheery blank slate. When had her son gotten so good at hiding himself even from them?

"I got us reservations at Scandia," River said.

"What the hell is a Scandia?" Roman said.

"I had to pull a few strings to get us in, but the food is supposed to be great. Frank Sinatra goes there sometimes. Diana Ross! It's Scandinavian. Hence the Scandia."

"Well, if Frank Sinatra goes there . . ." Roman jeered. "I'm not exactly dressed for anything fancy."

"It'll be great. Anybody who's anybody goes there."

Roman sighed deeply.

Half a block from the restaurant, a rather Dickensian-looking runaway sold narcotics to passersby. Inside, the restaurant was worlds removed, elegant even. Or at least, what seemed to pass as elegant these days, which meant entirely too much wood paneling for Emmeline's taste. The patrons were all very rich and very white, their whiteness reiterated by plaques of the coat of arms from what Emmeline presumed were various Scandinavian countries all over the walls.

This place isn't meant to be for us, she thought.

River strode up to the hostess, whose entire face gave the impression of being from somewhere where one regularly had to wear mittens.

"Johnson, party of five," her son said rather haughtily.

"I'm sorry, sir. One has to wear a coat inside," the hostess said with an ever-so-slight accent, looking sheepishly at Roman.

"He's a war hero," River said as Roman cut his eyes at him. "Literally just got off the plane not an hour ago."

"No he's n—" Rocco started as Emmeline pulled her son toward her. Rocco quickly yanked himself away.

"I don't make the rules." The hostess looked around for backup.

"Right this way, Mr. Johnson," an older man said, warmly. Wordlessly, he handed Roman a smoking jacket that seemed to materialize out of thin air.

They followed the man to the back of the restaurant past the packed rows of patrons. Cigarettes dangled from proprietary holders in thinning lips, their smoke wafting, mixing with the smells of lobster and Swedish meatballs. Most tables were polite enough to continue their conversations, others stopped and stared at them. River freely offered up smiles to anyone with whom he made eye contact, but it was clear that most of the older crowd here had no idea who he was. All they saw was a Black family with a returning service member.

"Thank you for your service," one older gentleman murmured to Roman, who flinched.

"He's our very own war hero," River said.

"Shut the fuck up," Roman mumbled.

"So you killed people?" Rocco asked as soon as they were seated.

"Jesus, Rocco," River said.

"It's war," Roman said. "I don't want to talk about it."

"In somewhat happier news, Mom left us," River said. "But now she's back."

"What?" Roman said.

"I didn't leave you, River. I left your father," Emmeline corrected him.

"Semantics," River said.

"When the hell did this happen? Was nobody going to tell me?" Roman said.

"I'm back home now," she said, feeling herself grow flushed.

"She had an affair," River said.

Emmeline glared at Odysseus. "I thought we decided to keep it between the two of us."

"I kept my end of the bargain," Odie said.

"Like your marriage vows, apparently," Roman said.

Emmeline was ashamed, but more than that she was embarrassed at having been so needy. For wanting so unabashedly. For starting something both she and Aaron somehow had always known deep down inside that she'd never finish. And now to be so laid bare in front of one's own children. She bit down on her lip until she could feel the slight metallic taste of blood.

"You just told on yourself. I was only guessing," River said. "But really, don't feel too bad for him, you guys, 'cause Dad stole my money."

Roman said, "What the fuck?"

"Boy, I know you back from a war, but you better show some respect for your mother," Odysseus said. "Act like you got some home training."

Emmeline felt a sort of guilty relief at briefly not having the attention on her own transgressions.

"And I told you I paid it back," Odysseus whispered, trying not to draw any further attention to themselves.

"What's wrong with this family?" Rocco said.

"Everything," River said.

Their waiter came and discussed the wine list with them. Emmeline smiled and pretended to be interested in notes and hints. River ordered for the table.

The waiter returned with a bottle of something that Emmeline determined to be expensive solely based on the very fancy French scroll across the entire label.

"I don't want to be here." Rocco eyed the plates of the people around them. Emmeline had to admit that Scandinavian was apparently very much not the mood she found herself in.

"Me neither," Roman said, and stood up.

"Are you kidding? Do you know how many people would die to be in here right now?" River leaned in and whispered to the table.

Roman glared over at River, who opened his mouth to respond and quickly shut up, thinking better of it.

"Welcome home, brotherman." A Black waiter clapped Roman on the back.

Roman grabbed up the bottle of wine and lifted it. "Cheers, family."

Then Emmeline watched as her son jettisoned the mandatory smoking jacket that had been forced upon him, placing it on the back of the chair.

"This doesn't belong to me," Roman said, and left.

CHAPTER THIRTY-NINE

MOST OF THE TIME PEOPLE DIDN'T EVEN KNOW ROMAN WAS DRUNK.

He had watched friends die, and he had maybe killed, and he hadn't stopped others from killing. He had seen the absolute worst of humanity. And the worst part was that he had done so willingly. In his anger, he had thought that war was better than whatever was at home. He had listened to the news, had seen the Black men who refused to go, and seen the boys who'd returned broken and ostracized. He had known what to expect and yet he hadn't known anything at all.

Nothing could possibly prepare anyone for all of that. Even after he'd deserted, most days he had not particularly wanted or expected to survive, had assumed that eventually he too would end up like the Kid, splayed open and left behind.

And yet here he was, not even two years later, back in sunny Southern California, making small talk and making beautiful things in his father's shop for fancy people who would never know the agony of watching a sixteen-year-old bleed out. The strangeness of watching somebody lose their warmth and heat, the deathly waxiness of a face that had just smiled at you hours before. So, sometimes, while he worked, he drank. So as not to be in his head. Then, sometimes, as he drank, he worked. Until, eventually, he didn't bother with the work at all.

"You can't live like this, RoRo," his mama said. Emmeline hadn't called him that since he was a very little boy.

Even with Rocco at home, the house was so quiet. The institution seemed to have done a number on his brother. Most days, Rocco would just stay in his room. Roman tried to talk with him, but he didn't quite know how. He would give anything for the chaos of the three of them chasing one another through the house, arguing, their bodies stretching and growing, feeling everything for the first time. Now, most of the time, Roman tried very hard not to feel anything at all.

The metal flask in his pocket accidentally clanged against the stairs as he headed down. It sounded a bit like a prayer gong, one he'd heard many times in Vietnam. He looked up to see his mother staring at him at the bottom of the stairs.

"When your father first got back . . . it was hard for him too," his mother started.

"I'm fine, Ma," Roman said.

"Maybe you two could talk about it. Together."

She grabbed him by his wrist.

"What if we have just Mommy and RoRo time, huh? We haven't done that in forever, have we?" Emmeline forced out a fake chuckle.

When they were little and his brothers needy and loud, every so often Emmeline would declare it "Mommy and RoRo Day!" and the two of them would go to the theater on Main Street, or out for milkshakes, where Roman could tell Emmeline all about anything and everything, uninterrupted by Rocco whining about how mushy the food was, or River constantly yelling, "Mommy, look at this! Look at this! Look!"

"Maybe later," Roman said as he maneuvered past her, the two of them in an awkward push-and-pull as his mother tried to block the door.

"RoRo, please!" his mother cried out.

He let the front door slam behind him.

ODYSSEUS POURED ALL the alcohol in the house down the drain. Roman bought more and hid it while Emmeline was out. Emmeline said she wanted them to have family dinners from now on, so they ate together as Roman sat quietly and his father chatted about the particulars of the store. As he ate, Roman struggled to remember where he might have hidden the airplane-sized bottle of vodka he'd stolen from the liquor store down the street. He didn't even particularly like vodka, but it would do. Why did they even sell those things? Little to-go bottles. Perfect for hiding. Perfect for drunks. But Roman was not a drunk. Roman was just a man going through something.

At the Suicide Bridge, as the light was fading and lovers and hooligans both contemplated their fates, Roman peered down into the arroyo below. Around them, the atmosphere was thick, so dense, you felt you could reach out and grab it, until it only just slipped through your fingers. He leaned and drank and tried not to think. He watched the young people around him, how carefree they were. Had he ever been that carefree?

Some nights, he never made it home. After nights in the jungle, nights in jail, a night under a bridge in Pasadena was nothing especially hopeless.

Nearby, along Colorado, the scaffolding would be going up any minute now for the Rose Parade. Volunteers scrambled to put the very final touches on with all those thousands of petals. Teachers even gave out extra credit to do so at some schools! It seemed such a very California thing, to get extra credit to build whole worlds with flowers.

At the bridge, he grew to know some of the others, some of them vets, like him, some of them dangerous, unlike him. Given the bridge's moniker, it was unsurprising that there were ghosts around, several of whom seemed to actually revel in their local notoriety, but Roman generally found the living far more annoying than the dead. A few local teenagers painted in defiant circles across the concrete.

"Shit, is that River Johnson?!" one of them yelled one night.

Roman was in the middle of counting the stars.

No. It's just me, he thought, but the words were too heavy on his tongue. He closed his eyes under their weight. He and River did look a bit like each other. It wasn't an uncommon occurrence that somebody confused him for his brother, the superstar. His little brother was more handsome though. Roman could concede that.

"Roman!"

Had he said his own name out loud? He felt a kick at his foot.

"What the hell?" Roman slowly raised his head.

There, hovering over him, was his famous baby brother. He was dressed as though he were trying to go incognito, which was even worse, given that a hat and sunglasses couldn't disguise one of the most famous musicians in the world. Even worse than whatever it was he thought he'd been doing at the airport. Especially since the sunglasses were expensive. Hat too. If River wasn't careful, he might get robbed around here. Why was he by himself? Why was he here at all?

"Hi," Roman finally said.

"Is that really all you have to say?" River said. "I've been looking all over for you."

Roman leaned his heavy head against his shoulder and looked at River. He'd filled out more since Roman had last seen him. Roman was still stronger, but in a fight, River might actually have a shot at beating him for the first time in their lives. Why was it that he immediately thought of fighting his brother? He struggled to keep his eyes open.

"What do you want?" Roman said.

"Look at you!" River said.

The others nearby had begun playacting in their various roles. The teenagers murmured and didn't kiss or touch at all, just held each other and gave furtive glances at River and Roman. The hooligan didn't even bother pretending to paint anymore, he just straight-up stared. All of them were more clearly besotted, not by the prospect of getting to second base or leaving a mark to stick it to the man but by the presence of River Fucking Johnson!

Roman rolled his eyes.

"Why are you like this?" River said.

"You don't know what I've lived through."

"We're all living through something . . . Mom and Dad are worried."

"Fuck them."

"I'm worried . . ."

Now the glorious, golden River Johnson squatted down low and took off his sunglasses so he and Roman were face-to-face. Roman was taken by simultaneous urges to hug his little brother and punch him in the face. Instead, he placed his hand on River's knee and pushed him off balance. River fell back on his butt, inelegantly splayed on the concrete. Everyone around them gasped.

"It's all right. He's just my brother!" Roman shouted to everyone before breaking out into song. "*It's a family affair . . .*"

"You're such a fucking asshole," River said.

"You think you're so perfect?"

"I'm not the one drunk off my ass in the middle of the Arroyo Seco, Roman."

"You stole Christmas's moves," Roman said.

"Anyone can dance any type of way."

"Pretty low, stealing from a dead kid, Riv . . . And why weren't you with Rocco that day?"

"Don't start."

"Where were you?"

"I said, don't start." At that, River actually sounded as though he were riled up enough to do something, even here in front of his adoring fans.

"Too busy with your little friend? What was his name again?" Roman made a very lewd gesture.

And before Roman knew what hit him, River hauled off and punched him square in the nose. Hard. Roman's nose bled in red rivers all over his shirt. Around them the others, at least those who were mostly sober, seemed to be on the verge of intervening, but on whose behalf?

"Not so golden after all, are we, Riv? I can't wait for the headlines: 'River Johnson Punches a Homeless Man.'" Roman laughed.

"You're not homeless. You're just my brother."

"You kicked me out the band!"

"You never wanted to be there in the first place!" River ran his hand over his head and tried to avoid eye contact with bystanders. "I don't have time for this."

"Of course you don't."

"You left me, Roman. All alone with them. What do you think that was like?"

"Are you crying?" Roman said.

"What? No. It's my allergies. Fucking Santa Anas." River sniffled and walked away.

Don't leave, Roman wanted to say. Why had he done that? *Fuck you,* he thought. Fuck River. Fuck himself. Fuck the dead.

"Riv, come back!"

River didn't turn around. Roman sang his latest hit single at him.

"Rocco would've sung it better!" Roman shouted. He pinched his bleeding nose with the bottom of his shirt so his stomach hung out the bottom. River turned around only briefly to look at him.

"Well, yeah. Maybe he would've."

═

ROMAN WASN'T SURE what exactly compelled him to follow River to the car, but he did.

"All right then," River said.

They passed by the house and instead got onto the 110. They hugged its curves and sat through traffic and switched lanes and freeways and landscapes and the entire time said nothing. River's song came on the radio, the one that Rocco could've sung better. Roman harmonized with his brother on the radio.

"Shut the fuck up," River said, and quickly changed the station. Roman knew how much River hated listening to himself. All he could ever hear was everything he could, or should, have done differently.

The facility was by the ocean. Immaculately landscaped with white people meandering here, there, and everywhere. Some of whom looked sullen, others of whom glowed radiant with positivity and affirmations. The fervor of recent converts to clear-eyed sobriety.

"Riv, really? Ain't another nigga in sight. I don't even see any Mexicans, or like a Chinese person, or whatever."

"There's one right there," River said, pointing to an older Chinese woman sitting on a bench reading.

"What am I gonna do in a place like this?"

"Whatever you need to."

And so, Roman found himself in rehab.

I can change, Roman thought. Maybe.

"Happy New Year, asshole," River said before driving away.

PART THREE

1972–1976

CHAPTER FORTY

1972

TO BE HONEST, I WASN'T SO KEEN ON THE IDEA OF MURDER. THERE ARE lots of ways to kill a man, but I wasn't sure I had it in me to do not a one. You could haunt a man so that he ran screaming into the road and got trampled by buggy, or car. Or you could scare him something awful, so that he has a heart attack and keels over right at your feet. Or if you were real patient, you could even slowly drive a man so mad, he went insane wondering if you were real, and took his own life. Some ghosts summoned all their purgatorial strength to physically grab up a body, to choke, or squeeze, or even rip it asunder, so that later, investigators wondered how such a thing was even possible and whole towns gathered to pray the evil away. I didn't think I had it in me to do any of that. Or least, not on purpose. I had always tried so very hard to be a good boy. Mostly.

But Racist Tom had it stuck in his head that we needed to avenge my death. That it was the only way for me to finally find peace in this world and move on to the next, according to him. For a long time, he insisted that we needed to do something.

"It's been several years now," Tom said. "We gotta do it while they're still alive."

"Do what?" I said.

How he knew what year it was, I couldn't tell since most of our days bled into one another. Time has a way of folding in on itself when you're dead. And anyway, I preferred my days to bleed rather than an actual bloodletting, I reckon. Ever since I told him of how I died, Tom seemed to be a little gentler, kinder to me, which didn't make much sense, but I'm not one to argue a gift racist in the mouth.

"Do you remember what town you were in?" he said. "At the very least, we can find those men and give them a fright."

The forest in which I died bordered quite a few towns, and there were several small rivers that ran through it. Sometimes, along the rivers, you could hear the songs of the old slaves who had drowned trying to escape to freedom. We decided they might be a good place to start, since they had been around for a hundred years or more. Maybe they could recall something of what happened to me, and who did it.

I wasn't sure that I wanted to see the men who killed me again. They were very ordinary men, but also very evil and I wasn't sure what of myself could possibly be restored in their presence. And to be really honest, I wasn't sure I wanted to go on to whatever was next.

"What if, instead of an afterlife, there's just a whole lot of nothing? Or worse?" I said to Tom.

"Then you're probably good," he said. "C'mon, let's go!"

Jim was the first dead slave we came across who was willing to talk. He must've been about twenty when he died, strong and young. He had many whip marks across every inch of his body and stood quite proud. The dead slaves tended to pay more attention to those of us who could've been their grandchildren or great-grandchildren.

"I remember the men what done that to you as if it were yesterday. One were almost seven feet tall with beady eyes. The other were very short, with a face like a weasel. I didn't get the best look at the rest of them, they all just were mostly ordinary white folk."

"Do you remember anything distinctive they said or wore?" Tom had taken it upon himself to be a detective like in the comics, he said. Or Sherlock Holmes. I saw Jim glance at the back of Tom's head where his brains threatened to spill out.

"They wouldn't be in the same clothes," Becky said, exasperated.

It was obvious that Jim wasn't very comfortable speaking freely in Tom's and Becky's presence. Quite understandably.

"One of them had a tattoo. An anchor and a turtle."

"A turtle?" I said, and Jim shrugged.

"He lives not too far that a-way," he whispered to me. "You trust them two?"

I wasn't sure that I did. But Becky, Tom, and everyone in the forest had become a kind of family to me. Not like the Johnsons. Or even Mr. Powell and Moses. But in the way that Mr. Farraday had, or Liz and Eliza. Most white folks could only ever really know you but so much.

None of us would've even spoken with one another when we were alive, but death makes strange families of us indeed.

Three men had sentenced me to death, one of whom had himself died not long after. The youngest of them, the tall one, a man named Orville, had been stabbed in the neck during a bar brawl on his nineteenth birthday.

"Serves him right," Jim said matter-of-factly.

According to Jim, the next closest murderer was called Ole Pete. We had to go around the outskirts of town asking after anybody called Ole Pete. The cabin we were directed to was not too far off the main road. Everything about it was a little worse for wear, including the old man sat on a rocking chair on the splintered porch. It had been many years, and he wore all of them badly, but still I remembered that face. Next to the front door was a shotgun. I wondered how many people he'd killed with it.

"Maybe we shouldn't," I said to Tom. "What if he's not the right guy?"

He was. Ole Pete had been the one who held me down. Knelt across my small body with the huge heft of his. I could never forget that face, the pressure of that knee. Still, the idea of getting any closer to him made every part of me uneasy, as though I still had skin, and he made it crawl. Two towheaded children around my age shrieked around the yard, spraying each other with a water hose. I had forgotten it was summertime.

"You're not a good liar," Tom said to me.

Becky longingly looked after the children playing. I could tell she wanted to join them. Or at least to go over and see if they would have her. Becky was as desperate as I to be loved.

Tom started toward them.

"Wait!" I yelled. But he didn't hear me. Or at least he pretended he hadn't.

He scared the children something awful, such that they dropped the hose and ran to the porch, screaming, "Pawpaw! Pawpaw!"

The birds who had been happily chirping all around yelled down at Tom, "What'd you go and do that for?"

"Their pawpaw killed my friend!"

Tom considered me his friend?

"It's true," I said, and the birds looked over at me pityingly before flying off in a misshapen V, having decided whatever came next was none of their never mind, I suppose.

The children cowered next to the old man as we approached. Ole Pete had reached for his shotgun and aimed into the forest, into whatever might have disturbed them. As we got closer, sure enough, there was the turtle and the anchor on his crepey biceps. Ole Pete lowered his shotgun and sat back down, as though he had been expecting us, or at least me, eventually.

"Go on inside," he said to the children.

"But Pawpaw!" the boy child said.

"What I tell you?"

"Yessir."

When the girl and boy had closed the screen door behind them, he addressed us.

"So . . ." he said, taking inventory of all my broken parts.

"You killed him," Tom said.

"Yeah, I done it," he said. "Niggers getting too many ideas in their heads these days. He touched that woman, you know?"

He pointed at me angrily. How could he still be angry over something that happened so many years ago? And me plenty dead as a result.

"His name was Christmas. And you didn't have to kill him!" Becky yelled.

"I didn't mean to touch her," I cried out. "I thought she was my friend."

"What white woman is your friend?" he said.

"I am!" Becky said.

He laughed and spat. "They get a little fame just 'cause they can carry a tune and forget their damn place. Puttin' on airs. Look at that nigger Poitier, or that Banana Day-O nigger!"

He sang a bit of the Harry Belafonte song mockingly, "*Daylight come and me wanna go home.*" Then he spat again.

"And don't even get me started on that Robeson nigger. Never mind that they're all a bunch of fucking reds!"

"You're an awful, awful man," Becky said.

The old man shrugged. "You gonna kill me? Go ahead. Otherwise, get off my damn porch and do your haunting elsewhere."

"Kill 'em!" Becky yelled with a surprising amount of bloodthirst.

Tom approached him menacingly. He reached his hands around the old man's neck. I should've stopped him. Or maybe not. Tom's hands shook violently as he began to squeeze, and the old man glared at me something awful, pure evil boring a hole in me. Never mind that he and his friends had already actually done so. I twiddled my intestines nervously. I'd never been party to such a thing as murder, at least not intentionally. I was still a child, after all. And what would happen to all of our souls after Tom got done? Even if Ole Pete did deserve it.

In the end it didn't matter, Tom couldn't bring himself to do it after all. Apparently shooting poor innocent animals was easy enough for him, but he couldn't bring himself to kill a pawpaw, no matter how vile the man was.

After that, Tom was all pissy for days.

"Let's go find the next guy," he said after he'd finished sulking.

"'Cause that went so well the last time." Becky rolled her eyes.

"I got a plan this time," he said.

According to Jim, the next murderer he could recall was named Quincy. By the time we reached him, Quincy had been so shrunk by age that he was hardly bigger than me. He wore thick eyeglasses and we watched as the mean ole son of a bitch grabbed his grandson's finger and squeezed it so hard that it nearly broke. Definitely a fracture at least. All of this for simply moving his drink. The kid started crying, and in response ole Quincy took a swig.

"Pussy," he said, and turned to the TV screen.

Onscreen, a rerun of *The River Johnson Show* came on, and Quincy started humming along as River came on the screen. He laughed heartily as River danced over to the stage. River was so charismatic that even old decrepit racists enjoyed watching him. For a moment I forgot who I was, and where I was, what I was in the middle of doing, and was briefly proud.

Then Tom pointed out all the bruises just under the grandson's skin.

"Excuse me, did you murder a small Negro boy singer many years ago?" Tom stepped into the room and drew himself up to his full size, which wasn't much, but he had accidentally been shot with a shotgun and was a bit gruesome. The man turned white as a sheet.

"I don't know what you're talking about, son," Quincy said.

"Sir. I'm dead as a doorknob," Tom said. "But I've gotten very good at telling when folks are lying."

Quincy quaked. "Who are you?"

"I'm . . ." Tom searched his head for something sufficiently dramatic. "I'm Death, come to get you, Quincy—"

Tom didn't know Quincy's last name, so he couldn't make it all official sounding. And Lord knows if Death were Teenage Tom, I'm not sure most people would be all that afraid, but Quincy sure was.

"I thought we were only going to teach him a lesson. I didn't know how far it was going to go! Honest!"

"Lies!" Tom yelled. He really had read too many of those detective books.

I couldn't bring myself to say anything to this man. I didn't remember his face at all, but I remembered a much younger voice, his voice yelling, "Get him!" As I ran and ran and ran for my life. He couldn't have been that much older than Tom at the time. But I'm not good at knowing white folks' ages. Or anyone's really, to be honest. When you're small, everyone much older than you seems ancient.

The man sank down into his chair. "Don't hurt me. My grandson's right here. He didn't do nothing."

"Neither did Christmas," Becky said.

"Christmas?" Quincy said.

"Me. Christmas Jones the Third, the prodigy . . ." I remembered Roman and Ms. Emmeline telling me that I shouldn't call myself a pickaninny no more, so I stopped it there.

The boy's gaze went back and forth between his grandfather and me.

"Is he a good grandpa?" Tom asked the boy.

"Tell them how I take you to the park and church and how we go hunting. Tell them how good I am to you!"

The boy remained frozen, his tears from earlier now starting to dry on his face.

"Dammit, boy! Open your mouth and say something already!"

He quickly moved to the farthest corner of the room from his grandfather. Then when he was at a safe distance, he looked over at Tom and shook his head no.

"Thank you, young man. You know, my gramps forced me to go hunting. I didn't want to hurt no critters that ain't hurt me, but he said no grandson of his would be a pussy. He's the one who did this to me, you know. Blubbered on about how it was an accident, but I don't think it were."

I hadn't known this about Tom. To hear the others tell it, he and his gramps tramped into the forest shooting whatever they could. But I guess it made sense. Tom always was such a strange combination of angry and sensitive, always crying. It made sense that he hadn't wanted to be in the forest in the first place. Had been hunting against his will when he died. And although I found it mildly irritating, Tom trying to save me, maybe he actually really did want to help. Still, I wasn't prepared for what Tom did next.

He reached inside ole Quincy and squeezed the man's heart, hard, like he was going to squeeze it until it was as small as it was empty. I could picture the man's heart flattening, oozing out the sides of Tom's hands. His grandson looked scared.

"Say you're sorry!" Tom had a gleam in his eye.

Surprisingly enough, ole Quincy looked more angry than scared, if I'm to be honest. He looked over at me, then back at Tom.

"Fuck you!" He spat. But since Tom wasn't flesh, it landed at his feet, across from his grandson.

"Wait!" I shouted, and turned to the boy. "Do you have somebody to look after you?"

I wouldn't wish being an orphan on anybody, even if he was the blood of one of the men who killed me.

"My mom should be back from the store any minute," the kid said.

"Do something!" Quincy gasped at his grandson.

The boy did not implore us to stop, did not intercede to save his grandfather. That alone told you all you needed to know, really.

So, Tom went on ahead and killed Quincy. It was a terrible thing to watch a man die, his mouth gaped open, eyes bulged as he went on to whatever came next, and yet it was far more peaceful than what he'd done to me.

When it was finished, Tom turned to me. "You're free!"

"You're free, Christmas!" Becky wailed. "Oh, I'm going to miss you!" Tears came to her eyes aplenty.

But I didn't feel free at all. Vengeance wasn't what *I* wanted. I wanted three little boys, a mother and a father. I wanted, no, *needed,* the Johnsons.

The fact that this man couldn't hurt another person was very good indeed, but it wasn't enough. Not now that I had been good and truly loved.

And then a curious thing happened—

Tom started talking excitedly: "I did a good thing! My daddy and grandaddy said I wouldn't amount to nothing. That I wasn't nothing but a piece of shit, but I'm good! And I ain't no pussy! I ain't shit!"

That was definitely not what I thought he meant to say, but I didn't have the heart to correct him, seeing how happy he was. I'd never seen him that happy in all the time I'd known him. Meanwhile, I felt a melancholy begin to take hold of me. Bigger than it had been before.

Tom looked very happy indeed. "I'm glad you can have some peace now, Christmas. Would you sing the song you sang that night? If you wouldn't mind."

So I sang.

Tom leaned back and sighed contently. And then, right before our very eyes, after I sang the chorus, he vanished mid-song.

"What just happened?" the boy said. I'd forgotten momentarily that he was in the room, so immersed in the song was I.

"Sometimes when dead people feel at peace, they go on to the next world," Becky explained. We had seen it once or twice before in the forest, though most of us there were not at peace and thus had been there a very long time.

"But I thought he was avenging you?" the boy said to me. "Shouldn't you be the one moving on?"

"Maybe I'm not at peace," I said, and knew it to be true.

"I am," the boy said. "My grandpa was an awful person. I'm very sorry he killed you."

"Me too," I said.

"Do you think you could keep singing, please?" he asked. "Just until my mama comes?"

I kept on, until the song ended and the kid's mother walked through the door.

"That was very beautiful," he said.

"Are you talking to yourself?" A woman came through the door who looked just like the man in the chair. She screamed upon seeing her father, and Becky and I decided it was time to go.

Outside, Becky and I looked at each other, 'cause here we were just the two of us again, with nowhere and nobody to call home.

"I mean . . . why Tom?" Becky fumed. "Why not us too? You're a good person. I'm almost a good person, I think."

Murder had not seemed the best way to get to heaven, or whatever was next for Tom, but perhaps sometimes the right thing to do was the wrong thing.

We were miles away, somewhere along a dirt road when Becky decided to throw a tantrum.

"I'm sick of this!"

"I miss my family," I said. "I miss the Johnsons!"

Becky screamed at the top of her lungs and I joined in with her. In the pasture, the cows lifted their heads and mooed.

"Please. My ears!" squeaked a worm as he inched by, tiny as can be.

We walked a great deal of time, mostly in silence, but after some time had passed, I began to sing the songs I learned at the Johnsons'. All those groups that Roman, Rocco, and River loved, whom Ole Pete would've called uppity, whom some Black folks and many whites called "a credit to our race"! As I sang, it made me feel closer to the Johnson boys. I wondered how they all were, especially Rocco. If he was happy, whether he'd ever forgiven me, whether he even could.

CHAPTER FORTY-ONE

THE WORLD WAS NOT QUITE AS ROCCO REMEMBERED IT. THE SHAPE OF his days felt too blobby, stretching this way and that. He had grown accustomed to the schedule of waking up at a certain time, taking his meds at a certain time, being told where to be, and to whom to speak, for most of his day. His world had been limited to the confines of punishment. He hadn't been at the house in Pasadena before being shipped off long enough for it to feel like home upon his return. What was absolutely certain was that he didn't want to go back to school.

"School's important, Rocco," Emmeline had pushed back.

"River didn't finish school. Roman neither," he said.

Upon his exit interview, his time served, the facility director had suggested a different direction.

"Working can give Rocco a sense of dignity, and purpose moving forward," he said as Odysseus and Emmeline flanked Rocco in the office that inexplicably had carpeting even on the walls.

"That sounds nice, doesn't it?" Emmeline said.

"Maybe Rocco can work with me in the shop!" Odysseus said.

"That sounds like an excellent idea," the director said. "Just in case you want an alternative, let me give you some pamphlets."

The man handed Odysseus the pamphlets, at which Rocco's father glanced only briefly before handing them over to Emmeline to put in her purse.

"It's been a pleasure getting to serve you and your family," the facility doctor said. "Give my regards to River."

As though Rocco had just simply been in a hotel stay funded by his famous little brother, and not imprisoned for something he hadn't done.

When the three of them finally headed to the car, rather than sit in the front passenger seat, his mama sat in the big bucket seat with him in the rear.

"Maybe we can rename the shop Johnson and Sons Millinery!" Odysseus said up front as he turned the key in the ignition. "It'll be nice to have you and Roman both with me, learning the trade."

Rocco said nothing. Making fancy hats all day didn't seem like his cup of tea, but surely it had to be better than what was in the rearview mirror. He had spent almost two years falling asleep to the wails of other children who'd been snatched up from everything they'd known on account of being too different, or too dangerous. Anything had to be better, right?

As they turned out of the long, dusty driveway onto the main road, Emmeline leaned over and grabbed his hand. Rocco wiped her tears away with his sleeve.

He didn't dare look back.

"I won't hurt you, Mama," he said.

"Oh baby, I know," she said, and started crying harder. "I know."

THE FIRST PROBLEM was that the shop was too loud. Rocco hated the way the steam hissed and shrieked as they folded and molded the beaver-fur felt. He hated how when he burned wool to shape it, the whole place smelled like burnt sheep (or at least how he imagined one might smell). He hated how he could never get the break line exactly as he wanted it, hated how frequently the bell rang letting them know that a customer was in, right as he was in the middle of setting the felt afire. He hated the way the lights bore down, bright upon the wooden hat blocks like spotlights on an assortment of little heads. It made Rocco desperate to close his eyes, except that one couldn't steam and cut with eyes closed. He hated how when his daddy was busy, he had to be the one to walk to the front to greet the customers. Before, when Roman was still at home and it got to be too much, as soon as Odysseus went out on delivery, or to make a phone call behind closed doors, Rocco would leave what he was doing and head to the parking lot outside behind the store. There, he often found Roman smoking a cigarette, or drinking from a flask.

"Want some?" Roman slurred.

Rocco shook his head. He didn't like how the world felt topsy-turvy after a few sips from Roman's flask. How he felt too big, or too small, or like he was hardly there at all. He'd had enough of that on all the drugs they'd put him on while he was in the first institution. Sometimes he still felt himself wiggling his fingers and toes to see if he was actually still here. Wherever here was.

"It's too-too." Rocco sighed, nodding back to the shop.

"Yup," Roman would say before taking another sip. He had been to rehab, but Rocco was pretty certain it hadn't stuck. Not that Rocco was complaining exactly. It was nice to have his brother around, even if he often stank like the bars in which they used to perform.

The two of them grew silent and listened for the bell up front announcing a customer's arrival.

"Guess I better get back in before he notices we're both gone," Roman said.

═

"JUST MAKE SURE you look 'em in the face and smile," his daddy said after someone called in a customer-service complaint. "Otherwise, people'll think you're shifty. Especially white folks."

Rocco especially hated how hard he had to work at not looking shifty.

Sometimes, being back home felt good, like on Sundays, when he, Roman, and his parents would all pile in the car and take a drive up the twists and turns of the Angeles National Forest. There, the motorcycle gangs in their oversized leather jackets with big patches announcing their allegiance would roar past, speeding up and down the mountain like they owned its curves, defying death itself. Odysseus would say the damn fools didn't have a lick of sense.

"I kinda get it," his mama would say softly.

"Me too," Roman said.

"They probably get lots of bugs in their faces," Rocco said, and everybody started laughing even though he hadn't meant to be especially funny. After Roman left for rehab, their Sunday drives felt different. Quieter. Eventually they stopped doing them entirely.

Eventually, Rocco couldn't take any more of the damned hats. Odysseus had left to do a delivery. One after the other customers piled into the shop, a deluge of demands, their orders, adjustments, demanding he look in their faces.

Where was his father? Rocco thought.

"Excuse me!" a lady yelled at him. "I need to speak to the owner!"

"OK," Rocco said.

Then he walked into his daddy's office, turned off the lights, shut the door, and slid down behind it. He heard the bell up front ring and ring and ring.

"What the hell?" Odysseus said when he finally returned. "What happened?" he asked as he pushed against the office door.

Rocco started to cry and bang his head against the door.

His father knelt down, circled Rocco in his arms, and rocked him for as long as Rocco could stand, before finally Rocco pulled away and said, "OK, I'll get back to work now."

═══

"MAYBE YOU JUST need something a little lower key?" River suggested during one of their phone calls. River was always good about calling Rocco, no matter where he was or what he was up to. At the moment, he was shooting a commercial for a soft drink.

"Maybe," Rocco said.

"Working for family would be stressful for most anyone," River said. "Roman needs to hurry up and get his shit together so he can be around to help you."

Rocco didn't think working for Odysseus was the problem. River could be uncharitable toward their parents, toward their older brother. Fact was, he wasn't there. River had left them all behind. He didn't see how they were all of them walking around the shattered glass of what they'd once been.

"Butterfly wings," Rocco said once with a sigh when they'd visited him in the institution. "Families are like butterfly wings."

═══

AFTER ANOTHER LONG day at the shop, when both his body and brain felt a whole lot like the tread-worn carpet in the back office, he walked up the front lawn of their house to see a man with a big camera lurking. Rocco had seen the man before. That time, Roman had been the one to shoo him away. Why couldn't they leave them alone? River was the famous one, and he wasn't even home. The man raised his camera and took Rocco's picture.

"Leave me alone," Rocco snapped.

He was tired and hungry and not in the mood. He hadn't been able to get lunch until later than usual, when his favorite taco place was closed. He was left with the PB&J Emmeline had packed him, grown soggy under the weight of an ice pack. He couldn't eat that. Just the idea of it made him gag.

His stomach gurgled. His brain turned. All this to say, he wasn't thinking right when the man raised up his camera and snapped again.

Rocco shoved the photographer across the lawn. Since he'd last lived at home, Rocco had learned how to fight. It was a skill needed among the brutality of the incarcerated, where kids like Victor roamed, knocking out grown-ups' teeth, and kids like Chad dreamed of medieval dismemberment. At that place, where he didn't have his brothers to save him, Rocco learned to depend on his own two hands, his own fury.

"Go away!" Rocco said.

The man raised up a camera and took another shot.

Rocco was about to smash his camera when Emmeline called from the porch.

"Rocco, baby, come inside. Let me speak to the man for a minute."

And with that, Rocco went inside, peeking only occasionally through the blinds until he saw Emmeline pat the man's hand, then he leaned over to pick his camera up, dusted himself off, and went on his way.

═══

ROCCO TOSSED AND turned all night, and when he tiredly stumbled down the stairs and into the kitchen, he already knew something was up. Odysseus and Emmeline sat at the table, the smell of cinnamon in the air. They rarely all ate breakfast together, and usually, these days, Rocco was the first to rise.

"Made you some French toast," his mother said.

French toast was definitely a harbinger.

"It isn't safe for you here anymore," his father said, cutting to the chase as he cut into his meal. "All it takes is for one of these guys to press charges and some asshole lawyer to say you got special treatment because of River and you never should've been let out."

"We're just afraid that next time they'll send you to jail for real," his mother said. "It's different for grown-ups."

"And River will find you somewhere nice. Really nice. With people your own age instead of hanging around your boring old folks." His mother tried to laugh, but she looked almost as miserable as he felt.

Rocco stood up. He felt the urge to run, but where?

"Baby, what do you think?" Emmeline said, grabbing his hand. Rocco looked down at it. He thought for a moment that maybe his mother was giving him an out. That maybe she even wanted him to say no and stay. She looked at him pleadingly. But pleading for what? Rocco couldn't tell.

Two years before, Chad had described to him a machine called a whirligig.

"Like the toy?" Rocco had asked, trying to picture something Chad had conjured up from childhood.

"Nah! Well, maybe a little bit, 'cause you spin, right? Your captors would place you into this cage thing that turned round and round, quick as shit, banging you up against things until you were sick," Chad had said.

"Baby?" Emmeline asked. "Tell us what you think."

Rocco didn't think much; in fact, he couldn't think at all at the moment. All he wanted was for the whirling to stop, to have a moment to catch his breath and rest his feet on solid ground.

CHAPTER FORTY-TWO

1973

DEAD DADDY, MEAN DADDY, DADDY WAS A ROLLING STONE—ROMAN had no energy for these Hollywood addicts and the way they all seemed to get off on their own sad-sack existences. Group therapy was a waste of time. Journaling was dumb. The food at this rehab was nearly as bland as most of the people in it. His therapist made eyes at him in between asking him how he truly felt about having a famous brother and how he'd felt growing up with a retarded brother.

"Rocco isn't retarded. He just thinks different," Roman said.

The woman crossed and uncrossed her legs.

"That's a lot of responsibility at a young age," she said.

"It was fine," he said.

"Let's revisit your first drink?" she asked. The top of her freckled bosom peeked out over the top of her peasant blouse. If Ilse Edelstein did anything more overt, Roman would have to tell her politely that she wasn't his type. Or that he was trying to take this sobriety thing seriously. Mostly.

"I don't remember it," Roman said.

"You're gonna have to open up sometime for this to work," she replied with a smile.

Roman did not want to tell this white lady his problems. Had no desire to wallow in war, abroad or otherwise.

"I'm having a lot of trouble with my stomach," he said. "Can you give me something for that?"

The woman sighed. "I'll talk to Dr. Friedman and see what we can do."

As he left her office, she rested her hand on his arm. "Let's see what you can remember tomorrow, shall we?"

The rehab center was largely comprised of single rooms, but a scant few were doubles.

"For those of us who are only SIPs. Somewhat important persons," Roman's roommate, Brad, had joked.

Because River had pulled strings to get him in, and because the rehab center was already booked and seemingly prebooked (how?), Roman had to share a room with the up-and-coming actor. Brad was not famous enough to have his own suite. What he did have was a supporting role in a film the studio was putting their full force behind.

"Apparently I give a tour de force performance!" Brad said mockingly. "They told me I need to get right before it comes out."

He laughed.

Australian, boyish, with a perpetual smirk, Brad looked like a very handsome stalk of corn. He was nearly as charismatic as River. He had already had sex with several of the women from group, even though that was most definitely not allowed.

"I think Dr. E wants to fuck me." Roman sighed.

"Yeah, I've heard that's her thing," Brad said.

Roman wasn't sure if Brad meant Black men or patients, but he didn't entirely want to know for sure. And anyway, he wouldn't be Dr. E's Mandingo. He didn't need his father in his head through that shit. He already heard Odysseus in his head, judging him throughout most of his day. What he ate—*shit.* What he said—*Didn't I teach you better than that?* What he wore—*Dear God, isn't there an iron in there?*

He could only imagine what the Odysseus in his head might say if he had sex with Dr. Ilse Edelstein.

Roman ran for an hour of his free time, preferring it to the games or things like paint therapy they scheduled in to pass the time. Eventually, having mostly run through all the women and subsequently met with drama or a deep chill during the group activities, Brad joined him. The two of them passed the time mostly in silence. Every so often, Brad would run out ahead of Roman, or Roman would best Brad, but neither spoke too much and that was just enough.

═

"CAN YOU HELP me read lines for this audition I just booked?" Brad asked one run.

"OK. I guess," Roman said.

They went over and over and over, with Brad flubbing the lines, or overacting, or something just feeling off.

"I've never auditioned sober before," Brad said, shaking.

"I have," Roman said, surprising himself.

"I didn't know you acted," Brad said.

"I didn't. I sang. A long time ago," Roman said.

"Were you good? How did you get through the auditions?"

"I was just a kid," Roman said. "And I guess, eventually, I started sipping a little here and there to get through all of it too."

Brad nodded. "See, I'm fucked."

"Maybe one of the girls can get you a pill or something to take the edge off?" Roman said.

There weren't too many men in the center with them, though Roman suspected it was because they were awfully close to time for the Super Bowl. Who the hell wanted to be sober when those parties rolled around?

"None of the girls are talking to me," Brad said. "Can you do it?"

Ordinarily, Roman would have nothing to do with this white boy's mess. But he was good and truly bored, and he needed something to distract him from the pain in his stomach. There was only so much to do in rehab. And he liked Brad. Brad was the first friend he'd made since the Kid. If they were, in fact, friends. Broken people often tried to fit each other's pieces into their own puzzles.

Still, Brad was funny and he didn't take himself nearly as seriously as everyone else in this godforsaken place with their family money or their headliner status. Brad had spent his childhood mucking stalls and riding tractors. True, he had been the glory of his hometown, but he'd been in L.A. long enough to know that didn't mean shit. He held on to his dreams only just barely, stardom by the skin of his fingertips in one hand and a bottle of whiskey in the other. Brad wasn't quite somebody yet, and thus didn't mind that Roman was a nobody, just his famous brother's problem.

Roman got along well with all the white-lady drunks, mostly because none of them wanted to seem racist. Racism was mostly out of fashion in the circles they all ran in. Though he suspected, out on the streets, all but Lonnie might have grabbed their purses closer as he approached. Lonnie was the daughter of a huge philanthropist whose name was sprawled across buildings throughout the city. Her sister had made the papers and was serving jail time for a truly shocking crime. Her great-grandfather was rumored to have run in certain unsavory circles. When, in group, Roman had shared his sad-sack war story, all the other women had been aghast, or in awe, but Lonnie didn't so much as blink.

Sally, Lisa, and Odette didn't have anything. Deirdre had half an upper that she was saving for a special occasion.

"Is this for you, Roman?" she asked. "Or is it for 'Detective Whit Mann, thirties, disarmingly handsome, just this shy of a con man himself'?"

So, she'd read Brad's script too.

Roman was terrible at lying. It was a miracle that the army recruiter had believed him. Or not. They needed to believe him. He decided it was better not to even bother lying, lest everything go sideways.

"He really needs it," Roman said.

"If he needs it that bad, he can ask me himself," she said.

Lonnie knew somebody who knew somebody who could smuggle something in. But the person in question wouldn't be on shift for at least three days.

Roman's stomach ached something awful by the afternoon. He rushed to the toilet and spilled his innards after speaking with Lonnie.

"Do you have any Pepto?" he asked Marcy. "Also, got any uppers?"

Marcy had LSD. She did not have Pepto.

"I might as well not even bother with the audition," Brad said.

"What about the nurses?" Roman asked. "Did you mess with them too?"

"Ask Trina." Brad sighed.

Roman went to the infirmary to ask Nurse Trina. His bowels felt raw as windows scraped bare after a good snowstorm. They at least had to have rubbing alcohol in the infirmary, didn't they? They had to.

Is the rubbing alcohol for Brad or for you? The Odysseus in his head sneered.

Roman's stomach was killing him as he approached Trina.

"Do you have any Pepto?" he asked.

"Lemme check," she said.

It was too easy. As she turned to the cabinet with all the locked medicine, he scoured the room.

There it was.

Across from him, Trina removed the bubblegum-pink bottle and poured it into a small paper cup. It was just enough time for Roman to swipe the rubbing alcohol. Trina was relatively new to the facility, or else she would have known better. Hell, almost anybody would've known better.

"Brad needs an upper," he blurted. "For an audition. He said you might be able to help."

Trina looked at him carefully.

"He says it's a big one," Roman said. "He doesn't want to drink."

The nurse rolled her eyes. Trina was only a tad older than Roman himself.

"You didn't need to do the whole act with the Pepto," she said.

"No, I really do need that. My stomach's wrecked."

Roman's stomach bubbled and burned. He gulped and waited for the coating to take effect. Trina passed him two little pills.

"So Brad doesn't drink," she said sarcastically.

═══

TWO WEEKS LATER, having gone ten rounds with himself, Roman drank the whole bottle of rubbing alcohol, scouring his insides entirely.

As they strapped Roman onto the gurney, Brad readied his bags, everyone having decided he was making solid progress and ready to return to life on the outside.

"Jackass. Don't die, OK?" Brad said.

Roman mumbled in response. Everything burned. He could only imagine what his father would say to this. Or worse yet, that he wouldn't say anything at all.

"Hey, I got the part."

That was the last thing Roman remembered before blacking out.

═══

ROMAN'S CHILDHOOD ROOM was larger than he remembered. Or maybe it was because the rooms in rehab had been sparse. Having been kicked out of yet another rehab (who wanted to get right in the middle of Utah?), he was back. He watched TV in the living room with his family.

It was the first time in forever that all of them had been home. Even River was on a brief hiatus from his show, from touring. It felt like they were almost as they once had been. Almost.

"That's my friend," Roman said as Brad appeared on the screen.

"He's very handsome," Emmeline said.

"The women in rehab all thought so too." Roman laughed as his mother sighed. He noticed that Emmeline didn't like when he actually gave voice to where it was he'd been. Like she preferred to pretend like he'd just been away at summer camp, or college, or on tour with River.

Rehab! Rehab! Rehab! Roman wanted to say.

"He's gonna plant drugs. Just you wait," Odie said. His father had a terrible habit of announcing the impending plot to a show, often incorrectly.

"Of course he is." River laughed.

"Shhh," Rocco said. Rocco was visiting for the weekend. The residence River found for him was lenient about comings and goings.

Onscreen, Brad stood over a dead body and inspected it for clues. Surreptitiously, he planted drugs just under the corpse.

"Didn't I tell you?" Odie slapped his leg and leaned back with a satisfied grin.

Everyone knew that Brad's character only did whatever was needed to get the bad guys caught. The studio film hadn't quite taken off as much as they'd anticipated, but as expected, Brad had indeed gotten rave reviews for his turn as a Confederate deserter.

"Shit, I wish I'd known you when I was prepping for the role," Brad had said only half-jokingly after Roman had shared his war story in group. "I probably would've got an Oscar."

Brad looked good. Clean. Fit. Fame suited him.

In contrast, Roman could feel the extra weight hanging off him like cans clanging behind the bumper of a car, "Just Married" written in shaving cream across the back window.

"I'm going out," Roman said, rising from his seat on the couch.

"But we're having such a nice time all here together?" Emmeline said.

"I'll come with," River said.

"I'm good. I don't need a babysitter, Riv," Roman said.

"Wouldn't mind some fresh air is all," River said.

"If you come with me, it becomes a whole production," Roman said.

"A production," Rocco repeated softly.

Nowadays River couldn't go most places without being followed by the paps or, more often than not, at least one member of his security detail. It was fan after fan, old and young alike doing horrible imitations of Christmas's move or singing River's songs to his face as Roman stood awkwardly off to the side.

Still, his brother stood there visibly pained, and Roman briefly felt bad for wounding him.

"Just trying to clear my head is all," Roman said to soften the blow.

Later, he wouldn't quite remember how he'd found himself at Mr. Robinson's corner store. His brain often felt as though it had black holes where the memories had been sucked clean through. He couldn't remember which bottles he grabbed and stuck under his shirt. He should've known that Mr. Robinson would've been on high alert, as it wasn't the first, or even the second time Roman had stolen from him. But before, Roman had gotten away with it, being both Odysseus's son and River's brother.

"You called the cops on me?" he demanded of Mr. Robinson. "Over twenty bucks of alcohol?"

"I told you I would next time, son," Mr. Robinson said sorrowfully. Roman almost felt bad, or he would've if the pounding in his head weren't threatening to kill him, if he weren't so fucking angry.

With his first collect phone call, he rang the house.

"Roman, aren't you tired of this?" Emmeline said.

He had been tired of himself for a very long time.

"It's not like I'm doing it on purpose?"

"Nobody is forcing you to steal. Or to drink."

"It's not that simple," he said.

"Your father says we're not bailing you out."

"Let me talk to him."

"He's not home right now."

"Since when do you listen to him, or anybody?"

His mother hung up on him. Roman begged the jailer for one more call.

He was surprised when Brad actually answered. Roman figured he wouldn't have caught him at home, or even in town.

"I need to be bailed out." Roman cut to the chase.

"I figured."

"You owe me one."

"You didn't have to say all that. I'll be there."

Brad picked him up. Roman whistled at the sky-blue 1962 Sunbeam Alpine.

"New car?"

"I always wanted one as a kid. Now I got it."

"Just call you Bond. Brad Bond."

Brad laughed.

"You're really sober?"

"It's hard, mate. But it's worthwhile."

"Pull over."

"What?"

"My stomach is bullshit these days."

"You shitting blood?"

Roman was not in the habit of looking behind him in the toilet.

"Had a buddy who started shitting blood," Brad said.

"What happened to him?"

"He ended up needing a blood transfusion," Brad said.

"Jesus," Roman replied.

"It's the drinking, you know," Brad said.

Roman said nothing and continued to stare out the window.

═

THREE OF THE rehabs blended together. Roman felt his insides ripped to shreds, felt even more pain with each detox, got sober for just long enough, went back home to increasingly less fanfare, and within a few months, ended back in rehab feeling himself once again torn asunder. After two years of this, even he was tired of his shit.

River decided they should try the first one once more. Maybe it would stick this time. It really was considered to be the best.

"I'm not gonna keep wasting my money on this bullshit if you screw this up again," River snapped at him over the phone. "You're such an asshole."

"Yeah, well. So are you," Roman said.

A week later, he found himself back in Dr. Ilse Edelstein's office. It had been two years since the first time he'd sat across from her. New sofa. Same shit.

"You got a new sofa," he said, melting into the Italian leather.

"The other one was a little uncomfortable, I'm told." She smiled, and Roman thought he saw a smirk poking through.

This time, Roman told her about the war, his desertion, and subsequent jail time, leaving out the part about the race riot. And about the Kid, leaving out the part about his ghost, of course. He told her about singing with his brothers, what happened to Rocco, leaving out the part about Christmas, of course. He left out that his dad had stolen from his brother. He left out his mom's affair. He sketched out just enough of a past to satisfy Dr. E's appetite for tragedy, for the why of it all, but he didn't fill in the color. You could trust anybody only so much with that information when your brother was River Johnson. Much less when the person listening was white.

"It must be hard being a Black man in America," she said. Roman resisted the urge to laugh at her Very Serious expression.

Thirty days later, he held her pale pink nipple against his teeth and threatened to bite as she stifled a moan as they sullied the supple Italian leather.

It was then that Brad appeared across from him on the couch in Dr. E's office.

"Told you you were her type, mate." Brad laughed.

"Fuck," Roman said.

"Yes. Please," Dr. E purred.

"No. No. No." Roman scrambled up as she looked at him, perplexed. "I gotta go."

"No need to stop on my account," Brad said.

Roman hurried down the hallway toward the rec room, where, on TV, the news anchor was solemnly breaking the news of Brad's untimely death.

"It's so awful," a new girl said. "I heard he was here a while back. Before he made it big. Like, isn't it weird and sad that he was right here?"

Roman couldn't remember what she did, or who she was related to. It didn't matter. He absolutely hated when people reached for whatever gossamer of connection they had to the public figure in question. He understood the human need of it all, but hated it nonetheless.

"'He was right here!'" Brad mocked the woman before looking back at the screen. "I look like a total douche in that photo."

"That's 'cause you are a douche," Roman joked.

"Excuse me?" the girl said.

"You should be nicer to me, Roman. I'm dead," Brad said.

"That's not funny," Roman said.

"Dude, what are you on? And how do I get some?" the girl said to Roman.

"Stay alive, mate," Brad said to Roman. "I mean it."

"But seriously, where'd you score?" the girl said.

CHAPTER FORTY-THREE

1974

JUST AS SEASON FOUR WAS ABOUT TO GET UNDER WAY, RIVER WAS TAKEN out to lunch at the Polo Lounge by the producers. *The River Johnson Show* had run for three seasons thus far, a respectable-enough showing, and one that had catapulted him into next-level superstardom. By now, River could barely make a move without security, he'd done a small international tour, was on with Carson himself! They sat at a table toward the back of the patio, under all the palms and pastel, on those uncomfortable white garden chairs. River didn't understand why people loved this place so much. As he ate his salad, he saw a beautiful young woman in full bloom, a model maybe, or an escort, seated with a much older decaying European man. She kept trying (and failing) not to stare over at River.

What could those two possibly have to talk about together? he thought.

"Have you thought about getting a nose job?"

River hadn't been paying much attention to the conversation at hand.

"What?"

"It's just . . . you're not a kid anymore . . . and . . ." He watched the executive producer struggle for the words to say.

"And I'm ugly now?" River asked. The executive producer himself was far more Cyrano than Christian.

"No, of course not!" the producer said. "But maybe we could make the nose a tad smaller, you know? I'm thinking more like a heartthrob nose . . ."

"What the hell is a heartthrob nose?" River asked. He had long ceased being timid around them after realizing how much money he'd made the network.

"You know . . . Like Bobby Sherman! Or David Cassidy!"

River raised an eyebrow. For one, he had heard the rumors about Bobby Sherman and Sal Mineo and wondered if either of them had. This town was so small sometimes. But more important, David Cassidy and Bobby Sherman were white men, with white noses. And River's nose came from the decidedly not-white Ms. Emmeline Johnson. It was beautiful on his mother and admittedly a little more awkward on him, at least right now.

"They want me to change my fucking nose!" he yelled into the intercom outside Arnie's office.

"That's racist, I think? Right?" Paul said, buzzing him in.

He controlled the urge to stomp through the hallways like a petulant child. Arnie's operation had grown in size, now taking up most of the top floor. In no small part thanks to River's success, Arnie was more in demand than ever before and with a wider variety of acts. Now even Paul's office overlooked Wilshire. Paul, with his self-proclaimed lack of ambition, had been promoted from front desk to executive assistant.

"What did you tell them?"

"That I'm not going to change my fucking nose! Did Arnie know about this?" River asked.

"Arnie's not in right now." Paul sighed.

River and Paul had become close enough friends that he could tell when Paul was covering Arnie's ass. That, and Paul was a terrible liar, which was a great trait in a friend but a truly lousy trait for being in entertainment, much less as an assistant.

"Is that why he had me take the meeting alone? Did you know about this?"

"Swear on my mother, I didn't," Paul said.

"You hate your mother," River said.

"Only because she married my father. And that's beside the point," Paul said.

"When's Arnie getting back?"

"I think he was off to Palm Springs for the weekend. As soon as he checks in, I'll have him call you."

"No. Call me to tell me he's there, and I'll call him. And don't you dare warn him, Paul."

After that disastrous meeting, River went so far as to go to a consultation with one of the most revered surgeons in town, who excitedly pointed out all the things that could be done, eager to be the one to re-sculpt one of the most famous noses in the world. But River couldn't go through with it. It was his mother's nose. His brothers' too. How much more of himself was he expected to lose?

"That would just be bad business to cancel the show over my nose, right?"

"Truly asinine," Paul said. "But . . ."

For a nose, they canceled the show midway through the season. After a considerable period of sulking and threatening to sue, Arnie suggested River leverage the show's success to get back out on the road, get some of that tour money.

"You love performing, Riv," Arnie said. "Fuck television. You don't need them. Go be a performer."

So here he was. But instead of his shows feeling like the exhilarating, life-giving thing they once had been, now they felt more like a consolation prize.

"Riv, come on, we gotta get going," Arnie said just as River broke from him, and the band, and continued toward the crowd waiting for him.

There were too many people around him all the time. People he paid. People he didn't. People who were trying to get him to sell something or buy something or be in something. He couldn't help but be good, he was River Fucking Johnson after all, but he began to feel himself float up elsewhere in the middle of it all, mid-show. As though he were watching River Johnson hit all the right steps, and sing all the right notes, tell all the right jokes, audience in the palm of his hand. He was very bored of being himself. He couldn't take his eyes off the girl in the cast, hovering around the periphery of the fans who waited for him after every show, who looked tired of being herself too.

As the others pushed against the barriers and reached out their hands, she stood back, taking them in as much as anything. He had the distinct impression that he knew that girl. He knew that mink. On her arm, peeking out under the sleeve of her mink, was a purple cast covered in signatures. It was entirely too hot for mink.

He walked toward the squealing fans.

He posed for a few photos, signed a pair or two, and hugged a grandma who didn't speak a lick of English and squeezed him so hard he thought his internal organs might burst, all the while looking at her. She stared straight back at him with a smirk.

When he finally got to the girl, he paused.

"Would you like me to sign your cast?"

"It's pretty full." She laughed. "It's for real broken. Itches like hell. Smells a bit too."

"I always wanted to break something," River said. "I used to daydream about everybody signing my cast at school."

"Don't break yourself, River Johnson. Don't let nobody else break you either."

Her gigantic eyes were very serious as she said that, as though a cloud had momentarily passed over somewhere inside.

"Do I know you?" he asked. "I feel like I know you."

"We met at Jonesie's house a few years back," she said. "Back when he was my old man."

And then River remembered the party in the hills where the two of them had briefly danced. Before she'd disappeared with that old-ass rock star, who had yet another comeback album climbing the charts at the moment.

"I remember," he said softly. "So is he still your old man?"

"He's still somebody's old man. Not mine." She laughed. "I'm Wendy, darling."

She stuck out her good hand and gave his a firm shake.

"Since when they got Black folks in Neverland?" River said. Was that funny? Would she think he was lame? People expected him to be confident, a superstar, whatever that meant. And she was used to hanging around people far more confident than he.

"Really, Neverland should've been all Black folks. We're fucking lucky if we get to grow up." She laughed. It sounded more like a bray, but it was a very warm laugh, the kind that made you feel like you were old friends with years of inside jokes.

"First star on the right and straight on till morning?" he said, lifting up the rope that separated the two of them and holding out his hand.

"It's second star." She laughed and grabbed his hand. "But fuck that movie. 'What makes the red man red?' I mean, come on . . ."

In the hotel, they'd rushed in through the back entrance. In the service elevator, making sure to avoid the paparazzi up front, River wondered if she expected him to kiss her. For somebody who had signed lots of breasts, he hadn't actually touched many. Not erotically. Women were a liability, according to Odysseus. They would want his money, or for him to make them famous. Or they would tell all of his secrets to the tabloids for a pittance. River felt his palms start to sweat and his voice go several octaves higher in the elevator as they approached the room. Maybe this was a bad idea.

He fiddled with the room key an embarrassing amount.

"Doors are tricky," Wendy said before the lock unstuck and he let her in.

═══

THEY TALKED FOR hours in the hotel suite. River showered and put on the plush complimentary robe. He didn't want her to think he was preparing for anything, or expecting anything, but putting on his pajamas seemed almost too familiar. He somehow felt less exposed with nothing between them but a robe. When he went to order room service, he was told it was too late, the kitchen was closed. The woman seemed massively annoyed that he had dared to ask, and thoroughly over her job.

"This is Elmer Fudd," he said gently, and Wendy raised an eyebrow.

You could almost hear the woman straighten up over the phone.

Their food would be delivered as quickly as possible. The woman paused, then said, "My mom is the biggest fan. She has all your albums. I mean . . . not that you're just for moms. I like you very much too, Mr. . . . em . . . Fudd."

"Thank you," he said. "Appreciate you. Tell you what, I'll leave you both tickets at the box office to tomorrow's show. Just lemme get your info real fast and I'll pass it along."

He quickly pulled the phone away from his ear as the woman shrieked.

Wendy laughed when he got off the phone. "Elmer Fudd?"

"Nobody would guess it was me. Isn't that the point?" River laughed. "I don't usually pull that . . . I'm not that kind of person."

"I didn't think you were . . . you wascally wabbit. You just about made that girl's year, far as I could tell. Hey, you want coke? I got some really good shit."

"Nah, I'm good. I gotta be up early tomorrow."

"Suit yourself," Wendy said, using a fingernail to snort the powder from a baggie hidden in her coat pocket.

Full of steak, good and drunk, and a little high, Wendy straddled him and began to kiss him. She pulled the robe off his shoulders. River looked down at her delicate hands against his bare skin.

"You're married?"

"What?"

"The ring?"

"Oh that. I stole it."

River briefly wondered if the girl might steal from him. He was in a very compromised position like this.

"It belonged to my mother," she said, only slightly reassuringly.

"Is she dead?"

"Oh no! I ran away. Ages ago."

"Are your folks looking for you?" River asked with great concern.

"No. I'm a grown-up now. Plus, my mother only cares about my stepfather. My stepfather is why I ran away . . ." She laughed, though there was a long sour note underneath. "The ring was one my real dad gave her . . ."

He'd always envied people who told all their business so freely. Who didn't wear their pasts tied to them like a hidden weight. River thought about his parents. He and his mother were talking more these days, mostly about his brothers. Rocco had been in a group home for a little over a year and he seemed like he was doing okay there, overall. Still, River felt shitty about it. He knew there'd been some nasty business with a paparazzo that prompted the move, even if Emmeline insisted it had been Rocco's choice. Roman seemed to mostly be staying sober after his most recent rehab stay, but their mother fretted about him and their father butting heads at the shop. And whenever River and his father spoke, it felt as though Odysseus was still in manager mode. Their most recent convo had consisted of his father lecturing him to joke around more in interviews. "White folks want the River Johnson from the TV show! Not some mopey Negro kid talking about his art too seriously."

"It's more than just white folks buying my records. And I'm not just 'some mopey Negro' kid anymore," River argued, but it was no use.

Odysseus and Emmeline had always tried to do right by their boys, and yet . . .

He felt as though he wanted this tiny girl with her seasonally inappropriate mink and her mysteriously broken arm to know everything there was to know about him. *I'm the reason my brother is in an institution,* he thought. *It's all my fault that we're not a trio. That my older brother's a drunk. That a ghost child is wandering the world all alone. All because I was selfish. My success is at the expense of my brothers.*

I'm an asshole, River thought, and took a swig of his drink, *I don't deserve any of this.* That's what he wanted to tell her, but he didn't, not exactly.

"There used to be a ghost that lived with us for a bit, when I was a kid." River hadn't told anybody about Christmas, except Milton way back when. He could hardly believe he was saying it to this girl he'd only just met.

"How did he die?" Wendy sat up to look at him.

"Lynched, I think? We didn't really discuss it. But he was so little . . . Couldn't have been more than ten."

"That's awful. Is he still with your parents?"

"Nah. He . . . left. It's kinda complicated."

Wendy nodded as though it were the most natural thing in the world to discuss.

"Maybe he just went on to the next life?" she said.

"Maybe. But I don't think so. Just a feeling I get. You know?" River said.

"Poor kiddo . . . I wonder how many of us there are like him out in the world . . . like, what if there's just a bunch of these little Black souls a-wandering?"

River didn't reply for a very long time.

Then, instead of talking, he reached for her and she sank into his arms, under his body, and the two of them together felt safe, except for when he accidentally bumped her cast a little too hard and she yelped. And while River had worried about being far more inexperienced than most people his age, certainly most people Wendy had been with, she reassured him by taking the lead.

Afterward, Wendy put on her underwear and got down on the hotel-room floor and began to fold herself into some sort of formation.

"Are you stretching?" River said.

"It's yoga! Have you ever tried it?"

River shook his head. He knew it was all the rage in circles he ran in, but he had never himself felt inclined to twist and turn his body into funky shapes while breathing deeply.

"It clears my head," Wendy said.

"Does your head often need clearing?" River said.

"Doesn't yours?" She drank from a mini-size Jack Daniel's bottle before inhaling and exhaling deeply. River did too.

"Breathe, River," Wendy said. "You're not breathing."

═

WENDY HAD SERVED as a "muse" to any number of music men who were old enough to be her father, or even her grandfather, which mostly meant that they'd sucked the youth from her supple skin until what was left was harder than she should have been at such a tender age. She had seen far more than River, which was saying something considering. She liked Carole King and João Gilberto and Dolly Parton and the Stooges. She liked Loretta Lynn but always made it a point to note disparagingly that she was a Republican. She loved Gilda Radner and Jane Curtin and was fond of yelling at River when aggrieved, "River, you ignorant slut!"

Wendy also really loved cocaine and alcohol and increasingly smack, all of which was in plentiful supply on the road. This was why she had on the mink coat at all times—Wendy was always cold.

"Hot dog!" she exclaimed when she was surprised or happy or both. Like when River surprised her with a beautiful dark-chocolate Lab puppy thinking she would get high a little less often if she had something to care for.

She raised the chubby puppy to her face and let it lick her lips.

"Black folks don't kiss their dogs like that," River said.

"This one does," Wendy said. "Plus, look at him! He's blacker than the both of us!"

They went to hidden bookstores and record stores and briefly took up jogging together.

They went to movies, often with River in outlandish disguises that amused them more than the movies themselves. River was partial to comedies, but Wendy loved black-and-white European dramas and blaxploitation. She decided to name their dog Shaft.

They were almost the exact same size, and River often woke up to Wendy putting on his clothes and insisting he try hers.

"You need a new look!" she said insistently.

"This ain't no drag show," River said. For just the briefest of moments, he thought of his very first visit to the Apollo. How the whole Johnson family had buzzed with excitement as they sat down to check out the acoustics and watch the Jewel Box Revue. How in awe he'd been. How very long ago it was.

"All the cool boys are wearing girl clothes," she countered. "Bowie's running around in lipstick."

"I'm not him."

"No. You're River Fucking Johnson," Wendy said. "And I think your ass would look perfect in my corduroys."

Wendy pushed him further and further with his look and eventually people took notice. In some rag, he was labeled a new "style star." Wendy shrieked and River laughed and that night they drank champagne and ate cake for dinner.

River had a notebook of songs he'd written here and there over the years, mostly too shy to share them with anybody but Wendy. He was thought of as a performer, not a songwriter. A pretty conduit for others' prettier words. Even the co-writer credits he'd received were mostly for rearranging the vocals here and there. Every song he'd brought to the label so far had been politely rejected. But when he handed Wendy the fading composition notebook that still said "River Johnson: Grade Nine" in which he'd accumulated bits and bobs of songs, a bridge here, chorus there, Wendy sat with it for a good long while.

"Here you are," she'd said finally, and smiled. "When you're ready. This is it."

From then on, whenever she thought he'd said anything particularly observant or silly or angsty it became a joke of theirs for Wendy to shout, "Write it!"

So he did.

═══

WHAT WOULD HIS parents have to say about her? Nothing good, he supposed. He'd never had that teenage ritual of bringing a date home. Still, he could hear Odysseus's voice in his head: *You don't need any distractions. You can't be getting anybody pregnant, River. There's different standards for us. We've worked too hard to get you to this point. You can't let no hussy get in the way of—*

═══

WEEKS LATER, DURING a weekend jaunt to L.A. in the middle of a cluster of East Coast charity shows, they met up with Paul at O-Sho. He waved River over and stood up to greet Wendy.

"I love everything about this," he said, gesturing at Wendy's sequined caftan, topped by her fur coat that somehow managed to look ever better for being worn in patches.

"River's never introduced me to somebody he's dating before," Paul said to Wendy. "You must be pretty special."

"I've never had time to date anyone," River said.

"So you've said," Paul said, eyebrows lifted.

Wendy was an especially large fan of the sashimi, and Paul was an especially big fan of Wendy's.

"She's fabulous," Paul said after she'd excused herself to the restroom. "I love it. I love her. Let's live in a throuple together. I'm only half-joking."

In the corner, a couple stared at River.

River nodded over to the bar at a pretty brunette with delicate features as though just barely water-colored on. If he were another man he might've been flattered by the intensity of her gaze.

The woman headed over to the two of them. Paul turned to look in the direction of River's gaze. "Oh fuck, it's her."

River didn't know if he should get up or stay put behind the safety of the giant booth.

"I painted this for you," the woman said. "I keep trying to deliver it to you, but you're never home."

River looked over at Paul wide-eyed as the woman presented River with a portrait of the two of them together. It was pretty well done and obviously the woman had spent hours and hours of her time. A painstaking amount of work. He was grateful, but still, how had the woman found him here?

"That's very thoughtful of you," River said, choosing his words carefully.

"I tried giving it to him a month ago." She gestured at Paul.

"Do you remember when we took the photo I used for this?" she said, gesturing to the painting. "I went to every show that tour!"

"Wow. I owe you a refund. The sound was shit on a few of those nights. Sound guys couldn't get it together at first. Or maybe it was just me," River joked.

"Every night was perfect." The woman beamed. "You're perfect."

"Well, we should get going—" Paul stood up. River followed his lead. The check would be dealt with swiftly enough.

"One question: Who is she?" the woman said, glowering in the direction of the bathroom as Wendy returned to the table.

═══

THE THREE OF them linked arms as they headed toward the valet together.

"I need a new security detail," River said solemnly.

"I'll call the company for you as soon as I get in the car." Paul nodded.

"I wish my parents would move." River sighed. "That house is too accessible."

What River suspected was that Emmeline didn't want to move in case the little ghost child made his way back to them. But it had been so long now. Surely Christmas had found another family by now?

"You know how parents are." Paul shrugged and lit a cigarette.

"Where's the Du Pont?" River asked.

"It crapped out on me again. That's the problem with old cars and old men alike." Paul giggled.

"How come you don't want me to meet your folks yet?" Wendy asked. River knew it was a sore spot, but he figured of all people, Wendy would be the one to understand how family had a way of twisting you about yourself. Never mind the fans. Appearing available was important when young women were half your audience. Not to mention the fact that Paul sorted through any number of death threats sent to Arnie's office on a regular basis. If they were particularly freaky, or the spelling was especially egregious, Paul would call up River and share it with him for a laugh. The more menacing ones they reported to the authorities, just in case. Still, they unsettled him, these people who hated him so deeply on account of his "stupid face" or the fact that he "tried too hard." The truly unhinged could find out his whereabouts on tour pretty easily, not to mention entirely too many of the letters started with "Dear Nigger."

"It's not like that," River said. "It's . . ."

"Complicated," Wendy completed.

River kissed the top of her head. "It's not you."

CHAPTER FORTY-FOUR

THE FIRST TIME AMERICANS LANDED ON THE MOON ALL THOSE YEARS ago, Roman, Rocco, and even Christmas had crowded around the black-and-white TV, adjusting and readjusting the antenna. Poor Christmas had contorted himself around the antenna so that the picture was less fuzzy, but every time he moved an inch, it all went to hell.

"Stay still!" Roman snapped at Christmas.

"But I can't see what's happening!" Christmas yelled back.

"Haven't you been to space before?" River asked. He just assumed that one of the perks of being dead like Christmas was that you could go anywhere, see anything. "What's it like?"

"I've never been," Christmas said quietly.

"But can't you? Can't you go anywhere?"

"I don't know. I never knew space was a place I could try to go. Maybe we didn't have space then?" Christmas said.

Rocco thought this was very silly. Of course they had space then, but Christmas was just a little boy, he had to remind himself. Rocco was much older. Why, just the other morning, he'd woken up in his own sticky. Nocturnal emissions, they'd called it in health class.

"Try it. Try to go to space now," River said.

Christmas had looked from River to Roman to Rocco.

"Try it," Rocco said. "Try it!" He jumped up and clapped around the room.

Roman looked skeptical. "He can't go to space. He's dead, not magical."

Rocco thought this was incorrect too. Wasn't the fact that he was here among them a kind of magic?

"He can too," Rocco said. "He can go anywhere, can't you, Christmas?"

This was the longest sentence he'd spoken in some time.

"No, he can't."

"Shut up!" Christmas said. He closed his eyes. They watched breathlessly as the baby ghost began to tremble.

"It's happening!" River yelled.

Christmas quaked violently, his whole body itself like a rocket. The house shook.

Rocco, Roman, and River looked on, mouths agape, preparing themselves for lift-off.

"What is going on down there?" Emmeline yelled from upstairs.

And then, Christmas began to cry. Big, fat tears. Real ones that landed on the shag carpet by the television.

See, Roman thought, *magic.*

"I don't want to go. It's too much nothing. I don't want to be in all that nothing by myself," Christmas wailed.

Emmeline came down the stairs. "Why is he crying? What happened?"

The boys all looked at one another sheepishly.

"What's wrong, baby?" Emmeline said to Christmas.

"I don't want to be in all that nothing by myself," he blubbered.

"What is he talking about?" she said.

"We were trying to get him to go to space," River finally spoke up.

The truth was that River, Rocco, and Roman had all been obsessed with space since handsome Ed Dwight had appeared on the cover of *Jet* six years before. A Negro? In the stars? They had run around with glass bowls on their heads, their arms stretched out from their sides, breath fogging the glass, ready for flight. Maybe one day they too could fly. They counted to lift-off and jumped off the couch. And Emmeline and Odysseus let them, 'cause it made them giddy too, River could tell. When it was announced that Dwight had not been selected for space, they put away their glass bowls and soured on NASA.

"That money should be going to the needy," Roman said. "Or to Black folks."

"Yeah," he said.

Still, they'd all wondered what it was like to be weightless.

With Christmas before them, it was maybe the closest the boys would ever come to space flight, to what was beyond.

"Christmas, baby, you don't have to go anywhere you don't want to go," Emmeline said. His mother was always tender in her words to Christmas.

They settled down and watched the white men soar to new heights. They floated and planted the red-white-and-blue and even the freedom fighters paused mid-protest in awe. One small step, one giant leap, blah blah.

Back then, Odysseus was still in California and they were still back home. His mother had held the phone up to the air between them and the boys had huddled close to the receiver. Even Roman, who was in a better mood then, before he had been unceremoniously dumped among a bunch of neanderthals in Catholic school. Or so he called them.

"Isn't it magical?" Odysseus had said breathlessly to them all, and for a few moments they didn't feel all the thousands of miles between them.

═

RIVER WAS THINKING of all of this as he sat next to Rocco on the grassy lawn of the group home. The most recent place in which River had placed Rocco was a beautiful house covered in elaborate stonework, a former mansion that some rich lady had left to charity and now was a residential facility for mentally ill young adults. The long distance from the iron front gate to the home itself was perfect for making sure no paparazzo could sneak any shots of Rocco. Not that any of them knew where he was, but just in case.

"I'm not mentally ill," Rocco said when River had shown him the brochure over a year ago.

"I know. But the place is nice," River replied. "You'll like it."

And he did. It had a huge front lawn on which you could sit in the sun and read comics, or play a game called bocce ball, though Rocco hated how sometimes other people cheated, because the rules were the rules and if you couldn't be trusted not to cheat at bocce, then who even were you? A rainbow of roses covered the backyard, and some of the other residents tended to them carefully as though each rose were a baby just born, with plenty of butterflies and bees and sometimes bunnies to celebrate.

"Are Mom and Dad still all weird and awkward when they visit?" River said.

"Everything is weird." Rocco sighed. "You're weird. Not me though."

He smiled impishly before bursting out into laughter, and River joined him.

"Mom said more words to Dad last time they were here. Oh! And he touched her back as they were leaving and she smiled at him," Rocco reported. "That's love behavior, right?"

"Yeah," River said. "It's something."

"So, they're something. I guess," Rocco said.

River nodded. "We're all something."

A plane flew overhead and Rocco reached up to trace its path with his finger. The best part about the place was that it was right on the flight path. As he'd grown older and River toured more and more, Rocco's boyhood fascination with butterflies had moved over to accommodate the particulars of passenger planes.

"I think that's a DC-10," Rocco said.

"I've been meaning to tell you! I started flying lessons!" River said to Rocco as they watched the contrail slowly smudge and fade.

Rocco nodded.

"When I've logged enough hours, you, me, and Wendy, we'll go anywhere in the world. I promise. Like we talked about."

Rocco could never remember them talking about flying planes and said so.

"You know, like space!" River said.

"The sky isn't space," Rocco said.

"But it's close," River said.

"Space is very big," Rocco said.

"So's the sky," River said.

"Not like that," Rocco said.

"When I'm up there, I feel both very important and like absolutely nothing at all," River said.

CHAPTER FORTY-FIVE

1975

EVEN WITH THE INCREASED DEATH THREATS, WENDY WAS IN A GOOD mood. River was about to perform at the Grammys for the very first time (though he'd been one of the top-selling acts for some time now, there was absolutely no reason he shouldn't have been invited to perform before). Word had broken to the tabloids of their relationship, and River's fans weren't happy. There were nasty letters filled with horrible ways in which the letter writers hoped Wendy might meet her end, one of which looked to be smudged with something like blood. Threats of kidnapping or maiming Shaft were reported to River's security detail and the police immediately. Wendy didn't fuck around when it came to her dog.

The harm people wished upon her got under her skin like a twelve-gauge needle, still she could handle it. That some of them addressed her politely as "Miss Wendy Love" before releasing a torrent of depravity entertained her even, if she was in the right mood.

Wendy didn't believe in much, but she believed in River. He was easy to believe in. River was the first person who had ever really loved her. Everything he wanted for himself, she wanted for him. The awards, the acclaim, even flight. That's how they'd wound up in this rickety old plane in the Torrance Airport (less likely for the paparazzi to be there, River said), with a cartoonishly mustachioed instructor who'd asked her if she had any cocaine, not fifteen minutes before they boarded.

For weeks, River had refused to let her accompany him, said it was off-limits, but she begged and begged and now here they were, the two of them, lifting off. Three, if you counted the instructor, who Wendy generally preferred to pretend didn't exist. River liked him though. Perhaps there was some redeeming quality she hadn't yet observed. At the moment, the pilot seemed more interested in River's brief time on the road with that famous guitarist who'd died tragically than in teaching River how to get them safely from point A to point B.

"River was a just a kid then," Wendy interrupted. She couldn't help but be protective of River, of what the world demanded of him, his life, his feelings, his time. Plus, Wendy knew exactly what it felt like to miss a childhood. To have the wrong grown-ups take more from you than they gave. Around them, the plane shook with the instability of ascent. They cut unevenly through the clouds until finally the whole Palos Verdes Peninsula spread out before them to the left of her, and ahead of them just a little ways across the ocean, Catalina Island.

"So, the Grammys! That's incredible, man!" the instructor said to River, ignoring her.

"Yeah. My dad's thrilled," River said.

"What about you?" the instructor asked. "You nervous?"

"I don't know. I'm . . . I'm tired, man. I've been doing this since I was a kid. Sometimes I wish I could leave it all behind."

Something about being up in the sky made River uncharacteristically open with a stranger, or perhaps it was all the hours he and the instructor had logged together approximating friendship.

"What else would you do?"

"I don't know. This maybe." River gestured at the cockpit, then turned back to look at Wendy. "What do you think?"

"I think you should turn back around and pay attention when you got me up in the air in this rickety-ass plane!"

The flight lesson came to its shaky, bumpy conclusion, which involved the instructor hurriedly taking over before what would have been entirely too fast a landing. The asshole had quick reflexes, even all coked up, Wendy had to give that to him. As soon as the plane finally came to a jolt of a stop, Wendy vomited on herself.

"Good luck with the Grammys, kid!" the instructor said to River before gesturing over at Wendy and making a face as she puked. "And that one."

═══

OVER THE LAST few weeks, Wendy had thrown up more than she had in her life before now, and that was saying a lot, given how she'd partied before River came along. Upon finding out she was pregnant, it was surprisingly easy to give everything up. Even alcohol, and she hadn't been to sleep without at least a nightcap, or two, since she was thirteen and sneaking her mom's liquor.

When she had finally summoned the courage to bring the pregnancy test over to River, they'd both looked at it in shock.

"Shit," River said. Wendy couldn't tell if it was a good shit or a bad shit. He repeated it again in disbelief, among a slew of other expletives, and she was briefly afraid he was going to ask her to "get it taken care of." The tears were already pooling in her eyes when River grabbed her up in his arms with a definitely more emphatic "Fuuuuck! We're gonna be parents!"

He'd gently wiped the tears away from her eyes and held her face in his hands. "This is a good thing, right?"

At that, Wendy'd nodded and burst into happy sobs.

River serenaded their baby every night as they fell asleep. At eight weeks, she read, the baby had ear folds but wouldn't be able to hear for another ten weeks. Still, why not?

Wendy was not an especially sentimental person, but she kept her favorite Peanuts comic crumpled in her fur coat, rumpled from years of folding and unfolding. In it, Lucy offers Snoopy psychiatric help for five cents. "Say to yourself . . . 'I am loved. I am needed. I am important.' "

This is how River Johnson and their baby made her feel. Baby. Embryo? Or was it a fetus now? Whatever. They were hers.

ON THE DAY of River's first performance at the Grammys, the second ultrasound revealed that the baby still didn't have a detectable heartbeat. The doctor had asked them to come in for another ultrasound, mere weeks after the first, "just as a precaution," which Wendy took to mean that either something was wrong or maybe it was just that she herself was wrong. And River took it to mean that the doctor was just being extra thorough given his celebrity patient. The baby hadn't grown much since the last ultrasound three weeks prior. Though Wendy wasn't sure how anybody could tell anything at all from the blurry image on the screen next to her. That was the future, she supposed. They were going to have to test her HCG levels.

Still, it was the doctor's opinion that this newfangled technology stressed new mothers out unnecessarily, her kindly older OB said as he tossed his surgical gloves into the waste. "I'm sure you'll be fine."

The phlebotomist stretched Wendy's arm across the padded table and took her fading scars in silently.

"I haven't done anything while pregnant," Wendy snapped defensively.

"I didn't say you had, dear," the older lady said.

She poked Wendy several times before finally finding a vein. Whether or not it was on purpose, Wendy wasn't entirely certain.

The Hollywood Palladium wasn't nearly as glamorous as it seemed on television. Still, several years earlier, the first time Wendy'd run away from home, she had made her way to the Palladium for Pop Expo '69 to see the MC5. She was almost embarrassed now at how enthusiastically teenage Wendy had yelled, "*Kick out the jams!*"

Tonight, the womblike velvet circles and the chandeliers looked different as all the world's biggest stars stood under them, instead of a bunch of unwashed wannabe teen rebels. Even dirty-ass Sunset gleamed a little differently as the limos pulled up to the front entrance and all the glittery people made their way inside. Wendy had pickpocketed a few times in front of here in another life, usually closer to the Chinese Theatre. When tourists bent over to take pictures of themselves matching famous hands in concrete, she and another runaway, Donna, ran distractions for each other. If only her old friends could see her now!

For tonight's Grammys, Andy Williams was the host. Wendy found him and the self-congratulatory nature of the industry all spectacularly boring. Still, she leaned in and told River, "My mother would absolutely lose her shit at all of this."

She had been cramping all day, but it wasn't much cause for alarm. Pregnancy seemed to be all weird sensations, worrying about said weird sensations, only to be told it was perfectly normal and feeling as though your body were no longer entirely yours. Still, the cramps were building in intensity. Far stronger than any she'd felt before. River stood up from their table to excuse himself backstage, to ready himself for his performance.

For weeks, she'd tried to persuade him to invite Emmeline and Odysseus; it was such a huge moment in his career. River had emphatically shaken his head no.

"They'll just make me nervous. I need to be able to concentrate," he'd said. She knew he wanted to impress his peers, to be seen as a legitimate performer, not just the cute child prodigy who became a television host ever so briefly. But why did River Fucking Johnson need to prove himself to anyone?

Plus, his parents would almost certainly think it was Wendy's fault he hadn't invited them. Didn't parents blame the girlfriend when a son excluded them from some major life moment?

"I thought things were better," she heard his mother say. "I thought everything was better."

"It is," River said. "This has nothing to do with you guys."

"Why are you still punishing us?" River's father said.

"Jesus, I'm not punishing anybody," she heard River say into the phone.

"But Riv, it's the Grammys—" Wendy had hardly been able to form a counterargument when River hung up the phone with them. "I get why they're upset. I don't understand—"

"We both have our family shit," he said gently. "I don't press you. Can you please not press me?"

"That's different," she said.

"Can we just have this moment be for the two of us?" River slowly reiterated.

She hadn't known if he meant the baby or the Grammys, but she'd held his face in her hands and agreed. "And a televised audience," she whispered, and they both laughed so hard she peed her pants.

═══

A WAVE OF pain hit that was so bad, Wendy thought she might actually pass out. She had to get to a restroom quickly.

"Wait? Where you off to? Riv's gonna be going on any minute," Arnie said.

"I'll be right back," she barely squeaked out. The pain was so intense that Wendy could hardly breathe.

She tried to hold herself upright as she pushed toward the back of the room, past the bar where a lovely pop princess they'd had dinner with earlier in the year tried to intercept her.

"So sorry, darling, I'm about to explode." Wendy air-kissed in the direction of the woman's cheek.

Until just now, she had carried the hope that the doctors were wrong. That her baby was simply so snug inside that they couldn't quite get a handle on her yet. Or perhaps she was actually a few weeks or so behind what they thought she was. Wendy had done everything right, all the dos and don'ts of pregnancy. This baby had to be all right. Wendy had willed it so.

The bathroom attendant smiled at her as she stumbled past two women in glittery dresses doing their white lines. The attendant wore a neat, bobbed wig and frosted shadow. The vest of her uniform just barely fit over her massive breasts, and the black skirt stretched over an equally impressive ass. She gave the impression of being maternal. Or maybe because she was a Black woman of a certain age, Wendy just assumed her to be so.

She sat down on the toilet, lifting her golden gown as best as she could around her waist. She was bleeding for real now, not just the spotting and cramping of earlier. She felt another wave of pain split her open and she cried out loud.

"You OK in there?" the attendant said.

"No," Wendy moaned. "No. No. No."

She looked down into the toilet and saw blood and tissue. Something strangely veiny and yellowish, next to it, a red clot.

"Do you need me to call the ambulance?" the attendant said.

"I don't know," Wendy said.

"Withdrawal?" a woman in the stall next to her said. "Fuck, I've been there."

"I . . . I think I'm having a miscarriage."

"Oh shit," the woman in the stall next to her said.

"I want my mother," Wendy cried. Her mother, who didn't know where she was. Or that she was even pregnant. Her stupid fucking mother, who had chosen to believe a man over her own daughter. Still, right now, she needed her, her mama.

"Can I open your stall door?" the attendant said.

Wendy hadn't locked it. "It's open."

The attendant knelt down next to her on the floor. She placed her cold hand on Wendy's bare back as Wendy held her head in her hands.

The white girls doing coke looked over from their perch by the mirror.

"Do you need something for the pain?" One of the glitter girls came over and stood by the attendant. "I think I got a Percocet. Would that help?"

"Pretty certain JoJo has heroin," Glitter One said to Glitter Two. "That would probably do the trick."

"This is the absolute worst of it," Glitter Two said, looking down at Wendy. "I've been there. I landed in the emergency room with hemorrhaging for one of mine."

The opening notes of River's latest single ripped through the Palladium. Even muffled, Wendy could hear him.

"River," she whispered.

"He's a dream, isn't he?" Glitter One gazed in the direction of River's voice. "I've seen him, like, ten times in person and every time I'm like, 'Goddamn, this man is incredible!' "

The attendant began to hum along with River's song.

"When I was in labor, I sang to help distract me from the pain. I know it's not the same, but maybe it would help?" she said.

In girlish pink scrawl, with hearts over the eyes, one of the death threats she'd received read, "Dear Wendy, darling. I wish you were a drawing so I could erase every single piece of you and you'd be powerless to stop me. I would start with your pretty legs, then your nice tits, then your smug stupid smile, I'd erase your teeth, one by one. I would erase and erase you until there was nothing left and the paper was worn holey. That's how you've made us real fans feel."

Wendy thought perhaps this was the girl making good on her promise. How could she still be alive through all of this? She looked between her legs and saw more tissue and then another sharp pain like a lightning strike to her body, and she felt something almost gelatinous pass from her body.

There it was, a sac. She was too afraid to look any closer, for fear of what else she would see, fingers, toes, her very heart outside her body. The attendant glanced in the toilet bowl and saw it too.

"Oh babygirl," she said, her black bob wig slightly askew.

"My baby!" Wendy cried.

Outside the bathroom, the crowd roared.

CHAPTER FORTY-SIX

IT WAS AT A PARTY IN LONDON, TWO MONTHS AFTER THEIR MISCARRIAGE, that River kissed the first man in his adult life.

They were all of them drunk and stupid high.

"Time to really get this shit started," a very famous rock star with swinging hips and trademark lips said to have come from some passing Black relative yelled as he put on Fela's *Gentleman*.

"*I no be gentleman at all,*" a B-list English rose sang, and swayed along with Fela's voice. A hit-making record producer with a trademark afro and a great affinity for skinny white chicks, who was not-so-secretly fucking a famous Black singer on the side, sidled up to her.

On deck was T. Rex, and Dibango's "Soul Makossa," and new kid Louisa Mark's single "Caught You in a Lie." They kicked off their shoes and drank and danced and did lines and poppers with each other into the wee hours until they collapsed on the orange couch in the sunken living room. And then, as though they'd reached some sort of witching hour, there was a palpable shift in the energy of the room. On the record player, Serge Gainsbourg and Jane Birkin moaned and writhed into their mics "Je t'aime . . . moi non plus."

"I heard that's really her . . . being pleasured . . . on the track," said a foulmouthed comedian whose trenchant political observations had gotten him banned in several states, waggling his eyebrows.

It felt too crass a choice for the waning hours of a party, too obviously transgressive. Plus, River preferred Gainsbourg with Bardot in "Comic Strip," but what did he know?

"*Woop shebam pow plop whiz!*" he sang aloud. He was, of course, very high.

Wendy leaned over and placed her hand on River's cheek, kissing him.

They hadn't been intimate at all since the miscarriage. River was afraid of hurting her any more than he already had.

Secretly, River wondered if somehow the fetus had sensed his ambivalence at the idea of being a father. How much would he have to give up? To grow up? He was still young, and his newest tour was selling out. Things were going well, really well, according to Arnie. How would his fans feel about him becoming a father? Arnie said a small percentage of his fan club was sending Wendy death threats as it was.

"I fucking hate my body right now," Wendy said after the bleeding and pain had mostly passed. "It's disgusting."

"Your body isn't disgusting," River said. Though maybe not as emphatically as he probably should have.

"It can't even do the one thing it's supposed to do," she said with more venom than he'd ever heard her spit at anything in the entire time he'd known her. Including Republicans.

And now here they were, with Wendy as beautiful as ever. He was overwhelmed by a desire to take her out of this place, to go somewhere just the two of them, where they could be as they once were.

Wendy turned and kissed the pretty brunette next to them who had just died in a horror film that was all the rage with the art-house crowd. River gripped his wife's leg as though she were a teddy bear, or a security blanket, needing the reassurance. That she would not leave him alone in this strange space, this strange state.

How was this all so wordless? How did everybody but River know what was OK and what was not? Or was it that everything was OK with this crowd?

River was famous, but he wasn't particularly debauched. He worked really hard. Stayed mostly sober. He left before parties got wild, content to cuddle up with Shaft while Wendy stayed out and partied. And now? The rock star kissed River's wife's thighs, pushing her dress up with his teeth, and River felt himself growing aroused. The rock star looked over at him.

"Goddamn," he said.

The rock star then reached over and grabbed at River's lap.

"I've never done this before," River whispered, but nobody seemed to be listening, or to care.

Soon they were all mouths and fingers and open longing. Everything and everyone was a blur. He was utterly intoxicated by the smell of the man's cologne, the musk, the stubble that rubbed against his cheek. He felt somebody unzip his pants and then a man's hand reach around him.

"Wait!" River said.

"It's OK," Wendy whispered to him. Or maybe to herself? "You'll be OK, Riv. We'll be OK."

River felt a great welling up inside him, and then a release.

═

SOMETHING THAT HE had shoved so very deep inside of himself stirred in the smooth and rough of that twilight. If before he'd been afraid to touch Wendy, after that party in London, they couldn't get enough of each other. He didn't keep his fantasies from her, just as she didn't keep hers from him. River had not been able to get the memory of that debauched night out of his head, and as they touched, they spoke of the others, male and female.

"What am I?" he'd said to her afterward. "Am I . . . what does this make me?"

"All it makes you is River Fucking Johnson." Wendy giggled and threw her arm around him. It was then that he noticed the newest track mark on her arm.

"Wendy . . ."

"I'm trying, River. I really am," she said, disappearing her face under the covers. She started singing mockingly as a means of shutting him up, and he let her, "*Someone saved my life tonight . . .*"

═

A WEEK LATER, she surprised him for dinner at Lutèce with an All-American football player turned up-and-coming actor and his girlfriend, who was on the fast track to becoming a legendary beauty, if not a particularly great actress, herself. The two were shooting a movie nearby. Together, after dinner, they all drank and increasingly touched one another's arms and thighs as they swapped stories in the back room at Max's into the wee hours. Eventually, Wendy's legs intertwined with the beauty's, who kept excitedly kissing Wendy on the cheek. The women not-so-briefly excused themselves to the powder room. As they waited for their partners, the football player threw his arm across River's chair, his thigh coming to rest against River's.

Well-built, with an athlete's body that had softened only a little for Hollywood, the former team captain's blond hair occasionally fell into his eyes as he spoke. Whenever he pushed the strands away with his hand, River felt all the blood rush out of one head and into the other. They talked awkwardly about politics, and the people they knew in common, until their girls came back disheveled and newly coked up. On the model's collarbone, he could see a trace of Wendy's lipstick.

"So what do you think? Should we move this upstairs?" the football player said as though rallying them all for a big game.

Everyone murmured their assent. It was safe, wasn't it? Very cosmopolitan of them, even. There were no rules. Not for people like them. It was the '70s!

And besides, not a one of them would tell a soul. Everyone had something, or someone, to lose.

The deepest shame flooded over River the next day. He walked over to Wendy and buried his face in her neck as she brushed her teeth. "You don't have to do this for me."

She gargled and spat before turning to face him. She put her hand on his cheek gently. "Oh Riv, I love you. But who said this was for you?"

"I just . . . I feel all twisted around." He nuzzled into her palm.

"Write it down," she said, hocking another load of Colgate into the sink.

TWO WEEKS LATER River returned from an interview to find Wendy in a hotel room in Madison, Wisconsin, folded over on the floor, Shaft pawing at her chest. He raced over to her body, pushed the puppy out of the way, and began CPR. Foam pooled at the corners of her mouth. Spilled out her nostrils. River wiped it away with his shirt before placing his mouth on hers, willing her to breathe. After several failed attempts, he ran over to the phone and dialed the front desk.

"Somebody help! Please!"

Then he dialed 911.

River massaged her heart, willing her back. "Come on, Wendy!"

"You're wasting your time, babe," he heard her voice say from across the room. Scared River near out of his skin.

"The fuck?"

Wendy sat in a chair with her feet up on the table. He stared at her ghostly form while still holding her not-yet-cold body.

"You can see me?" She leapt up excitedly. "Hot dog! I'm a ghost!"

He started crying.

"It was an accident, Riv," she said gently. "Too much . . . Stopped my heart."

"Did it hurt?"

She didn't answer him.

"I'm so sorry, Wendy. I'm so sorry I let this happen to you."

He could hear the ambulance sirens growing closer and closer.

"Oh come off it, Riv. You didn't let anything happen to me. I did this to me. Don't be a martyr."

Shaft walked over to the chair in which Wendy sat as though he could feel her.

"Riv, what if you just, like, stopped performing? If it's not making you happy anymore, why keep doing it?"

"I can't."

"But what if you just . . . did? You don't have to be anything other than who you want to be, you know?"

"It's all I have now," River said.

"Well, that's melodramatic, Riv."

"Wendy. You're fucking dead!" he shouted at her. "I think I can be as dramatic as I want."

"You don't think I know that?" Wendy laughed. "I'm the dead one."

River didn't want to get into an argument with his dead wife.

"Anyway, I just thought I'd ask."

Just then, there was a knock on the door. The hotel security was accompanied by police and paramedics. River noticed the police officer taking note of who he was. There was a good chance this would be in the papers the next day. Maybe the evening news. Fuck.

"What happened?" the paramedic said. "I need you to move out of the way, sir."

"Little rough with me, aren't they?" Wendy said as the paramedics struggled to clear her airways. River hadn't thought to clear the floor of

Wendy's drug paraphernalia. He saw the police officer take inventory of it all. The gray-haired man bent over to touch the needle with a latex glove.

"Well," Wendy said. "This part is kind of a bummer."

River whispered, "Don't go. Don't leave me."

He felt the tears rolling down his eyes.

"It's OK, Riv. You're OK," Wendy said, looking at him so intently he thought she might actually be able to see the heart breaking in his chest. "You're OK. Just as you are. Do you get what I'm saying?"

Before he could answer, she said, "Oh . . . and River? Write it down."

She giggled and then she was gone.

═══

"MAN, FUCK RIVER Johnson. He's a coon!" It was a deliberate challenge. Everyone backstage knew River was in earshot.

The young man running his mouth wasn't much older than River himself. He was part of the stage crew at the venue, chest puffed, with creamy skin that would pass even the most stringent of paper-bag tests. The brown curls upon his head flopped this way and that, with barely any kink to them at all. Only his nose and the shape of his mouth gave away that he was Black. The young man was the kind of pompous that came with a lifetime of being fawned over and told that he was better-than. River should know.

River walked over to the young man. "Excuse me, what did you just say?"

Normally, River was not one for confrontation. He had too much home training, too much media training, too much at stake for righteous anger. But today, Arnie had begged him to take something, uppers, downers or, hell, both. They could cancel the rest of the tour after this, if that's what River needed, but River just had to get through tonight. Wendy's overdose had not yet made the news. In Ireland, the Protestants and the Catholics were fighting. A very popular interfaith Irish band, the Miami Showband, had been intercepted at a fake checkpoint on their way home to Dublin from a concert, and several members were killed. What was one drug overdose in light of that? He didn't know whether to be angry or relieved. Wendy's death had meant something to him. Everything. How could it not be in there? Her mink coat still lay across the fainting couch. He had slept in it for part of the night, feeling like some feral, hibernating creature until the heat had become absolutely unbearable. When he found a pill in the coat's pocket before heading out to rehearsals, without even caring what it was, he took it.

The man squared up to River as behind him people murmured at him to knock it off. River himself would only have to snap his fingers for the man to be dragged out right then and there. Onstage, the openers riled up the crowd, getting them pumped for when River, the star, would take the stage.

"You ain't singing for the people. Our people," the young man continued, emboldened by having captured River's attention.

"The fuck you mean?" River heard himself say.

"Man, you know as well as I do, your shit's for white people."

And then, River lost it. He began to yell in the man's face and had to be held back. It cut deeper than River would ever acknowledge. Hadn't Mr. X said many years earlier how the Johnson brothers were such good little Black boys, so well-spoken, so palatable, with definite crossover appeal?! Hadn't River spent his entire goddamn life wanting and working so hard to be good, to be liked, to be loved by everyone, and at what cost to himself?

River was one of the most famous Black men in America, in the world even. People had screamed out his name and he had performed his music in places where they hadn't so much as ever seen a Black person in the flesh before. What to say in his own defense? Wendy would know what to say to this fucker.

"I am our people!" River beat his chest and yelled at the young man, feeling a surge of adrenaline just beneath his skin, the drugs, maybe, or something else. "Me!"

Our people. Fuck all that, River thought and walked out still wearing Wendy's mink.

"Hello, Wisconsin!" he howled as he went onstage full of fury and grief and loneliness. "This is for Wendy."

Wendy who had seen him, who had always loved and accepted him exactly as he was.

At any other time, his backstage outburst might've made it into the papers, except that it was quickly overshadowed by the fact this had quickly become the best-known live performance of his career. And, some would argue, one of the best live performances ever.

CHAPTER FORTY-SEVEN

ROMAN AND HIS FATHER HAD NEVER TALKED ABOUT WAR. ABOUT HOW what you saw hollowed you and couldn't nothing quite fill you back in afterward. About the shame stuck deep under your fingernails that never seemed to come clean, what you'd done, or hadn't, to survive. The way it rewrote who you were, who you'd been, who you were going to be. Maybe there was a pride in it for some, but not for Roman.

Roman'd been jealous of his little brother for so long, for everything he had, what he didn't, and now all he felt was deeply sorry for him. Roman wasn't sure what a miscarriage felt like, but he figured it had to feel like losing something important. Like going through a tiny war, without anybody commemorating your loss but you. River's Wendy had lost something important, but so had his brother. And then, just like that, River lost her too. His brother had helped him when Roman most desperately needed help, had even sent a very fancy floral spray to the funeral home, having remembered that Brad and Roman were good friends. Shouldn't Roman do something?

He decided to call River while his father was out on the bank run. More privacy than when they were at home and his father or his mama could walk in at any minute. He rang figuring River's help would answer and he could leave a message for River to call him back. Roman had met Wendy only once, when he'd flown up to one of River's shows in San Francisco, but he knew her all the same. That was a woman hungry enough to swallow the whole world, and haunted enough to throw it right back up, he'd thought.

"Hello?" River said.

Roman hadn't expected River would pick up at the first ring, before he'd even had a chance to collect his thoughts.

"Hey. River. It's me," Roman sputtered. "Roman."

"I know who 'me' is." River laughed.

Roman was surprised to hear his brother laughing.

"Wait. Why are you calling in the middle of the day? Is Dad OK? Is Mom?"

"What? Yeah. Everyone's fine," Roman said, even though they both knew that hadn't entirely been true for a very long time. "How are you?"

"Oh you know . . ." River said.

"I'm coming out to you," Roman said, surprising himself. River had just closed escrow on a new place in the Village that he'd purchased as a surprise for Wendy before she died. The idea of his little brother in that big old empty space all alone, save for his staff, seemed unbearably sad.

River paused for a very long time. Roman thought he heard his brother sniffling on the other end.

River said, "I just got her ashes . . ."

"I can help you spread them . . . if that's what you want. If you don't have other plans with her family, or whatever."

"She didn't have one. Not really," River said. "Anyway, gotta go now, but Paul will call and arrange everything for you and . . . whoever wants to come."

"OK," Roman said.

"OK," River said.

IN WAR, AMONG the dying, more often than not, men cried out "Mama!" There was a reason for that, Roman supposed.

Emmeline wrapped her fingers through his for takeoff and then again for landing. River's friend Paul stood waiting for them outside the gate.

"Riv wanted to come get you himself, but he had a last-minute meeting pop up. And he didn't want to send a driver."

"How is he doing?" Emmeline said.

"Oh, you know River," Paul said. "We had to force him to cancel the rest of the American tour. There were only two dates left. He needs to rest up for Europe anyway. He runs himself into the ground. Wendy was good at getting him to slow down every once in a while . . ."

"That poor girl," Emmeline said.

Paul sighed.

Roman felt his mother place her hand over his. He resisted the urge to pull back. She was trying. They all were.

"I'm gonna let y'all have your privacy," Paul said as he dropped them off in front of what was presumably River's building.

River answered the door to his new penthouse in a sweatsuit. Had he taken a meeting like this? Roman couldn't even picture his brother owning sweatsuits. River's hair looked longer than he usually kept it. His under-eyes held all of their shared baggage and then some. Stacked cardboard boxes formed a labyrinth behind him.

"You came." He looked at Emmeline and then at Roman.

"I told you we would," Roman said.

"Paul dropped us off," Emmeline offered. "He wanted to give us some time to catch up."

Roman couldn't remember the last time he'd seen his little brother look this helpless. He looked down to see the USPS package in River's hand.

"You order something?" he asked.

"They shipped her through the mail," River said, his voice cracking. "In a bag like . . . like . . ."

Roman nodded and swallowed back tears.

"I don't want to just put her down. She's . . . I can't open it."

"You don't have to," Roman said. He had known war and he had known loss, but this was different.

Emmeline gently grabbed the envelope.

"We'll hold on to her for you," she said. "For now, you need to sleep."

River slept and slept, and Emmeline and Roman did their best to unpack and place things in some semblance of order for him. Roman found it soothing, organizing all of his brother's things. Whenever they came across something that was obviously Wendy's, they put it in a box away from the rest for River to go through when he was ready. Every few hours, Paul ordered food from River's favorite restaurants and brought it over.

"He needs to eat," Paul said. "I ordered three of everything he usually gets, for you and your mom."

"Thank you so much for everything," Roman said. "He's lucky to have you as a friend."

"Oh, don't I know it." Paul laughed.

Roman hadn't had a close friend since Brad's passing. Bars were places to be avoided these days, and with them all the friends he might've made therein. People flocked to him. He was just charming enough, and looked enough like River, that folks could tell who he was. He never promised access to his famous brother, but proximity was all most of them cared about, and before he was sober, that was friendship enough for him. Now in the evenings Roman sat quietly between Emmeline and Odysseus watching Cronkite until he excused himself to his room to read, or sometimes jerk off.

═

TWO WEEKS LATER, Roman sat across from his brother in the almost entirely unpacked living room. Emmeline had gone out for a walk to get some fresh air.

"Are you sure you wanna go alone?" Roman asked. "It's New York, Mom. You gotta keep your guard up."

"Oh please," Emmeline said, and let the door close behind her.

River had stumbled into the room several minutes later. "Where is she?"

"She went out for a walk. She'll be back soon," Roman said.

"No . . . I mean Wendy," River said. "I think maybe I'm ready now."

Roman went over to where he and Emmeline had carefully stored the USPS envelope that contained the remains. He brought it over to River, who sat with it in hand for what felt like forever.

"I'm so mad at her," River said. "So fucking angry."

"I know," Roman said.

"I feel like shit, being mad at her," River said.

"It's gonna feel like shit for long while, no matter what," Roman said. "Might as well allow yourself to feel what you feel."

Roman wondered if River wanted him to say something about addiction, something to make him feel better about Wendy's death, but he couldn't think of anything that didn't sound stupid. Wendy was an addict. She died. Roman was an addict. He lived. River had loved them both as fiercely as he could. Luck was the only thing that separated them, really.

"Did you see her?" Roman asked. "After she died?"

Roman thought of Brad on the couch across from him after his overdose.

River nodded. He inhaled and began to unseal the envelope in front of him.

"For a short bit," he said, looking down at the ashes before him.

"Maybe you'll see her again?" Roman said.

"She'd have come back by now, if she were coming back," River said.

"You talk to Dad yet?" Roman asked.

"He called and was all like, 'Everything happens for a reason, son.' You know he doesn't even believe that bullshit himself. You would think he of all people would know better."

"Dad's just shitty at emotions," Roman said.

"So shitty." River laughed.

"Speaking of which, Riv, I never said thank you . . ." Roman started.

River paused for a long moment before speaking, his eyes welling. "I owed you one. Maybe if I hadn't kicked you out of the band . . ."

"It's OK, Riv. We're OK," Roman said, wrapping an arm around his brother's shoulder. And he realized he meant it.

River held his portion of Wendy's ashes in the palm of his hand.

"How is this all that's left?" he said.

There was nothing Roman could say to that.

═══

THE NEXT DAY, Emmeline, Roman, and River journeyed to the waterfront to spread Wendy. Nearby, just under the dilapidated pier, a group of teenagers sat precariously on the craggy rocks, sharing exactly one bottle and one cigarette between them. Roman noticed the smallest of the bunch pointing at River, then the others quickly turned to look in their direction.

"Is this legal?" Emmeline asked.

"Probably not," Roman said.

"Not that Wendy would have given a fuck," River said, and laughed. "She was happy here."

"I'm sure it's seen better days," Emmeline said, kindly.

"Nah, that's why she liked it," River said, looking out at the Manhattan skyline before them. "Plus, it's private."

If his brother noticed the fans starting to gather several feet away from them, he gave no indication. In the near distance, a stocky, middle-aged man readied his camera lens.

"Not that private, Riv," Roman said and nodded in the man's direction.

River emptied the baggie into the East River and the three of them scrambled as the wind blew Wendy's ashes back toward their faces.

Roman squeezed River's hand and Emmeline held the other and the three of them stood there like that until a passing jogger yelled at them to move the fuck out of the way.

CHAPTER FORTY-EIGHT

1976

"I'M SO LONELY," RIVER SAID.

They could still hear the caregivers down the hall chatting loudly about River Johnson's visit, about how the speech pathologist had just missed seeing him, how she should hover in the vicinity if she wanted a peek. River looked on the verge of tears.

Rocco held his hand for just a second. "Me too."

He had seen the newspaper headlines, but he had not gone with his mother and brothers to spread Wendy's ashes. Rocco knew his parents thought it would be too upsetting for him. Maybe it would've been.

"Sometimes I think about how we're in this whole year that somehow doesn't have any piece of Wendy in it. At least in '75 she'd been around for most of it, you know?" River said.

"I'm sorry about your Wendy," Rocco said.

"Me too," River whispered.

River leaned over and began to cry on Rocco's shoulder, and didn't stop for what felt like an eternity. Normally, Rocco would've been very uncomfortable with River's body heavy and heartbroken against his, but he didn't dare say anything. Rocco knew that his little brother didn't let the world see him like this usually. Probably not even their parents, or Roman. That this was something sacred and brotherly, just between the two of them.

It's OK. Cry on me, River, he thought.

"You dating anybody?" River said after some time had passed. He wiped his tears away on his sleeves.

Rocco shook his head no.

"You should get yourself a girlfriend!" River sat up excitedly. He began to rattle off descriptors of several of the girls in the group home with him. Only one or two of them was cute. And most of them Rocco found very annoying, on a good day. Still, Rocco liked that River thought of Rocco as having a future. As worthy of loving and being loved. Nobody else had ever suggested as much, not even his parents.

NOW ON TV in the rec room, on the dance show, River took the stage and began to perform.

The lights and the fog machine onscreen were too much. Rocco watched for as long as he could, then he closed his eyes and danced along with his brother. He did the steps Odysseus had taught them all those years earlier, and then River did the Christmas moves. The ones he had performed for them that first night in the forest, only now River did them in sky-high man platforms that made him appear larger than life, even though he was the very shortest of all the Johnsons. There was a pang, somewhere deep inside, that Rocco was not right there beside his brother.

True, he did not like the lights or the crowds, but Rocco loved singing and he knew he was good at it, maybe even better than both of his brothers. His head lifted, uvula reverberating, arms flapping in sync to a beat or across the black-and-white keys—that was when he felt most himself. Sometimes, if he'd had a good week, they even let him play piano and sing for everyone in the home for dinner.

The new girl stood up and danced along with him. Along with River. Every so often, a sound would escape from somewhere deep within her as though the music commanded it, as though her words were trapped but still joy escaped. She had freckles and short red hair that looked like she cut it herself with craft scissors. Not quite a pixie, but the general idea of one.

And she was nonverbal, caregiver Cathy made sure to tell them all. "She can hear you, but don't be offended if she doesn't respond to you."

"Sit down," Daisy demanded.

Daisy was the bossiest person in the group home because she had been there the longest and also because she had a very hard time regulating her emotions, it seemed. Daisy had been there since she was eighteen. Now she was a little over thirty.

Rocco was twenty-two. He tried to imagine several more years of being in this place. If maybe he might end up like Daisy after a bit. Celebrating his twenty-first here hadn't been too depressing. River had bought out a very fancy bar nearby, where they all went to drink and dance. Rocco'd even had a martini "shaken, not stirred." Like Bond himself! Still, he didn't think he wanted to celebrate turning thirty at the home; that seemed more depressing somehow. The new girl looked closer to his age than Daisy's, far as he could tell.

"Stop it, Alice! Stop it, Rocco!" Daisy yelled as the two danced on.

So Alice was her name. Maybe Alice could be his girlfriend, he thought. If she wanted.

═══

ROCCO DECIDED TO woo Alice. He spent the next few weeks learning everything he could about Alice, a bit of reconnaissance. Alice loved blue Otter Pops; her mouth, when she actually opened it, was blue as the ocean or the sky or first place, and this seemed auspicious. He supposed blue could also be the color of sadness or loneliness, but after so many years of feeling both, he felt excited by Alice's blue tongue and all the possibilities therein.

Alice liked the meatloaf and the salmon, but not the chicken breast. At dinner, when the breast was placed before her, she'd eat around it, nibbling at her corn and her mashed potatoes and then for dessert she would point emphatically at her bowl until she was given an extra scoop of ice cream.

Alice had bruises on both thighs, big purple, brown, and yellow welts that formed because when she was overly frustrated or excited, when everything inside was too much, she beat against herself like a drum, hard and unyielding, until her knuckles grew white or somebody intervened. Her eyes were too close together, too short a distance across the bridge of her nose and they were the color of murky water, but Rocco liked how sometimes in the rec room she closed them and tilted her head back as if listening to a symphony. The beauty of her eyes was in their fluttering, lidded and light. This was Alice in several parts.

The next time they told Rocco to play them something after dinner, he sang and played only for Alice. He had learned the song for exactly when this occasion would present itself, had asked River to send him the sheet music. "*You make me feel like dancing. I wanna dance the night away.*"

Alice sat not with the others but on the stairs just outside the room, her head tilted back, her body moving to the beat. When he finished, she opened her eyes and looked at him.

The next activity scheduled was roller-skating. Every month, the home took several of them in a large van to the local rink, where instead of the loud music and flashing lights, Rocco remembered from similar outings with his brothers, they dimmed the lights and played music softly or not at all. He liked to listen to the rolling wheels, their forward momentum, the beats in a series of step, push, step, across the worn wood.

The rink was musty. Carpet garish. There was a snack spot, where you could get nachos and soda and undercooked cookies that still mostly tasted (gloriously!) like dough in the center. They would line up in front of a grumpy teenager while their very own Nurse Ratched told him their shoe sizes from off a list and he would hand them a pair of dingy tan roller skates with blue or orange wheels and the size stamped on the back.

Rocco got the skates with the orange wheels and told the kid he wanted blue.

"That's what we got," the kid said.

"I want blue. Those are blue." Rocco pointed behind the kid at the remaining skates with the blue wheels.

"That's what we have left in your size, buddy."

He felt his frustration rising. He hated when people who weren't like him spoke to him as though he were a child. The blue-wheeled skates did exist in his size; he'd had them last time.

"Go check," Rocco said.

"Manners," caregiver Cathy said. "Rocco, you're holding everybody up."

Rocco felt himself starting to flap. This was not how this was supposed to go. He was going to wear blue skates to match Alice's blue tongue, because blue was her favorite color. But when the other kid behind the counter handed Alice a pair of size-9 skates with orange wheels, Rocco decided maybe it would be OK to be orange after all. Also, Alice had big feet for a girl. He added this to his list of Alice facts.

They laced up in front of the lockers with tiny little baby locks, just big enough for shoes or secret treasures. There were other groups there too, some of whom had people in wheelchairs or walkers. He watched a man tentatively walk out to the very center of the rink, gripping his walker tightly. He began to move in very small circles as the DJ began his set.

"Stick to the edge, Ralphie!" a woman yelled.

Ralphie ignored her in favor of his slow, steady circles, his own little worlds.

Skates laced, Alice bolted out to the floor, surprising Rocco. He had thought she would be tentative, one of those people who spent half the time with their fingers outstretched as though in limbo between either the wall or the floor. She glided easily, one foot slightly lifted in front of the other, elegant. Then, as she warmed up, she did a spin, like Dorothy Hamill. On her third time around, she stuck out a leg and went very low to the ground, a human protractor.

On the bus ride over, Rocco thought he'd offer to hold her hand if she fell. Alice did not need his hand. In fact, just as Rocco began to pick up a bit of speed, Ralphie veered away from his small circles and darted in front of him. Rocco hurtled straight into Ralphie's walker and tumbled forward, landing right in front of Alice, who jumped over him as though they'd planned it, as though he were merely a setup for a great trick.

From the sidelines, somebody clapped, and Rocco felt his plans for the evening grow further out of reach, beyond his fingertips, as though Alice were the wall or the floor from whence he scrambled to rise.

He sulked in forward circles and some backward ones too. All was lost, he thought.

Daisy scooted in small steps in her skates. Her wheels were blue and her feet were only a size 6, which seemed entirely too small for someone of her height. No wonder she could barely steady herself.

"Hi, Daisy," Rocco said.

"Please be quiet, I'm concentrating," Daisy said. She scrunched up her nose at him. "That's too much cologne."

Rocco didn't much care for cologne himself, but women seemed to like it. He had been told that this was what girls liked. He didn't remember who had told him exactly, just that he had always known it to be true. He'd asked his mother to send him some in his most recent care package. He could feel a headache coming on, and his allergies were killing him, but for Alice, he would endure.

"This is very nice cologne!" he told Daisy before skating off.

What did it matter what Daisy thought of him? It was only Alice who mattered, Alice who had momentarily disappeared.

Suddenly, there was his brother through the speakers, urging him to dance.

"River!" he said aloud to nobody at all.

It was one of River's lesser hits, too much production for Rocco's taste, perhaps to mask the fact that River sounded tired. Rocco imagined a late studio night and a take that had finally been settled on to fill an otherwise solid album. Rocco tried to make up for River's lack of vocal enthusiasm with his own.

He was swaying to the beat when a hand slapped against his. Why couldn't other people keep their damn appendages to themselves? There was plenty of space and Rocco's knee still ached a bit from his spill. He felt the hand again and turned to berate its owner, only to see it was her, Alice. She stuck out a blue tongue in his direction. Then skated off.

The next time around, they skated together. Alice matched her pace to his, her pinkie against his in just the lightest bit of pressure that made him spin.

She turned to face him and skated backward for a bit, almost knocking into Daisy, who was still plodding in baby steps against the wall, and, with that slight bit of disturbance to her equilibrium, fell flat on her ass.

"Alice, you asshole!" Daisy yelled.

Alice reached for his hand—a question. The final song of the skate session came on, Carl Douglas's "Kung Fu Fighting." Rocco had really been hoping for something slower, more romantic. Still, Rocco took her pinkie in his—an answer. Then they both fell.

═══

THEY ATE MEALS together and drew together and went on walks together. They watched movies together and smiled and did puzzles together. Outside, they found a family of bunnies together and Rocco ran to the kitchen to get carrots so they could take turns feeding them. The carrots were almost as large as the bunnies themselves but still happily they chomped. It was a perfect day. Alice tilted her head back and took in the sun as the bees and butterflies flew from flower to flower around them. Rocco meant to stay by her side, but it was all too much. Too-too. He ran away from all of them, bees, bunnies, flowers, butterflies, from her.

Later, he had trouble telling her why he'd run. All the things he preferred to forget. When he went to open his mouth to explain, instead of words it felt full of bees. He flapped his arms. She beat her thigh. The next day at breakfast, she sat not next to him but with Daisy.

"Alice!"

She ignored him.

"Alice!" He pounded on the breakfast table.

"That's enough, Rocco," Ratched said.

Afterward, he followed her to the garden. She pretended not to notice him behind her.

When she sat down again near where they had seen the bunnies, he sat next to her. She refused to look over at him.

A bee buzzed entirely too close to his ear, and Rocco yelped. Then as he jerked away from that bee, another bee attacked. Alice peered over at the sting and grabbed his arm closer. She rolled up his sleeve like he was giving blood. He felt his heart pumping loudly.

"Too loud," he said.

She took the stinger between her nails, wiggling it just-so until it was out and only a drop of blood remained. She didn't release his hand and he didn't want her to.

Was it even possible that Alice was real? She was always in his brain, moving through his cerebellum. He felt her behind his eyes, in the back of his head, the thought of her fingertips and her mouth, the weight of her lips pressing down on him from the very inside of his body.

"May I kiss you?"

She leaned in closer to him. An answer.

First their lips touched, then Alice slid her tongue into his mouth. His first thought was to recoil as their spit mingled. Alice's tongue was larger than his, and it took a minute to figure out how to move his tongue with hers. It was very weird at first, but then it felt like a kind of momentary magic. How could something so unsanitary, so very gross, be so great? This is what it meant to have a girlfriend?! No wonder River had wanted this for him! Rocco finally understood all the love songs he'd ever heard all at once.

Still, that was enough magic for now. He pulled away first and Alice, quite splotchy across her freckled chest, sat across from him beaming. He knew then that he was hers. And she was his. She reached for him again, and Rocco understood then why people promised each other forever. And suddenly he understood how very much his brother must've just lost.

Alice picked up a nearby dandelion, and blew.

CHAPTER FORTY-NINE

THE SICKNESS BAG ON THE PLANE DID NOT HOLD NEARLY ENOUGH. Definitely not the two appetizers and glass of champagne Emmeline ordered once they reached cruising altitude. She had thrown up shrimp cocktail halfway across the Atlantic, having thoroughly embarrassed herself among the other passengers in the first-class cabin as they snacked on their fruit medley and caviar and discussed their stocks with strangers. It was her first international flight. So much of Emmeline's youth had been about survival, she hadn't had time for adventure. It felt as though it were only now, as she rounded the corner into middle age, that she was able to fully breathe. River wanted to fly them out private, but Emmeline insisted that she didn't want her son to waste that kind of money on her. No matter how much of it he had.

The blond stewardess whisked away Emmeline's puke, holding it gingerly between her fingers and away from her perfectly starched blue suit. Emmeline had desperately wanted to be attended to by the lone Black stewardess whom she saw board the plane. She smiled as the girl with her close-cropped afro did the safety spiel, hoping to catch her eye as she cheerfully mimicked inflating the life vest.

"Gladys, you're needed in coach," the blonde had said, and the girl disappeared through the curtains behind them.

Rocco squirmed in the seat next to her. When they first sat down, he had wadded up a bunch of tissues and shoved them so deep in his ears that Emmeline thought Rocco might actually reach his brain. Even so, every time the plane rumbled, he looked around.

"We've should've taken a Concorde," he muttered.

"Are you excited to go to Europe?" she asked him.

This was the first time she and Rocco had been together for so long, just the two of them. She tried to shake the feeling of guilt, of having failed her boy. Of having left him to flounder, to be raised by caregivers and therapists. Still, he seemed good. Better than good even.

"I miss Alice." Rocco shrugged.

"Your friend?" Emmeline said.

"My *girlfriend*!" Rocco insisted.

"Right. Of course. We can make sure to get a few lovely souvenirs for her," Emmeline said, holding her son's hand. "Maybe River can sign a few things too . . ."

"Pepé Le Pew," Rocco said, taking his hand away from hers and turning his head toward the window. It was what the boys had said to one another when they were little and one of them stank. Emmeline firmly shut her mouth until the stewardess came back around to offer another glass of champagne.

"May I have a mint, please?" she mumbled, trying not to bowl the girl over. She and Rocco were the only Black people in first class, and God forbid she had rancid breath. Everyone might think all Black people had bad breath, were uncouth, threw up on planes. She hated how aware she was of her skin in places like these, how she wanted to peel it off and see what it felt like to be so at ease.

After their meal, the stewardess passed around cigars to everyone in the first-class cabin. Rocco took one, though Emmeline knew that he didn't care for the smell. And to be honest neither did she.

Still, why not? Emmeline thought, and dangled the still-wrapped cigar from her mouth like a mafioso.

A DRIVER WITH a robust head of graying hair, very deep-set eyes, and a gut that hung just slightly over his belt held up a placard, EMMELINE E ROCCO JOHNSON.

He looked up and down at Emmeline and Rocco as they approached the limo.

"Hi! I'm Emmeline Johnson," she said, and stuck out her hand to shake his.

"Sì?" The man looked at her skeptically as he shook it. "You?"

"Mio fratello è River Johnson, il cantante," Rocco said.

"Ah!" the man said and clasped his hands together and smiled. "Buonissimo!"

Emmeline looked over at her son in wonder.

"When did you learn Italian?" she said as they climbed into the back of the car.

"People in Europe don't like it when you don't try to speak their language, so I learned several important phrases in Spanish, French, and Italian."

"Like 'My brother is River Johnson'?" Emmeline laughed.

"That's an important phrase," Rocco said as they headed away from the airport.

═══

RIVER MET THEM at the hotel that night after rehearsal. Emmeline held her youngest tight to her chest and marveled at how much he'd changed since the last time she'd seen him two months ago. His eyes were a bit sunken, but his skin was clear with a fresh layer of stubble. At certain angles she thought she caught a glimpse of the grandmother who hadn't wanted her, and the mother who had but died anyway.

"What are you staring at, Ma?" River laughed.

"My baby's a man," she said.

River kissed her on the cheek. She felt something rub up against her leg and looked down to see the brown dog, Shaft. He had grown even larger since she'd seen him last. Not just a puppy but an actual dog.

Rocco emerged from the bathroom and stared across the room at his brother. Then he rushed over to pet the dog.

"Hi, Shaft," Rocco said to the dog. "Buona sera," he said to his brother. River walked over to Rocco and patted Rocco's shoulder as he pet the dog.

"The gang's almost all here," River said.

"Almost," Emmeline said. She was still holding out hope that Odysseus would come. Roman was due in early the next morning.

After River showered, they went out to dinner, and drank plenty of wine and ate food more savory, more decadent, than anything Emme line had had back home. She and River walked through the cobblestone streets arm in arm, through all the white people who stared as they passed. Rocco walked slightly ahead with Shaft, who was an absolute hit with even the well-heeled Italian donnas. They heard the flashes of cameras, and River tilted his head this way and that, angling himself for what would be the best photo. River had given his security detail the evening off.

"Family only," he said.

"Is that safe?" Emmeline said.

"We've got Shaft." He laughed.

"*Shut your mouth!*" Rocco'd sung.

"Mama, would it be all right . . . do you think . . . would it be all right if, next time, I wasn't with a woman?" River said in a rush.

Emmeline considered what her son was saying, was trusting her with, and waited for some time before responding.

"I'm sorry I wasn't there when you needed me," she said, batting away a fly.

"That's not why—"

"Let me finish," Emmeline interrupted. "What happened with Rocco wasn't your fault. And I know I wasn't who you needed me to be. When you needed me."

She turned to look at him and placed her hand on his cheek. "I'm here now. Is what I'm saying."

River nodded, and she wiped away one of his tears.

"Mio fratello è River Johnson, il cantante," they heard Rocco say to a slim woman in Gucci heels. How did these European women balance so effortlessly on the stones? Emmeline felt like an elephant thudding along, trying desperately not to twist her ankle. She'd already rolled it a few times.

The paps came closer than usual.

"Smile, Mama," River said.

═══

THE NEXT DAY Roman flew in. Odysseus wasn't with him.

"Dad isn't coming?" River said.

"Good to see you too, bro," Roman said.

"God, I need a shower," Roman said. He leaned in to hug Rocco.

"Pepé Le Pew," Rocco said.

"I can't believe him," River fumed. "This is the biggest tour I've ever done. This is everything *he* wanted . . ." He trailed off.

"He's got to tend to the shop, River. Business has been slow, and you know he doesn't want us living off your money in any way . . ." Emmeline said gently. "You know how proud he is of you."

"Yeah, well, he's got a real shitty way of showing it," River said.

She couldn't argue with that. At twilight, she and Odie had taken to going on walks together. As they moved their bodies across town, they frequently fretted about their boys. Together, they'd dissect their weekly visits with Rocco after joining him for picnics on the lawn at the group home. Odie extolled Roman's work ethic and Emmeline told him he should compliment Roman more to his face. To all of their surprise, Odie did. In church basements and meeting halls, they celebrated Roman's chips. Still, Odie struggled with what to say to River, his youngest, whom Odie had lovingly held up so high, his weight at dawn, pumping and lifting the boy higher while River giggled.

"You gotta find a way to get through to him, Odie," she told him.

"The boy is stubborn as all get-out," Odie said.

"Wonder where he gets that from." She laughed.

"Why are we doing this again?" Odie paused to take a breath.

"It's good for your digestion," she replied, slipping her hand in his.

They passed their elderly neighbors walking their dogs. Exchanged pleasantries with the young couple who'd moved in next door. When the couple had a baby girl, they brought over a small gift.

"It goes by so fast," Odie said wistfully to the young mother covered in spit-up.

"Too fast," Emmeline concurred as the baby cooed.

Roman threw an arm around his brother. "Who needs Dad when you got the world?"

Roman started chanting, "*River! River! River!*"

Rocco and Emmeline joined in, the three of them growing ever louder while River looked around embarrassed.

═══

LATER THAT NIGHT, backstage, Emmeline and her boys sat in the greenroom waiting for the concert to get under way. River was not the kind of artist who showed up mere minutes, or even an hour, before he was supposed to go onstage. He was prompt, sometimes even early. He signed all the posters and posed for fan photos, asking women, children, and even grown men about the minutiae of their day before they came to this place to see him. Everyone walked away feeling special. Emmeline was proud of how respectfully River acknowledged everyone at the venue and the road crew.

I've done something right, she thought.

"My face hurts from smiling so much," River said as he plopped down on the sofa. He reached for the bottle of champagne that had been left and put it by his side, out of Roman's reach. It wasn't subtle. Roman had been mostly sober in the wake of his friend Brad's death, with over a year's worth of AA meetings and chips under his belt, still the last time he'd relapsed had been ugly enough that Emmie couldn't blame River for being cautious.

River ran through vocal exercises, all those vowels darting here and there on the scale, and occasionally Roman or Rocco would join him and they would laugh. Muscle memory, Emmeline supposed.

Rocco grabbed at the dish of brown M&M's set out on the coffee table, the only kind River would eat well before anybody else was talking about the dangers of red dye #2, or was it #4?

"I made sure they had only those for you," River said.

"Those are the boringest. Most boring? Whatever," Roman said.

"An M&M will not kill me," Rocco said succinctly.

There was a knock at the door. Paul stood there in a red velvet suit. "Why hello, Johnsons!"

River walked over to Paul, and the two of them embraced.

"You trying to upstage me?" River laughed.

"Oh please," Paul said.

Emmeline had not forgotten the myriad kindnesses Paul had done for River and their family in the wake of Wendy's death. She grabbed him and held him tight to her bosom. "It's so good to see you again."

"Much better circumstances this time," he said quietly.

"Indeed," she said.

"So, Riv, you'll let me know when you're ready for makeup and hair," Paul said.

River nodded.

"There's one more thing," Paul said. "I've got a VIP fan club member who really, really wants to meet you and flew in from out of country."

"But we already did the meet-and-greet?" River said. "Can they wait until after the show?"

"He paid a lot of money, River," Paul said.

River mumbled, "All right. You can send him in."

Odysseus stepped into the doorway.

River and his father stared intensely at each other for a long time before River teared up.

"What about the shop?" River said.

"It'll be there when I get back," Odysseus said. "Probably."

"Better be," Roman said. "I still need a job."

Rocco lifted up the dishes of M&M's. "River got only the brown ones so the chemicals don't kill us."

"That was very thoughtful of him," Odysseus said.

Emmeline walked over to Odysseus and kissed him. She squeezed her husband's butt mid-embrace.

"Gross," Rocco said.

═

TWO HOURS LATER, they all gathered as River got strapped into a harness that was about to lift him up above the stage while pyrotechnics flanked him. Bold colors. Sequined suit. Platform shoes. No shirt. Every inch of him sparkled.

"My boys." Emmeline wrapped her arms around their shoulders. River kissed his mother on the cheek.

"I hope you enjoy the show. Wish me luck."

River cracked his neck, shook his arms out. Pumped himself up to the sounds of the crowd's applause. They began to chant his name with a near religious fervor. Emmeline peeked out and saw the sea of faces begging for River. Some of the girls looked downright delirious. Boys too.

"You don't need luck, Riv. This was always going to be yours," Roman said.

And for a moment Emmeline thought her son looked at his little brother with something like awe.

"Always," Odie said, and patted his son on the shoulder. River turned to him, suddenly tentative.

"Dad, would you love me even if I quit music?"

"What the hell kind of question is that?"

"Would you?"

Odysseus paused for a moment but only just. It was the wrong thing to do. Emmeline knew that River would take it as a no, not simply a moment to collect one's thoughts.

"Never mind. I just . . . never mind," River said.

"Of course. I love you, River. Of course." Odie leaned forward to hug his son, only to be blocked by one of the makeup girls dashing a last pouf of powder across River's forehead while a harried junior member of the hair team sprayed an overzealous final blast of oil sheen.

"They might love you more," Roman joked as River's name arose from the very bowels of the crowd. A hush briefly came over the audience as the lights dimmed and the band began to play.

River turned to them and grinned. "Showtime!"

Everything was perfect. And yet Emmeline couldn't shake a feeling of unease. Simply everything was too good right now. It was just her anxiety. Sometimes good things just happened, and that didn't mean that something bad was around the corner. But Emmeline had never known life to be otherwise. When she was a girl, she had gone out for a Sunday drive with her parents in their new Model B, and within forty minutes she didn't have parents anymore. She'd had her very first best friend, Bettina, and within a year Emmeline didn't have her anymore. She'd loved a beautiful ghost child, and within two years Christmas too was gone, and her family in tatters. Hers was a life of people being snatched from her. Was it any wonder she either gripped too hard or not hard enough?

Rocco leaned into his mother's shoulder.

On the other side, Roman rested against her so that she was flanked by two of her boys as they watched her third. Odysseus stood slightly off to the side, hands on his hips, like the anxious stage parent he'd once been.

Then the curtains opened, and River rose. The entire stadium of fans stretched out their hands.

CHAPTER FIFTY

"OH, HOW I WISH I STILL HAD SKIN," BECKY SAID. "HOW NICE IT MUST be to feel the sun on a day like this."

After Tom avenged my death and went on to whatever was next, Becky and I decided that the only way for the two of us to find any peace was to take matters into our own hands, as Tom had. So, we left my murderer's house in search of a new family. We agreed that we wouldn't settle until we found somebody who would take in the both of us! For many miles, we walked, and hitched rides with unsuspecting truckers. We even squeezed into a motorcycle sidecar, and my innards unfurled in the wind like a flag for several county lines!

Finally, we made our way all the way to the coast. New Jersey!

"Let's go in the water," I said.

"But I don't know how to swim," Becky said.

"Neither do I! But we'll be OK."

In the world of people like us, sailors with stab wounds palled around and the drowned cleared their gargled throats and implored us to stay on land.

Still, the two of us walked toward the water, past the children building sandcastles and the men tossing a football. The Atlantic foamed at our feet.

"Can you feel anything?" Becky asked.

I closed my eyes and tried to feel something, anything. I thought of what it had been like to feel sun and rain and breezes. To feel hugs and tears and bottom pinches. I tried to remember what it had been like to have a whole body full of nerve endings.

And then I could feel it. Water!

I told Becky to close her eyes and place her thoughts in her fingertips and toes, in the very soles of her feet.

"Wait. I think . . . oh my goodness!" Becky squealed. "It's so cold!"

"It is, isn't it?" I laughed.

A flock of seagulls argued over an abandoned picnic. "Mine!" they all yelled at one another.

"Can't we just share? There's enough for all of us!" one of them yelled slightly off to the side. He was a lovely bright white, but missing a leg.

"You're such a ninny, Frank!" was the response.

"Poor Frank." Becky laughed.

Frank glanced over at us, embarrassed. Then, with a rocky start that required a few extra hops on his one good leg, he took off and away, but not before yelling at his people, "Screw you guys!"

Frank had given me the absolute best idea! I don't know why I hadn't thought of it earlier! I looked over at Becky. "What if we kept going? Like, around the world?"

I thought of what the Johnson brothers had asked me about where I had been. If I had been to space. If I had even tried. The world, the universe, was so huge, and I had only seen such a small little bit of it. What was there to stop me from seeing more? Maybe I *should* try to touch all the stars along the horizon.

The cruise ships lined the coastline, bulky and imposing. Becky followed my gaze to where they sat.

"Could we?" She seemed to ponder.

"Why not?" I said.

This is how we came to board the *Endeavor*. We walked up alongside the families with their chubby stacks of luggage and small children who ran up and down the boarding plank, their parents distracted by a quick passport double-check. We waited behind an elderly duo like us, who looked back at the pair of us and giddily said, "This is our honeymoon! We didn't meet until we died!"

"I want to see home one last time!" the older woman said in a very thick accent I couldn't place. She reminded me of somebody who had been a washerwoman or a seamstress in one of those large factories in the North. Her body stooped as though permanently on task.

"And I've never been to Europe!" the man said. He too had a thick accent, but more local than not. All-American ruffian.

"How lovely!" Becky said. "We're going to see the world too! Would you like to be our parents?"

I didn't think we should just ask the first couple we saw to be our parents! We didn't even know how they died, if they were good or bad!

"Oh, we're entirely too old for children!" the washerwoman gently said.

Every once in a while, I thought of how old I might have been had I lived. Sometimes, I lost count. I thought I might be as old as the two in front of us were, but maybe that was too old?

The cruise ship was of two worlds, with the living and the dead overlapping in the same space. Generations passed through the casinos arm in arm, as Becky and I did.

Out on the decks, the living quickly started on their tans. It was there that I saw a dead woman who looked African, as though she'd once had skin as dark and beautiful as a night at sea. There were rotted iron chains around each ankle. She folded her arms behind her on the deck chair and lifted her face to the sun. If you looked very, very closely, you could see an ever-so-slight imprint of a soul on the plastic deck chair, life. Or, afterlife, as it were.

I walked over to her. She opened her eyes and looked up at me.

"You're blocking my view, child!" she said. It was a language I didn't speak, but I understood it nonetheless. This was one of the pleasant things about being dead.

I stepped out of her way and sat down next to her. Then I saw them! A family of four, brown-skinned and elegant, mother, father, and two daughters around my age. The four of them wore matching afros like crowns of curls. The white people aboard stared as the family made their way toward the deck chairs. The dead stared too.

"They're letting darkies on this thing now?" a bloated dead white man said.

The older couple who had been in front of me and Becky as we boarded laughed. "It's a new world, you know!"

The dead white man huffed.

One of the dead Africans rolled his eyes at this idiot as we dead Black people, New World and Old, gathered together to watch this family, their defiant incandescence!

"Look at them." The slave woman sat up and stared, marveling at the dainty crook of the woman's neck, the tiny ears from which a not-insubstantial pair of diamonds dripped. The mother's caftan floated a bit in the breeze, making her look like a butterfly. The ancestors admired the proud way the elder girl dove gracefully into the water while the little one cannonballed and popped back up with the loudest laugh. These girls didn't wear the word "no" in their bodies, or across their faces. If they noticed a few of the white kids being dragged out of the pool by their parents, they didn't acknowledge it.

We murmured appreciatively.

"Wowie! Who would've thunk it?!" An old man missing his teeth, with a neat bullet hole through his chest, clapped his hands as though the family were itself a performance.

I took to following them around the cruise ship. Becky complained, "Why do we always have to go where they go?"

"You don't have to come with me!"

She grumbled but didn't leave my side.

How beautiful it was to be a family!

On a particularly rough night at sea, as grown-ups surfed the hallways and women stumbled to casinos in their dress heels, the wind blew everyone sideways. But inside their room, I could hear the little Black girls giggling.

How wonderful to feel so safe, I thought.

I was disappointed when we reached our first destination and everyone disembarked. I lost the family in the crowd, and Becky insisted that we go sightseeing with a group taking a bus tour of the city. We got off and meandered around the famous ruins. A bunch of half-naked olive-skinned men and women sat among us laughing and fucking and pontificating on the meaning of life, pausing momentarily to mock the tourists with their corpulent bellies and very tall socks. I felt almost protective of these people with whom I'd been traveling, but only the ones who had smiled at and been warm to my family. This is what I'd taken to calling the mother, father, and two sisters. Mine.

Perhaps they could be my new Johnsons. Perhaps they could be home. I resolved to not lose them when they next disembarked.

At the next stop, the family took a ride on a gondola, and so Becky and I took a ride on the gondola. Venice was sinking, the gondolier told the tourists, to whom it was fresh news, although Venice had been sinking for quite some time.

The mother smiled and pulled the father in closer as the little girls shrieked and splashed canal water on one another. The dead souls who'd met their end in the canal rose up and heckled the gondolier and the tourists for disturbing their peace.

Back on the boat, the father rubbed the mother's feet while the kids played in the pool for an hour before dinnertime. I felt a pair of eyes on me. I looked to see if anybody else was around, but it was only me and the bartender serving drunks in the corner.

I quickly ducked out of sight.

When I popped back around, there she was. Even more beautiful up close, her face framed by several tiny moles in a constellation.

"Hello," the mother said.

I was dumbfounded.

"Can I ask a favor of you, please?" she said.

"Anything," I whispered.

"Can you stay away? Please. Please don't come near my family? I just . . . I don't want them knowing . . . I want my girls to be happy. Free."

"I'm free," I whined. "We could play together!"

"We're trying to leave all that behind," she said gently.

"All what?" I asked. "I'm good. I promise," I said. "I behave. I won't make no trouble for you." I thought briefly of the Johnsons and Rocco somewhere away. I didn't mean to lie to her, I would be better. I could be.

"It's not your fault, baby. I had to tell my own sister to stay away. Grandmother too . . . our house was set on fire when I was a girl."

"On purpose?" I said.

She bit her lip and nodded once again. "You know how it was . . . how it is."

And indeed I did.

"You've must've been such a beautiful little boy," my not-mother said sadly.

DEJECTED, REJECTED, I could barely lift my head to look at the world around me, which continued on as though I hadn't experienced what I thought was one of the most devastating days of my existence—little did I know what was to come.

"They weren't that great," Becky said. "What kind of woman tells her grandmother and sister to stay away?"

"Right," I said. But I still felt protective of the beautiful woman and her beautiful family. If I'm to be perfectly honest, I secretly hoped that they might change their minds.

We wandered around the piazza and stopped by a fountain. Tourists threw pennies into it and wished for things big and small.

"Make a wish," Becky said.

I shrugged.

"Wishes don't come true," I said.

"Well, I don't agree. I'm going to make a wish," she said.

We were not the only spirits around. A group of unpleasant very old dead men sat by the fountain trying to lift up women's skirts or knock small children into the water. Then the lot of them would laugh and laugh as the living tried to figure out who or what had assaulted them.

"Stop that!" Becky said.

"Fuck their wishes," one of the old men said in Italian. I was not quite certain why he had not already gone to the bad place, but maybe he was only a little bad and not quite bad enough for eternal damnation.

I wish I could say I did something, or at least told them not to speak to my friend like that, but I was too depressed. Becky threw a penny in as a toddler tried to point out the seemingly magical flying penny to its mother, who was far more concerned with an errant string on her shirt. It splashed only a little before sinking down, just as all the wishes around it had.

Across from us a huge billboard read: IN CONCERT: RIVER JOHNSON AT SAN SIRO!

"Hot dog!" I said to Becky.

"What?"

"It's River! My River! He's here!" I said, pointing at the extra-large photo in which River was posed triumphantly, ready to take over the whole wide world, or at the very least Milan.

"We gotta go!"

"Christmas, wait!"

San Siro was quite far away from where we were, and Becky and I were terrible with directions. The dead Italians were most unhelpful, and generally spoke entirely too fast. I found it easiest to consult with the dead Moors to tell us how to get from Venice to Milan. Even though they had been dead for many years before the advent of the locomotive, they were quite familiar with the trains and happily directed a fellow Blackamoor to the nearest station.

We took one train to Verona, then got off and took another. When we exited the station we wandered, looking for something that resembled a stadium. Some of the folks we asked for directions to the stadium assumed us to be stupid Americans, thought we meant the Colosseum, and somewhat gleefully told us we were in the wrong city entirely. We walked with our heads lifted toward the sky, past the crumbling buildings, looking for something new. Neither Becky nor I had been to a stadium before.

As we neared the stadium, the crowds were dressed in costumes that resembled some of River's most famous, or concert tees that had his face sprawled across them. It was very strange indeed to see River across a number of people's bosoms. Three different people fainted as we made our way through the crowds. At first I thought it was the sight of us, but no, it was just that River Johnson was near, that soon they would see him. If I'm to be entirely honest, I felt a little like those girls myself.

A stadium was a very big place and not at all like the places I had performed at the height of my fame as the Pickaninny Prodigy. It stretched for what felt like a whole city block or two, and thousands of people crammed in shoulder to shoulder, most of whom could barely see the stage at all. Gigantic screens flanked both sides of the stage and the audience murmured as the opening act, a white woman who danced and shook across the stage in sparkled skivvies, did her best for a crowd who wanted only to see River. So much so, that in the middle of her act, the Italian fans began to stomp their feet and chant, "*River! River! River!*"

"He's coming!" the singer said during a dance break, slightly out of breath and visibly exasperated.

Becky and I climbed many steps to get closer and closer to the front. I suppose we could've floated, but we didn't want to draw any extra attention to ourselves. The sun had set by then, and living people tended to be much more easily spooked by the sight of us at night.

Then, the lights went out. Onstage, a series of explosions as a mass of dancers came out and writhed and the familiar bass began. Everyone around us shrieked. Then they began to chant, "*River! River!*" Which with their accents sounded more like "*REE-ver!*"

In silhouette, he emerged, arms outstretched in his signature pose on a raised platform that felt as though it were miles above the crowd, even though it was probably only about fifteen feet.

"Becky, look!" I said.

But I didn't have to tell her; her mouth gaped as she watched, transfixed.

"Oh!" she said, holding her hands to her mouth in awe.

And then he did it! My moves! Onstage in front of all these people!

"I taught him that!" I shouted. "Me!"

I have never felt more proud of anyone in my life.

River Johnson put on a hell of a show.

I looked back to make sure that Becky saw exactly what me and everybody else in the crowd saw: magic.

"Becky?"

And just like that, she wasn't there. I followed what I thought was the back of her head through the crowd, but it belonged to an Italian wartime miscreant.

"Becky!"

I searched everywhere. There were many people in the stadium, living and dead. Those who heard turned to look in the direction of my voice, but only briefly. One living Becky, having heard me, even screamed back, "What?!"

While I looked, River performed and occasionally I stopped my search to marvel at the boy who'd been my brother for a time. After a few too many such occasions, the concert was nearly over and I still hadn't found her.

I found myself in a horrible spot. I needed to make sure I saw River. I was ready to belong to the Johnsons again. I was prepared to beg for forgiveness if I needed to. But Becky was my family too. If anything, by now, I'd known her for far longer than I'd known the Johnsons. We were tethered to each other at this point, murdered orphans in our shared afterlives.

I pressed on, looking in all the nooks and crannies that could hide a little girl. I went back out front and even onto the field, which had been slightly muddied with the footprints of River's most adoring fans. I shouted across the tops of the exiting concertgoers' heads, "Becky!"

Backstage, a lady passed by with all of River's costumes on rolling clothing racks, saw me, froze in place, and then slowly backed away as though I were a rabid dog. Where was Becky? Where was River? There was the cacophony of excitement, and outside of the stadium the horns of taxis and cars log-jammed while trying to exit. I frantically searched for Becky through the rafters. I couldn't find her anywhere.

Eventually, I found Becky in a place I hadn't thought to look: under the stage itself, by the hydraulics that lifted River skyward.

"You were going to leave me," she said quietly, lifting her head from her hands only briefly to look at me. She had been crying. "I thought I'd make it easier on you."

"I wasn't," I said, trying very hard to control my anger.

"Nobody ever wants me for long," she said. Which was ridiculous, because Becky and I had been wandering the world for a long time together at that point. Although, I am not sure if it was months, or years, or decades, as when you're a little kid and dead, time is even harder to detangle than the knots in a street urchin's hair, or the cord of a really good pair of headphones.

"Becky, we have to go find River," I pleaded. "We can both stay with the Johnsons. It'll be wonderful. I promise. They're good people. Let me introduce you to him at least. You'll see."

We hurried through the people backstage, searching for River. We didn't do anything to conceal ourselves or to try to blend in; time was of the essence. Time was all that stood between us and home.

Except . . . too much time had passed. I didn't know just how long I'd been looking for Becky, but in that time River had boarded a tour bus and left Milan.

It was too late.

Becky and I stood quietly in the empty parking lot. An old Algerian man bent at the waist and swept up the beer bottles and cigarette stubs.

"Just because nobody likes you doesn't mean nobody likes me! They love me! The Johnsons love me!" I cried.

But deep down I was terrified that maybe Becky was right. What if the Johnsons were afraid of me still, after that no-good, very bad thing I'd done?

I'm not proud to admit this, but in my anger, I shoved Becky and she shoved me back, our sadness and fury making our spirits respond as flesh. We tussled and huffed and finally we broke apart and began to cry.

The old immigrant stooped and whistled River's song.

Into the bin, the bottles clanged, discarded.

"River!" I shouted, but he was gone.

PART FOUR

1976–1981

CHAPTER FIFTY-ONE

AFTER MY MISS WITH THE JOHNSONS, BECKY TRIED TO CHEER ME UP AS we continued on to the rest of the ports. There was so much to see, so much to do—screw family! We don't need parents, she argued. We could stay up until all hours dancing, or singing, or talking as loud as we wanted. We didn't have anybody telling us what to do, or where to go, how to be. Becky belched loudly. A living person felt the slight breeze across his ear and turned to look at who, or what, was responsible.

"See!" she said triumphantly. "What would a mother have had to say about that?"

I belched loudly too. Becky did it again.

A passing old couple saw us and shook their gray heads.

We went back and forth like that throughout the night, trying to one-up each other until eventually we grew tired and fell asleep in the lifeboats swaying under the stars.

One of our first trips after Italy was to Greece. Becky loved walking up to the ancients. She asked many questions, and they gave her unsatisfactory answers.

"Why are we dead and still here?" she asked them.

"Fucked if I know," a tiny man in a toga replied. "It happens."

"I thought you guys were all supposed to be wise?" she said.

"Many of us are quite dumb, I assure you." The man laughed.

"Can we go to the beach now?" I said.

"But don't you want to know why?" a frustrated Becky said to me as we dodged poop along a cobblestone road.

"Of course!" I said.

But unlike Becky, I never thought these dead white men had any answers for me.

═══

WE CAME TO travel to all kinds of places near and far, and sometimes I forgot entirely about being loved. We walked along the Great Wall and spoke to the ancients who'd died building it. We watched as the pharaohs cussed out construction workers laying the foundation for an American fast-food joint across the street from the pyramids. We played in the water at beaches bluer than any I'd ever seen before, on the smallest of islands, where we ran into indigenous ghosts who'd died so that spoiled heirs and heiresses could get away for the weekend.

Get away from what? I thought.

We met former kings and queens, most of whom were not especially interesting, and we met toddlers who had died of malnutrition. I observed that a great many people died all over the planet to make a few Europeans very rich. We met people who had died trying to shove things in freaky places, or who had fallen asleep while smoking, or who had started fights and instigated feuds they hadn't won.

After quite some time a-wandering, Becky and I found ourselves in a barren stretch of land somewhere in the middle of nowhere, full of open sky and dried grassland. A place that I have since come to learn is called a steppe.

"Where are we?" I asked.

"I don't know, but it's kinda ugly," Becky said.

We had been to large portions of Eurasia by then, two of us exploring the big world before us. This particular stretch could've remained unexplored, in my opinion. Becky's too. Still, we walked.

We walked through a field of tulips amid wild horses and marveled. Becky and I stretched out our arms, catching the wind in our fingertips as the horses rushed past.

Men in military uniforms with funny fur hats, and even funnier mustaches, argued heatedly among themselves as to what had gone wrong the day they died. It seemed to me a very, very long time to keep arguing over who had screwed the pooch in battle.

Finally we came upon a clearing. Here, scaffolding supported a large rocket covered in bright-red Soviet letters near old train tracks. A gathering of international newsmen and their cameramen busied themselves setting up their equipment, reading scripts and wiping their sweaty pits.

Something big was to happen soon, and the living and we dead could feel it, both.

Nearby, three cosmonauts sat in a circle chatting. Their faces were bruised, but otherwise they looked in pretty good shape for people who had died hurtling through the atmosphere.

"Say, what's going on?" Becky interrupted in her characteristically blunt manner.

"We are sending first Negro to space!" the cosmonaut said in English. "From Cuba!"

That was very big indeed! I thought of all the magazine covers the Johnson boys had of Ed Dwight tucked away in their bedroom. I felt the phantom pain in my chest where the Johnson boys resided. What were Rocco, Roman, and River up to now?

"How was it up there?" I said. "In space?"

"Beautiful. We are beautiful stars," a cosmonaut named Eugene continued to speak in either English so accented I couldn't understand it or some sort of Russian even the afterlife couldn't translate, or perhaps it was just nonsense.

"Death scramble his brains," another cosmonaut, Vlad, said by way of apology.

I decided I should tuck Eugene's answer inside myself for later, should I ever see the Johnsons again. Perhaps River or Rocco might still want to know. Or maybe grown-ups didn't care as much about these things. And they weren't boys, they were grown-ups now, weren't they? Far as I could tell, growing up meant dropping the cool parts of yourself that really loved things like space, or dinosaurs, and forgetting to pick them up after too long.

"The Black's name is Arnaldo Tamayo Méndez, you know him?" the lady cosmonaut said.

I did not know this man and so I shook my head.

"You know, he was orphan!" Vlad said cheerily.

"We're orphans too!" Becky said, growing even more excited.

"Oh boy!" I said.

Suddenly, the rocket engines roared to life. We jumped back, as around us, cameras flashed furiously, and the fire began.

"Shhh, this is the most dangerous part," the lady cosmonaut said.

PART FIVE

1981–1983

CHAPTER FIFTY-TWO

1981

THE ABANDONED PIANO SAT ON THE SIDEWALK. AROUND IT, MOVING ropes fluttered and flopped with each autumnal gust of wind. As though somebody had given up mid-move and left it there. It was such a rich-people thing to do, but River was himself stupendously rich, and living in a rich-people area, where people discarded perfectly good things that were only moderately out of fashion. Like bookcases with the wrong stain for this year's trends, black-and-white televisions, and, apparently, perfectly usable instruments. He imagined the owners had decided to spring for a new baby grand, or a child had not panned out to be a prodigy after all, or somebody's nana had died and her cherished piano was not the inheritance anyone had expected or wanted. The wooden upright was a little weathered, but no more than most you'd find in a church or a school music room. It looked majestic next to the pile of smelly black trash bags. River pressed his index finger down on the ivory and a shiver tingled up his spine. He pressed another key, and again he felt it, the past, his past. At least, it felt like his. So much so that he checked underneath to see if there were carved initials.

Still, he didn't touch it again for two days. I'm no thief, he thought. I have too much damn money to steal a street piano. Surely somebody needier will claim it.

When several days later the weather forecast was rain, something in River couldn't bear to let the piano sit there and get destroyed. He had exactly seven hours to get the piano up to his apartment. He thought at first to enlist his assistant's help, but his assistant was out of town on a last-minute family emergency. River had wanted to ask more but didn't want her to think he didn't believe her. He wasn't that much older than she, and it felt odd having another person whose job it was to do everything for him that he didn't want to do. Dominique felt like a sister or friend some days. Other days, he could feel a whiff of resentment as she brought in his dry cleaning and placed it down dramatically, so the air whiffed out of the bag in a pffffff. She had been to college and he had not. She had a habit of saying "Back when I was in school" and then she'd relay some tale of youth and excess and friends and university-adjacent hovels, and River felt a pang deep in his gut that he had never been young. Not like that. Maybe he'd go back to school one day, he thought. Whenever this all ended.

He had one photo of himself up on the wall. From the European tour, captured for a magazine. Roman had looked up at it in his foyer, the piece of art River had acquired for the place, and said, "Narcissist!"

They'd both laughed. River loved it because he looked bold and ballsy, confident. The woman had captured him midair, sparkling above the crowd. In reality, he didn't feel particularly sparkly at all. It was hard for him to make friends. Hard to know who wanted to actually be his friend and who simply wanted to be near the sparkle. He'd made a handful of friends in New York, and that was more than he'd ever really had in his adult life. Wendy had been right to love this place. He had found home here.

His friends started disappearing right as the piano appeared.

Why were they dying, nobody knew. River had sat with one such friend in a hospital room. Georgie had been plump and jovial in that way that plump people were often expected to be, though he had confided in River once that he thought it was because he'd been so desperate to be liked in school, so desperate to fit in, so desperate to hide in plain sight. He was the funny kid and he kept it up through college, and even here in this new out version of himself, where he could be whoever, still he tried to make 'em laugh. That's how you disarm them, he added. He said it like a jaded old starlet.

In the hospital room, River had sat by Georgie's side as they waited for his parents. There was a group of them who kept vigil, feeding him ice chips, making Georgie laugh, singing songs, trying to put Georgie at ease even as some of the doctors and nurses noticeably stiffened upon entering the room.

"Aren't you River Johnson?" one of the janitors said as she emptied Georgie's waste. Plump Georgie had wasted almost clean away. She began to hum River's most recent hit single. It was his least favorite of all his singles to date, which meant of course that it was his most successful and thus ubiquitous.

"Omigod! I knew I recognized you from somewhere." Georgie grabbed River's hand and they all started laughing.

Disarm 'em. Make 'em laugh, River thought.

"Welcome to *The River Johnson Show*!" Paul said, imitating River's old introduction. When River was ready, Paul was his entrée into New York's scene, taking him to Ninth Circle for "the steak," then Paradise Garage. The first night Paul tried to take him to the baths, but that was too much, River said. He didn't want to get caught. Couldn't afford to.

"You could afford anything in the whole wide world, River," Paul had said with a laugh. "Plus, it's a great place to make friends too!"

That's where Paul had met Georgie, who then became River's friend too. Georgie wasn't their first friend to get sick, but he was the closest. They sat together, crying, laughing, and waiting under the fluorescent lights until Georgie's parents arrived from Idaho and kicked them all out.

There was something that ran in the papers not too long afterward. A paper of ill repute, one nobody respectable took seriously, but a paper nonetheless. The writer hinted that River was gay, that he had the new gay cancer. That he had been seen leaving St. Vincent's looking forlorn. RIVER JOHNSON'S TRAGIC BATTLE the headline read.

"You have to get a girlfriend," Arnie said.

"What?"

"Just for now. Until this blows over."

"Which part of it?"

"Stop being stubborn, River. This is your career we're talking about. I'll find you somebody. Just keep a low profile, OK?"

River scoffed at Arnie of all people telling him to keep a low profile, but he listened.

Eventually, after much hemming and hawing, River had been set up with a beautiful up-and-coming actress. She was funny and warm and wry, and he took her out dancing. He would never have taken a real date somewhere so public. It was the place where people went to see and be seen, and it was almost assured that they would be photographed. She held his arm as they passed the velvet ropes. They glittered together under a disco ball big as her afro, and in the bathroom he had taken a bump. He was pretty certain she had too. She was a blast, and he was genuinely enjoying their night together when she went to kiss him on the dance floor. It was a good kiss. The right amount of tongue, pressure, that brief electricity of two bodies meeting. He should've been delighted. Instead, he felt like absolute shit.

"I'm flattered . . ." he tried to whisper into her ear. Though for a brief flash he could picture their future, a spectacular wedding, a marriage long enough for a child.

The actress smiled and threw her fingertips to the ceiling as if to catch the glittering lights. She tilted her head in the direction of a photographer who sat in one of the booths, snapping them.

"I got you, River Johnson," she said.

It was one of the sweetest things anybody had ever said to him in his life. He started crying right there on the dance floor of the Limelight. Lots of people were on drugs, so nobody paid him much mind. The actress rolled her head back, closed her eyes, and rapped every single lyric along with Debbie Harry to "Rapture" like a little prayer given up to the rafters of the former church.

Georgie had been buried earlier that day. Nobody understood anything about this new disease, just that it seemed to afflict primarily the homosexuals and the Haitians, according to the very few news articles that had been printed thus far. None of them had been invited to Georgie's funeral, and even if River had been, best to stay away from your friends for a bit, lie low, his agent had said.

Instead, River danced.

═══

WHAT MIGHT HIS life have been if he hadn't become famous? At parties, he got drunk and pleaded with strangers, "Please, call me Riv."

After one such party, where he found himself unable to stop thinking about how much Wendy would've fucking loved it, River stumbled into his penthouse and retrieved her fur coat from the back of his closet. He nuzzled into the one spot where some faint whiff of her remained. Then he crawled with it, like a security blanket of sorts, under the piano.

Upside down, his fro pressed into a halo atop Wendy's beloved mink, and the world a whirl around him, River marveled at the piano's underside, at all the work that went into creating the thing which creates things. He had turned himself topsy-turvy. All he needed to do was right himself.

The first ghost he saw was not of Georgie but of his friend Murray. Murray wore suits, but looked just as great in dresses, and lipstick, and even got River to try wearing a bit of mascara. Eventually, he lost track of Murray and thought that the city had gobbled them up. He didn't realize just how thoroughly Murray had been masticated. Murray appeared beside River at the piano in an elegant dress that had belonged to their grandmother, their eyeball shot clean through.

Alvin was one of those Puerto Ricans who looked Blacker than River and sounded wholly Nueva York. He called River nigga affectionately and River wasn't sure he liked that, but he liked Alvin. They had danced for hours one night at the Saint, the both of them being attracted to each other in the middle of all that whiteness, and even made out a little bit. But when the lights in the club came on, they'd just laughed about it and both had gone home alone. Alvin used too much tongue for River's taste. River wasn't really Alvin's type. Every time they saw each other, Alvin joked about it, and somehow their friendship became even stronger through rejection. Alvin appeared next to the piano with his tongue white, his sarcoma bright, his face gaunt.

The third ghost was Simon (yes, two of his ghosts were also Chipmunks, but he didn't have any friends named Theodore). Simon was knifed outside a bar near Christopher Street. Beautiful, tall, Black as the sky, blue as a bruise, red gashes across his torso and face. He'd been robbed, but the robbery hadn't been the point.

It was a violent year in New York. A dangerous time in his adopted city to be both Black and gay. Gay Cancer. Black Death. He and his friends already were or were becoming statistics.

A plague on both my houses, River thought.

═══

HE TOOK TO speaking with some of his dead friends as he tinkered.

"Not working." Murray sat atop the piano and twirled their pearls.

"OK, then what should I try instead?"

"Fucked if I know, I'm not the musician you are!"

"Yo, you gotta make it more upbeat," Alvin said. "Give the people something we can dance to."

"But disco's dead," River lamented.

Two years earlier, in Chicago, before a Sox game, an entire stadium of red-faced young white men had stormed the baseball field to crush and destroy all those records with their Black and brown and queer smiles. They jeered and danced around the burning. The joy in their faces akin to those River had seen in lynching postcards. River had felt their chants of "*Disco sucks*" through his body, wrapping itself around his neck. He thought of Christmas and remained shaken even after he'd changed the channel.

Their reasoning was that music was too much. Too overproduced. Too shiny. Too cheesy. Or in plainer terms—entirely too gay and Black.

"Fuck those honky haters," Alvin said.

"Personally, I think you should do something unexpected . . . like . . . like a rock opera!" Simon said. "Go big!"

"Nigga, what?" Alvin said. "And you ain't even the one who got their brains stomped out."

"So rude . . ." Murray said. "What about an album of standards?"

"He's not some aging has-been!" Simon said.

"Standards are standard for a reason. They're great songs. Hello, Cole Porter? Gershwin?"

Murray floated as though in their own musical number with Fred Astaire.

"You should do something like the kids are doing with the turntables," Alvin said. "Something funky fresh."

"Am I funky fresh?" River said.

They all seemed to pause to consider it.

"You might be better off with the standards," Simon said.

River thought of all the times he'd done what he was supposed to because other people said it would be good for him.

"Write it," he heard Wendy's voice say in his head.

Fuck it. River thought, and then he wrote.

═

RIVER PUT ON a beanie and sunglasses and a sweatshirt hoping to blend in as well as he might. His security guard trailed behind him as he exchanged a few pleasantries with his doorman Milos. He reminded himself to remind his assistant to pick up a gift for Milos's new baby girl. Or was it a boy? Shit. How the hell had he forgotten already?

There was a chill in the air as he walked under the scaffolding, thinking about chord progressions and lyrics. Murray, Simon, and Alvin had sung along in harmony to his most recent composition. More voices made it better. Layered like that, it was haunting. And not just because they were dead.

Still, it was missing something. He was so deep in trying to find what he was missing that he didn't see the man coming the other direction in his trench coat and suit.

"Sorry, man," he said, and intended to keep going. There were increasingly plenty of yuppies in this section of town, always too important to look where they were going, always a bit too loud. People whose days revolved around numbers and how to add more zeros for people who already had so many. Wendy would've mocked them.

"River?" the man said.

He had assumed at first it was a fan and cursed the fact that he hadn't gone for the baseball-cap-and-hoodie look instead. Fuck. He hoped the man wouldn't ask for a picture. He hadn't expected to look up and see his childhood friend. His first kiss.

Milton smiled at him and River didn't know whether to hug or shake hands. In spite of himself, he glanced at Milton's hand to see if there was a ring.

"You're a yuppie!" River laughed.

Milton shrugged. "I'm in law school. Just came from my internship. If you're trying to disguise yourself, that's a pitiful attempt."

He laughed. River was surprised at how deep Milton's voice was. How sonorous. In his head, Milton was forever fifteen, with a voice that couldn't make up its mind from sentence to sentence on which side of the adult/child divide it landed. Not that Milton was ever Barry White by any means. It was just a man's voice. Now Milton was a man, and a beautiful one at that.

"I'm on my way to get coffee? You want some?"

"Are you inviting me with you?" Milton said. "Am I getting invited to hang out with *the* River Johnson?"

"Oh shut up." River laughed. How was it this easy between the two of them after all these years? Shouldn't this be more awkward?

"I mean, the bodega's just around the corner. I like the coffee there as much as anywhere. And my place is just . . ."

The air lingered with the awkwardness of their first and only kiss. He probably didn't even remember it, River thought. They were boys then. People experimented. He probably had a girlfriend now. Maybe another law student. Somebody who'd been to college, definitely.

"You get your own coffee?"

Not usually. Usually, his assistant did.

"I'm a very down-to-earth famous person, Milton," River joked. "I've even been thinking about doing my own grocery shopping."

Milton laughed and stood next to River. "Let's go then."

"Wait, one sec," River said, and dismissed his security guard, Shawn, who put up only a little bit of a fight.

How weird and wonderful to find home where you least expect it. Somehow, Wendy had led him back to Milton. *Don't get ahead of yourself, River,* he thought. *It's just coffee.* Maybe Milton was actually a total douchebag now. How much could they even have in common? Young Milton hadn't wanted to be anything like his father, and yet here he was. Even so, River could use a friend. Somebody who knew him before.

"Hey, how far is your place?" he said to Milton.

"Not very. Why?"

"I've been shut in mine for days, working. I wouldn't mind a change of scenery."

"Curious about how the other half lives?"

"Something like that." River laughed, thinking of his ghosts.

═══

THE ELEVATOR WAS down. It took eight flights of stairs to get to Milton's apartment. River was in good shape, he had to be for his performances, but still. Eight floors. He tried to mask how breathless he was when they reached the landing. Maybe he should've just taken his chances with Milton seeing his ghosts.

"Yeah, it's a lot." Milton laughed. "I swear that fucking thing is broken more than it's working. I'm sorry, I should've warned you."

The inside of Milton's apartment was remarkable for how unremarkable it was. Nice and neat, a bookcase lined with books, mostly textbooks, some with the "used" stickers still on them, and records. A framed poster of *Butch Cassidy and the Sundance Kid,* a Hockney print from a semi-recent show in San Francisco, and a Hopper print from the Whitney, were the only decorative items. There were dishes in the sink, but not an obscene amount, and a bag of cat food under the windowsill, next to a few wilting plants.

"You have a cat?"

"I'm technically allergic," Milton said. "But there's a stray who I think is two-timing me with several of my neighbors. Three-timing? I don't know."

"Better at feeding the cat than the plants, it looks like."

"Tricky fuckers. I'm trying to be an adult here."

River sat down on the plain couch in the living room. The only substantial piece of furniture in the room. It felt comfortable, like the kind of couch friends crashed on when they weren't sober enough to go home. It was a spartan student's apartment. River had never had one of those. He'd hired a designer to do his apartment while he was on the road. It wasn't entirely his sense of style, but he figured maybe one day he might grow into the kind of person who wanted a couch as a piece of modern art, one that looked like a bunch of clown noses stuck together.

"I have to say, it's a little intimidating trying to decide what music to put on for one of the most famous musicians in the world," Milton said, flipping through his sparse record collection.

"Oh shush," River said.

Milton settled on *Breakfast in America.* River only liked a few of the songs off the album, but he wouldn't dare say so, lest he embarrass Milton.

"How's your folks?" Milton said above the opening notes of "Gone Hollywood."

"They nearly got divorced, but they seem good now. Happier than I've seen them since before we moved to California, maybe?"

Milton nodded. "And your brothers?"

"Rocco's good. He's really happy. He's got a girlfriend going on several years now. At the group home where they live. And Roman's staying sober these days. I try to call him once a week or so, when I can . . ."

River felt himself grow a little nauseous thinking of how the last time he'd spent any significant time with Milton it was before the decline of the Johnson Three, right before their world burst open.

"When I was with you . . . before we . . . that's when the bullies got to Rocco and everything went down. And at my party . . ." River started. "I'm sorry I was so cruel to you. I blamed myself and I blamed you. And I thought if I had just been where I was supposed to be . . . I didn't mean to hurt you."

"Did it hurt? Yes. I was devastated," Milton said. "I was crazy about you, Riv . . ."

River felt himself holding his breath.

"And it was my first time feeling that way about . . . about anyone."

River felt the tears welling up in his eyes. He had no right to cry. It was he who had hurt Milton, embarrassed Milton, hurt everyone he ever cared about in some form or fashion.

"It took me years to not hate myself . . ." Milton looked him in the eye.

"I hate myself sometimes," River whispered. "Most times."

"Well, don't do that, stupid." Milton wiped away a tear and laughed.

"I still have the starfish," River said softly. The golden starfish paperweight Milton and Holly had gifted him on River's birthday so many years back sat atop various pianos over the years, giving weight to lyrics here and there, this scribble, that idea.

"What happened to Holly?" River asked.

"Her parents moved our senior year, and we kept in touch for a little while until we went off to college and broke up freshman year like everyone does. You know how it is . . ."

River did not, but he could imagine all the same.

"I was awful to her," River said.

"Won't argue with that," Milton said. River liked that Milton didn't try to make him feel better, that he let the past be the past but he didn't sugarcoat who they'd been. It made it easier to be here as he was now.

The A side of the album came to an end, and they decided to switch to Prince's *Dirty Mind*. The kid had swaggered onto the *SNL* stage in his sequin leotard and fringed go-go boots, hints of his thighs flashing as he twirled. River would've been jealous if he hadn't been so damn delighted.

"Do we think he said 'fuck'?" Milton said.

"Oh he definitely said 'fuck.'" River laughed.

Milton grabbed him by the hand, and they danced as Prince sang "*I don't want to die I just want to have a bloody good time!*"

"Look at you hitting them notes!" River said, and Milton turned beet red.

Milton and River talked for hours as their coffees grew cold and the sky grew dark. They watched a television movie that was absolutely horrible, and Milton told River about the people he'd loved, his parents for whom he was never enough, how he'd fallen in love with New York after moving there with an ex, and then deciding to go to law school after a few years of floundering. The ex was the one who had bought the Hockney and Hopper prints.

"I stole them out of his moving boxes." Milton giggled. "I wasn't even all that attached to them, but I didn't want that fucker to have them."

River imagined how lovely it must be to share a home with somebody, even if they were a fucker. He and Wendy had shared a life for just a bit, but they'd never not been in hotel rooms. They'd never had the ability to get into the rhythms of domesticity. He'd never kissed the back of her neck as she washed dishes. Not that Wendy would've washed dishes.

They continued to talk as the city grew sleepier outside.

Soon, they too fell asleep, and whenever River moved, Milton brought his leg to touch him. It calmed River down. Somehow, just his touch of Milton's calf against River's felt both comforting and like the most erotic thing in the world. He felt himself grow hard and tried to will it away.

When Milton's alarm went off and he readied himself for class, River decided to do a yoga flow on the floor to wake himself up.

"What are you doing?" Milton brushed his teeth and stood in the doorway watching him.

"I learned it from a friend . . . A girl I loved," River said, feeling the need to be open and honest with Milton, although he wasn't sure why. With Milton, he felt . . . in bloom.

"Wendy," Milton said.

Of course Milton knew her name. It was the title of River's most recent single, more acoustic than anything else he'd done in his career. He'd refused to sing it on any late-night shows and only a handful of times in concert 'cause his voice always cracked when he got to this part:

beside me beside me beside me
what is there, who else is there
besides you besides you besides you
The why or the how, don't matter much now
No, don't nothing matter much now to me

"She must've been special," Milton said.

"She really was."

CHAPTER FIFTY-THREE

1982

LUCY LOUDLY CRUNCHED ON APPLES AND LAUGHED MORE HEARTILY than anyone had any right to. Lucy had come to the U.S. for a new start after quite literally burning her house down and all her worldly possessions with it in England. She had a daughter who didn't call her back and an ex-husband who did, but only when he wanted money, or to yell at her for ruining their lives. Lucy had a tooth missing from a bar fight that she refused to get fixed, a mauve scar across her wrist from the time she'd tried to kill herself, and skin grafts from the fire that Roman hadn't seen but that Lucy said were the reason she mostly wore pants. Lucy helped him through three relapses to date. The first of which was not all that long after he'd gotten out of rehab.

Roman had not wanted a sponsor. Had not seen the value in some grizzled old white man telling him all about how he drank himself nearly half to death and then found Jesus and every day was a struggle but if Roman just prayed and surrendered and got right with the people he'd hurt then everything would be OK. At least that was how Roman had imagined it would go. He had not thought that he would find himself in the hands of a small snaggletoothed British woman who looked like something out of a fairy tale.

Lucy had walked up to him after a meeting and taken a liking to him. Roman had been hoping for the fatherly Black man, or even the excessively sweaty Latino man closer to his own age, to approach him. He had gotten used to people approaching him, directly confusing him for River, or saying "Your brother's famous!" As though that were an introduction, an invitation to immediate friendship. He'd mastered the proud-but-benevolent smile when somebody mentioned they were a huge fan. Secretly, he had hoped somebody in the church basement would look at him and see music, would approach him ready to fawn, and instead he'd have a real and true friend to tell his whole good-for-nothing sad-sack life story. He had been looking for a father or a brother, a compadre even, not this little British witchy woman who'd lost so much, laughed the loudest, and didn't give two fucks who his brother was. Lucy earnestly and passionately argued that all music had turned to shit in the '70s.

Even so, Roman had not seen Lucy angry until now.

"No," Lucy said. "Absolutely not."

The reason Lucy was angry was that Roman was in love. He had been fully sober for almost two whole years after a series of fits and starts, brief relapses here and there. At least he wasn't thirteenth-stepping, right?

"Am I not allowed to be in love, Lucy?" He laughed. Lucy didn't laugh back.

"It's only gonna end bad, yeah? You've come too far to fuck it all up like this," Lucy said. "Feels like you're just finally getting the hang of it, Ro."

"I've been sober for nearly two years already!"

"Of being you, I mean," she said. "Being alone."

He'd had a series of pretty dysfunctional quasi-relationships over this most recent year or so of sobriety, the worst of which had ended with him raiding the liquor cabinet of the woman he was seeing while she slept. He'd sat in her bathroom holding a bottle of her cooking vermouth for what felt like an eternity before setting it down and walking out her house without so much as retrieving his shoes. Lucy said the problem was that sober Roman couldn't bear to be by himself, and so he would hop into a relationship with damn near anyone who would have him. And given his proximity to River, there was always someone.

Lucy was not in the habit of mincing words, and Roman liked this most about her. She was not an altogether bad-looking older woman herself, and every once in a while she would enter Roman's head briefly as he pleasured himself. But most of the time, when he was in his right mind, he would push her out of his head as quickly as she'd come. He loved Lucy in a way, but not that way. He knew better. Usually.

Katherine, Kit, was as though Roman had manifested her from an actual dream. A real-life dream woman. She was tall and brown with beautiful doe eyes; everything about her was exquisite, her delicate ankles and wrists, her pendulous breasts, not to mention she was possibly the smartest woman he'd ever met. She was studying for her PhD at Caltech. A Black woman at Caltech! A PhD! Roman had forgotten what in, but assumed it was something sciencey. She had entered the shop one afternoon as Roman steamed a big hat.

"That's a mighty big hat you got there," she'd said, and laughed and snorted at herself as though she'd just said the funniest thing ever. He would later find out that Kit was constantly snorting at her own jokes, once so violently he was positive he had seen actual snot materialize in her nostrils that she attempted to surreptitiously wipe away with her pink chiffon blouse. It was not nearly surreptitious enough, but Roman loved her by then.

Kit needed a hat for a wedding. Not hers, she said. And Roman thought it meant something that she made sure to mention as much. She looked up at the wall, which Odysseus had made a practical shrine to River.

"You guys favor each other," she said.

"Yeah." Roman sighed. He was used to women coming in and trying to get River's number or hanging out with him for a month or two only to find out that what they really wanted was an in to River, or VIP tickets for a concert, or merely to say that they had been to River Johnson's childhood home, knew his brother, had kissed him, maybe more. He had dated a few celebrity or celebrity-adjacent types, but when they discovered that he was perfectly content to spend the day in his father's store making hats, that he occasionally woke up screaming in the middle of the night having dreamt of dead children, they often drifted away. Sometimes after a few good months, more often, a few great nights. So Roman had learned to keep most women at an arm's length. He went to their homes or hotel rooms or apartments. He opened only the smallest parts of himself to them. Or stuck only the smallest parts of him in. Whichever they or he preferred in the moment. Kit, though, Kit was different.

"It must suck being River Johnson's brother," she said, taking in all the photos.

"It's not that bad," Roman said. He was not especially in the mood to share.

"Hmmm," she said, and left it at that.

"You're Roman, right?" she said.

He grunted in response.

"You don't remember me," she said.

"Remember you?" Roman said. He was focusing on not burning his hand as he shaped the hat. "I'm sorry, we get a lot of folks coming in."

She rocked a little bit to one side, a little bit to the other and sang, softly, beautifully. He still didn't know her. Something about her did feel awfully familiar. He momentarily allowed himself to look down. The woman had the longest legs he'd ever seen.

"Would you like to go for a coffee?" she said.

"Miss, you haven't told me what kind of hat you're interested in yet."

"I can tell you over coffee, can't I?"

"Look, I'm very flattered but I'm too busy to leave the shop right now. Plus, I'm not big into coffee."

"Is that code for you don't date Black women?"

She laughed at herself. It was a very witchy laugh. Or was it bewitching? Nah, she actually sounded a bit like the Wicked Witch as she cackled at herself. Roman flushed and burned the tip of his finger. He yelped.

"Fuck. I'm sorry," she said. "I was only joking. Do you have ice?"

"I'll be OK."

"You gotta at least run cold water over it. Hold on just a second."

She practically sprinted out the store as Roman shouted after her, "I'm fine!"

It might in fact have been at least a second-degree burn. After she'd disappeared from view, Roman rushed to the bathroom in the back of the shop and ran cold water over it.

"Hello!" He heard her voice from the front again. "I've come to the rescue!"

He walked back up front. With a bit of a huff, and a lot of frantic energy, she thrust a bag of ice at him. But not a baggie, not something appropriately sized, but rather the kind of ice bag one would use to fill a cooler. The counter was already wet with condensation.

"I went down to the liquor store."

It was the liquor store that Roman knew almost as well as he knew his store. Where he'd bought candy as a kid and stolen vodka bottles a year ago, and where, eventually, he'd had the cops called on him. Odysseus had told the owner, Mr. Robinson, that if he so much as let Roman in the liquor store again, he'd take a bat to the whole place. Mr. Robinson had been one of the first business owners to welcome Odysseus to the neighborhood.

"I'm not allowed in there." Roman just let it slip out. He had no reason to tell her and yet something about her was disarming. She had the kind of face that made you want to feel known. Or maybe it was just that she was lovely. In her awkward, snorting, frantic way.

"Why not? Did you steal from them as a kid or something?" she said.

"Worse. As an adult," he said.

"A bad boy, then?" She leaned in and touched his hand to look at where he'd burned it. He was surprised by her touch.

"No," he said firmly, but he did not pull his hand away.

"I'm surprised it didn't make the paper." She nodded up at River on the wall.

"The owner and my dad were friends before I fucked it up."

"Do you like tea?" she asked.

"It's all right I guess."

"OK. Tea it is. Shit, I'm running late for my class. I've got to go, but I'll call you with the details."

"What about the hat?" He shouted after her. "Where do I know you from? How are you going to call when I didn't give you my number?"

The little bell chimed as the door closed.

Later that week, she called the shop, and they arranged for tea at the Huntington. She told him all about her studies in a field he didn't understand anything about. Roman wished he had been to college, wondered if it was too late to go. He had always been a good student; in some alternate world he could see himself across from her, perhaps as an astrophysicist. He'd always liked planets and flight. Hadn't all the Johnson boys dreamed of the stars? He was turning thirty soon and already he felt somehow that the world had passed him by. He liked that she didn't speak down to him, that her life seemed full and complex, and she seemed confident in a way that had little to do with her looks, though she was extraordinarily beautiful. He liked the way her eyes lit up as she told him about her research.

"Are you ever going to tell me where I know you from?"

"You hadn't guessed it yet?! The Sertrelles!"

"Holy shit! The Sertrelles! But there wasn't a Kit in the Sertrelles. Minerva, Kiki, and . . ." He searched his brain for the third sister.

"Joan. And I went by Kiki, instead of Kit, when I was younger."

"KikiKit," Roman said. He didn't know why he said that. Sometimes he blurted out things that he probably should've just kept in his head, but she laughed at it good-naturedly.

"I don't know how you guys didn't get famous," Roman said.

"Neither do we." She laughed. "We were good, weren't we? We got so close. So many different times. It's such a nasty business though, isn't it? I think I'm happier now than I would've been. Maybe. I don't know. Is your brother happy?"

"I think so. I'm not sure. We're not as close as we could be," Roman said, and shrugged. "Plus, he's busy."

"There's still time," KikiKit said.

"For what?"

"To get close. If you want."

"Yeah . . . So how are your sisters doing?"

"Joan's great. She's married. Still living back home. Has three kids who are practically feral. But I think she likes letting them do whatever 'cause our parents were so strict with us. And Minerva . . . Minerva passed not too long ago. Heroin overdose."

Roman sat back in shock. He remembered another version of himself many years ago imagining what a future with Minerva could look like. Or at the very least a kiss.

"I remember how sweet you were on her," Kiki said.

"Was I that obvious?"

"Boy, your tongue practically hung out your mouth every time she was nearby!"

They both laughed and then grew quickly solemn.

"Fuck."

"All those years of working so hard, and all that rejection. And so young? Never mind all those leeches and the leering when we were just girls. I think it really did a number on her. On all of us really . . ."

"None of that shit is healthy for a kid," Roman said.

"No. Not at all," KikiKit said. "Sorry for dumping all that on you."

"Don't feel sorry for that. That's what friends are for," Roman said.

"Are we friends?" KikiKit asked, eyebrows raised.

Roman shrugged. "It's just nice to see somebody from home. From before."

She nodded.

"Do you miss it? Performing, I mean?" Roman said.

"Sometimes," she said, and left it at that. "I like what I'm working on now, though."

KikiKit had come out to California to get away from it all for a while after her sister's death, and to continue her studies. That's how two Black kids from the Midwest had ended up in a hat shop in Pasadena. That and she was curious to see if that hat shop really was owned by River Johnson's father, per local gossip.

"I'm a ghost from your past." She laughed.

"A welcome one," Roman said.

"So tell me about you. What have you been up to for the last . . . decade or so?"

Because she had been so open with him, he only hesitated for a little bit before he told her what had happened when he went AWOL, and later in the jail, and about the drinking and the years in and out of rehabs and basements trying to get ahold of this thing that had a grip on him, that might always. He told her how he had always hated helping out in the shop as a kid, but now he found it comforting, making beautiful things. Hats as a form of art. He hadn't finished high school, but he could probably pass the GED test easily enough. He liked her, so he told her more about himself than he'd ever told anyone on a first date. If this was, in fact, a date?

"My brother is a superstar and I'm a high school dropout alcoholic," he said.

"Those things aren't mutually exclusive," she said softly but firmly. "And besides, you're assigning value to him and not to yourself. You are valuable. You are not a disease or a degree or a platinum record."

He hadn't known what to say to that. She grabbed his hand across the table. The one that had been burned by steam. *Ouch,* he thought, but he didn't dare say a word, because in her hands he felt known.

That was how it started. There were dates all over town. Long walks spent talking about everything and nothing at all. A trip to Griffith to see the stars. Sometimes they'd burst into one of the songs from their youth and just harmonize with each other, notes floating between the two of them. A hike in the canyons that had always been just around the corner but to which Roman had never been, the Millard Canyon waterfall. The day was a little too hot and their bodies were sticky and funky by the time they finally reached the main event. They took off their shoes and stood on the smooth stones at the water's edge. Here, Roman leaned in to kiss her and she let him get close, so close, before backing away and falling into the water behind them.

"Oh fuck, are you OK?"

"I'm fine." She laughed. Then Roman launched himself into the water behind her.

"It's only fair," he said.

If she needs to take things slower, I can do it slower, Roman thought.

She leaned over and hovered near his face, their mouths almost touching but not. They just held it in the space between, neither of them leaning in closer. Finally, KikiKit pressed her mouth against his. They kissed until she pulled herself back and gasped. Then she ran directly under the waterfall itself and squealed with delight.

The water rushed around their feet as KikiKit stretched her arms up to the sky as if receiving a gift, or perhaps giving one. How much more beauty was there just around the bend? This, this is why he had survived the war, survived himself. How wondrous!

He could not stop thinking of KikiKit and everything lovely about her.

"I'm about to turn thirty soon enough. I think . . . maybe I'm finally ready for something real?" Roman said as he took a huge bite of pecan pie.

"I worry that you're not far enough along in your recovery as you think. Besides, just because the two of you have the same damage doesn't make it a good idea . . ." Lucy said at their weekly diner meeting.

"But Lucy, I think she might be the best idea," he said, leaning in.

Lucy threw her head back and cackled like a fairy-tale witch. He could see her silver molar glisten before she bit into her apple.

"Idiot."

The way Lucy said the word was almost multisyllabic, in her mouth it rang out like a song. Idyyiott.

CHAPTER FIFTY-FOUR

1983

THERE WAS A MARK ON MILTON'S LEFT SHOULDER. HE NOTICED IT while showering over at River's place. This had become his regular shower routine, wash his hair, then all his bits and bobbles, and finally try to hold the panic attack at bay while he checked for lesions. Up until this very moment, death had not left its mark on him.

It's here, he thought, and promptly vomited in River's toilet.

"You all right in there?" River shouted.

"Just drank a little too much last night," Milton said.

"Lightweight!" River laughed and began to sing, "*I got the sweetest hangover, I don't want to get over . . .*"

Milton toweled off and got dressed in the bathroom. Milton had grown up with money. In fact even in California, he was likely upper middle class, or possibly even a little rich, though it seemed to him awfully gauche to claim as much. But River's place was something else. River was an international superstar. Sure, he hadn't had a huge hit in a few years, but that hit and the ones before it had been literally everywhere. Everything in River's place was kept just-so, thanks to his house manager, Joy, and his personal assistant, Dominique, not to mention all the myriad other people who kept River's life going. River trusted Joy and Dominique with everything, and they delivered, moving in and around his place felt, but unseen. Perhaps this was why Milton was afraid to walk around butt-naked. River mocked how Milton seemed so shy, intent on covering up after they just spent the evening exploring each other's bodies.

"I just had my tongue in your ass!" River laughed.

"Shhh." Milton went to hold his hand over River's mouth as he giggled.

"Nobody's here but us," River said.

But Milton had the feeling that was never exactly true. He remembered the stories River had told him when they were young, about a brother ghost who lived in their house. Anybody else would've laughed at River and called him a liar, but while Milton never saw anything, occasionally he thought he felt a tingle, a breath, once even a laugh, a loud one, while he sat in River's apartment studying and waiting for him to return from some meeting or another. This, even though he knew River had paid for both the penthouse and the floor beneath him. For the sake of privacy, of course, he'd said. They shouldn't have been able to hear a soul.

The dead didn't scare Milton as much as they had when he was young. His favorite ex was Paolo, with whom he'd spent a glorious time at Fire Island years ago. And now Paolo was dead, and several of the others from that July where they'd all danced at the Sandpiper, and fucked on poppers to Blondie. Paolo had been his very first, the one who had made him finally come out to his parents. He'd been broad-chested, olive-skinned with dark, curly hair and eyes like seafoam. And then, last year, Paolo was the first person he loved, who was his age, that he'd seen, body a fraction of what it was and skull shrunken in an ostentatious coffin that swallowed him whole.

It's coming, Milton thought then. He hadn't let go of the thought since.

"You all right, Milton?" River asked, noticing that he'd grown quiet.

"You know how it is," Milton said. And indeed, River did.

═

LATER THAT DAY, Milton rescheduled a meeting with a client and walked the three blocks to the local clinic, one of several he went to in rotation, lest they think him a hypochondriac. He and River had been exclusive for the last two years, and still, he couldn't shake the thought that it was only a matter of time. He had friends who were vehemently against the closing of the bathhouses, who considered it a full-on assault on a community that not that many years earlier had fought so hard to simply exist and gather in peace. Milton hadn't frequented the bathhouses, although he had gone to one once, when he was first starting to realize who and what he was. It was not quite for him, though he'd marveled at the glistening bodies, the very freedom of it all. He'd hooked up with two different men, one of whom he recognized from his Civ Pro II class. After, he'd felt not satiated but empty. It wasn't for him. Milton was a romantic through and through. Then, when a friend finally dragged him out after a night of studying, Milton met Paolo at 12 West while dancing to Sylvester's "You Make Me Feel (Mighty Real)." It felt fated, until it didn't.

Now he sat in the waiting room for a blood test across from a man old enough to be his grandfather. Instead of focusing his gaze on the ground, as the young man next to Milton was doing, the old Black man smiled across at Milton, holding his gaze.

"I didn't think I'd even make it this far, to be honest," he said, unprompted. "I was a gay-as-a-goose Black man in the South at the height of lynching, you know?"

Milton nodded, though he did not, in fact, know. He wanted to tell this man that his boyfriend was Black, but then thought that would be stupid, or awkward, or both. The old man had an elegant walking cane that he gripped as he leaned forward in his chair to talk to Milton. He could see that the man had once been very beautiful indeed, still was in a way, even with all the markers of old age.

"I left the love of my life to come to New York. But I had to. I was dying down there anyway. Just slowly."

"I can only imagine," Milton said. Jeez, why was it so hard for him to converse like a normal person sometimes?

"You kids think you invented it all. But let me tell you. We did it all first! You ever hear of the Daisy Chain?"

Milton shook his head no.

"The Clam House?

"Y'all don't even know!" The man slapped his knee and laughed so hard he began to cough. His cough began to rattle his whole body about, such that Milton was about to rush over to get a nurse, until the man put his hand up and said, "I'm OK!"

"Say, you know that move that River Johnson do?" The man did a little wiggle and tilt of his body, as if to do what he could of the dance move from his chair. "I only seen one other boy do that in my life, way back in the day. Before you and that boy River was even in your Daddy's nut sack. River Johnson stole that move somehow. Nothing else like it. Boy who created it first been dead since the thirties, last I heard. That boy was something special he were . . ."

"Are you saying that River Johnson stole his whole act from a dead kid?"

"Ain't that something?" The man laughed. "It sounds crazy, I know. But crazier things happen all the time. I ain't mad at him though. River is doing my peoples proud." The man leaned over conspiratorially. "You know he's a fairy, right?"

"You don't know that for sure!" Milton was terrible at lying.

The man chuckled and winked. The nurse called for the other man in the room, who continued to look down at the floor as he walked toward her, his knees visibly trembling. They sat in silence for a few, each of them contemplating their respective fates, and the fate of the man who'd gone before them.

"You said you left the South back in the day because of lynching . . . Isn't this just lynching by another name?" Milton asked in earnest. "We're dying and nobody's doing a thing. Nobody seems to give a shit at all."

"Maybe," the old man said. "But honey, I lived. I'd do it all again in a heartbeat. For a good long while, I got to live!"

"Moses Powell?" the nurse said, and the old man looked her way.

"I'm coming!"

═══

MILTON WALKED HOME, dodging the black trash bags strewn along the sidewalk, the people even younger than himself with their boomboxes, their breakdancing, and their loud laughter. How could anyone laugh at a time like this? he thought. Their world was ending.

"Arnie thinks I should I do a fucking musical!" River said as Milton walked through the door. "Like, what am I gonna do, prance around at the Winter Garden dressed like a cat?"

"Riv . . ." Milton leaned down and gave him a kiss on the cheek. "What if instead you did that gala or fundraiser or whatever that Paul's been talking about, for AIDS research?"

"I thought you hate Paul?"

"I never said I hate Paul. I just said he can be annoying sometimes."

"Same thing . . . Besides, you know I can't do that."

"Why not? People are dying. Our friends are dying."

"It would be career suicide for me, Milton. Are you kidding me? I can't just walk onstage and go, 'Guess what guys! You were right! I'm a faggot! Here to raise money for all the other faggots dying of our little faggy disease!' Nobody wants to hear anything racial or even remotely political from me."

Milton stood, mouth agape. He couldn't believe the words coming out of River's mouth. He felt sick. He felt . . . disgust?

"Are you really that fucking selfish, River?"

Milton had never once raised his voice at River before. He was River Johnson, his beautiful childhood crush, the one who got away, one of the most recognizable voices in the world. Their first big fight was over the NDA that River had him sign. Three pages.

"What is this?" Milton had said.

"You're the lawyer." River laughed.

Milton didn't consider it a laughing matter. He signed it eventually, but not until after a few choice words were exchanged. Still, he'd never raised his voice, even when he probably should have.

They'd argued, like any normal couple, or at least any normal couple in which one party was one of the most famous people in the world—everything revolved around River's schedule, and Milton never got to hang out with his law school friends anymore (his law school friends had no idea he was dating River Fucking Johnson, and for obvious reasons he couldn't tell them what he was up to. "I'm studying this weekend!" only went so far as an excuse after so long). River was out until all hours with fans and hangers-on alike and somehow Milton was just supposed to trust that it was strictly business?

Their nastiest fights were reserved for the fact of River's refusal to be out to his brothers and father. Two years of being somebody's secret would drive anybody mad. But they always made up, followed by some grand gesture on River's part (for the really big fuck-ups) or just a hand extended to the other across the couch after a protracted silence that had wounded them both more than either cared to admit.

"Yes, well, very famous people tend to be selfish. How else do you think we get famous?" River said snidely. Milton knew that it was a sore spot. That River held all kinds of feelings he should probably work through with a therapist about being the brother who got it all in the end.

"Don't give me that shit," Milton said. "You're better than that. You have to do something!"

"I can't!" River crumpled into himself and appeared to be on the verge of tears. "My dad worked so hard . . . and my brothers . . . It would destroy everything."

"You're a coward!" Milton screamed.

". . . I don't want to be," River whispered.

"Then don't be! Who even are you?" he asked River.

"I . . ." River stopped and stared. Milton waited for him to say something. Anything. To fight for him. For them. Instead, River just shrugged.

"You know what? Fuck it. It doesn't even matter anymore. I'm done," Milton said, and turned to walk toward the door.

And like the emotionally stunted, petulant child he fucking was, River repeated Milton's words back at him, mockingly high and whiny.

"Wowwww," Milton thought he heard another heavily accented voice say, all Nueva York, even though it had just been the two of them in the room, or so he thought. "Yo, for real, River? For fucking real?"

Milton didn't even bother turning around to look back and see who, or what, it was.

CHAPTER FIFTY-FIVE

IN VIETNAM, WE MET MANY OF THE RECENT WAR DEAD, SOME OF WHOM especially liked to play tricks on the living, crashing cars, scaring former generals who'd sold their souls and land and lived. There were many dead American soldiers, but even more Vietnamese who had only been in the business of living at the wrong time and place.

As we visited Ho Chi Minh Square, I saw a dead teenager reading a book and something inexplicable deep inside of me told me to go talk to him.

"Hullo," I said.

"I'm reading," the boy said.

"Where did you get that book?"

It looked so familiar. And then I realized where I'd seen it before. In Roman's backpack. He'd just been assigned it in school before I'd left the Johnson family home.

"From a friend," the boy said.

"Do you like being dead?" I asked. It was the first time I'd ever actually asked anyone that question before.

The boy shrugged. "Don't have much of a choice, now do I? You're asking too many questions, little boy. Now, can I please go back to this chapter?"

"Was the friend who gave you that book Roman Johnson of Pasadena, California, United States of America?" I asked.

"Jesus Christ, are you him?" the Kid said, his face suddenly lighting up. "You're his family's dead kid. The adopted dead brother."

The Kid burst out laughing.

"Why are you laughing?"

"Well, I told him we dead don't all know each other, and now here you are!"

The Kid kept laughing harder and harder.

"How did you meet him?" I demanded. "Where is he now?"

"How else? The war! And back in California I'd guess. I don't know. I don't, like, have his address or whatever. That fucker never bothered taking my body home. I died helping those fucking ingrates."

Then he started digging through one of the books; to anyone living it might've looked like the pages of an abandoned book flapping in the breeze. "Hey," he said. "Give this to him. Tell him he left it in *Siddhartha*."

"Where's that?" Becky said.

The Kid pulled out a photo of the Johnson brothers and me on the roller coaster at Coney Island. I mean, you couldn't much see me, but I was there as a bright speck of light, seated right next to Rocco!

"Look Becky! That's me!" I shouted.

Becky peered over, looked at the picture, and nodded, though I could tell she was dubious, or maybe jealous.

The Kid kept laughing, though it sounded an awful lot like weeping. "What a small, small world, indeed."

═

"DID YOU HEAR him?" I asked Becky later that evening as we floated along a river with a man selling wares by boat. The man was missing both his legs, and sometimes that made people feel very sorry for him and buy much more and other times they shivered and moved swiftly past without so much as looking him in the eye.

"Hear what?" Becky said. She was trying very hard to remember what it was like to taste a pear. The man had what looked like the most delicious fruit.

"He called me Roman's dead brother! Brother!"

"Yeah . . ." Becky said, annoyed at the interruption. "You keep talking about the Johnsons, but what about me? We're family now. They left you."

"No, they didn't."

"Yes, they did."

"I hate you!" I said. "I would be with them now if it weren't for you!"

Becky grew very, very quiet and we didn't talk to each other for the rest of the boat ride.

Later, under the stars, I turned to her and said, "I don't hate you."

"I know," she said.

"You were right. We are family. We've been family longer than I ever had any other. The Johnsons. Mr. Farraday. Even my dearly departed mama. You're my real family, Becky Hargraves. I love you."

The only people I loved even remotely more than Becky were Rocco, River, and Roman, and my mother, and Ms. Emmeline. Oh, and Mr. Odysseus. Even if he had cast me out of their paradise.

"I love you too." Becky smiled at me. Fireflies flickered around and through her body.

"Not in the gross grown-up way, though," I added.

"Ew, no," she said. I was glad we agreed.

In New Zealand, we happened upon rows and rows of lavender. We walked among the dead Maori children playing between the stalks and living tourists and found ourselves in a remote part of the field. Here Becky lay down between two rows and I joined her.

"This place is perfect." Becky sighed. "I could spend forever here."

Becky turned and excitedly smiled over at me. "I can smell them!!! Christmas, I can smell lavender right now!!!"

She bent a stalk closer to her face. Then flung it into mine. "Isn't it marvelous?!"

"I can't smell it," I said.

"Try harder," Becky said.

"You know, Ms. Emmeline is the best ever. She'd take us both in. I'm sure of it!" I grew ever more excited at the prospect of returning. "Then you could have a family too."

"This day is perfect," she said contentedly.

Becky wasn't prone to sentimentality, but it was hard to argue.

Then I sneezed quite forcefully. That I was still plagued by allergies, even in death, seemed woefully unfair.

When I opened my eyes, Becky was gone.

"Becky? Becky?"

And just like that, she was gone and I was alone. Again.

I cried and cried until the stars came out and the ants crawled across my knees and the bees buzzed all around and tried to cheer me up before they got caught and yelled at to "Get back to work!"

When I awoke, I was here, and I had a strong feeling that I should be there. I got up from the field and began to walk toward home.

PART SIX

1984–1995

CHAPTER FIFTY-SIX

1984

FAR AS ROCCO COULD TELL, "INDEPENDENCE" MEANT GETTING PAID less than peanuts to package supplies wearing a hairnet and a face mask that bothered his face something awful. All day, he kept pulling down the mask to breathe, for just a moment, before his new supervisor would tell him to put it back up again.

"We have to keep conditions sterile," she said very slowly. "Sterile means no germs."

"I'm not stupid," Rocco said.

"No one said that you are, sweetie," she said, continuing to speak to him as though he were a petulant toddler before walking away.

It was the first job Rocco had held outside of working for his father. The group home had arranged an interview of sorts at a place meant to "foster independence" before transitioning to meaningful employment in the larger community. That morning, Rocco felt a sort of pride in being hirable, in navigating the city bus to the warehouse and punching in.

"She thinks we're very stupid," a wisp of a young man next to him whispered. The man too spoke slowly, but because the words seemed thicker on his tongue than not. He rolled his wheelchair closer to Rocco. "She's a bitch."

"A bitch," Rocco repeated.

"It's not so bad though," the man said. Rocco patiently waited as he forced out the words. "The work sucks. But when I'm at home all my mother does is make me watch her stories with her all day. At least here I get to talk to people. I'm Mac."

Rocco tried hard to meet the man's eyes. This is how you made people trust you, according to his parents and his old behavioral therapist. If they trusted you, then you made friends. "I'm Rocco."

"Anybody ever say you kinda look like River Johnson?" Mac said.

"No," Rocco said, surprising even himself with the lie.

═══

MOST DAYS, ROCCO and Mac sat across from each other packing gauze into boxes. Rocco imagined where it might go, which hospitals might use it to stanch which wounds. Maybe they were helping to save lives, in a way, he reasoned, maybe they were doing important work. He said so aloud to Mac.

"But what if they're using them to . . . save murderers?" Mac said. "Or . . . escaped Nazis?"

Rocco didn't think that was likely, and he wasn't sure exactly what to say. He kept packing the gauze, albeit a little more slowly, just in case.

His coworkers had varying degrees of ability. Rita was mute and blind in one eye, but when somebody said something funny, she had the best laugh you ever did hear. Janet often wandered away from her workstation until their supervisor guided her back and sat her down.

"No," Janet would say.

Rocco hated the work itself deeply. Everything about it was demeaning. But he grew to view Mac and Rita and Janet as friends of a sort. And if he worked long enough, maybe he could even save up to buy Alice a ring. Sure, he could ask River to pay for it, but it wouldn't be the same. It had to come from him. For Alice, Rocco would pack all the medical gauze in the world.

═══

ONE NIGHT, HE came home excited to tell Alice about the day's kerfuffle between Janet and their supervisor, only to find Alice under her covers, barely able to move. For months now, Alice had not quite been herself, quicker to anger, sleeping for hours on end. She had rarely cried in the years he'd known her and yet just these last few months she'd burst into tears at least seven times. Something was very wrong, Rocco thought. Cancer, maybe? Some illness he didn't even know existed? Still the laws of probability dictated that the actual answer was the most readily apparent. And once, the condom had broken. Just once. But once was enough, right?

"I think you're pregnant," Rocco said to her. "Either that, or you have cancer."

In response, Alice angrily inflated her cheeks like a chipmunk and raised her arms like parentheses at her stomach, which Rocco took to understand that she thought he was calling her fat.

"I didn't say that!" Rocco said, then he took her in more carefully. "Well . . . maybe you are a tad rounder?"

Then Alice stormed away and wouldn't communicate with him for a whole week. He hadn't brought it up again after that.

And now, for the last few days, she'd been either vomiting or unable to eat much. Whenever somebody suggested she go to the doctor, she'd empathically shaken her head no.

"What's wrong?" Rocco said.

Alice grimaced and grabbed at her head as though she wished to take it off her body entirely.

"Maybe you just need to eat," he said gently, pulling the covers off her. "Eating will help. Plus, the Farris Brothers are coming!"

The Farris Brothers were everyone's favorite, a quartet of older Black men who sang barbershop songs and danced like the olden days. They had opened for some big names, but mostly made the nursing- and group-home circuit these days, according to Maurice. Maurice was the oldest, and Rocco's favorite. The Farris Brothers' eyes sparkled when they danced, and the youngest brother, Otis, still attempted to hit the high notes, with varying degrees of accuracy. Rocco never remembered the names of the middle two, but found them worthy additions overall. Sometimes they danced with the caregivers, and even stupid Cathy softened as she shimmied with Otis, who must've been a looker back in his day. He still was, save for a very large mole on the side of his face that Rocco wished to scrape off. This seemed to be what age did, build and harden across one's skin, across one's heart. And yet there was so much that was still soft, like Maurice's hands when he shook Rocco's. Rocco tried to get out of the handshake, but Maurice swiftly gripped his hand firmly, a friendly stealth bomber. When Maurice's prolonged touch felt smooth and comforting, Rocco thought maybe he had getting older all wrong. Maybe life was soft and hard in all the unexpected places, and that was what made you at the end.

Anyway, the Farris Brothers were coming. Rocco convinced Alice that she should get up and go with him to dinner.

Maurice and Otis and the middle children sang a Ray Charles song. Bossy Daisy sashayed and sang along with the refrain to "(Night Time Is) The Right Time."

"*Baby! Baaaabbbbyyy!*" middle brother #1 sang.

"Go on, Wallace!" Otis called out.

Oh yes, that was his name. Rocco tapped out the beat under the table. Alice looked miserable. She grimaced and let out a guttural moan.

Ever the professionals, the Farris Brothers didn't miss a beat, though Rocco did notice Wallace look over in their direction.

"Don't be rude," Daisy said. "Alice is being rude."

"Shhhh," Rocco said to them both. He patted Alice affectionately on the back. Her eyes a-flutter, she lifted her head to the ceiling as she always did when Rocco played piano. Except she didn't stop there, Alice fell all the way back, down to the floor, where her head slammed down hard with a sickening crack. Her body jerked for a moment and then went still. Rocco leapt up and yelled out, "Alice!"

The Farris Brothers leapt up into action, with Maurice getting to Alice's side before Cathy did. He was quite spry for an older man. Maurice had been a medic in the war, he told Rocco.

"Her pulse is way weaker than it should be," Maurice said. "Get her oxygen right now!" he yelled at the staff.

"Get her oxygen!" Rocco repeated.

"Call the ambulance," Ratched yelled at one of the younger nurses, who scrambled. It had been some time since there had been a real emergency.

"Call the ambulance," Rocco repeated. He held on to Alice's hand tightly, tighter and longer than he'd ever held anyone before in his life. Her freckled face hung to the side.

"Gotta give her some space, son," Maurice said gently, but Rocco refused to let go.

═══

THE AMBULANCE CAME and took Alice away, and instead of going back to performing, the Farris Brothers instead led a prayer for Alice.

"Dear Heavenly Father, please lift up . . ." Maurice searched to remember her name.

"Alice!" Rocco filled in.

"We lift up Alice to you and ask that you keep her safe and give her strength so that she comes back home."

Rocco didn't think God was logical, but there was also the way that two dragonflies made a heart with their bodies as they mated, and how else could something that beautiful just be the work of the universe at random?

═══

LATE THAT NIGHT, the door to his room creaked open. Before, Rocco had been in a sort of twilight sleep, neither here nor there, his thoughts racing and his body stirring, and her, only her, racing through his mind. He sat up.

"Alice?"

There was no shadow across, no footsteps. He lay back down and pulled his blanket over him tighter.

"Boo!" the familiar voice said, and laughed.

"What took you so long?" Rocco said.

═══

AFTER HE GOT over his initial excitement, Rocco was mad as hell at Christmas and didn't much want to talk to him. Christmas had left him when he needed him most, had left all of them. And right now, he only had space in his head for worry about Alice, not anger at Christmas. The two emotions pushed against the sides of his body until even his fingertips stiffened and he felt like a dam about to burst. He began hitting the side of his head with the flat side of his palm, harder and harder at his temple.

"No," Christmas said, and grabbed Rocco's hand.

He had forgotten how strong the little boy was. For that was how Christmas now appeared to Rocco, a very little boy.

"No," Rocco repeated.

"I'm so sorry." Christmas began to cry. The room shook and it felt like a slight quake, as though there were a passing freight train, or truck, but instead it was just the force of two little boys aching.

"How did you find me?" Rocco asked.

Christmas had snuck into the Johnsons' house, but nobody was home. It was very quiet, too quiet. After hours of waiting for somebody, anybody, he saw the phone number and address to Rocco's group home written in faded pencil on the kitchen wall. He'd asked all the other spirits along the way for directions, gotten lost a few times, but what was a hundred more miles after all these years?

"You're my best friend," Christmas said.

"Alice is my best friend," Rocco said. He knew it wasn't nice, but it was true. He hadn't seen Christmas in fourteen years, and he had loved Alice from just about the moment he'd seen her. Whatever hole Christmas had left, Alice had filled it up, and then some. He wanted to give Alice the world, or at least whatever he could buy of it with his hours at the medical supply company. He imagined where she might be now, if maybe something he'd packed might be used at this very instant to save her, to keep Alice with him. He instantly regretted all the times he'd taken his blue surgical mask down when the supervisor wasn't looking.

"Who is Alice?" Christmas said.

So Rocco told him. She was love. She was home. And now, she might be dying.

CHAPTER FIFTY-SEVEN

INSTEAD OF BEING SHORT AND KINDA STUBBY THE WAY HE WAS AS A boy, now Rocco must've been well over six feet, maybe even closer to seven! Though being still rather small myself, and my head ever so askance, I'm quite terrible at estimating these things. As if to apologize for his height, his body curved in on itself ever so slightly, like one of the roly-polies we used to play with in the Johnson backyard. How badly I wished I could take Rocco into my hand and hold him away from any harm to come.

"What is it like to die?" Rocco asked me. He had a mustache that looked a whole lot like a caterpillar across the top of his mouth. I wondered if he still knew the names of all the butterflies that ever were, though it was definitely not the time to ask. "You never told us anything about it."

And so, finally, I did. I told Rocco about the very bad, horrible thing that happened on one of the absolute best days of my short life. The day I sang opera.

As I told Rocco, I started grabbing at the rope about my neck and gulping for air, as though my lungs still needed it, as though I were still up on that tree.

"You must've been really scared," Rocco said quietly.

"I was in so much pain, I kept passing out and waking up from the pain until finally I didn't anymore."

When I finally came to again, I saw Liza and Elizabeth and Mr. Farraday blurred beneath me. Elizabeth threw up and Mr. Farraday gripped her hand. I tried to wave, but nobody saw. Plus, my hand was now missing.

"We can't just let them get away with this!" Liza said.

"We have to leave now," he said. "It isn't safe here. Not for any of us."

"Hello!" I yelled from wherever I now was. "Elizabeth! Liza! Mr. Faraday! Fanny!"

I kept yelling their names as loudly as I could until the trees began to shake, stirring a family of squirrels from out of their nest.

"They can't hear you, baby boy," an aged squirrel with long gray whiskers said, crawling very close to my face. "You're . . . you're elsewhere now."

"You can talk?" I cried out. I felt heavy and light at once.

"Of course I can!" the squirrel declared, as though he'd suffered some grave indignity. A bluebird flew by and inspected him.

"You're dead," a crowd of ants sang in a chorus, like a work song, as they crawled on my hands and ears.

"Sorry, they don't have any tact," the squirrel gently said. "Brain's too small, I suppose."

"You don't have to stay up here," the bluebird sang, floating in the air in front of me. "If you focus real hard, you can get out of there, and get down."

"Out of where?"

"Your body," the bluebird said. "No need for it anymore."

I focused as hard as I could. It took time. The animals cheered me on with every attempt. And eventually others came and cheered me on too. Then finally, I was on the ground. My entrails around me, my head hung to the right, but I could move and float and I had even made some new friends in all my attempts. Now that I was good and dead.

I COULD TELL that Rocco wished he could actually hold my hand, and I desperately wanted to feel my fingers interlaced through Rocco's own.

"You're my best friend too," he said to me.

"I know," I said.

"I don't want Alice to be in pain," Rocco sobbed. "I love her."

"I know."

I am too young to care much for all that mushy romantic stuff, but I imagine that being in love with somebody must feel like I do about the

Johnsons, like you would travel to the very ends of the Earth just to make your way back to them.

"Look!" I said, remembering the photo the Kid had given to me. "Roman brought it with him to Vietnam and accidentally left it! His friend gave it to me!"

"You went all the way to Vietnam?" Rocco said incredulously.

"I'd go the whole wide world. I'd go the whole wide world just to find [you]," I sang.

"Where'd you hear that song?" Rocco said.

"On a cruise!" I said.

"You went on a cruise?" he said.

I settled in to tell him of all the many places Becky and I had gone, and all the people we'd met, and how, somehow, they took me right back here, to him. To home.

A few hours later, the caregiver, Cathy, whom Rocco detested, cracked open the door to Rocco's room. She opened her mouth to speak, but didn't. Then she opened it again. We couldn't bear to wait, not a minute longer.

"How's Alice?" Rocco blurted.

Cathy leaned against the doorway staring at him intently. "Alice had eclampsia."

"What's that?"

"She almost died. But she didn't."

"What does that mean? Where is she? Why isn't she back home?"

"Alice is resting now. She . . . Alice just had a baby . . ." the nurse said.

CHAPTER FIFTY-EIGHT

"NO OFFENSE TO BETH, BUT YOU NEED A SHARK," RIVER SAID. "AND somebody in disability rights."

They could pay for the very best, both he and Odysseus argued for days on end. But Emmeline's old friend was increasingly becoming one of the foremost attorneys when it came to advocating for women's rights. A few of her cases had even made the news. More important, Emmeline trusted Beth not to tell their business to a single soul.

As far as Emmeline was concerned, Beth knew what it was to have a child misunderstood by the world around them. To fight for every single resource and counselor and teacher to see her child. Beth read all the books, did everything she could to get the girl into speech therapy with any number of doctors who claimed to the have the answers that would unlock her. But maybe Edie didn't need to be unlocked, Emmeline thought. What if Edie was just fine the way she was? Still, Beth was not afraid of gnashing teeth and deep seas.

The meeting at Rocco's group home would take place that Wednesday, and Beth would be beside them.

═══

THE MILK REFUSED to come in. The nurse massaged Alice's boob, squeezing at the ends harder until something dense and yellow emerged and the nurse forced what little there was of it into the baby's tiny mouth.

That's not enough, Alice thought. How is she going to eat?

"It's OK. We'll keep trying." The nurse patted her hand and smiled as though she'd read Alice's thoughts. "Sometimes it takes a little bit. But you'll get there."

Alice waddled back and forth to the restroom in the mesh diaper, rough and pressing into her still-swollen, still-bleeding body, creating little rashes. Her nipples were cracked and sore. Still, her baby was the most exquisite being she had ever seen, with her perfect little button nose and the long eyelashes and full lips she'd gotten from Rocco. She'd thought the baby would have curly hair, or even an afro, but for now it lay flat and plastered across the girl's head, auburn in hue. She was red and slightly crusted in the way that newborns apparently were. Alice had never been more in love. The nurse trainee, who still wore braces, brought Alice a baby name book during her lunch break and pored over the first few pages with her as the baby slept. Not five minutes in, Alice immediately knew they didn't have to read any further. She pointed down at the top name on the page—Angeline, for everything about her was a miracle as far as Alice was concerned.

═══

UPON ENTERING THE small office, Odysseus grabbed Emmeline's hand. They were going to do this together.

"We will go to the news with this," Alice's mother said to the director before Odysseus and Emmeline had even had a chance to sit down.

"I'm sure we can come to some sort of an understanding," the director said.

"This happened under your care," Alice's mother said.

"We thought Alice was sterilized," the director said. "Most of our residents are."

"Why on earth would we do that?" Alice's mother said. "And aren't residents supposed to be under adult supervision?!"

"They are adults," the director said.

═══

ALICE'S PARENTS CAME once a month, and even they had not realized Alice was pregnant. Her mother had told her that she was eating too much, and that she mustn't get too fat. It wasn't good for her health. Alice's parents had five other children to look after. Alice was the oldest. When her little brother was born, she remembered her parents waiting with bated breath as he reached each milestone and hugging each other.

"He's normal," she remembered her mother whispering into the phone on a call with her grandma. "Thank God!"

It'd hurt.

Alice would make sure her Angeline felt loved no matter what she could or couldn't do, what she could or couldn't say. And Alice did have a language all her own, if anybody in her family had bothered to listen. Rocco had.

"I KNOW THIS is hard. But they're in love," the director said. "They've been together for years."

Beth blew into the room like the force she'd become. "My apologies. What did I miss?"

She kissed Emmeline on both cheeks and patted Odysseus and Rocco on the back.

"I love Alice." Rocco beamed. "With all my heart."

"I don't want him in the room. Get him out," Alice's mother said. "He makes my skin crawl."

Emmeline summoned everything in her power in her attempts to not reach across the table and claw the woman's eyes out.

"You need to watch how you talk about my son," Odysseus said. Emmeline could see the woman tense up further. Could see in her mind the white woman's thought bubble that labeled her Black husband "threatening."

Alice beamed at Rocco.

She reached across her parents and grabbed Rocco's hand before the girl's mother intervened.

Alice's mother raised her voice. "He . . . he took advantage of my girl."

"I did not!" Rocco yelled at her.

"There is no evidence to support as much," Beth stated clearly. "Many of the carers at the home have stated on record that they believe Rocco and Alice have been engaged in a mutual relationship for years."

"Of course they're gonna say that!" Alice's mother seemed to be on the verge of tears.

═══

NO, ALICE THOUGHT. Nonononono. This is not what she thought this was about. She thought her parents had come simply to meet the new baby. To celebrate. Isn't that what people did when a baby was born?

Alice had not known she was pregnant, but nobody had ever really told her much about sex or babies or any of that stuff to begin with. She knew that her mother and father had assumed that she would never be able to get married, or to have a family. That they assumed the only people who could ever really love her were the ones who were already related to her. They assumed so much about her that she began to assume it about herself.

═══

ALICE ROCKED BACK and forth in her chair and moaned. Her mother reached out an arm to stop her.

"Let's redirect the discussion for a minute to discuss a course of action for the baby?" Beth interjected.

"We're giving it up for adoption. Alice can't possibly keep it," Alice's mother said.

"Her," Cathy, the caretaker mumbled.

"Her what?" the woman said.

"The baby . . . not it. Her," Cathy said more clearly. Cathy was on their side, Emmeline thought, even though she knew Rocco thought Cathy was sorta racist. Emmeline drew from Cathy's support a kind of comfort. Her son was not bad, and even this other vaguely racist woman saw his heart clearly.

═══

ALICE GROUND HER teeth and pushed her palms into her mother's ears.

Listen, she thought. *Listen to me.*

She knew she shouldn't. She knew that. But they were not going to take her baby away. She pulled at her mother's ear so hard her purple clip-on came off and her father grabbed Alice's furied fists with his hands.

"Alice, stop that!" her mother said. "Stop right this instant!"

Rocco began to hum Alice's favorite song. He knew exactly how to calm her down. He was, after all, her person. She felt everyone's eyes on her. She hated it so much. Rocco kept humming, and her heart rate slowed, even if just a little.

"WE CAN'T SUPPORT a child here, but I think we might be able to help you secure at-home care for Alice."

"No," Alice's father said. "That's not possible. We've tried that before. This is the best place for her. Adoption is what makes the most sense. We're still her legal guardians. It's the right choice for Alice moving forward."

It was the first he'd spoken all meeting. Emmeline had forgotten the man was even on the other side of Alice's mother.

"You can't possibly believe that this place, which you contend was grossly negligent and allowed your daughter to be taken advantage of, is also the same place she needs to stay to receive the best care. Surely those two ideas are at odds with each other?" Beth said.

"It's not fair that they have her here." Alice's mother glared across the table at Beth.

"She's here purely as an old friend," Emmeline said.

"For now," Beth followed up.

"Bullshit," Alice's mother said.

It had not gone unnoticed by Emmeline that the meeting had become mostly a verbal volley between mothers.

Rocco shouted, "We're right here! It's my baby and Alice's baby. Nobody else's."

"He has to leave." Alice's mother fixated on Rocco.

"I'm not going anywhere," Rocco said.

"Your son is River Johnson, is he not?" Alice's mother said, not even remotely subtly.

"What does that have to do with anything?" Beth said.

"We want to have Alice's expenses here paid for at least the next ten years and any additional counseling services she might need as a result of this assault."

"Let's not use those words," Beth said.

"This is completely unethical," Emmeline cried out. "And if you think she was assaulted here, why would you want her to stay? That doesn't even make sense!"

"My son did not assault your daughter." Odysseus stood up and raised his voice. Emmeline grabbed on to his thigh to calm him.

"Do you think the courts will see it that way?" Alice's mother said.

They all knew she had a point. Regardless of how gentle Rocco was, or how much he loved Alice, how famous his brother was, he was still a Black man. One with a history of violence, according to his files. Over a decade ago, a little boy paralyzed. And now this . . . a white woman who could not technically say yes . . . it wouldn't play well in front of a jury. Emmeline saw Beth do the mental calculations. And Emmeline saw Christmas, the stoop of his neck, the innards that trailed, his missing hand, that hand of American justice. There were too many boys like him even now. Rocco could not be one. Would not be one.

═══

"MY BABY," ROCCO pleaded with them all before turning to Emmeline. "Please. I'm her daddy!"

"We'll take custody of the child," Odysseus said before Emmeline could respond. "No need to involve anybody else."

Rocco looked over at his father gratefully. Odysseus hadn't stood up when they'd taken Rocco away and yet here he was now, fighting for all of them.

After a long pause, Beth opened her mouth and said softly, "I think we should have both Alice and Rocco return to their rooms for now. Before we continue this discussion."

═══

NOW ALL OF their parents and the director crowded into Alice's small room. Alice walked over to Angeline and held her daughter tight against her chest. Alice's short, reddish hair hung over her forehead and into her eyes as she beamed down at her daughter, who suckled contently. She kissed the tips of Angeline's little pink fingers. Love meant something else entirely now, something she couldn't possibly have even fathomed before.

"The baby's not that brown, is she?" Alice's father said softly.

"They get browner," Alice's mother said.

"Alice is a good mother," the director said ruefully. "She loves her."

═

IN THE END, Beth got them the baby. The facility's lawyer's got Alice's family to agree not to sue, but only if Rocco could no longer stay there, which meant that, for now anyway, Rocco was coming home. Beth would hammer out the rest of the financials with their lawyer after discussing it with River's legal and financial teams.

═

ALICE'S MILK FINALLY came in as they took her small, squirming girl from her. Alice bit and scratched and threw whatever she could as the milk flowed and leaked through and soaked her shirt in two uncontrolled circles. Her own father held Alice down to help a nurse administer a sedative. He was hurting her wrists. How could her father do this? How could anyone?

"Mmmmm—" She struggled to form the word she needed. *Mine. Mine. Mine.* That was her baby! Hers! Her flesh and blood! The love of her life!

She looked up and saw Rocco's mother looking as though she might vomit as she stood in the doorframe. Their lawyer stood next to her, squeezing her hand.

"Is all this necessary?" Emmeline said. Still, she did nothing to stop them.

"I promise to take care of her, Alice," Emmeline said, tears welling up in her eyes. "Mother to mother. I promise."

"Here. Take her." The nurse quickly passed the baby to Rocco's father, who held his granddaughter like a football, ready to run.

═

"YOU'RE INCREDIBLE, BETH." Emmeline leaned her forehead against her friend's. "Thank you for this. For her. There are no words."

"You're pretty incredible yourself, Emmeline Johnson," Beth said. "I've got to head back, but you've got this. I'll give you a call later."

They pulled apart and Beth shook Odie's hand, who grabbed hers in his warmly.

"You know, she reminds me of Edie a bit," Beth said softly.

"Are we doing the right thing?" Emmeline asked. Beth paused for a great long while before she spoke.

"I don't know . . . but . . . you'll make it the right thing." And with that she quickly headed down the hallway, back to where Edie would soon be coming home from her day program, and Beth would be there to greet her.

===

WE WERE SUPPOSED to be family, Alice thought. All of us, together.

She wriggled out of her father's grasp and punched at the air around her until her arms gave out on her, the sedation finally kicking in.

Alice screamed until she felt her flesh tear and fill with blood. The noises in her throat garbled and stopped. Then Alice felt herself fading away.

CHAPTER FIFTY-NINE

THE SPIRIT OF THE JOHNSON HOUSE WAS ALL HUNCHED OVER LIKE. A few of the clay roof tiles were absent, like after a long performance when half the fake eyelashes went missing from Liza and Elizabeth's faces. The old Mr. Odysseus would never have stood for such a thing, but maybe this old Mr. Odysseus figured out a few missing house eyelashes weren't that big a deal. Being there felt like waking up after a long sleep away, when you're still making sense of the shapes and colors all around you, only it was the Johnsons themselves I was trying to discern. How were they here? How were they real?

This is how I came to find myself once more amid the Johnsons and once more a part of a real-life family!

After everything that had happened in the meeting about Angeline, the Johnsons had rushed to get some of Rocco's belongings from the group home. I watched silently as they quickly grabbed the items River had given Rocco, especially any letters River had written, because otherwise the staff might sell them for money, or to the press. Everything else could be sent for later. In all the commotion, I didn't know how to rightly reintroduce myself, and I was all of a sudden deeply afraid that maybe they hadn't forgiven me after all. Plus, Rocco was so upset he could hardly speak. He picked up a dried dandelion stem that was resting on a small desk and clutched it to his chest.

A piece crumbled off into his hand.

I tried to catch it and, ever so briefly, I did, suspending dandelion bits and bobs midair.

I followed behind at a short distance as they made their way to the car, hiding briefly behind a tree when Ms. Emmeline turned to look in my general direction, then paused and stood at attention like a prairie dog.

"What are you looking at, Emmie? Did we miss something?" Mr. Odysseus said.

"For a moment I thought I just . . . it's nothing," she said, and shook her head.

After they loaded up Rocco's belongings, in all the commotion I quietly entered the trunk unnoticed. I would have the car ride to steel up my resolve, to ask the Johnsons if they could ever possibly love me as a son, and brother, if they could be my home once again. The car ride felt like the longest trip anybody's ever taken, and also the shortest.

We pulled up to the house on Mar Vista, and Ms. Emmeline walked back to the trunk.

"Hi," I said as she opened it.

"Oh shit!" she said, startling backward and clutching her chest. I was briefly terrified I might actually have killed her this time, being as that she was now a lady with wrinkles and gray hairs and a heart with more wear and tear on it than the last time I'd surprised her.

I wasn't sure she'd remember me after all these years, and she herself was always telling the boys, "When you assume, you make an ass out of you and me," so instead, I stuck out my good hand.

"I don't know if you remember me. I'm the pickani—" I started, out of habit, before remembering that she and Mr. Odysseus didn't like this word. "I'm Christmas Jones the Third."

Before I could finish, Ms. Emmeline screamed and ran over to hug me, as though I were a real boy! And instead of either of us falling right over, I sank into her arms and for a moment I swear on my very life and death that I felt the pull of skin, the thump of a heart, the think think think of a brain, but maybe it was just her body in mine.

"Oh my God! You're back! You're here! With us!" she said, as if there were anywhere else I'd rather be. Of all the beautiful things that Becky and I had seen most everywhere in the world, there was nothing more beautiful, more magical, than being in Ms. Emmeline Johnson's arms.

Mr. Odysseus was next. I didn't know what to say to him, and I reckon he didn't know what to say to me either, 'cause he just stared, tears pooling at the corners of his eyes. His hair looked much thinner than the last time I'd seen him, and his face had started to droop a little downward in that way the years have of making people's cheeks like pockets with something heavy in them—life itself, I reckon.

Then finally he wiped the corners of his eyes and said, "Hello, son."

"I'm sorry!" I said to them both, feeling the waves of sadness as they crashed against my missing heart. "I didn't mean to do it, Ms. Emmie. I promise! I never meant to kill him."

"Kill who?"

"That boy who hurt Rocco!" I said.

"What? You didn't kill him. All these years you thought you killed him?"

"You didn't tell him, Rocco?" she said.

"He didn't ask." Rocco shrugged.

"Oh, you sweet boy, that kid's doing just fine. He owns a car dealership in Altadena, or was it Arcadia? Last I heard. Married with a kid and everything."

"But I hurt him bad?" I said.

"You did . . . but he would've hurt Rocco bad too, and in a way he did, didn't he? Lotta things worse than being in a wheelchair. He stole all those years right from under all of us. Way I figure, we can't get those back neither," Mr. Odysseus said.

"You ain't got nothing to be sorry for," Ms. Emmeline said through tears. Right then and there I felt as though Ms. Emmeline might actually be magical, my very own Blue Fairy, like at the end of *Pinocchio,* for with her I felt once more like a real boy!

"I don't remember you being so small," Roman said.

Roman was much thicker than the last time I'd seen him, solid and slightly distended in both the right and wrong places, with big muscles and a belly like Santa's. He hadn't grown any taller though, not like Rocco. I'm not sure I would've recognized him in passing. He patted me on the shoulder and I swear I felt the pads of his fingers graze my skin!

"Maybe now that you're grown, you don't know big from small," I said.

"Maybe you're right." Roman chuckled.

I poked at his belly and nearly stumbled clean through his body.

"Yeah. Yeah. I traded my beer gut for a love gut." He laughed. I don't know what that means, but Roman seemed very happy, which made me happy. Then, all of a sudden, I felt unbearably sad because I wondered how I might've looked old. Would I be round like Roman? Or tall and skinny as a streetlight like Rocco? Would I have kept my hair? I would like to think so.

When Becky was extra sad, she used to say growing up was just decaying while your heart stayed beating, and weren't we lucky to have dodged all that? She tried very hard to convince us both.

"Oh, I wish River were here now," Ms. Emmeline said.

"He's very busy being famous," I said.

"That he is," Roman said.

Angeline said nothing, 'cause she's a baby. She was little with a face that looked either surprised or as though she'd sucked on something sour. She didn't cry but often looked like she wanted to but was afraid to let the sound out. Or maybe that's just how your face looks when you lose your mama and you don't even get a whole week with her. Maybe Angeline's face would be like that forever, I thought.

Rocco's face didn't look much different from hers, and not just on account of the fact he and Angeline favored each other.

We sat down to dinner and Roman grabbed everyone's hands in a too-long prayer and thanked the Lord for my return. I don't know when he got religious, but Rocco whispered he's got a girlfriend who goes to church a lot.

"So, what have you been up to, Christmas?" Mr. Odysseus said, and everyone at the table laughed in that way that grown-ups do and you're not quite sure which part is the joke. But I think maybe the joke was time itself.

I didn't rightly know where to start, so I started at the beginning. And sitting there next to the Johnsons felt just like when Becky and I were in the lavender and the world was so beautiful. I was suddenly deeply sad that Becky had left before she could experience just how lovely it was to sit at dinner with the Johnsons when a little bitty baby lets out a loud fart and everybody at the table accuses one another and Ms. Emmeline sternly says, "Really, boys? Pass the peas."

Then Ms. Emmeline let out the biggest guffaw of all and kissed Angeline on both her little baby cheeks.

I thought maybe, just maybe, this was peace. Surely this must've been the way Tom felt, and Becky too before they moved on to what was next. And for a moment, I felt as though I'd been hornswoggled. I had just made my way back to the Johnsons and it felt entirely too soon to be spirited away already! And River wasn't even there yet! But maybe it wasn't so bad, maybe wherever I might be headed was as soft and lovely as this moment. Maybe Mama might be there too.

If I inhaled deeply enough, I was certain I could smell the pot roast that Ms. Emmeline had made, even the very cinnamon sprinkled across the steamed carrots that Rocco kept pushing around the plate.

Angeline made itty-bitty baby wah-wahs, like a kitten mewling, and Rocco kissed the bottoms of her pale feet before sniffing the top of her head.

"Can I try?" I asked. Apparently, baby heads smell very good.

"Try," Rocco repeated.

I leaned over, taking care to keep my innards from spilling on her, and her big eyes grew wide and fluttered up at me. I had the thought then that it would be wonderful if the very last thing I smelled before leaving this place was a small baby's head.

Instead, I felt something very cold and damp indeed. I couldn't shake the feeling that something very big was about to happen. Was this it?

"Wait!" I cried out to whoever might be listening.

CHAPTER SIXTY

RIVER FELT EVEN MORE ALONE THAN HE USUALLY DID. SOMETHING about knowing all of the Johnsons were back in California together, and he was out here in New York. His mother had called him, explaining the situation with Alice and that her parents had demanded that River pay her group-home fees in exchange for keeping quiet—a "tidy sum" is what Emmeline said they called it. River was tired, but at this point he always expected people to need him for something.

What he didn't expect was Christmas returning. When Emmeline had told him, he felt the tears immediately well up inside him . . . He would fly out there as soon as this album was done, as soon as the tour was over. It was time to go home. But first, he had work to do.

He cried more than he had in his whole life to date. For everyone. For himself.

Murray, Simon, and Alvin crowded around him as he full-body heaved with each sob.

"You get dropped from your label?" Alvin said.

"Did Milton die?" Simon said. "Oh, I hope not! I liked him." The slashes on Simon's face sometimes reminded River of Bowie's on *Aladdin Sane*. It was not his favorite Bowie album, but Wendy had loved and played it until the record warped. It was only now that he was able to hear "Watch That Man" without tearing up at the thought of her.

"Milton was cute for sure," Alvin said in his thick Boricua accent. "And I don't even fuck with white boys like that usually."

"You can't fuck with nobody at all now." Simon started laughing at his own jokc.

"What? No—Milton's not dead!" River snapped.

"You insensitive knaves!" Murray scolded the other ghosts. "There, there, River. Whatever happened. It'll all be OK."

═══

"WRITE IT," WENDY had said. And for the first time in forever, songs flowed from him. He wrote for his friends. For his brothers. Even a song for his new niece. It was the first album on which he had songwriter credits on every single song. Not shared with a billion co-writers. All him.

He sang love songs, and he knew what it meant to love.

He sang breakup songs, and he knew what it meant to break. To have his heart torn from his chest as a result of his own idiocy, his own cowardice.

He turned his speakers all the way up so they vibrated the floors and bathed in the sounds of regret and renewal.

He sang of heartbreak and thought of Rocco, and Roman, and Christmas, and his father.

He sang of loss, about all his dead friends. Then he put it to a dance beat so nobody knew just how very sad the song was. That was the key.

He kept himself up at night thinking about the men he'd touched and who had touched him. Which of them were dead or dying? Was he to be next? Was that what was growing inside of him? Is that what this feeling was? Or just good old-fashioned regret?

"I can't stop crying," he told his therapist.

"Then don't," she said. Which felt like a waste of a session, but whatever.

Murray and Alvin and Simon were his chorus whenever River hummed at his street piano. He wrote songs with all of their voices in his head.

And when he finally finished, when the songs felt perfect, he did something blasphemous. He crawled under the old upright and carved his name. He understood it more now. The urge to leave some piece of yourself behind on something that might outlast you. That should outlast you. And wasn't music just that? A piano as time travel, all those black-and-whites bringing you back into the past, forth into the future.

He felt something within himself finally burst loose. An unburdening.

He sent the label the demo and waited. Held his breath as he walked around blue as Joni, as hydrangeas, as Cookie Monster.

They loved it. Him. Thought this album had the potential to be the biggest of his entire career to date. He needed to start filming music videos for it as soon as possible. Music videos were what was hip now, the old white men told him.

He left the set of one such video and showed up on Milton's doorstep. In costume.

"What the hell are you supposed to be?"

River looked down at himself. "It's a whole thing. For the music video."

"What music video?"

"They want something that's going to get a lot of airplay on MTV. All the cool kids are doing it."

Milton held the door tightly.

"What do you want?" he said.

"I'm about to release the biggest album of my life and everybody's up my ass about how great it is, and how great I am, and . . . and the only person I want to share any of this shit with is you."

Milton raised his eyebrows but said nothing. He opened the door and walked back inside his apartment. River followed behind him.

"I'm changing . . . I'm trying to anyway," River said.

"I only have water and Dom to drink," Milton said, his head half-buried in the fridge. "I need to go grocery shopping. Don't open the bottle of Dom. I'm saving that."

"Water's fine," River said.

Milton poured him a glass and then reached for the Dom Pérignon himself.

"Fuck it," Milton said.

"What were you saving it for?"

"Something that felt worthy, I guess," Milton said.

"And that's me?" River joked. Milton just raised his eyebrows and didn't say anything.

"I want to be worthy of you," River said.

"You're River Johnson," Milton said, with more than just a hint of sarcasm. "You're worthy of whoever you want."

"Please . . . I'm trying . . ." River said.

For the next hour or so, River Johnson turned his innards inside out and let Milton see it all. He told him about Christmas and that disastrous day with Rocco that changed their whole lives. He told him not only about Wendy's OD but those moments afterward, when she was dead and they had just a few more minutes together; he told him about Murray, Alvin, and Simon, who thought Milton was the best thing that happened to River and also refused to leave the apartment, not that he wanted them to.

And to River's absolute astonishment, Milton believed him.

"Is Christmas where you got your signature move?" Milton asked.

"How could you possibly . . . ? Yes. He taught it to us."

"There was a really old man in the clinic from the South . . . said he'd only seen one person do that before you. A little Black boy who died way back in the day."

River laughed at how very big and small the world could be and how even time itself was everything and nothing at all.

"Riv. You should know something . . ." Milton said, growing serious. Too serious for River's liking.

Milton had slept with another man while they had been broken up.

"Just one," he said defensively. "And we were careful. And I got tested afterward."

River felt his stomach tighten. He nodded. He felt sick, but he would not allow anything else to mess this up. Not even himself. Not anymore.

"I don't care. I mean I do. I'm human. But it's in the past, OK?"

He sat on Milton's couch, dressed and made-up as an alien, begging him to love him.

"Phone home," Milton said, extending his forefinger like E.T. River extended his back so that they touched.

"Yo, there's gonna be a show at the Apollo . . . to kick the tour off . . ."

"I'll be there." Milton grabbed his finger and brought River toward him. As they kissed, the metallic green makeup covering River's face smudged all over them both.

═══

AT THE APOLLO, with Arnie and the rest of River's team backstage, Milton sat in front, next to River's parents and Rocco. Roman stayed home with the baby and Christmas. River introduced Milton as his good friend from junior high.

Emmeline clasped Milton's hands in hers. "Ah!! It's wonderful to see you again. I'm so glad you two were able to reconnect out here. It's hard for River to get close to people these days, you know! You remember Milton, Odie, right?"

"You were a good kid. He used to talk about you all the time," his father said to Milton, who smiled over at him. "Having lifelong friends is rare these days. Are you in the industry as well?"

"Not quite. I'm a lawyer now," Milton said.

"Doing what?" Odysseus asked.

The answer was fighting for AIDS patients. Fighting for dignity in death. For access to drugs that had been made available abroad. Milton had decided to do something.

"Civil rights law," Milton said.

"Good man," Odysseus said.

River knew it wasn't enough, but it was a start.

Just let me tell them one step at a time, he'd begged Milton.

"After the tour!" River offered.

"After the tour," Milton said.

As River danced and sang, and shared funny little anecdotes about the many years of fame in his short life thus far, like how on his first tour, he was stabbed in the hand by a very famous late guitarist's (RIP) girl, the crowd roared. People had to be stopped from mobbing the stage. River could feel the energy from all 1,500 seats. They loved him. Every single one of them. He smiled down at Milton. At Emmeline and Odysseus. And especially at Rocco.

He surprised himself by pulling Rocco up onstage with him, where they sang together, harmonizing across the lyrics and years. And rather than being afraid of the immense crowd, Rocco had eaten them right up. Had held them in the palm of his hand with a grin and his beautiful voice. Had come to life up there in a way Emmeline said she hadn't seen since they'd had to move him from the group home. God, what a spectacularly beautiful voice his brother had, even still. River threw his arm around Rocco and they swayed.

"THESE JUST CAME in for you," Dominique said the next morning. River stumbled in after spending the night celebrating with Emmeline and Odysseus and Rocco in their room at the Plaza. Arnie had even cried as he hugged River after the show. Paul too, but Paul had always been an unabashed crier.

"You did great, kiddo. So great!" Arnie said, wiping away tears.

"Arnie, you really are a weepy little son of a bitch these days," River said, and they both laughed. Arnie had helped raise him, maybe even more than his parents in the later years, so it made a kind of paternal sense. "Thank you. For everything. Always. Except the whole taking-ten-percent-of-my-money part. Fuck you for that."

"River! Language!" Emmeline said, but she still laughed along.

"Riv." Paul had held him in the tightest embrace and smacked his ass after. "You fucking genius."

Milton had gone home earlier, against Emmeline's insistence that he stay with them and celebrate into the wee hours. Milton said he had a last-minute motion to prepare, but River suspected Milton left to give them some time alone as a family. As far as River was concerned, Milton was family too. As he left, Milton tightly hugged everyone goodbye, even Odysseus, who'd had a few and thus brought him in far closer than anyone expected with an awkward series of, if not fatherly, then at least avuncular, back pats. Milton promised he'd be over to help River pack for the first leg of the overseas tour.

"Don't be a stranger!" Emmeline yelled as the door closed behind him.

The Johnsons continued to pop champagne, and Rocco sang and sang, reliving the concert with River.

"I was good, huh?" Rocco said with the biggest grin River could ever remember seeing across his brother's adult face.

"So good," River said, beaming right back at him.

Now, hours later, River's head felt as though he were the very Liberty Bell itself, and just one more ring might crack the whole thing open. Never mind that Dominique was entirely too chipper for this early hour and those were way too many cardboard boxes in his foyer.

"I waited for you to get here to open them!"

She took the box cutter and gingerly cut across the tape at the top, being careful not to accidentally carve into the contents of the box itself.

There they were. His album. The one that felt the most his. Like his beating heart carved out and given to anyone who would listen.

Dominique turned the album over in her hands, taking in the artwork. Meanwhile, River ripped into the plastic wrapping on one of the records. It was not the cover art he was most interested in, though it was pretty perfect. No, there was exactly one thing that had to be absolutely right. That meant more than the whole rest of it.

In the liner notes, tiny on the inside of the cassette case, only slightly larger on the record sleeve, there, River had written something big: "For my brothers, the Johnson Four."

"Everything look good?" Dominique asked, peering over his shoulder. "Shit. I thought you only had two brothers? Did they fuck it up?"

"No. It's perfect," River said.

CHAPTER SIXTY-ONE

THERE WERE ALREADY RUMORS STARTING. THE SAME RAG THAT HAD published River coming out of St. Vincent's had published a photo of Emmeline and Odysseus carrying the swaddled baby around town. "River Johnson's Love Child."

"Make up your fucking minds." River had laughed at the headlines.

Of course, River didn't take it seriously; River never had to take anything seriously, Roman fumed. He and his brother were cool these days, better than just cool even. Still, the old resentments were hard to let go.

A reporter had tracked down the agreed-upon payments to the facility for Alice's room and board. Although the Johnsons as a whole suspected the girl's parents had leaked at least some of the information to shame them. Or perhaps somebody at the facility. A story about River Johnson was worth a lot of money to many people. River's PR people had spun it as mere charity, but the tabloids kept prodding.

At first, Roman was livid. Why should he be the one with the love child? The irresponsible one? The one who couldn't keep his dick in his pants? Yes, it was true that he had in fact had a scare or two, or OK, maybe four, himself. But still.

"We'll all help, Roman," Emmeline pleaded. "And we don't want them to drag Rocco all through the news. Please. River can't do it. Obviously . . ."

"I don't know how obvious that is," Roman said, just as his mother sighed.

"With you she can lead a quiet life. We'll give her a good life."

Is this what his mother thought of him? A quiet life? What the hell did that mean?

He decided to call Lucy. What would his sponsor have to say about all this? Should he tell her at all? What if she decided to go to the tabloids to confirm the story? He scoffed at himself; he'd told Lucy a great many downright scandalous things. Lucy would never betray him.

They sat in the back corner of a pie house in Los Feliz. Lucy had recently moved into a condo off Vermont with her newest boyfriend. The traffic on Griffith Park Boulevard alone would've driven Roman crazy, but Lucy seemed to love everything about it and the man. "We can sometimes hear concerts at the Greek!" It was the first time since he'd met her that she'd been in love, and everything about her seemed softer, lighter. She was wearing a dress that even showcased her scars from the fire. It was the first time Roman had ever seen her legs.

He glanced down and she caught him.

"Jay loves my legs." She shrugged shyly.

Roman told her about the baby in whispered bursts between the waitress's comings and goings. They'd each ordered a peach pie and coffee. His middle brother had a baby. His youngest brother was rumored to be the father. His parents wanted him to say it was his. Not to mention, apparently, the baby was half white.

"I'm white," Lucy said.

"No shit. But I don't have to raise you. Plus, I don't know anything about babies."

"Being a parent isn't something you're ever really ready for," Lucy said.

This was not what Roman had thought she'd say. He assumed she'd rant about what a terrible deal it was. How it was a threat to his sobriety. How his parents shouldn't have asked such a thing of him. Lucy's youngest daughter had recently started taking her calls again; perhaps this was what had made her sentimental.

"I don't even know how to change a diaper," Roman whined.

"It's just shit," Lucy said, and laughed. "That's the least of it. Let's be honest. This child will need a lot. But I think you're ready to give a lot. You're far more than you tell yourself you are, Roman Johnson." Lucy smiled.

"God, I liked you much better when you were miserable," Roman said, and they both burst out laughing.

Lucy grabbed his hand across the table. "You don't have to do anything you don't want to do. But this . . . maybe this could be good."

===

ROMAN LOOKED DOWN at Angeline's face. She was splotchy, with weird patches of dryish skin, and her fingernails were so very, very tiny. Babies were supposed to smell good, Roman had heard, but Angeline's diaper needed to be changed like five minutes ago. She squirmed in her own shit and settled in his arms. Christmas floated above, looking at the baby, who seemed to track his movements with her eyes. He came in close and hid his face behind a hand.

"Peekaboo!" Christmas said.

The baby laughed.

"She can see you?" Roman said.

"Duh," said Rocco.

"Boo!" Christmas said again, and Angeline laughed louder. Then she scrunched up her nose and mouth like she'd both tasted something incredibly sour and smelled the foulest thing anyone had ever smelled in all of eternity.

"Is something wrong with her?" Roman asked, growing concerned as she grew redder in the face.

Then, a rather specific squirting noise came out, and she unclenched, looked back up at them, and smiled.

"Eww," Christmas said.

"You wanna change her diaper?" Emmeline said to Roman.

"Not especially." He laughed.

"It's very gross," Rocco concurred.

"I can't wait until River comes home and we're all together!" Emmeline said. And they all murmured in assent. River's latest album was doing so well that he was being jetted off here, there, and everywhere. Each time he called, it seemed as though he were in a different time zone. Roman was genuinely happy for his brother. He wished he could have always been, but it'd taken some time, and lots of meetings and therapy and self-reflection to get there.

For the first time in a very long time, it felt like they were a family.

═══

STILL, ROMAN FOUND himself twisting and turning over how to tell KikiKit. Most women wouldn't want to be with a man with a child, much less one that wasn't his. And certainly not one who practically came with her own NDA. Plus, Kit was a professional; would she be willing to saddle herself in that way? He loved how dedicated she was to her research, her spontaneity. He braced himself for the absolute worst.

It pained him to think of how much he might miss Kit's smile as he wiped baby powder onto Angeline's bottom. As he mixed up the formula for her bottles he thought of how Kit had squealed under the waterfall after they kissed. And as he sucked up Angeline's snot with the nasal aspirator, he thought of the one time KikiKit had laughed so hard, her own snot had made a surprise appearance. He laughed, and little Angeline smiled up at him and reached out her tiny little pudgy arms, as if to say, *Closer!*

He found himself good at taking care of a baby. Found comfort both in its rhythms and its surprises. But he grew resentful at times. Why had Angeline come just as he'd found happiness? He had to tell Kit, but he wanted to hold on to her just a little bit longer. As long as he could.

═══

"YOU HAVE A baby" was the first thing she said to him. A bit accusatorially, he thought.

"I didn't know how to tell you," Roman whispered. "She's my brother's."

"River?" Kit said. "I thought he was . . ."

Roman brought his index finger to his lips. "Rocco. She's his. And now, as far as everyone else is concerned, she's mine. It's . . . complicated."

"Family often is," Kit said. "I need some time to think."

"I get it," he said.

═══

ROMAN WAS PUSHING Angeline's stroller through the local grocery store when he saw KikiKit in the aisle between the eggplant and asparagus. She was examining tomatoes on the vines painstakingly, and the woman to the side of her was growing frustrated waiting for her to move out of the way. He ducked behind the peaches and nectarines. He had only just learned that nectarines were just peaches without the fuzz. He would have to remember these things to tell Angeline when she got older. There was a whole world out there for her to know.

KikiKit spotted him first as he attempted to look consumed with a choice of white nectarines. She pushed her cart over to him, and Roman held his breath until their carts were nearly touching.

Roman looked up. Kit looked tired but otherwise good. She reached out to grab one of Angeline's tiny, perfect fingers, and Angeline held KikiKit's finger in her improbably strong baby grip.

"Angeline," he said.

"How absolutely perfect she is," KikiKit said.

Kit tried to tug her finger from Angeline, but Angeline refused to let go.

"May I hold her?" Kit asked. Roman nodded.

Kit lifted Angeline up out of her stroller and brought the baby close to her chest. Angeline reached for Kit's dangly earrings.

"You better be careful. She almost ripped my mom's earlobe the other day." Roman laughed.

"And her mother?" KikiKit said carefully.

"She's in a group home," Roman whispered. "Her parents don't want her in Angeline's life . . ."

He trailed off as an elderly Chinese lady with a chunky hearing aid walked past, deciding on cabbage. She probably had no idea who he was, or what he was talking about, but he had learned you could never be too sure.

"How horrible," Kit said.

"I know . . ." Roman started. "Angeline's a good baby though. Hardly fusses at all. And she sleeps pretty well."

"You don't have to sell me on her like she's a car, Ro." Kit laughed.

"I haven't been able to sleep at all since I told you," Roman said. "I wanted to give you space."

Kit looked up at him and nodded. "I haven't exactly been sleeping well myself."

"I don't want to lose you. I can't," Roman said. "I mean . . . I'll respect whatever you decide. But I . . ."

Kit buried her face into the top of Angeline's head. "She smells divine."

And then, how easily Roman pictured it: the three of them in front of a Christmas tree opening presents. He pictured Kit's surprise and delight upon meeting Christmas himself. Or at a park, with Kit pushing Angeline down the slide, only for Roman to catch her. He could see the two of them arguing over whether Angeline should be allowed to go to a sleepover. And staying up until she came home from her first date. He pictured them at Angeline's first concert, maybe one of her uncle River's shows, atop Roman's shoulders as Kit reached up to feel the music and to hold Angeline steady. Perhaps Angeline would be like Rocco and her mother, Alice, and a little different from the other kids at school. Or a lot different even—Roman didn't even know what exactly Alice's diagnosis was. Maybe kids would ask her why she was so brown and pull her curls, or why she was so light compared to the rest of her family? Maybe he and Kit would have to fight to protect her. There was so much to be afraid of, and still he pictured the three of them as a whole, happy.

And as though she could hear exactly what he was thinking, Kit smiled up at him and an understanding passed between them.

"Don't let me forget to buy some almonds. I feed them to the squirrels outside my window sometimes. They're quite picky actually. For squirrels."

They chatted as they walked through the aisles, picking out milk and coffee and salmon and oatmeal and formula and trash bags. Kit preferred Sara Lee to Wonder Bread, and he preferred red grapes, while she preferred green. She liked chicken breasts, while Roman found them bland.

"That's just 'cause you haven't had them prepared right," she said, matter-of-factly.

"My mother would fight you over that statement," he said, and laughed.

What a thrill it was to walk through the aisles, to smell her perfume and look at her tank top as it fell down her shoulder to expose a pink bra strap, while she reached for the wrong applesauce, the right almonds for her picky backyard squirrels.

How positively and inexplicably erotic when they loaded all their items on the conveyor and the cashier looked at the three of them and asked, "Together?"

CHAPTER SIXTY-TWO

1985

IT WAS A SPUR-OF-THE-MOMENT THING—RIVER CALLED ROMAN AND asked if he and Rocco wanted to go flying with him before he took off for the tour. He'd passed all his tests and flown many, many hours and now he could fly not just himself but other people too! Plus, River's thirtieth birthday was soon; he didn't want a party, or anything major, just to meet the baby, and this.

"Can I come?" I tried not to beg. I had now been on big airplanes with many people on them, but never a small one flown by my very own brother!

"Yes, Christmas. All the Johnson boys," River said brightly over the phone, and my phantom heart warmed in my open chest.

"So how about I come to meet my niece first, then we go out?"

"I can't go, I have to be here for Angeline," Rocco said solemnly. "Tiny babies shouldn't fly in tiny planes."

Tiny planes seem to me exactly where tiny babies should fly, but what did I know?

"It's OK, Rocco. You boys should have fun together," Emmeline said. "Just for a day, she'll be fine with me and your father."

"We got it," Odysseus said. "You're all still here, aren't you?"

He laughed heartily at himself as Rocco looked on skeptically. I thought Emmeline and Odysseus were the best grandparents I'd ever met, though I hadn't known too many. They cooed and oohed and aahed and bought all the toys and even changed Angeline's poopy diapers. The whole house felt like a hug now that Angeline was in it. I should have liked to have had them as grandparents maybe even more than as parents.

Roman looked at Rocco, then over at his parents as baby Angeline nestled, milk-drunk and satisfied, in the crook of Odysseus's arm. "All right."

Several days later, River barged through the door, shouting, "Where is she? Where's our princess?"

Roman came into the foyer from the kitchen, a burp cloth slapped across his shoulder. "Hello to you too, Riv."

"I like your accessorizing," River said, and laughed.

"Oh, this old thing?" Roman twirled the muslin cloth around his head.

"Do I smell bacon?"

"Dad's cooking breakfast," Roman said.

"What about the shop, shouldn't you guys be there?"

"Way I figure it, we can afford to take the day off." Odysseus popped up behind Roman. He walked over to River and gave him a hug.

"How's things been?" Odysseus asked, but before River could answer, Rocco came down the stairs holding Angeline, who was wearing a bow almost as big as she.

"Angeline, this is your uncle River Johnson," Rocco said formally.

"Oh wow. Oh she's so, so beautiful," River said, on the verge of tears. He reached out his arms to hold Angeline, and Rocco hesitated for a moment before gently placing her into River's arms.

River held her awkwardly, as though she were a football.

"That's not how you hold a baby, Riv," Roman said, and laughed.

"I don't want to break her," River said.

"I think you should sit down," Rocco said, nervously hovering.

Meanwhile, Angeline squirmed and looked up at River skeptically. I'm not sure if it's 'cause she too thought he might drop her, or because of the unwieldy bow, or because that's just kinda her default face.

"When you get older, I can't wait to spoil you rotten, and tell you all the stories, and take you all the places," River said.

After a few moments of staring into Angeline's impassive face, he said, "I don't think she likes me."

"Oh, don't be silly, Riv. She just needs a little more time is all," Emmeline said, placing her hand on River's back.

"Just you wait, I'll be your favorite uncle yet," River whispered, nuzzling his face into her head. And at that, Angeline wrapped her baby finger around River's, scrunched up her face real tight, and grunted.

"Does the favorite uncle want to change his first diaper?" Odysseus said, and everybody laughed, even Angeline.

THAT AFTERNOON, IN front of the airfield, a bunch of young kids rapped loudly over the comings and goings of private planes. From what I know about planes, I don't believe all that exhaust was great for their voices, but they didn't seem to care. Maybe they thought this was a place to be seen by the kind of people who had private planes, people who could cut through the sky without issue, people who made things move.

"Is that who I think it is?" A young man with gray eyes and short, sandy locs looked over at River.

"Yo! River Johnson?" His friend, squat and darker-skinned, jumped up from the stairs on which he sat.

"Yeah?" River said. He wasn't often alone these days, but he'd given his new bodyguard the day off. His bodyguard was a very nice man named Cooper, and I think you'd have to be either a very nice person, or a very foolish one, to be willing to step in front of any manner of danger for somebody you're not even friends with.

But still, I was happy River had somebody to protect him from the sort of thing that happened to me. Every place had good people and bad, but some places were like a loose tooth, just a little wriggle was all it took to reveal the decay at the root. Maybe if I had a Cooper to guard me, I would still be alive and very old, indeed. As old as Odysseus, or maybe even older! I can't remember.

"Shiiiit. I just wanted to see if it really was you?"

"In the flesh." River smiled.

The gray-eyed kid walked up to River and extended his hand into a very complicated handshake that River could only half keep up with.

"Do I got something to show you?!" the stocky one said.

"I should get going. I'm here with my brothers. We're kinda on a time crunch, my dude."

"Oh, they're gonna wanna see this too!" The boy reached into a crate full of records, flipping through several in the bag until he pulled out a very familiar one like a prize.

"Got it at a yard sale!"

It was the Johnson boys' very first record, the one they'd cut at the studio with Theo Celestine. Before we moved, before what happened with Wayne, back when they were just three little Black boys in a backyard singing.

"Wowzers!" I shouted. Rocco gave me a look that meant I needed to keep it down around the living.

"This shit is wild," Roman said. "There are only a handful of these roaming around I think, right?"

River nodded. "Collectors pay a lot for one."

"Watch this!"

The kids scribble-scrabbled the record on the turntable so that the Johnsons' notes scratched and stretched and shortened until their grooves held some other music entirely. I'm sure a fancy collector person would've been very mad that some kids scratched up a rare record like that, but people like that don't always see what could be, only what's been.

Mr. Odysseus didn't like it, but as far as I could tell rap wasn't that different from Shakespeare. And only a little bit more crass.

On the turntable, those boys continued to cut the brothers up and make them anew. Rocco joined in on the chorus. Then River and Roman joined him.

"Yoooo!" The stocky one began to jump up and down like his very feet were pogo sticks as my brothers harmonized with their childhood selves.

═══

YOU WOULD THINK around an airfield there would be plenty of dead people. But I only saw a few leaning against some planes from around the 1940s. Their bodies were plenty broken and atop their floppy heads they wore those floppy-ear flying hats like in the pictures. They nodded in my direction. I separated from the boys and walked over to them briefly.

"Hi!" I said, and then suddenly grew shy. I hadn't thought in advance about what I might say next. Or whether they were nice men or racists. But I was dead and there wasn't much to be scared of so I said, "What are you guys up to?"

"I like watching the new planes landing and departing," the guy with the floppiest hat said.

"They're so different and yet so the same," another guy said.

"Doesn't it make you sad?" I asked. "Being reminded of it all?"

"I reckon I'd be doing the same thing even if I'd survived," he said, nodding over at a bunch of elderly men smoking cigars perched not twenty feet away in lawn chairs. In their laps, some of the men had cameras, others had composition notebooks that they looked to be scribbling details in every time a plane took off.

"Do you ever see crashes?" I asked.

"See far more landings," the floppiest guy said.

I nodded.

"Christmas! Let's go!" Rocco called out.

"Brother time!" I shouted excitedly as the boys all buckled in, and all three of them laughed. I suppose I should stop calling them boys, as by now the Johnson brothers were men, with facial hair and smelly, smelly pits and their share of disappointments and triumphs alike. I wondered what my face might've looked like if I'd got to be their age. Would I have the lines that crisscrossed Roman's eyes far too early? Or would I have the slight something extra that Rocco was starting to have just at the tummy? Or perhaps, like River, would I not look very different at all? Somehow, River looked younger than he ever had. He had deep smile lines, but for once they looked carved out of the real deal instead of from smiling 'cause all those people paid him to.

The four of us crammed into River's new plane with its knobs and switches and compass-looking things. All those flying instruments looked a little like the sound boards in a music studio.

"What kind of plane is this?" Roman said.

"A Beechcraft Bonanza. A36!" River exclaimed.

"I don't know why I asked. It's not like I know planes." Roman chuckled.

River placed his hand on Roman's shoulder. "I can teach you if you'd like. Maybe we could go out together."

"Yeah. Maybe." Roman smiled.

"Do you ever think about what if we never moved to California?" Roman said wistfully.

"Doesn't matter. We're here now," Rocco said very matter-of-factly.

"Should I do a rap album?" River attempted to beatbox.

"Please don't do that," Rocco said.

"Yeah, what he said," Roman said.

We rose higher and higher still, and as we did, it reminded me of the paintings Becky and I saw in Europe with all their strokes on top of other strokes, lovely and chaotic, until the more you pulled away it made a sort of sense. Or the raps those kids did, past, present, and future all sliding around together on a turntable or a dance floor. There were clouds and beauty and everybody and everything living and dead layered over one another like so many little flecks.

"Oh boy!" I said.

"Happy birthday, Riv," Roman said.

CHAPTER SIXTY-THREE

EMMELINE WAS SO DEEP IN THOUGHT THAT SHE DIDN'T NOTICE THE brunette with big glasses, her dark hair hanging loose around the shoulders of her boxy sports coat, waving at her frantically from across the movie theater lobby. The woman was younger, but not as young as the students out front protesting a movie in which a rich white kid takes pills to make himself Black to get into Harvard on scholarship, the protesting of which seemed to Emmeline an especially fruitless endeavor. The kids would be better off going about their lives, not walking around holding signs against a movie that would almost certainly do well financially, because that was the world they lived in, wasn't it?

Maybe age had hardened her to these things. Though she didn't feel hard. In fact, she felt softer than she ever had before. And it was getting harder to remember things these days. Just the other day she found a pen in the refrigerator. Last week, she found herself unable to remember the word for the thing that sucked up dirt and left life clean. Now she couldn't remember why she knew this young woman.

"Mrs. Johnson!" the woman rushed over. "How lovely to see you!"

Where did she recognize her from?

"It's me! Rachel! From Aaron's office! Dr. Takahashi?"

The girl gave her a warm hug.

"It's been ages!"

The young woman seemed genuinely excited to see her. Emmeline glanced over at Odysseus, who gave a tight smile.

"Rachel! Have you met my husband, Odysseus?"

"I don't think I ever did," she said. "Gosh, you guys must be so proud of your son. I can't believe just how insane his career has been. Can you believe I didn't put two and two together until I saw an interview of his and they were showing some old family photos and I was like, Oh my God I know her?"

"We are very proud." Odysseus beamed.

"You went to Caltech, if I remember correctly?" Emmeline said as the young woman slowly came into mental focus.

"You do indeed," the woman replied.

And suddenly, next to her, with a paper bag full of half-eaten buttery popcorn, there he was. He'd gone gray in spots, mostly near the temples, which gave him the unfortunate effect of wearing a toupee. His eyes creased in the corners, tiny little whiskers, as he smiled gently at her. They hadn't done that yet last time she'd seen him.

"Hi," he said.

"Hello, Dr. Takahashi," Odysseus said.

Emmeline felt sick to her stomach, which only slightly overrode her excitement at seeing Aaron Takahashi again. In all these years, she hadn't seen him after that last phone call. Occasionally, she'd imagined what they might say to each other one day when they were older and wiser. When she was strong enough to not come a little undone at the sight of him.

"How is Rocco doing?" Aaron asked, carefully directing his question at Odie and avoiding Emmeline's gaze.

She felt dowdy in her sensible heels, and the cardigan that covered her shoulders, not from the cold, just from the eyes of anyone who passed. They were designer, gifts from River, who said Emmeline should treat herself more. But even these designer clothes did not have the sexiness of Uptown, or Downtown, or wherever the kids thought was cool these days.

"He's great. He's home with us."

"Glad to hear it."

Rachel put her hand on the small of Dr. Takahashi's back. An emerald glistened from her un-manicured finger. Her grandmother's ring. It fit her perfectly.

"You're married?" Emmeline asked Rachel.

"So it's kind of a funny story, right? Ages ago, Aaron and I started hanging out after work, and I don't know, we just kinda clicked or something. And we, like, saw each other off and on while I finished my PhD. After my dissertation, I asked him if he was in or out. Because I had no intention of wasting valuable energy pining over him instead of focusing on my research."

Rachel laughed heartily. "And here we are."

Emmeline didn't find it to be a particularly funny story. Quite typical on the surface, in fact. Man starts dating his assistant. Still, Rachel was lovely and warm and brilliant. Shrinking her didn't make Emmeline any bigger.

"Here you are," Odysseus said, putting his hand on the small of Emmeline's back. "Congratulations!"

"What a gorgeous ring," Emmeline added. Aaron stared at Emmeline. He was beautiful, but also, when she looked hard enough, he was just a man.

"Thank you! It was his grandmother's! We're actually moving next month. I just landed a tenure-track gig at the University of Michigan."

"And what about your practice?" Emmeline asked.

"Sold it. Ready for the next stage in my life I guess." Aaron looked at her carefully.

She nodded.

"Michigan was the last place we lived before we moved the boys out to California," Odie said.

"I'm a California girl through and through, so I'm a little terrified of the winters. Did you enjoy it?" Rachel asked.

"Gosh. Our lives were so different then," Emmeline said. "But we were happy, weren't we?"

"We were," Odysseus said.

They exchanged further pleasantries. Turned out they had all just come from seeing *2010: The Year We Make Contact*.

"I'm not sure I understood a lick of it." Rachel laughed.

"I find the older I get, I'm not sure I understand anything at all," Emmeline said, and all four of them laughed.

═══

IN BED THAT night, Odie leaned over and asked her, "Do you still love me, Emmie?"

Over the years, every so often they'd check in on each other like this, but tonight, after seeing Aaron, the question felt heavier than it had in a long time.

Several years ago, Odysseus had a small heart attack. And it wasn't until she was in the hospital room with him and the doctor was going over his charts that she found out that it wasn't his first or even his second. How many things had they kept from each other over the years? When the doctor left the room, she'd leaned her head against her husband's and said, "No more secrets, OK?" And he had agreed.

"Of course. Always."

In all of her searching and yearning, it was Odysseus who had made her feel most loved, most at home in her own skin. Odysseus had seen her, even when she herself wasn't looking. And what a beautiful life they'd created together. What beautiful lives. She held his cheek in her palm before moving her hand to his chest. His skin was still so smooth. Just a few lines around his eyes and mouth where the years had crept in. Her husband really was still so very lovely. She felt his heartbeat under her fingertips, his heart, that most sturdy and delicate thing.

"I . . . *I'm so in love with you,*" she sang, and they both began to laugh.

"Girl, you better leave the singing to them kids." Odysseus snorted and slapped his thigh at his own joke. He then reached for her hand.

THE NEXT MORNING, Emmeline overheard Odysseus talking to River on the new phone Roman purchased and insisted on setting up, even though they told him their rotary phone worked just fine. The speaker flooded the room with whoever was calling so that his or her voice somehow managed to be larger than life and tinny at the same time. River was in England now. Or was it France? Either way, he was winding down as she and Odie started their morning coffee.

"Been in the papers a lot with that actress, I've noticed. She's a pretty girl . . ." Odysseus said.

"She's very fun," River said with what sounded like genuine affection.

"You two getting serious?"

River laughed as though Odysseus had said the funniest thing ever. But to Emmeline it sounded like Odie was being earnest. How was it possible that her husband didn't know? He had to!

"Say, I've been thinking, Riv," Odysseus said. "Since everything went so well in New York, why don't you do something with your brothers? Maybe a double album? Or just have them on background vocals?"

"Maybe."

"It might be nice. A reunion of sorts. Show the fans how you started."

"Maybe," River said again.

"How about you come home for Angeline's baptism next weekend? If you can . . ."

"I'm supposed to be in Italy next week . . . I'm sorry, when did we start doing baptisms in this family?"

"You boys were all baptized. And Roman's got a little more Jesus in him after that last rehab. Or maybe on account of Kiki. Either way, I think seeing you might cheer Rocco up. He keeps bringing up your performance in New York to anyone who'll listen. And that plane ride. Plus, he's still pretty down about Alice."

"Of course he's still upset. He was in love with Alice," River said. Emmeline thought her son sounded exasperated, but River and Odie often sounded exasperated with each other.

"Bring whomever you like," Odysseus added after a pause.

CHAPTER SIXTY-FOUR

RIVER KISSED THE RANDOM SOFT, HAIRLESS SPOT ON MILTON'S UPPER arm. He let his lips linger on Milton's pale skin and stared into his eyes, which drifted ever so slightly in the early morning and late at night when he wasn't wearing glasses to wrangle focus. He was often struck by how absolutely beautiful Milton was. Where age had filled and hollowed him, carving him into adulthood. And underneath it all the same boy, same brain, same large heart he'd had when they were kids. *My God! He's mine!* River thought.

"I love you," River said.

"Yeah. Yeah. Yeah." Milton laughed. His eyes twinkled as he reached for River, pulling him in closer. River kissed him and closed his eyes. Milton was home. They stayed in bed, legs intertwined under the white striped hotel linen.

"What if I got the Johnson Three all back together for an album?" River said.

Milton laughed.

"I'm serious! You saw how excited Rocco was up onstage with me! It could be fun. Or at least, like, do a few shows together."

Milton cupped River's face in his hands. "I think that sounds beautiful. It could be really good for you guys. But let's take things one step at a time, yeah? Plus . . . if you tour with them, what would that mean for us?"

River paused. "I was thinking . . . let's tell them together when we go to the baptism."

"To visit your secret love child?" Milton started giggling like it was the funniest thing ever. "Are you sure I should go? Maybe it's just a family thing."

"You are family. And my dad said, 'Bring whoever you want.'"

"What do you think he meant by that? Do you think . . ."

"What I think is that we should get going. I wanna stop by the café along the way. This hotel shit is hot garbage."

"Such a coffee snob," Milton said, and pulled the blankets back over his head while River started the shower.

When he got out, having sufficiently scalded himself clean, he saw Milton reading the paper that had been delivered earlier that morning.

River peeked over Milton's shoulder at the article he was reading. Apparently, back home, Bayard Rustin had just given an incendiary speech.

"What do you think of this?" Milton asked as he began to read the content of the speech aloud as quoted.

" 'Today, Blacks are no longer the litmus paper or barometer of social change. Blacks are in every segment of society and there are laws to help protect them from racial discrimination . . .' "

River lifted an eyebrow and Milton paused.

"Go on," River said.

" 'The new . . .' " Milton paused at the forbidden word. "The um . . . new . . . N-words."

"Did Rustin actually say 'N-word'?" River asked, laughing at him.

"No . . . will you let me continue? 'The new N-words are gays. It is in this sense that gay people are the new barometer for social change . . .' "

"Well, I don't know if I agree with all that, exactly. Not in that way. But what do I know? I'm just a gay-ass nigga," River said, laughing. It was the first time he'd called himself that word aloud. Well, one of them anyway.

Milton started cracking up.

"Hey! You can't laugh at that, white man!" River joked before they decided on breakfast at the pasticceria the concierge said had the best espressos in town.

As they walked along the cobblestones, every so often Milton's pinkie would brush against River's, and he'd grab it with his pinkie, but only for the briefest of moments before they turned the corner. Once they were on a more public-facing street, a few fans stopped River to ask for photos, for which he graciously posed as Milton stood off to the side. The usual paparazzi walked backward, making awkward conversation as River and Milton walked forward. They shouted for River to smile. He did. It was easy. He was happy. Mostly.

But how desperately he wanted to be able to take Milton's hand in his own. It mightn't even be a big deal here. Men were much more openly affectionate outside of the U.S. Still, he had to be careful.

"Il suo amante?" he heard one paparazzo say to another.

"Migliore amico!" Milton said, slapping River on the back as they turned to enter the pasticceria.

Something by Giorgio Moroder played over the café's speakers. "Utopia—Me Giorgio," maybe? Milton bobbed his body to the beat and beamed all goofy and shit over at River.

What would it be like to be here, just the two of them? To walk around without complete strangers demanding River's attention? Increasingly, he found himself daydreaming about when he got old and lost his voice and nobody cared about him anymore. At least, not like this. No more telephoto lenses or helicopter shots, even when he was out on a yacht in the middle of the damn ocean. When his existence became the kind of thing a certain kind of holier-than-thou teenager discovered while flipping through the one hip record store in town with the unfriendliest of clerks, a place smushed between coffee and consignment shops. Could he give it all up? For Milton, he could. He would. One day, he and Milton would have a proper romantic vacation. River would be much braver then. As brave as Milton deserved. Together they would be old and crusty and happy. How lovely it might be to finally leave it all behind.

THERE WAS JUST one last interview before they headed back, on a very popular Italian show with a notoriously obnoxious host. River's publicist had gone over the prepared responses, and reminded him to remain calm no matter what the man asked of him.

"What's the point of even going on the show then?" River snapped.

"To show everyone you're game. You can laugh at yourself. That there's nothing to hide," his publicist Hannah said, and patted him on the back encouragingly as though he were about to be thrown into a game. Without padding.

Milton thought the show was a terrible idea. River didn't dare call Paul and ask his opinion. As much as Paul and Milton didn't particularly like each other, they always seemed to agree somehow.

"He's an asshole, River. And besides, what if they skew your words in translation?"

As usual, Milton was right. He always was. River couldn't say he hadn't been warned.

═══

RIVER TRIED TO look into the man's eyes as they spoke, but he kept fixating on just how inky black the man's hair was. It was as though somebody had poured an actual bottle of shoe polish on his head. Surely the man didn't think this was a good look? And even more surely he made enough money for a decent stylist?

"What do you have to say about the rumors you have a secret love child?" the man said.

"Anybody who knows me knows that rumor is absurd. My brother had a baby, and I'm thrilled to be an uncle. In fact, I'm set to head back to the States later on today, so I can spend some time with my new niece."

River waited for the translator to communicate his answer. He suddenly couldn't wait to be home among the palms and the smog and snowcapped San Gabriel Mountains. Couldn't wait to taste an orange from the tree in the back. He would try harder with Odysseus. He would hold his new niece. He would hug Emmeline tighter. He hoped that Christmas was still there with them when he got in.

"Will the famous River Johnson be changing diapers?!" the man said with a laugh.

River mimicked rolling up his sleeves in preparation, "Uncle River Johnson, reporting for diaper duty!"

How stupid he always felt with these things. In the corner of the set, he could see Hannah baring her teeth, a Cheshire cat reminding him to grin. He smiled at the audience, who laughed at whatever the host had just said to them in Italian.

Then, the host played the audience at home a clip from River's very first appearance on TV. River, Rocco, and Roman singing together in harmony on local television. The Johnson Three. He remembered how happy he'd been that day. How perfect they'd sounded together. Before everything changed. Two weeks later and a boy would be paralyzed, his brother placed in a facility, and not too much longer, another brother off to war. Then it would just be River. Solo.

He wished he could transport himself inside of the TV, inside of that moment so many years ago, and stay there forever.

"How do your brothers feel about your astronomical success?"

"They're very happy for me, of course! My success is our success."

"Your brother Roman has had his struggles with drugs, no? Much like your rumored dead girlfriend, Wendy Evans."

"My brother served his country. His country didn't do right by him."

"Yes. Vietnam was a tragedy, of course. But your brother, he had a dishonorable discharge?"

"As I recall, many of your countrymen were quite vocally against the war," River said, trying to maintain his calm.

"And what about Wendy? You haven't spoken publicly with anyone about what happened. It was reported that you were the one who discovered her body. That there was drug paraphernalia in the room?"

"Wendy was a beautiful, sensitive soul, and her demons unfortunately got the better of her. I loved her deeply."

"Did you pay for Roman's rehab because you were afraid he would end up like Wendy?"

"My brother's health is a private matter."

"Speaking of health, I've read that your other brother viciously hurt somebody as a child and had to be institutionalized, but now he's out and allowed to roam free?"

"I'm confused. I thought we were here to talk about me?"

"We are. As you said, your success is their success."

"Keep my brothers out of your mouth. Everything I have, everything I am, it starts with them, you dig?"

"Let's switch gears . . . what of the rumors that you're a homosexual? You have been photographed going in and out of hospitals known to treat AIDS patients."

River felt himself sweating under the hot studio lights. He looked over at Milton, who stood frozen next to Hannah. Milton looked ready to vomit.

River got up and walked off the set, toward his team, struggling to remove his mic. And then, he watched himself double back and calmly face the camera. *Enough running,* he decided. *Enough.*

"Honestly, so what if I were?" he said.

CHAPTER SIXTY-FIVE

THE WHOLE HOUSE WAS ABUZZ. EVEN THE BABY SEEMED TO FEEL IT AS she jumped higher and higher in a bouncer precariously affixed to the doorjamb.

"River should be here any minute, and there's still so much to do! He hasn't been home in ages!"

"It'll be fine, Emmie." Odysseus kissed his wife on the cheek. "He's our kid. We wiped his ass. Everything doesn't need to be perfect."

She peered in the plastic grocery bag and back up at him. "Are you kidding me?"

"What? What did I do now?" He was starting to get seriously annoyed with her.

"Odie, I thought I told you to get Dreyer's, not Breyers."

She had definitely not told him this, but he wasn't about to start a fight in front of Roman's girlfriend. Odysseus liked Kit for his son; she brought out something softer and lighter than he'd seen in Roman since he was a boy. Kit seemed to be the helium in Roman's balloon. Or maybe that was Angeline's impact. Babies had a beautiful way of rounding out even the hardest of edges. His own included.

"What does it matter?"

"River prefers Dreyer's. And what is this Neapolitan nonsense? Seriously, Odie, did you listen to anything I said?" Emmeline grumbled as she unloaded the groceries he had just plopped on the newly remodeled kitchen island.

"You'd think River was royalty," Roman said, and rolled his eyes. He and Kit sat across from them at the far end of the kitchen island near where Angeline bounced.

"I mean, he kinda is, in a way." Kit laughed and poked at Roman's stomach. Magazines were always crowning River the prince of this or the king of that. In the world's eyes anyway, River was larger than life.

The phone rang loudly in the other room.

"I'll get it!" Emmeline scurried out of the kitchen, not that it appeared that any of her sons were in a rush to answer the phone.

Odysseus opened the cupboards and started putting away the canisters of powdered formula they kept for Angeline. Rocco came into the kitchen, kissed the top of Angeline's head as she bounced, then peered into the freezer.

"But River doesn't like Breyers," he said.

"Your mom just reminded me." Odysseus sighed.

"He likes Dreyer's," Rocco said. "It's even in his rider."

Emmeline came into the room all a-fluster. "River's missed his flights. Nobody seems to be able to get ahold of him."

═══

HOURS LATER, CHRISTMAS sat next to Rocco as he rocked the baby. More to soothe himself than Angeline, Odysseus suspected.

"Was he flying commercial or private?" Odysseus heard Roman ask. "Could he maybe have just borrowed a friend's jet last-minute? Check with all the usual suspects."

Odysseus thought the young woman's voice on the other side of the phone sounded frustrated.

Dominique had sent a car to pick River and his friend Milton up after the JFK to LAX leg of his flight. It was not like River to not show. Not like him at all.

There had been an explosive interview in Italy, Arnie told the Johnsons when Roman called him to see if he knew anything about River's whereabouts. River was probably just blowing off some steam, Arnie said with clearly feigned confidence.

"What kind of explosive?" Odysseus heard Roman ask. Odysseus motioned for the phone.

Rocco apparently hated the static and echo of the speakerphone and briefly went to cover his ears with his hands.

"Hello? Arnie? You still there?" Roman yelled at the speakerphone.

"Shhhhh," Rocco grumbled. "Too loud."

Arnie paused for a great long while. "I'll fax over the transcripts as soon as I get them."

"We don't have a fax machine here. Can you send it over to the shop?"

"Sure . . . just call me when you're there. And I'll send it."

"Arnie, this interview—are we in damage-control mode?" Odysseus asked. But Arnie hung up the phone without giving an answer.

"This isn't like him," Emmeline said.

"What's wrong?" Christmas said.

"Shhh," Rocco said. Whether it was because he didn't want to upset them or because Kit was in the room and hadn't yet seen or been introduced to Christmas, Odysseus wasn't sure.

Roman started toward the door, then doubled back to kiss the top of Kit's head. "I'll be right back, OK?"

"I'll come with you," Odysseus said.

"Nah, it's OK. I got it, you stay here with Mom," Roman said. "Call Paul. Maybe he knows more about River's flight."

"I'll call Paul," Emmeline said. "Do you have his number?"

"Call Arnie back and get it. He'll have it," Roman said. Odysseus found himself unable to think. He was grateful to his eldest for taking charge of the situation.

"Something's gone terribly wrong. I know it. I just feel it," Emmeline said, pacing the floor. His wife began to hyperventilate before Christmas hopped up from his perch next to Rocco, walked over next to her, and held her hand.

"River . . ." Emmeline whispered aloud. Like a prayer.

CHAPTER SIXTY-SIX

THERE WERE NOW DIVERS ALONGSIDE THE ANCESTORS IN THE OCEAN. They hadn't found River's plane. Odysseus preferred to think River was somewhere up in the clouds, still flying. The grief pressed down on him. As though he were the one underwater and couldn't swim. Had he taught River to swim? To build a fire? Had he not taught his boy everything he needed to know to survive?

"I made you!" he'd yelled at River once. River was his flesh and blood. His whole heart out into the world. This is my River, given for you. Oh, how he wished he could take it all back.

"Can you see him? Try hard as you can," he said to Christmas.

"He's not here. Maybe he's heading home? Or maybe he's still alive?"

Odysseus began to sob violently. Christmas wrapped himself around Odysseus and he could feel the slight chill of the child around him. He imagined his baby boy so cold, plunging into the water, and he wept.

He'll come, Odysseus thought. He's heading home. All the rest of his boys had made their way home; of course River would too.

It became a thing he asked Christmas every day for six days straight. At first it was just Odysseus, but then Emmeline too seemed to be nearby whenever he'd ask.

"Christmas, can you see him?"

"Can you feel him, maybe?" Emmeline asked.

Christmas looked at them pityingly.

"It doesn't quite work like that," he said.

The divers finally located River's and Milton's bodies two weeks later.

The Johnsons called up Milton's parents using an old phone book from when the boys had been in each other's class. Milton's mother answered the phone.

"Who is it?"

Odysseus couldn't find the words. He felt himself inhale, then sharply exhale. Emmeline sat frozen at the dining-room table.

"Leave us alone. I already told you. No comment." Milton's mother slurred her words before slamming down the phone.

Emmeline took the phone from Odysseus and dialed again. He leaned in close to her.

"Don't you people have any goddamned decency?" Milton's father said upon picking up.

"Hello, Mr. Cohen. This is Emmeline Johnson. River's mother. I don't know if you remember our family from . . ."

The voice on the other end paused before responding, "I know who you are."

"I just wanted to say I'm terribly sorry . . ."

Mr. Cohen sighed. Emmeline hesitated for a moment.

"River loved Milton immensely. The last time I spoke to them, they sounded really happy. I just wanted you to know that. Your boy—"

"My boy wasn't . . . Milton wasn't like that."

There was a long silence between them.

"If you need any assistance with the funeral arrangements. We would be—"

"That won't be necessary. Sorry for your loss, Ms. Johnson."

"Sorry for yours, Mr. Cohen. Please extend my condolences to your wife. You're both welcome to come over any time—"

The phone clicked. Emmeline stood there with the dial tone. Odysseus knew he should touch his wife, hold her, something, but he wasn't sure either of them would recover if he did. There were things to do. Arrangements to make. He gently took the phone from her hands and placed it back on the receiver. People might call. They needed the line free. Death came with a lot of business at hand.

Still, Odysseus hoped that maybe with the delivery of River's body to LAX, River would come to them.

═══

ROMAN WAS THE one to identify River, who did not look like himself at all. The ocean had its way with River's body, and Roman was very glad his parents did not have to see his brother like that. That was no way to see your child, or anyone at all. Christmas had accompanied him. Had squeezed his arm when the coroner had pulled back the sheet. And when Roman had found himself mute with grief, Christmas had faked a response to the coroner in a voice somewhere between boy and man, which felt strangely appropriate.

"It's him."

Emmeline and Odysseus both slipped so deep under the weight of their grief that they couldn't so much as eat or dress. Roman was to be in charge of everything. It was Roman who sat across from the slight funeral director with just a few little froey curls at the top of his head. Roman couldn't tell if he'd forgotten to shave them or if he was stubbornly holding on to whatever remained. He looked at the curls as the man spoke of astronomically priced coffin finishes and linings and the cost of transport, which made Roman imagine his brother on a bus between the living and the dead. When Roman was done deciding the particulars, he took Roman down to the room where River had been prepared for the next life.

"I did what I could," the undertaker said apologetically. And Roman nodded but couldn't quite bring himself to look once again. He closed his eyes and clamped down, breathing in deeply before turning away. Christmas peered over at River.

"We'll have a closed casket," Christmas said on Roman's behalf, his voice cracking a bit. If the undertaker noticed a difference in Roman's voice, he didn't say a word. Perhaps he saw Christmas but didn't say anything about that either. Perhaps he thought that kind of sadness made children of adults.

In the car, on the way back from the mortuary, Roman and Christmas listened to the radio, which now played River's entire catalog nonstop. Even the ones most people hadn't heard of, and some of the ones they had heard and hadn't liked well enough for the songs to chart. Roman heard the grieving over the airwaves, people from around the city, the world over even, sharing recollections of River's role in their first kisses and first concerts.

"We played his song at our wedding," one woman cried on-air.

River never got to have a wedding, Roman thought. It shook him out of his stupor and instead made him very angry at all the things his brother wouldn't get to do and see and be.

"Why isn't he here? Why isn't he like you?" he asked Christmas.

Christmas went quiet for a moment.

"It's not fair. It should've been me," Roman whimpered.

How many times had Roman taken himself to the brink of death and back? In Vietnam, and then again as he drunkenly stumbled through Pasadena actively willing cars to hit him, spent late nights with dangerous people doing dangerous pills under a bridge nicknamed Suicide. How many times had Roman been an absolute piece of shit, to women who had tried to love him, to friends who had tried to keep him, to his parents and Rocco and River? What sense did it make that he was here and River was not? What sense did any of it make?

"You have to take care of Angeline," Christmas said gently.

Christmas reached over and held his hand, and for the briefest of moments Roman thought he felt his little-boy fingers, felt the chill that ran through the length of his body, felt the world beyond in his fingertips, and said a brief prayer that his baby brother was OK, wherever he was.

═

YOU DIDN'T KNOW HIM! Rocco wanted to shout from the back of the limo. How weird it was that so many people lined the blocks for his brother. His father and mother held each other in the seat across from him, and it seemed as though they had both gotten very old and very frail over the last few weeks. Next to him, Roman held Angeline, who was a good little baby. Perfect.

"You're not supposed to bring babies to funerals," Roman had said.

"That's weddings," Odysseus said. "People don't want to hear a baby wailing over vows. Nobody cares if a baby wails during a funeral."

"She's a very good baby," Rocco said. "The best."

Rocco was thrilled that he got to see Angeline whenever he wanted. Roman was going to move into the house down the street, and that was where Angeline would stay, with Roman and his girlfriend, Kit, for now. Rocco could sleep over whenever he wanted to hold and feed the baby at all hours of the night. Roman's girlfriend was very nice, and Angeline seemed to like her, which meant that Rocco liked her. Sometimes, Angeline was too loud and Rocco had to leave the room, but over the last few days whenever she started crying, so too would Rocco. Yesterday, Roman had lain down by Rocco's feet and started to cry too. Rocco missed his brother, but also he missed Alice, very deeply. He missed her smile and the way she held his hand. He saw her in the baby's eyes and her ears. He wanted to call Alice, but knew he couldn't. He needed Alice. To tell her how the house was quiet and loud and how he thought he'd see his brother again, but his brother was nowhere to be found. He wanted to tell Alice how he couldn't sing because it made Roman cry and sometimes his parents too. He wanted to tell her how their baby had begun gnawing on his foot and sometimes he thought his heart would burst from how much he loved her and how much he missed his brother and he didn't know how he could hold so much in his heart at once, but oftentimes now he heard it very loud in his ears and he went dizzy and couldn't breathe, and he thought it was then that finally his heart had exploded and he was dying and maybe then he too would find his way to wherever River was.

The crowds clapped alongside their limo and held up records and signs and flowers and danced to River's music in the impossibly bright day. Hands reached out to touch the limo and the hearse carrying his brother's body in front of them.

"It's not like he's in there," Rocco said.

"It makes them feel close to him," Emmeline said.

Angeline burst out crying at the top of her lungs. Chaos wasn't good for babies. Rocco didn't much like it either.

"They really loved him," Odysseus murmured.

"They did," his mother said.

Christmas played peekaboo with the baby to calm her down.

"Peekaboo!" He came out from behind his good hand. Roman started laughing.

"It's a ghost saying boo!" Roman kept laughing, and they all joined until they gasped for air.

THE CHAPEL ITSELF was full of people and somehow both rowdy and somber. It felt like entirely too many to share in a mother's pain. And yet, Emmeline's boy had been so loved. People crammed their way to the front. A teenage girl several rows back wailed louder than baby Angeline.

"He was one of us," an older man said, clasping both her hands. "He showed the youngbloods they too could make it."

Emmeline nodded. "Appreciate you saying that."

There were so many strangers watching their every move as they walked down the aisle to the very front. Photographers ran up in front of them and stole a few shots. Not to mention the ones who had been out front calling each of their names, like family.

"Over here, Emmeline!"

For a moment, she'd thought it was somebody she knew.

The portrait of River at the front was one Roman had selected, Emmeline supposed. She knew it wasn't fair to have left everything to him, and yet neither she nor Odysseus could so much as brush their teeth, much less pick out all the ways in which to bury their son. They could've had Arnie, or Dominique, or Paul, or River's people at the label do it, but it seemed like the kind of thing that should be left to family. It was River, not as a grown-up, but as a teenage boy, in one of the publicity stills they'd taken right before his rise. River smiled at the camera impishly, ready to fly. It was a good choice.

Emmeline sneezed. There were flowers in every single inch of this space where there weren't people. And all kinds of colognes and perfumes mingling together, forming a kind of sensory overload. It was a miracle that Rocco sat still, calm even, with all the people and all the sounds and all the noise. Her boy surprised her sometimes. They all did. The pews were scratchy and not especially comfortable. She leaned over and told Odysseus so.

"What?" he said a little too loudly.

"Never mind."

Christmas sat next to her in the large pew that had been roped off for their family.

"There are a lot of people here," he said.

"So many," she said.

"A lot of people like me . . ." he clarified. "Dead people."

"Really?" Emmeline said. "For River?"

"Mostly. Yes," Christmas said.

"Do any of them know where he is?" Emmeline asked.

"I don't think so," Christmas murmured.

And then the service started. It was mostly a blur. Bible verses that

River wouldn't have cared about. Songs he would've sung better. People whom Emmeline hadn't known, who had known her son, and well, it seemed. A girl called Dominique, one of his assistants, shared a story about River's kindness when her father had died. Arnie, River's business manager, had said through tears how he'd watched her boy grow up, grow into himself, how he thought of him as a son.

"Maybe I was a little bit in love with him, in retrospect," River's friend Paul said, holding back tears. "But weren't we all?"

And then her boys came to the front. River, Rocco, and Christmas too. They sang, in harmony, and she grasped Odysseus tightly and he her. Later, news reports would say how magical it was that it sounded like River was right there with them, singing. Christmas sang River's part. He told Emmeline, with tears in his eyes, that he sang it even better than he'd sung "Amami Alfredo" from *La Traviata*. Emmeline didn't know what that meant, but she knew it was important.

When Christmas hit the high note, the hairs on her body stood up and a chill went through her. And briefly in that cathedral she could see all the dead boys who had gathered around to pay their respects to hers.

Emmeline wept for all of them, living and dead.

ODYSSEUS LOOKED AROUND, let out a primal wail, a yawp, and clutched his heart, which betrayed him by still beating.

CHAPTER SIXTY-SEVEN

THE PAPARAZZI HAD CHASED THEM ALL THE WAY BACK TO THE HOTEL. Hannah immediately got on the car phone with the record label and dropped possibly more F-bombs in one conversation than River'd heard in his life to date. And he had been on the road for most of the last ten years! Alongside them, scraggly men on motos pounded their limo windows, flashing and snapping, blinding them every few seconds.

"Velocemente!" Hannah yelled at their driver, who responded unfavorably in rapid-fire Italian none of them could understand and yet perfectly understood.

In front of the hotel, the fans gathered had doubled in number.

"What a fucking shitshow," Hannah muttered.

As soon as the interview had ended, Milton had grabbed River's hand and hadn't let go since. River leaned his head against Milton's shoulder and felt both deeply exhausted and exhilarated. They'd only had a few moments like this before the hordes descended.

There was a song in his head. A good one even. It might be his best song yet. For Milton. For love. For home. God, how he couldn't wait to be home!

"Don't answer any questions," Hannah said as they exited the limo into the crush of people. "Just keep walking. And no more surprises, all right?"

Already, his hotel phone was ringing off the hook. It was Arnie, River supposed. He didn't want to get yelled at. Not yet. He was happy. Really, genuinely happy for the first time in years. Ecstatic, even. Also, he was terrified.

"What if we took a little plane ride? Just the two of us? Just for a few hours?" River said.

"I don't know, Riv," Milton said. "Shouldn't we get going? Hannah's gonna be pissed."

"Hannah's already pissed! Everyone at the label's already pissed! Fuck 'em all." River felt a bit high as he paced around the room. He lifted the phone from the receiver and slammed it back down before taking it off the hook entirely.

Milton nodded at the phone. "Riv! What if it's your parents calling?"

"Please. Let's just go. Everything's going to be insane when we get back. I just want . . . I want to feel free. Just for a bit. Please?"

Milton softened, walked over, and kissed River gently on the lips. "As you wish."

THE FOG WAS rolling in heavier and heavier now. It hadn't been so bad earlier. How was it so dark already? River checked his instruments.

Milton had not wanted him to get a plane. He had taken a Xanax just before they took off. He always took a Xanax.

Milton slept. River looked over at him, patted his thigh, and smiled. Milton looked over at him with the sleepiest of smiles and closed his eyes again. The plane bumped a little but not too much. Then it bumped again, startling Milton awake.

"You good?" Milton said sleepily.

"I'm not sure."

"Check your frequencies, Riv." This was the extent of what Milton knew about flying.

River struggled to get his bearings. He couldn't tell where the horizon was.

"Something's wrong," he said frantically.

"Call control or whatever," Milton said. He held his ears. River assumed, like him, that he'd felt them pop.

"Fuck."

"Pull up!" Milton said.

"I can't. I can't tell." River started hyperventilating. "Oh my God."

They were falling, and fast. Too fast. The oxygen masks dropped down, plastic dancing in the space between them.

"I love you," Milton said, and grabbed his hand. "Calm down. Think clearly."

River thought of his brothers. "This one's the one," Roman had said of Kit over the phone. "She's everything."

And he was an uncle! He was supposed to see baby Angeline's first few steps! Roman had been bragging about them on the phone incessantly. River was supposed to go home and love on her, to lavish her with wisdom and presents. To wrap his hands gently around her sweet baby cheeks and relish the beauty his brother had made.

And he promised Rocco he would take him flying again. He always kept his promises to Rocco.

"What is it like, Christmas? Dying?" he'd asked him once when they were little together.

No, not yet. He wasn't going to die today. There was still time to right themselves. There was still too much to do.

He'd told his mother he'd call her as soon as he got in safely. He pictured her waiting by the phone. And his father? River had hurried him off the phone as soon as Odysseus started pestering him about the next album. Why hadn't he taken his time? His dad's voice rang deep and sonorous in his head. Sound energy to electric energy, his love in waves across the wires between them. Had River said "I love you" back this time?

Milton put his mask on. Then River's.

"I love you most," River said.

They plummeted.

We're running out of time, River thought. There's no more time.

The impact was a searing pain like nothing he'd ever felt before.

OK, he thought. OK.

Then he felt himself being held. Wendy? he thought. No, not her, so many hands reaching out to touch him.

Fans? He felt so disoriented. Not fans. No. Ancestors.

Where was Milton? And then there next to him was Milton, being held.

Were they dead? Was this death? There was some weight of them both floating down steadily, together.

There were so many Black folks down here, swimming, floating. He noticed their worn metal shackles. Their tattered frocks. Two little girls, sisters maybe, with matching afro puffs, played a game of patty-cake. He thought he saw a white woman float by in a fine burgundy gown, something from near the turn of the century that should've been entirely too heavy to swim in. His old friend Murray would've loved that dress, River thought.

A jellyfish swam by, bioluminescent. River had first learned that word from a nature documentary he'd watched with Rocco in his hotel room after they'd fled that first facility.

He thought he heard a school of fish say, "Pardon us, sir. We're quite late." Very posh accents. There were two giant octopuses in a lovers' quarrel, it seemed, and when the female went to storm away, the male grabbed her with all of his tentacles and pulled her in close. "Ma chérie. Ma petite chouchoute."

And then! Porpoises! Just like the ones he'd seen so many years ago with his brothers in that old diving ride at Coney Island. Five of them hummed a tune among themselves as the posh fish quickly scrambled out of their way.

The coral in pinks and greens and blues was like something out of a picture book, or the issues of *National Geographic* that Milton piled up on their coffee table. But how could he see it all without goggles, without scuba gear? How could he understand this whole universe in front of him?

A crab scuttled from one corner to another across the ocean floor.

"Is Lucas with your Annemarie?" the crab shouted to a nearby eel.

"You gotta keep better track of your kids, dude." The eel slithered.

Oh my God, how beautiful it all was! How absolutely transcendent!

"Milton! Babe! Isn't it incredible?"

Milton looked over at him and smiled, pointing at two indigo-colored starfish splayed across a coral reef.

"Yeah. Yeah. Yeah," he said.

And then they were both gone.

CHAPTER SIXTY-EIGHT

THE FIRST NIGHT ANGELINE SAW ME WAS A CHRISTMAS IN WHICH ONE could reasonably argue she deserved coal. She'd tiptoed out of bed to eat one of the cookies left for Santa. She knew it was naughty but figured he'd already delivered her presents by then. And if Santa was still in transit, surely he wouldn't turn back because of a nibble or two?

Odysseus and Ms. Emmeline's house had grown even creakier through the years. Angeline'd stepped softly down each stair, daring them to tattle on her. Her gifts were not yet under the tree, so eating the cookie was a gamble indeed.

Santa was running late. CP time, Ms. Emmeline had said earlier, when at midnight there were still no presents. Really, it was because Rocco and I had been tied up in a game of chess, neither of us wanting to bring the game to an end.

I begged to be on Santa duty that year. Santa never existed for me when I was flesh, and now! The irony! I was Christmas! I gleefully carried the presents with me from out the basement and into the living room. As I placed one of the boxes with its red-and-gold wrapping paper under the tree, I shook one to see what it might be. I was fairly certain it was a train set. Hopefully not now a broken one.

Across from me, Angeline bit into her grandfather's homemade chocolate-chip cookie with the walnuts she had sprinkled in as he lifted her up to the mixing bowl. I watched as she closed her eyes to savor the bite. From what I could tell, her grandpa's cookies were worth missing presents for.

When she opened her eyes, there I was.

"Hi," I said.

She screamed, loudly.

Everyone came thundering down the stairs. Roman in the satin do-rag he used to lay his curls and a nightgown that made him look like Scrooge McDuck (Rocco and I had become especially fond of the entire Disney Afternoon lineup that year). Ms. Emmeline followed in a flowing silk kimono. Rocco rubbed his eyes in his ratty oversized favorite concert T-shirt from River's last European tour.

Odysseus slept.

Angeline's mama, Kit, wielded a bat taken from Roman's childhood room. She was bleary-eyed but ready to swing.

I looked up at all of them expectantly.

"What's wrong, babygirl?" Roman said.

She lifted her finger and pointed at me.

"There's a ghost," she whispered.

Roman began to laugh hysterically.

Emmeline sat down on the stairs. "Child, you nearly gave me a heart attack."

Rocco walked over and ate a cookie from the pile before plopping onto the faded couch.

"River, those are for Santa," Emmeline said.

Rocco just shrugged and didn't even bother correcting her.

"That ain't no ghost, babygirl, that's our brother," Roman said to Angeline, and I beamed.

At first, I could tell that once she got over the fright, Angeline'd been disappointed that the ghost before her wasn't her storied uncle River. But she quickly warmed up to me, as having somebody her age to play with around all the adults was nice. I told her stories from when she was a baby, when she could last see me. I couldn't do everything she could, but I did enough. After school, sometimes she would show me what she'd learned in her piano lessons on the worn piano the Johnsons had shipped from River's place in New York. She'd run her fingers underneath, feeling the letters of her uncle's name. One day, while Emmeline was very distracted, Angeline slipped underneath the seat and carved her own name next to River's in her childish scrawl.

"Look," she whispered to me. "Now I'm here too."

Then she started giggling.

"You can't tell a single soul," she told me conspiratorially. And I didn't!

She begged Roman to take her over to her grandparents' house more and more so we could play together, until it was decided that I could stay at Roman's house with Angeline for as long as either of us wanted.

I told her my stories, all the stories of my travels around the world and my friend Becky. I told her of my short, mostly unhappy, life and all the happy and unhappy stories about her family that the rest of them refused to tell, either because it hurt too much or they'd forgotten. Or because adults never remember anything right.

Most of what she knew of her uncle River came from me, or the television, which Roman turned off as soon as River appeared.

Every once in a blue moon, River's friend Paul came to visit with his new partner, Bryan. Then the Johnsons and Paul would laugh and swap stories about River and the old times. The Johnsons had also started a very robust foundation in River's name, and Paul would give his two cents about which charities they should fund, having become a pretty massive philanthropist in his own right. At Paul's most recent visit, as they were saying their goodbyes, Ms. Emmeline grabbed Paul's hand and thanked him for helping River with "all the Wendy business."

"Pool girl . . . I'm not sure where River is at the moment, but you know he's been keeping himself busy."

Then Paul gripped her hand, and Bryan looked kinda sad and uncomfortable, but Ms. Emmeline wasn't, not one bit. For a little while, in her brain, River was still here with us.

"Who is Wendy?" Angeline asked.

"She's dead," Rocco said.

"Like Unc—" Angeline started, but before she could finish, the rest of the adults told her to hush and stay in a child's place.

Around the tenth anniversary of his death, there was no escape, no turning the TV off, very few places you could go without hearing the music of River Johnson. Angeline listened to all of her uncle's albums on her new yellow Discman, the CD spinning round and round in its little world. I marveled at how all that sound could come from something smaller than your hand.

How far technology had come from Mr. Farraday's Victrola!

"Don't play it when your dad's around," Kit whispered. "It makes him too sad."

Angeline told me that at school, it was a running joke that River Johnson wasn't dead, he was just on some deserted island. It was a conspiracy theory that had gained more and more traction. River wasn't real to those kids, just a person who had once been famous, before their time, and now was dead, or not. River had been seen in Vegas. Somebody said he'd jumped from his plane with a parachute just like D. B. Cooper, never to be seen again. Somebody swore they'd seen him in Alaska. Emmeline saw this on the news and we were all afraid she might cry or get angry, like she sometimes did upon learning, once more, that River was dead, but instead she'd laughed and laughed like it was the funniest joke nobody'd told.

Anybody who knew River knew there was no damn way her son would be holed up in Alaska, Ms. Emmeline said.

River sightings were more common when Angeline was very little, after his death, when his fans were more rabid. But they'd popped back up again as his name was in the news. A young Black man gone too soon as we neared what would have been his fortieth birthday. Onscreen, River was frozen in time and in the '80s, with a slightly more than unfortunate hairdo that had been all the rage back then, I told her.

Even so, her uncle was beautiful, but that hair was definitely hideous, she said.

"Why is Christmas a ghost but not uncle River? Or Mommy's sister Minerva?" Angeline asked on our first Christmas Eve together as her parents tucked her back into bed.

At one point, this would've made me very sad, but not now. I had come to love my life with the Johnsons. Sometimes, Ms. Emmeline and I worked in her garden for hours as Rocco let ladybugs and caterpillars crawl across his hand. When he wasn't with us in Ms. Emmie's garden, Rocco worked as a part-time ranger at a botanical garden nearby. Roman and I sang together as he worked in the shop, since Odysseus had passed it down to him. Odysseus's hands had grown gnarled with arthritis like the trees in my forest, and I tried to help him massage them so that he was no longer in pain. Even Kit had grown used to me, after that very first time when she'd swung a fireplace poker at my head. Kit was a very kind woman indeed. She and Roman never married, but they raised Angeline as their daughter together.

"Some people live on in our hearts instead," Kit said to Angeline.

"That's a very stupid answer," Angeline said. Angeline was a child who appreciated the concrete, facts, logic.

"Go to bed. The sooner you go to sleep, the sooner Santa will come," Kit said. Another nonanswer.

Angeline finally asked me the next day before dinner why I was dead, and still around, and her uncle River wasn't. But I wasn't sure what to say. I still didn't fully understand how the universe worked myself. I was only a child, after all.

"But maybe River was very happy? Sometimes when dead people are finally very, very content they disappear," I said with a sigh.

"Aren't you?" Angeline said.

"Almost. I think?" I said. "Definitely the closest I've been."

"Don't go yet. I like you very much," Angeline said. Then we spun around circles until we made ourselves dizzy, and Odysseus's ham was ready, and it was time to go inside and eat holiday dinner.

═

AS ANGELINE GREW, she neglected me a bit. I pouted only a little because I knew she felt bad about it. We still hung out at her grandparents', but she got busy with school and life and her skateboard friends, and an invisible little dead boy tagging along like a little brother wasn't something easy to explain to anybody else. When I did come over, we jumped on the trampoline while she told me everything about getting older, mostly how much it sucked. This was the slang the kids her age were using, and as far as I could tell everything always sucked! She told me how she felt either angry enough to punch a wall or so happy she could spit, and there was no buffer in between. And to add insult to injury, the boys at school were loud and stupid and kept commenting on her new boobs, which she despised.

She bent her concrete-skinned knees, and I listened as though growing up was like all of my stories about traveling the whole wide world. She told me about her period (which did indeed sound ghastly, if I'm to be quite honest) and how it meant she could have a baby, technically, but screw that, she didn't want to do that. So gross! It was day three and only now did she feel like a human being again. Only now could she come out and play.

"The miracle of life" her health teacher called it, and when the teacher turned back to the slides, the boys sniggered and threw spitballs up at the ceiling.

"What miracle?" Angeline asked me, and bounced higher still. "What is so miraculous about this shit?"

I laughed and laughed. Rocco came outside and plopped down on the trampoline next to us.

"Hi, my baby."

"Hi, Uncle Rocco."

Rocco was her favorite in the whole family except for me. She knew her uncle was different and special, and she loved the way he taught her lots of things she'd never thought to know, and the way he didn't kill bugs, not even ants, and how together we spoke to butterflies, and how absolutely perfect his voice was when he sang to her. I don't think the Johnsons had yet told her that he was her actual father, but I suspect there was something deep inside her that knew.

Rocco and Angeline bounced together, higher still. Angeline reached for Rocco's hand.

Nearby, Angeline's boombox played a series of dueling pretty-boy bands, movie soundtrack ballads with the same co-writers, and a song about Tootsie Rolls! After that she shouted at the top of her lungs, angry as can be, even though she didn't have much to be angry about far as I could tell, "*And I'm here, to remind you, of the mess you left when you went away!*"

When that song faded to a close, the DJ said somberly by way of introduction, "RIP, my mans. One of the greatest of all time, River Johnson. Gone but not forgotten." Angeline briefly stopped bouncing and went over to turn the song up louder, and for a little while, it was as though River was out there with the three of us.

Ms. Emmeline stood in the upstairs window watching. Angeline waved at her grandma, but to be honest, I wasn't entirely sure Ms. Emmeline even knew who we were in that moment. Just an hour earlier, she'd called Angeline Bettina.

Still, I was the happiest I'd ever been. It was the happiest day I could remember in a very long time. I was home. I felt myself getting very, very sleepy. The sleepiest I'd ever been. I felt as I had when I was a child and I'd wanted to stay up with the grown-ups but my body wouldn't let me.

I still am a child though, aren't I? A very, very old child, but I've known older.

"Christmas?" Angeline said.

ACKNOWLEDGMENTS

So much of this novel was forged in and from the mess of life, the heaviness of grief, and the wonder of birth. I'm so thankful to have had editors who were indefatigable in their work toward making this chonkster the absolute best it could be, but who were also so deeply kind in allowing me the space to grieve, and to revel. Chelcee Johnson, I appreciate you so very much. Sydney Collins, you are an absolute rock star. Jennifer Hershey, thank you for believing in this book from the very beginning. There are so many people who contribute to putting a novel out into the world, and I'm so deeply grateful to every single one of you at Ballantine.

David Doerrer, agent extraordinaire—for always seeing the potential beauty in the chaos I foist upon you. I'm so truly lucky to have you not just as an agent but as a friend.

Lyn Miller-Lachmann—for your careful and enthusiastic read, as well as your vulnerability in sharing the ways in which your story has intersected with Rocco's. Thank you for ensuring his story felt as authentic as possible, as well as historically accurate.

Dr. Sneha Kohli—thank you for taking the time away from your busy schedule to share your expertise with me and for allowing Adam the space to share so much of his lived experience on the pages of your incredible dissertation, "Understanding the Lived Experiences of Autistic Adults."

In order to do my best to honor the varied lived experiences of people across the spectrum in telling Rocco's story, both historically and at present, I tried to focus mainly on books that centered the voices of the neurodivergent whenever possible. Of particular interest for further reading might be *We're Not Broken*, by Eric Garcia; *Sincerely, Your Autistic Child*, edited by Emily Paige Ballou, Sharon daVanport, and Morénike Giwa Onaiwu; *Funny, You Don't Look Autistic: A Comedian's Guide to Life on the Spectrum,* by Michael McCreary; *NeuroTribes,* by Steve Silberman; *Unmasking for Life,* by Devon Price, PhD; and *Look Me in the Eye,* by John Elder Robison.

Sean Daily—thank you for your tireless work in getting mine into the hands of people who are equally passionate about storytelling.

Kelly McWilliams—you are one of the absolute best friends a writer could ask for. Thank you for reading and loving on the Johnsons draft after draft, for being the best hype woman for this book and me, and for your incredibly detailed notes even as you were busy with your own work. I adore you. I'm so glad we get to birth Christmas and Walter into the world together, and I'm so excited for the world to see what you're cooking.

Elise Bryant—thank you for being you, for your endless encouragement, for your love, for your work. And for being there with a shoulder to cry on, sweets, and all the top-tier rom-com books, when I so desperately needed an escape. I feel so blessed to have met you and to have you as my dear friend. My little family is so lucky to have yours.

To my fellow writers, thank you for the inspiration, the friendship, the laughter, and the encouragement, with special shout-outs to Dawnie Walton, Danielle Jawando, Iva-Marie Palmer, Hannah Sawyerr, Brandy Colbert, Justin A. Reynolds, and Mateo Askaripour.

To the bookish community—from Bookstagrammers, to book bloggers, to bookstore owners, to my readers—thank you so much from the bottom of my heart to everyone who has taken time from their busy lives and work to uplift and affirm mine.

Sonali Kohli, thank you for our Urth dates, your friendship, and for sharing Sneha with me. Sophia Dalton, thank you for sharing Sonali with me. I'm so truly grateful to you both for your love and support throughout it all.

Jus Christian, thank you for being you, and for getting hyped about this story when it was more blob shaped than not. I remain so incredibly thankful that we were thrown into that box together all those years ago.

Liz Wong—thank you once again for being my oldest friend and for letting my baby terrorize poor Cliff when we so desperately needed a getaway.

Jack, Elizabeth, Helena, thank you always from the bottom of my heart for being such wonderful friends, for your encouragement, and for Ixtapa.

Hyemee Han—I could not have survived these last few years without you and your incredible family. Period. There are no words for the extent of my gratitude toward you. I love you. You are the most beautiful soul, and you deserve all the beautiful things.

To my parents—thank you for never saying no to buying a book, for raising us to see the beauty in difference, for all the years of sacrifice that I didn't quite understand as much as I do now. Thank you for everything you did to help me make my deadlines even with a new baby, and for being the absolute best grandparents ever.

To my sister—I'm so proud of you. I don't say it enough, so I will here for everyone to see. Omi is so lucky to have you as a mama, and I'm lucky to have you as my sister. Thank you, and thank you, Reza, for allowing me to take over your kitchen, eat your food, and for allowing my baby to aggressively adore his cousin while I write.

To my niece—my first time holding you remains one of the absolute best moments of my entire life. Thank you for the joy, laughter, and wonder you bring into all of our lives. I hope you read and enjoy this when you are much much older.

Derek—there is no way this story exists without me loving and having been loved by you. Thank you for seeing me even when I myself wasn't looking, and for this incredible little person we created together, for whale and shark and "more more more bones!" I'm so very happy we found and keep finding each other. King/Smith families—thank you so much for your enthusiastic support, and for him.

My sweet, sweet baby boy, you are every good thing about this world. Thank you for choosing me to be your mommy and for giving me and these pages an even further sense of purpose. How wondrous the world with you in it!

And finally to Kevin, wherever in the universe your stardust might be—it's not *The Black Kids 2: Electric Boogaloo* but I think you would've liked it.

ABOUT THE AUTHOR

Christina Hammonds Reed's debut YA novel, *The Black Kids,* was a *New York Times* bestseller, a William C. Morris Award finalist, and a California Book Award Silver Medalist. She lives in the Los Angeles area with her lovely little family. *The Johnson Four* is her adult debut.

@christinahammondsreed

ABOUT THE TYPE

This book was set in Minion, a 1990 Adobe Originals typeface by Robert Slimbach. Minion is inspired by classical, old-style typefaces of the late Renaissance, a period of elegant and beautiful type designs. Created primarily for text setting, Minion combines the aesthetic and functional qualities that make text type highly readable with the versatility of digital technology.